Waking Sapphire

Book Two in the Dream Traveller Series

T J Gristwood

ISBN: 978-1-326-48323-4

PublishNation
www.publishnation.co.uk

Dedication

This book is in memory of Loxley, my familiar and friend, who is sadly missed but fondly remembered. And dedicated to all the party people out there who have inspired me on this magical journey. You know who you are.

Thanks also to all the various DJ's who download to Mixcrate and supply me with endless trance, dance, drum and bass and ambient tunes to help me travel to all the right places whilst I am writing.

Also by this author

Sleeping Sapphire

Prologue

Sapphire Whittaker opened her eyes and let out a contented sigh. She had gone down the rabbit hole and entered a whole new world... a world full of magic and wonder, so different from the home that she had just left. She was lying on a large four-poster bed covered with a white canopy that lifted gently in the breeze. Daylight spilled through the open doors from the balcony to her right, and warm air touched her skin with a gentle caress. Sapphire Whittaker, dream traveller and recently transformed thirty-something woman, was now in a new land – a magical world called Shaka, where she could begin again.

Crossing over had been an amazing journey through a wormhole filled with lights and visions, which had saturated her mind in a kaleidoscope of spinning colours. Flashes of the last few weeks had spun through her head as she had travelled across time and space to join the man she loved. Her body tingled all over with the anticipation of finding him again. Fox, her guardian and lover, the magical man she had recently met, would be waiting for her here on this strange new world. As she pushed herself up slowly, and tried to clear her head from the intense pulsing that was pushing inside her skull, she looked around for any trace of him. All was still, save the throbbing of the magic surrounding her and filling her body with excitement.

She noted that her pretty summer dress and the obsidian necklace were the only things from her previous life that had travelled with her. She lifted the necklace from between her breasts and held it for a moment, emotion washing over her as she felt its warmth in her palm. She would miss Pearl, Charlie, and her other friends so much, but she had done the right thing – the only thing she could do now that her life had changed so drastically. The magic that filled her was growing by the day, and it was no longer safe for her to remain on Earth. She did not know what this new future would hold for her but she knew that it would be by Fox's side, and that was all that mattered right now.

1

As she pushed herself off the bed and stood slowly on slightly shaky legs she felt a presence by the door. On turning her head to see who it was she was suddenly overwhelmed by a rush of pure, undiluted and unconditional love. Fox stood in the doorway. Tall, sexy, and utterly gorgeous, he smiled at her – a smile so wide and filled with happiness that it struck a chord in her chest, which fluttered and danced like a butterfly. His wild amber eyes flashed with sparks of gold light; his hair was tied back so that it tumbled behind him in a cascade of braids and dreadlocks. He reminded her of a warrior from years gone by, strong and dominant, waiting to claim his prize.

He took long, purposeful strides towards her and stopped just inches from her body, heat radiating from him as he reached out to touch her. He hesitated for just a moment before he took her hands into his own, licked his bottom lip, and spoke in the deep, sultry voice that made her weak at the knees.

"Hello, Sapphire, it's so nice to see you again. It has been too long." Her own smile grew wide on her full, pink lips as she clasped his fingers tightly. He bent his head down and brushed her lips with his own, his tongue gently licking her top lip with the slightest of touches and making her tremble. He pulled her towards him urgently and moved his hands to hold her head firmly before kissing her again, this time with an urgency that made her head spin. Their bodies were locked together. His groin pushed fully against her and moved just slightly, so that she could feel just how happy he was to see her again. He kissed her for some time, devouring her like a man in a desert drinking water for the first time, before withdrawing slowly and leaving her breathless.

"Welcome home, my love," he whispered softly as she stared up at him with wide eyes. "I've missed you."

Chapter One

The strong sun of the planet Shaka was shining brightly above a beautiful natural pool and casting golden rays of sunlight across its surface. Shadows cast by the canopy of tree branches, which surrounded the edges, gave it the appearance of a dark, bottomless blue.

Fox lay on his back, arms stretched out either side of him, as he floated silently in the water. He was completely naked, and basked in the warmth of the sun on his face and the coolness of the water surrounding him. It felt wonderful, and he was completely at peace. As if it were a halo of dark braids and beads in the water, his hair moved gently around him like seaweed. His body felt as light as a feather. His eyes were closed, but he was completely aware of everything around him: the energy of the land, the beautiful woman sitting by the water's edge. He could feel the strong pulse of her magic. It vibrated in his solar plexus and in his heart, for he was inextricably linked with her – his woman, his love.

He smiled and opened his eyes again. Of a deep amber, with a black ring surrounding each iris, they flashed with sparks of gold. Fox lifted his head, allowed his legs to drop beneath him, and trod water for a moment while looking over at her. She was lying back on her elbows, her face turned up to the sunlight and her brown legs stretched out before her. She wore a white dress that fitted her curves perfectly, showing off her wonderful, voluptuous breasts. Her long dark-blonde hair fell heavily down her back like a cascade of silk, her eyes were shut. He noticed a faint smile was on her lips. He watched her for a moment, his body relishing the feeling of being naked in the water. A waterfall splashed droplets of crystal-clear fresh water behind him into the pool, creating a gentle background noise that soothed his mind.

He felt a surge of emotion fill his body. He was the happiest he had ever been. He relived the moment she had returned to him, to his world, and had stepped back into his life forever … the most wonderful moment of his long life. Sapphire the dream traveller, his love – and, hopefully, some day his wife – had crossed over to be with him on the planet of Shaka.

She had been here for some time now. They had embraced their new life ferociously, clinging together with a renewed passion that had lasted weeks. This was one of the few times they had left his house and ventured out, such had been the intensity of their joining. They had made love over and over again, wrapped in each other with a longing that was so deep and and so full of desire that it had consumed them for a while. He had in fact lost all idea of what time it was, or even what day. That was irrelevant to both of them right now.

Today, however, they had ventured out to refresh themselves in the beauty of Shaka, and to take in some much-needed fresh air. Sapphire had wanted to stretch her legs and take some time out from their coupling. He had agreed reluctantly: his stamina was immense, and he could have continued to keep her in his bed for several more weeks. She, on the other hand, was still mostly human. He swam back towards the edge of the pool, his feet finding the bottom as it inclined upwards to the gradually sloping earthy bank that allowed him access on to the grass. Sapphire opened her eyes and turned her head to watch him as he stepped out of the water. Her eyes grew wide and hungry as she took in the full glory of his naked body. He stood for a moment, letting her take in the view: he was a wonderful golden brown, the colour of his skin highlighted by the water as it slipped from his hair and down his body in droplets.

"Now there's a sight for sore eyes," she said.

He chuckled as she reached for a towel and threw it across at him. He caught it in mid-air and smiled at her seductively as he started to rub his body down with slow, tantalising strokes.

"Are you sure you do not wish to swim, my love? The water is cool and wonderful. It would refresh you."

She laughed, a light, happy laugh. She was sitting up now, and wrapping her arms around her knees.

"No, I'm fine just here watching you."

He walked slowly towards her while wrapping the towel around his waist, water droplets still dripping from his hair. She licked her lips in approval. God, this man was gorgeous. He sat next to her, stretched out his long legs, and leant back – as she had earlier – on his elbows, and closed his eyes.

"Are you hungry, Sapphire?" he asked her.

"Saf ... Call me Saf, Fox. It makes me think I have done something naughty when you call me by my full name all the time."

He chuckled softly.

"But you are very naughty, my love, and as beautiful as any sapphire. I prefer to call you by your full name."

She reached across and placed a soft kiss on his lips, tracing a pattern with her fingertips across his chest as she did. He shivered.

"I'm only naughty when I'm around you." She whispered. They stared at each other for a moment, a smile firmly planted on both their faces.

"Would you like to take a walk to the village? We could eat at the tavern, and I could introduce you to some of the local people. Bear wants to meet you. He has been nagging me constantly to let you out of the house."

She lowered her eyes for a moment and bit her bottom lip nervously. "I'm a little anxious about meeting strangers ... but that would be nice, and I suppose I'll have to venture out at some point."

He ran the back of his hand across her cheek softly. "You have nothing to fear, my love. The people of Shaka are kind, friendly, and gracious. They will all embrace you and love you as I do."

She looked up into his eyes and smiled sweetly. "You make me feel like some precious object, Fox."

He laughed. "And you are, my beautiful woman. Come, I will get dressed and we can walk to the village. It is not far from here."

She nodded and handed him his clothes – soft leather trousers and a loose-fitting shirt. He dressed quickly. She watched his muscles ripple and move gracefully as he pulled his trousers up (he went commando) and slipped the shirt over his head. It hung low over his hips and gave him the appearance of a medieval knight. He reached down with his hand to help pull her up.

She gasped a little as he pulled her into his chest and wrapped his arms around her, squeezing her tight. She breathed in his scent of patchouli and sandalwood ... warm and wonderful.

He kissed the top of her head and mumbled into her hair, "Well, I for one am ravenous."

5

She laughed at him and they headed off out of the wooded copse leaving the pool behind them. The towel and blanket vanished as they ambled down the small pathway ... magic.

They walked slowly, hand in hand, along the pathway that led away from the woods where they had just been resting. The landscape was now a blanket of fields filled with crops on either side. Everything here seemed to be verdant and full of life. Sapphire was slowly beginning to understand the nature of this world with its abundance of magic. The sky was clear, except for a few odd clouds that drifted across the blueness. She looked up at the planets in the sky ... such a different landscape from Earth. It was still making her gawp every time she took in the view.

"Are you happy, Sapphire?" Fox squeezed her fingers gently.

She paused before answering. "Yes, of course I'm happy. We are together again." He sensed she was holding something back from him.

"But ...?"

She looked up at him, a slight frown on her forehead. "I feel overwhelmed by all this. Quite frankly, it feels like I'm in a permanent dream now. I miss Charlie and Pearl, but I know it will take time to adjust."

Fox felt an underlying sense of sadness coming from her words so he let go of her hand, placed his arm around her shoulders, and pulled her gently into his side.

"I understand completely, but you will make new friends here. I know you will."

The frown slowly disappeared and she smiled back up at him, seemingly reassured by his comment.

They continued to walk for a while before the landscape began to change and Sapphire could see a cluster of buildings appear before them. The village was small, but people were milling around and going about their business. As they drew closer she found herself hesitating a little. She was indeed nervous.

Two women standing by a well on the edge of the village stopped to look at them as they grew closer. They were drawing water from the well and collecting it in wooden buckets. They were young and dressed in what looked like peasant clothing: clean and tidy but plain and practical. Both were very pretty, with long blonde hair. They smiled and bowed their heads as they approached. They both curtseyed as Fox stopped for a moment.

"Good afternoon, my lord. Blessings to you on this day."

Fox smiled at them and nodded. "And to you, my ladies."

Sapphire could see the glint in their eyes. It was obvious they found Fox just as tantalising as she did. She fidgeted a little. His arm was still around her shoulders, and he gripped her a little tighter in response.

Men and women were busy with herding small animals and carrying goods to various places. Each person seemed to have a purpose. Everyone stared at Sapphire and Fox. Sapphire lowered her eyes to the ground. She felt as though she stuck out like a sore thumb. Well, actually ... she did stick out, and it was making her feel as if she really didn't belong there. On feeling her palms become clammy she pulled on her inner strength to find some confidence and to stop herself spiralling down into having a panic attack. It had been a very long time since she had felt this nervous.

They quickly reached the tavern, a wooden building with a large door frame that sat low on the horizon like a wizened old man waiting to welcome her into another world of magical madness. Fox paused, his hand resting on the handle of the heavy, studded door. He hesitated before opening it, turned to her, and kissed her lightly on the lips.

"Are you ready to go inside?" he asked her.

She nodded silently and took a deep breath to steady her nerves. She suddenly felt like the new kid at school about to enter her classroom for the first time. It sucked. Stepping inside the tavern was like going back in time: nothing like The Swan pub in the village she had lived in on Earth.

The tavern was a little darker inside, but had a light and happy atmosphere. It was full with mostly men – but a few women were seated at the many tables scattered around, eating and drinking with their partners. Several young serving girls wandered around the tables with trays of drink and food. As they walked towards the long wooden saloon-style bar silence dropped like a stone and hit the floor, creating an unnerving stillness. Had she just entered The Slaughtered Lamb in *An American Werewolf in London*? Every single person was staring at them and smiling – thankfully – but silent.

Fox lifted his head high. "My people, this is Sapphire. She is my woman. I hope that you welcome her to her new home with open hearts."

Sapphire was horrified. His declaration of her being his 'woman' in front of all these strangers made her feel oddly uncomfortable.

Everyone smiled and bowed, and she heard the words, "Welcome," and, "Blessings to you both," as if they had just announced something much more than her arrival here on this new planet. The tavern returned to its normal chatter and bustle just as quickly as the silence had fallen.

Sapphire let out a sigh, her heart bouncing around in her chest like a pinball.

Fox smiled at her and kissed her lightly on the forehead. "Stop stressing, my love. Let's eat." He ordered drinks and food and they found a table by one of the bay windows.

Sapphire felt detached, as if she really was actually dreaming now. None of this felt real to her. Spending the last few weeks with Fox at his home had been another thing altogether: she had been sheltered from this new reality she found herself in. Now she just felt awkward, and missed her home with a burning in her throat.

Fox held her hand across the table and watched her intensely. He sensed her shift in mood and could feel the weight of it hanging heavily between them.

"I know this must be difficult for you, Sapphire. I understand it is all strange for you right now, but in time life here will become normal and you will be happy again."

She smiled back at him softly, wanting him to make the strange, uneasy feeling in her chest go away. She knew that the decision she had made to cross over from her world to his was going to be tough, and that there really was no alternative after what had happened there. But it was turning out to be harder than she had thought – far harder. She was human. These people were something else, of which she knew nothing as yet, and she felt like a fish out of water. Perhaps the honeymoon period was fading, and she was suddenly realising that she had made a terrible mistake.

Fox stroked her hand with his thumb, making small circles with the pad across her palm. It sent shivers up her spine. He always had that effect on her. She would just have to suck it up and get on with it. This was her decision, and the only choice she had so that her friends back home could be safe. It had been a necessary sacrifice so that she could find out exactly what was growing inside her, and how she could deal with the changes now taking place in her life.

"It's all a little weird for me, Fox. I don't feel that I fit in very well. I miss my old life, my TV, my job ... eating burgers and drinking beer with my friends. You know ... normal stuff."

He smiled at her and let go of her hand as he leant back in his chair. "I cannot imagine how hard it is for you right now, my love, but I promise you this: your decision to come here and stay with me on Shaka was the right thing to do. You were no longer safe on your world, and the danger you faced there was growing every day you remained. In time you will learn to trust your decision and know it was the only solution."

Sapphire nodded. She suddenly felt very tired. The happy feeling she had had by the pool earlier had gone, and she wanted to return to his home and bury her head under a pillow in bed.

One of the serving girls appeared beside them with a tray laden with food and drinks. She smiled at them both and started to unload the tray. Fox thanked her, and she curtseyed and left. Sapphire looked at the food, her appetite suddenly gone.

"Please, Sapphire, try to eat. You are making me feel very sad."

She looked into his beautiful amber eyes and sighed deeply.

"I'm sorry ... I don't mean to be like this. I'll be fine."

He frowned at her and reached for his tankard. The plates were full of bread, cheese, fruit, and what looked like ham. She picked up some bread and started to eat. It was delicious, but it reminded her of the home-made bread Pearl made. The burning in her throat appeared again. Fox watched her with sad eyes. She knew she was fucking this up. Even now, with the perfect man by her side, it seemed she was incapable of holding down a relationship and making a partner happy. She had never been lucky in love – before Fox had appeared, anyway. The thought was somewhat depressing.

"So this is the beautiful Sapphire? You have let her out at last, my friend."

Sapphire jumped in her seat and looked up to find herself staring at the wide, grinning face of a huge hulk of a man. He was towering over her, his hands on his hips. He must have been six feet seven inches tall at least, and almost as wide.

Fox chuckled and pushed his chair back to stand. "Bear, it is good to see you." They embraced and slapped each other's backs with bravado.

Sapphire continued to chew the piece of bread in her hand before she choked on it. The man was positively huge. His dark ruffled shoulder-length hair and a full beard gave him the look of a Scottish warrior: all he needed was his kilt and he would be straight out of *Braveheart*.

"Yes, this is my Sapphire. Sapphire … this is Bear, my good friend."

Bear stared at her with a sparkle in his eyes, she could feel herself instantly start to blush under his scrutiny.

"You mean your only friend. I can see why you have fallen so hard, Fox. This woman is a beauty, and with ample assets too."

Fox punched him on the arm. Sapphire could not help but smile. This man was intimidating, but funny at the same time.

"Be polite, Bear, or I will have to teach you a lesson in manners."

Bear laughed loudly, causing the other customers to turn and stare at them. "I'd like to see that, my friend." He grabbed a chair and swung it around so that he could sit with them.

Fox returned to his seat and grabbed a hunk of bread. Bear joined in, and Sapphire watched now with some amusement as they tucked into the food.

"So, Sapphire, now that you are here how long do you intend to stay and keep my friend company?" Bear was looking at her now with curiosity, and stuffing handfuls of food into his mouth as he spoke.

Fox watched her, and waited for her response.

She fidgeted in her seat. "I intend to stay quite some time."

Bear smiled. Fox visibly let out a sigh of relief.

"That is indeed good news, Sapphire. I shall look forward to spending time with you, and learning about your world and stories of your life."

She laughed shyly. "There is not much to tell, really, Bear – but of course it will be lovely to get to know you too."

The food had disappeared just like that. She had only managed to eat one piece of bread: Bear had demolished the rest. Fox called the serving girl over for more food to be delivered. Sapphire sipped the cool liquid in the tankard. It tasted sweet, like honey … delicious. As the drink slipped down her throat she began to feel the weight that had been bearing down on her shoulders since they had arrived at the tavern start to lift.

Bear was laughing at something Fox had just said, and she smiled at them. It was good to see him with a friend – to see a glimpse of his world, his life. She had selfishly been so wrapped up in her own misery of missing her friends that she had forgotten the times he had spent with her on Earth, risking everything, trying to fit in to be with her. She felt a new swell of emotion rise up from her belly: love. She did love him, and she would try to make this work. In time she would settle in, and everything would be OK. Perhaps it was the drink, perhaps it was hearing her man laugh again with his friend, but something changed for her then while she was sitting in this strange tavern with a new acquaintance and her gorgeous, magical man. She would be OK, just as Pearl had said.

They ate and drank heartily. Sapphire dug in now. She wanted to fit in. She ignored the bustle around her, and tried not to notice the stares in her direction. The drink – which tasted strongly of honey – was going down well, and she was starting to feel a little tipsy. Bear and Fox were chatting between mouthfuls of food, and it felt oddly familiar to her: not unlike sharing a beer with her friends at The Swan. Time slipped by quickly, and she noticed that the tables were now illuminated by candles that lit the tavern in a warm glow. The softness of the candlelight gave the inside of the tavern a welcoming ambience, and she realised that the day had quickly passed by.

Bear, now seemingly satisfied after demolishing several servings of food, sat back in his chair and gulped down his drink. She had lost count of how many he had drunk.

"You must come and visit my home sometime, Sapphire. I have a wonderful cook: she can rustle up the most amazing food. I will show you how we truly entertain on Shaka."

Fox laughed. "I am not sure she is ready for that just yet, my friend, but of course we will come and visit you soon."

Sapphire felt her eyes were starting to go blurry, and her head was swimming a little. She realised with a smile that she had become unwittingly and quite unexpectedly drunk. Fox smiled at her with dark, amused eyes from across the table.

"Are you OK, my love? You look a little strange."

Sapphire chuckled and took another sip of her drink. "I'm good. What is this, by the way?" She lifted her tankard, and it sloshed a little as her arm wobbled slightly.

"Mead, made from honey. We have an abundance of bees here in the village."

Sapphire nodded, a grin on her face now. "It's good," she said, and chuckled again.

Bear laughed loudly and slammed his tankard down on the table. "The golden nectar, Sapphire. It will soothe the soul – and also give you a thumping headache if you are not careful."

Fox was smiling at her, and starting to realise that she had perhaps had a little too much.

"It is stronger than the alcohol you are used to on your planet, my love. Perhaps it is time to go home now."

Sapphire laughed and threw her hair back in a swish. She suddenly felt as if she did not have a care in the world and wanted to dance around naked. She had always been a lightweight when it came to alcohol, usually to her detriment.

Bear watched her, an amused grin on his bearded face. "You may have to carry her, Fox. She looks quite intoxicated now."

Sapphire pushed her chair back to stand. She needed to pee. As she stood up she staggered slightly to one side and giggled again. She caught herself on the table and knocked one of the tankards over.

"I'm fine," she reassured Fox. "I just need to use the bathroom."

Fox jumped up, laughing, and ready to catch her. "I will help you, my love. Here, take my arm. I have misjudged your ability to consume our magical mead … apologies."

Sapphire hiccuped and grinned, a little hazily.

Bear also stood, and they grabbed her either side and helped her across the tavern. People were laughing and talking loudly now, and she didn't care one bit that they stared at her even more as Fox and

Bear directed her across to the toilet. Sapphire was glad of the help. All coordination seemed to have left her legs, which now had a mind of their own.

Bear stopped by the bar and allowed Fox to half drag her the rest of the way. Her legs had suddenly become quite useless. Visions of the scarecrow from *The Wizard of Oz* filled her head, which made her laugh more. Fox was laughing softly as he pushed the door open and helped her in. She flopped down on to the toilet seat and looked up at him, still giggling.

"I think I'm drunk," she confessed.

He kissed her gently on her forehead and nodded as he helped her to pull down her underwear and get her seated on the toilet properly. He hesitated before leaving to let her go about her business in private.

"Will you be OK?" he asked her.

Sapphire's head was hanging down low, her hair around her face. She hiccuped again, but nodded and giggled a little.

"I'm fine. I won't be long."

He laughed again and shut the door behind her.

She swayed from side to side on the toilet seat while she blissfully relieved herself. She felt positively intoxicated. After eventually sorting herself out she pushed the door open again to find Fox leaning casually against the sink, his arms crossed over his chest. He looked utterly gorgeous, as usual. Sapphire narrowed her eyes at the sight of him standing before her. The alcohol coursing through her veins gave her the sudden overwhelming urge to grab him and have her wicked way with him. She lunged at him clumsily and stumbled slightly. He caught her as she tripped over her own feet and laughed loudly.

He folded his arms around her and held her close for a moment. She snuggled into his chest. The warmth of his body and the steady beat of his heart against her head calmed her enough to regain some sense of balance once more.

"I think it might be a good idea to go home now, Fox."

He was chuckling, and stroking her hair softly. "As you wish, my love."

A shiver of warm air ran across her body, and they were suddenly standing in his bedroom. It was dark now. The room was lit with candles and the balcony doors were open, allowing the moonlight to wash in. He sat her down on the bed and held her arms to steady her.

"Wait here a moment," he said.

She watched him walk out of the room. His graceful stride made her feel flushed and restless. She laughed again, flopped back on to the bed, and stretched her arms out above her head. The mead had caused her whole body to become totally fluid and warm. She relished the feeling of drunkenness and giggled to herself. All memories of feeling uncomfortable and out of sorts from earlier that afternoon had been completely removed. God bless alcohol.

Fox suddenly reappeared next to her. He was smiling with amusement, a cup in his hand.

"Here, drink this. It will make you feel a little better," he said encouragingly.

She pushed herself up slowly with a slight sway.

"But I feel fine," she insisted.

He laughed and passed her the cup. "I am not so sure, Sapphire. Drink this, all of this."

She reached out for the cup and sniffed the contents as she smiled at him.

"More mead?"

He steadied her hand as she took a sip. "No, my love ... something to ground you a little."

She wrinkled her nose up, although the liquid was very pleasant and slipped down her throat with a cool sensation.

"But I don't want to be grounded. This is fun," she protested.

He watched her lifting the cup up to her lips and encouraged her to drink more, with the smile still firmly on his lips. His eyes flashed darkly and seductively at her.

"Yes, this is fun. It is good to see you smiling again. You will feel even better in a minute."

She finished the drink. It was cool and refreshing – almost like lemonade without the fizz. Her head began to clear slightly and the swaying stopped. She felt a new buzz in her stomach creating a tingling throughout her body from her head to her toes.

"Better?" Fox took off his shirt and stood beside the bed in just his trousers. Sapphire felt her horny button bleep back on with a vengeance. She licked her lips, lay back with her arms above her head, and stretched.

"Much better," she said.

He laughed and crawled on to the bed so that he was on all fours above her. She watched him as he slid his hands up under her dress and pushed the material slowly up her body.

"I had forgotten how easily you fly, my love. It was most amusing, but I like you when you are at least conscious."

Sapphire smiled, then frowned suddenly on remembering how drunk she must have looked in the tavern.

"Did I make a fool of myself?"

He bent down and kissed her exposed thigh softly. She shivered in response. He looked up again and pushed her dress up above her navel.

"No, my love. You were fine … no harm done."

She brought her arms down, placed her hands either side of his head, and pushed her fingers into his wonderful, wild hair.

"I doubt that," she said, and giggled again.

He laughed and kissed her stomach. She closed her eyes and held his head as he ran his tongue across her stomach in tiny, light circles.

"That feels good," she sighed.

He chuckled and slid his hands up further as he pushed the dress up over her breasts. She shuffled, laughing, so that he could lift the cotton dress up over her head, and then she was blissfully naked except for her knickers. He brushed her hair away from her face and stared into her eyes for a moment. The intensity in his amber eyes was suddenly fierce, and she knew he meant business. She reached down and unbuttoned his trousers, pushing her hands inside to feel the warmth of his skin and the evidence of his growing arousal.

Fox let out a soft moan and lifted his hips so that she could push his trousers down further to release him. He kicked them off and pressed his body against her. The heat from him made her tremble slightly: skin on skin, soft and hard. She was vibrating like a triangle… such an exquisite sensation. He kissed her, probing with his tongue and – after using one hand to remove her underwear – she was suddenly as naked as he was on the bed. Their energy started to lift, as it always did when they connected. Her eyes rolled, and she could see flashes of white start to sparkle around them.

His fingers traced a line down her thigh sofly and slowly, teasing her skin with their touch. He rolled to one side so that he could still kiss her, but could also stroke her body lightly as she lay flat on her back with her legs now limp and fluid. He started to work his finger magic, playing her like a skilled musician tuning his favourite instrument. He moved to her cheek, her neck, her earlobe, kissing and whispering to her in his strange tongue ... she really must learn his language so that she would know what the hell he was saying. As he continued to caress her she felt her energy start to lift higher. The heat in her groin pulsed intensely, and made her feel light-headed almost drunk again. He lifted his head and stared at her for a moment.

"You are so beautiful, Sapphire ... I could do this to you forever."

She giggled and ran her hand across his chest, the fine hair soft beneath her fingertips. Without warning he lifted her over on to her side so that she had her back to him. She rolled easily. Her body was totally pliable within his hands. He spooned her, pushed her leg forward, and pushed himself inside her very gently.

She gripped the pillow beside her and gasped. He claimed her neck with his mouth and wrapped his arm around her waist so that she was held firmly within his grip. With a slow, luxurious rhythm he pushed himself completely inside her. She was more than ready for him, and pushed back so that he could fill her body completely. She was once again in Fox heaven. He held her tightly and began to make love to her, leisurely, slowly, holding her waist close and kissing her neck ... sucking and licking with a flick of his tongue.

Sapphire felt herself slide, as she always did when Fox was inside her, into the most amazing place. Her whole body was on fire now, with every cell responding to his touch. She could feel the almost burning urge to climax growing inside her, but held it back slightly and enjoyed the ride.

His hand moved from her waist to her breast, where he pinched her nipple gently and made her whimper again as it sent a new pulse of wonderful sensations down into her groin. She could feel him growing harder inside her. He whispered her name softly, which made her quiver against him. He was still moving back and forth against her, with his cock filling her inside and his fingers playing her from the outside.

This was all too much. She felt her body start to throb. Her energy fizzed inside her, and the warmth of her climax started to spread upwards like a trail of fire. She felt it explode like a firework, with waves of heat spreading up from her groin to her belly and chest. She cried out and pushed back against him as she came hard, her whole body shaking now. He groaned against her neck and sucked hard one last time before he flipped her back over so that he was towering above her.

She opened her eyes and gasped. He was surrounded in sparkling gold light. His eyes were almost black, and filled with a hunger so desperate to claim her she felt as if she would implode at any moment. He growled a deep, guttural sound in his throat and then pushed himself back inside her, which made her cry out again.

Fox took her then, hard and fast. His own need to come urged him into a frenzy. He threw his head back as his hair whipped around him in a wild dance and he called out her name one last time as he climaxed inside her, which made her head spin out of control. They were lost for a moment in gold sparks, which lifted them up off the bed still wrapped around each other.

Sapphire clung to him before she felt them bounce back on to the bed. Fox was panting like a dog in her ear, his body hot and hard against her. As he regained his breath he laughed softly and released her slowly, and allowed her head to fall limply to one side. The room was dark and a cool breeze caressed her naked body, which soothed her soul.

She smiled and closed her eyes. His hand was placed gently on her belly, and his face nuzzled into her neck. Life was suddenly so much better. They fell asleep wrapped in each other's arms, sated and soothed. Sapphire's sense of equilibrium had returned and it felt damn good.

Chapter Two

Sapphire woke from a dreamless sleep. She had not dreamt at all since her arrival on Shaka ... her travelling days seemed to be over for now. It had been a wonderful respite from her time on Earth, when she had been out of control. The magic here was obviously keeping her safe.

She opened her eyes slowly and stretched her body out. Every muscle felt as if it had been worked hard. She smiled as she remembered Fox claiming her last night. She reached out for him, but found an empty space in the bed next to her. He was gone. She sat up and blinked. The day was bright and clear outside, and a warm breeze blew softly in from the open doors by the balcony. It was the first time she had woken alone since she had arrived. She yawned, pulled the sheet up around her breasts, and wondered where he had gone.

"Good morning, my lady. I hope you rested well."

Sapphire jumped out of her skin. A young woman was standing next to the bed holding a tray of food. She was smiling at her warmly.

"Fuck! You scared me."

The young woman laughed and placed the tray on the edge of the bed. "I am sorry, my lady. I did not mean to frighten you. Master Fox asked me to attend to you today, as he has been called to see his father and will be gone for a while."

Sapphire nodded, suddenly very conscious that she was naked with just a sheet wrapped around her.

"Oh, OK ... thank you."

She was a pretty young thing, with big dark blue eyes and hair the colour of midnight that hung in soft curls around her face. She lingered by the bed as if waiting for her orders.

Sapphire's stomach rumbled loudly. The girl laughed and pushed the tray towards her. "There are pancakes and some herbal tea, and some eggs and ham, my lady. It sounds as if you need to eat."

Sapphire smiled at her. She had a warmth about her that radiated in a light purple aura.

"I am Kitten, by the way, but you can call me Kit."

Sapphire reached out for the plate full of food ... It smelt amazing. She was suddenly very hungry.

"I'm Sapphire, but please call me Saf."

"I know who you are, Sapphire, I mean ... Saf. It is a pleasure to meet you at last. My lord has told me many things about you. I have been eager to make your acquaintance."

Sapphire nodded and tucked into a pancake. It was warm and sweet ... delicious. She wondered where the hell Fox had been hiding the young girl all these weeks. The thought made her blush slightly. They had hardly been acting as if there was a young woman in the house somewhere hiding in another room ... God, she hoped she hadn't been hiding in another room.

"Are you all named after animals here?" she asked her, trying to make light conversation to ease the slightly awkward atmosphere.

Kit laughed, a light, tinkling laugh that made Sapphire smile more. "Not all of us, my lady – but yes, most people on Shaka are named after the animal they are connected to."

Now that was a piece of interesting information. Perhaps this girl could give Sapphire some insight to the strange new world she now lived on. Sapphire patted the bed next to her and shuffled over a little so that she could sit. Kit hesitated for a moment, then sat down and watched Sapphire consume the food eagerly.

"How do you know Fox?"

Kit smoothed her skirt across her thighs and blushed a little. "He is my lord: I am his servant. I have worked for him since I was a little girl ... he is the kindest master."

Sapphire could tell she was a little smitten, but who wouldn't be?

"Oh, well, it's nice to meet another female. I'm a little out of touch with what's what here on Shaka at the moment."

Kit laughed again. "Yes, I am sure. Master Fox has been keeping you hidden from us. We have all been dying to meet you. I am most interested in hearing about your world ... we have never had a human here before. My mother has told me stories of the dream travellers but, of course, no one except Fox has ever met one. You are quite the curiosity."

Sapphire stuffed a strip of ham into her mouth and sighed. She was a curiosity now, was she? "Mmmh, well ... it's probably about time I let everyone know that I'm pretty normal, really."

Kit smiled broadly. "Oh no, my lady, I can see how wonderful you are. The magic surrounding you is truly beautiful: so different from anything I have ever seen."

Sapphire stopped chewing. What exactly could she see?

"Really? That's news to me," she said.

Kit laughed, and said, "You talk funny."

That was an understatement, to say the least. They both laughed. Sapphire liked this girl. She was sweet, and easy to talk to.

"So, Kit, did Fox say exactly how long he might be?"

"No, my lady – but he could be some time, as his father often has business with him that can take many days."

Sapphire picked up the mug of herbal tea and took a sip. It was sweet, and tasted like cinnamon and honey. It reminded her of Pearl.

"Well, then, we can have a girl's day out. That would be nice. You can fill me in on what there is to do around here."

Kit licked her bottom lip, suddenly looking a little nervous.

"My lord has told me that you must not leave the grounds, my lady."

Sapphire raised her eyebrow. "He did, did he?"

Kit nodded solemnly.

"Well, we shall have to see about that."

Kit stood and brushed her skirt down. "Would you like me to run you a bath, my lady?"

"Saf. Call me Saf ... and yes, please, that would be lovely." Kit smiled and curtseyed and left the room.

Sapphire shook her head at the gesture, which seemed so outdated. It seemed that all the women curtseyed here. Or was that just because Fox held some status in this land as a guardian, and as his 'woman' people were treating her with the same respect? But then she was living a new life on this strange new world, and who was she to question their customs?

After bathing in the most wonderful hot water filled with scented oils of rose and geranium Sapphire dried and dressed in the clothes Kit had laid out for her. She looked down at the long velvet dress in a deep blue and wished that she had brought some jeans and a T-shirt

20

with her. This medieval look was beautiful, but not really her. She sighed, and dressed. It did feel wonderful – and the material was soft to touch and fitted her, as always, perfectly. She brushed her hair out and let it hang down her back to dry.

On walking back into the bedroom she found Kit tidying the bed sheets.

Kit looked over her shoulder and smiled warmly. "You look beautiful, Saf. That colour really suits you."

Sapphire laughed and did a little twirl. "Yes, it feels lovely, but I would kill for a pair of jeans right now."

Kit frowned. "Jeans? What are they?"

Sapphire walked towards the bed, noting that the bed was now freshly made with a scattering of rose petals across the pillows. Perhaps the girl was a hopeless romantic.

"I would love to show you, Kit, but I guess there are no shops around here that sell them."

Kit stepped back from the bed, happy with her work. "Oh, we have shops here, my lady, but I am not sure they would be the same as the ones you have on Earth."

Sapphire regarded her with amusement. "I very much doubt that they would be, but I would love to see yours. Let's take a walk in the garden, and then you can show me."

Kit looked down and fiddled with her hands. "I am not sure Master Fox would be happy for me to do that, my lady."

"Saf, please call me Saf, Kit."

Kit looked up again and smiled, her whole face lighting up. "Well, I suppose it would be OK for a little while. The town is not far, and we could ride there. Can you ride?"

Sapphire smiled broadly now. "Yes, I can, actually. I'm a little rusty, probably, but that would be great fun."

Kit bobbed her head in agreement. "I will show you the stables."

Sapphire was eager to see where the horses were kept. She had not noticed any stables before, but then she had never really ventured very far from the house – and Fox had only taken her to the woods to the far side of his home, then to the tavern yesterday.

They left the house. The air outside was warm, and filled with fragrance from the flowers that grew in the garden. Everything was well kept: the lawns were lush and green, and the flower beds abundant with buds and flowers.

"Who keeps the garden so tidy, Kit?"

The young woman almost skipped alongside Sapphire. She was just a little taller than her, but that wasn't difficult with Sapphire being so tiny.

"Oh, I do. I love the garden, but then everything grows well here. It is the magic in the earth, you know."

Sapphire watched her. She seemed so full of life, a childlike innocence glowing around her.

"Tell me about that. How does it work?"

They stopped beside the fountain, which threw purple and silver water into the air. When the light hit the fountain it created a rainbow of colours that shimmered around its edges.

"This world was born from magic. Everything around us grows from it. Our land, our crops, the animals, and the people all resonate at different levels of magic."

Sapphire smiled at her. "So what exactly are you?"

Kit giggled. "I am not sure how to explain, my lady – I mean, Saf. I suppose you could call us Indigo people, although on your world you may liken us to Elves."

Sapphire laughed. She was living in a world of creatures like in *The Lord of the Rings*. She had a sudden amusing thought.

"Christ, I hope you don't have Orcs here as well."

Kit frowned for a moment, clearly not understanding the term.

"I mean bad people. Elves are the good ones on our world, and the Orcs are the bad ones."

Kit smiled. "Oh, I see. Well, yes, we do have some creatures on our world that are not so pleasant, but they do not live here. They are far away."

Sapphire sighed. "Well, that's good to know."

Kit indicated that they should turn towards the back of the house.

Sapphire looked up at the impressive building. Fox certainly lived in a grand house.

"Tell me, Kit … Fox's father is a magician, right? What is Fox's role? Apart from looking after my sorry ass, of course."

Kit continued to walk as she showed Sapphire the way around the house, and they now stood in a large courtyard.

"Conloach is a magician, yes, but he is also king. Fox is our prince. They are royalty."

Sapphire stopped short. Holy shit, she was dating a prince. This really was turning out to be a fairy tale. Perhaps she was dreaming again. Perhaps this whole thing was one big dream… quite the unexpected bonus. Or headfuck, depending on how you looked at the situation. She laughed at the irony of it all.

Kit seemed surprised by her response. "They rule our kingdom, Saf. They have done for thousands of years. It has been peaceful since Conloach came to rule our lands. I do not remember when Conloach first came to this land and claimed it as his own, but I have heard tales of the battle that took place and how he changed our kingdom for the better. The ruler before was a cruel man."

Sapphire nodded. This was getting really interesting. "Wow … really? That's pretty wild … a battle to claim his kingdom. This really is a place of legends isn't it?"

Kit smiled and nodded, excited now. "We have many legends, Saf. In fact you are one of them – which is why it is such a pleasure to meet you, of course."

Sapphire was a little taken aback. This girl seemed to have known she was crazy different before she even did. "I'd like to hear about that sometime."

Sapphire suddenly found herself standing in front of a series of buildings that were quite obviously stables. Kit led her to one of the stable doors, which was open at the top. She whistled softly, and the head of a beautiful dark brown mare appeared over the wooden frame. It nickered gently and nuzzled her hand.

"We have libraries filled with books that tell the tales of our land. I can show you one day, if you like."

Sapphire watched her stroke the mare's head. The horse was beautiful, with deep brown eyes.

"Yes, I would like that."

Kit opened the door and led the horse out. "This is Amber. You can ride her, Saf. She is gentle and sweet. I will take Midnight. He is a little feistier … I am not sure it would be wise for you to ride him just yet."

Sapphire reached up and patted the horse, who responded by pushing against her softly.

"OK, that sounds like a good idea. It's been a while since I rode."

Kit left her to hold the mare and went to the stable next door. She stepped inside and then reappeared, leading the biggest, blackest horse Sapphire had ever seen. Sapphire stepped back a little, suddenly afraid. Kit chuckled softly.

"Do not fear. He will not harm you. This is Master Fox's horse ... he is a beauty, isn't he?" The stallion stamped his foot and snorted: he did remind her of Fox, all sexy and tall.

"I will show you where the saddles are. Then we can ride to Calafia."

Sapphire laughed. "Calafia?"

Kit nodded and started to lead the stallion across the courtyard to the tack room. "Yes, our city. It is where our king lives."

Sapphire nodded and followed her across the courtyard to the tack room. They saddled the horses, and Kit showed her how to adjust the straps.

It had been a long time since Sapphire had ridden. Kit jumped up like a nimble ninja and looked across at Sapphire, waiting for her to mount. Sapphire grabbed the reins. This was going to be fun in a long dress. She noticed that Kit had hitched her skirts up, showing bare legs that were brown and lean. With some difficulty Sapphire managed to haul herself up on to Amber. The horse stood still, patiently, as she untangled her legs from her long dress and pushed her feet into the stirrups. She was wearing flat shoes that were soft and made from leather. They felt like slippers ... not quite the riding boots she was used to wearing, but they would have to do. Kit did not offer her a riding hat and she felt like it would be an insult to ask. She just hoped she wouldn't fall off and smash her skull open. Positive thoughts were needed at a time like this.

Kit smiled at her. "Are you ready, my lady?"

Sapphire nodded and smiled broadly. This was going to be fun.

They headed off at a gentle trot, with Sapphire feeling the horse beneath her respond to every little movement. Amber seemed to know the way, and was doing all the work. Sapphire just held on and followed Kit. As they headed out of the garden and towards the path Kit looked back over her shoulder, her curls bouncing as they trotted.

"It is not far to Calafia ... depends on how fast we go, really."

Sapphire patted Amber's warm neck. They were trotting quite nicely.

"OK. I'm game, Kit. Let's go for it."

Kit laughed and gave Midnight a kick. The stallion took off like a greyhound released from its cage. Kit was obviously an accomplished rider, and had no fear.

Sapphire sighed. "What the hell," she thought. She kicked Amber gently and the horse responded immediately. Her strong legs moved them up a gear into a canter. Sapphire put her head down and gripped the reins tightly. She felt the wind whip against her face and the strength of the muscles of the horse beneath rippling against her thighs as they moved with a grace and speed she had forgotten. She laughed loudly and tried to keep up with Kit, who was flying ahead. This was the best fun she had had in ages.

They cantered for some time, following the path that turned into a wider road. The fields whipped past either side. Sapphire urged Amber forward. This horse could move, and she gripped tightly with her thighs to keep her balance. She rode well, the memory of her childhood riding days was coming back. She had been a good rider when she was young, and had little fear when it came to speed. It was totally exhilarating being up high and feeling the wind against her face. They rode for about half an hour with the horses keeping up the pace, seemingly full of energy. Perhaps they were magical, too, and could keep going for hours. Eventually they began to see life ahead of them: a few small cottages dotted around at the edges of the road. They passed several people and Kit waved at them as they went by.

As they turned a bend in the road Sapphire gasped at the view. Ahead of them was the most incredible sight she had ever seen: a huge castle that spiralled up with turrets and beautifully coloured glass windows. There were a lot more people around walking and riding to the gates. Kit had slowed Midnight down to a trot as they approached and Sapphire pulled up beside her, a big grin on her face.

"You did well, Saf. You are a good rider to keep up with Midnight."

Sapphire laughed. As they slowed down further, to a walk, she noticed that people were moving out of the way for them as they stared up at Sapphire with wide eyes. They reached the gates. A tall wooden studded door indicated the somewhat forbidding entrance to the castle.

There were two men, one standing guard on either side of the door. They both held swords big enough to chop off a head in one swing. Kit reined Midnight to a stop, and Sapphire did the same with Amber. She was a little out of breath now. Her energy was high, and she felt amazing - the ride had done wonders for her. They dismounted, Sapphire a little ungracefully. She was trying not to fall flat on her face from catching her feet inside the long dress. Kit was smiling at her and watching Sapphire struggle, her big blue eyes flashing with amusement.

"I know, I know. I'm a little out of practice … need to get up the gym."

Kit laughed. She had no idea what she was talking about. They led the horses to the gateway. There was a long wooden bar to one side of the gate, with several other horses already tied to it. Bales of hay and fresh water buckets were along its length. A young lad stood to one side, brushing one of the horses. Sapphire stifled a laugh.

"Is this the parking for horses?"

Kit smiled at her and shook her head. "I do not understand you, Saf."

Sapphire smiled. "Never mind. I assume we leave the horses here, don't we?"

"Yes. They will be taken care of while we are inside the castle gates. We cannot take them in." They handed the reins to the young man, who tipped his head and smiled at them both. Sapphire stopped abruptly.

"Shit. I have no money. How are we going to shop with no money?"

Kit turned and regarded her, a little confused. "You do not need money, my lady. You are the prince's woman. You can have whatever you wish."

Sapphire raised her eyebrows. "Now that's pretty damn cool," she thought.

They walked through the gates, with the soldiers bowing as they passed. In fact everyone was bowing as they passed. Sapphire found the whole thing a little strange and, quite frankly, unnerving. Kit seemed to take it all in her stride. She placed her arm into the crook of Sapphire's and led her into the opening courtyard of the castle entrance.

Sapphire looked up. Some way ahead, the castle towered above them. There were streets leading off in all directions, and people everywhere going about their business.

Kit looked at her with a kind smile. "Where would you like to go first, Saf? I can take you to the dressmaker's, we could visit the jewellery shop, or I can take you to the market where they sell fresh food and delicacies."

Sapphire found her mouth opening slightly in awe. This place was amazing. It was just like being in the eighteenth century, but with magic. She noticed that the air here seemed to hum with an underlying current of energy. She felt it in her belly.

"You choose, Kit. I will follow."

Kit bobbed her head, her curls jumping up and down as she did. "Then the dressmaker first and the jewellery shop second, I think. We can pick up some food on the way back. I need some provisions for supper."

Sapphire was really getting into this now. She was ignoring the stares and taking in her surroundings, and soaking up the atmosphere with relish. They arrived at a shop that looked as if it belonged to Tudor times, with a window display showing beautiful dresses and skirts in all the colours of the rainbow. Kit pushed the door open, and Sapphire followed behind. The energy inside hit her at the same time as the strong smell of roses and jasmine. The interior was lit with soft candlelight, and everything seemed alive. A woman behind the counter beamed at Kit. She was perhaps in her fifties, but obviously age here was a different thing altogether. She had long dark-blonde hair intricately braided and piled up on top of her head. She was also very beautiful, which seemed to be the normal trend here on Shaka.

"Kitten, it's wonderful to see you. How can I help you today?"

Kit walked to the counter and leant over. She placed her head in her hands and her elbows on the wooden countertop.

"Something extra special today, Violet. I have brought you a very special lady here, who would like to take a look at your clothes."

Violet smiled warmly and nodded. She glanced back at Sapphire who was standing still, looking around her at the kaleidoscope of colours and textures.

27

"And who is that, my dear?"

Kit giggled. "Her name is Sapphire. She is the prince's new woman."

Violet gasped and clapped her hands with glee.

Sapphire suddenly felt a little weird. Violet bustled around the counter towards Sapphire, who stepped back a little in anticipation of contact with her. The dressmaker stood before her, clasping her hands together like an excited child. Her eyes were flashing a deep violet, beautiful and oddly mesmerising.

"Oh, my goodness, this is an honour. It is wonderful to meet you, Sapphire. Please take your time … try on whatever you like. I am at your service."

Sapphire raised her eyebrow and smiled weakly. Violet's enthusiasm was slightly overwhelming. She was not used to being treated like this and wished Fox had warned her of her new status on this world, which was much higher than on the one she had left behind.

"Thank you. That's very kind of you."

Violet moved in a rush of skirts to find things to tempt her. Kit, obviously enjoying herself, swung around and beamed at Sapphire. Very quickly Sapphire found herself in her underclothes with an array of dresses, skirts, and tops to try on. She had picked out a few items, but Kit and Violet had been handing her other things she would never have thought of trying.

It was just like shopping with Charlie, with all the enthusiasm and giddiness. She felt a little sad at the thought of her friend. Charlie would have loved this. Perhaps not the outfits, but the whole experience of people rushing around after her. As she stepped into a particularly beautiful green skirt and fitted bodice she wondered how the hell this had all happened so fast.

Kit stepped into the dressing room and, very much the attentive servant, started to lace the bodice up for her from behind. Again, this was something Sapphire found very strange.

"This is also a good colour for you, Saf. You have such a wonderful figure – so curvy, but tiny. It is no wonder our lord covets you so."

Sapphire felt a faint blush spread across her cheeks. Kit looked up from under dark lashes and smiled a little teasingly. "I can find you some beautiful underclothes if you like. That will please him."

Sapphire laughed a little shakily. Everyone must know that their lord was rather practised in the art of seduction. "If you like, Kit."

Kit finished tying the bodice and stepped back to look at Sapphire in the mirror. They both stared at her reflection. She did indeed look beautiful. The material was heavy and wonderfully soft. It contoured her hips perfectly, and the bodice was stitched with tiny diamonds and pearls – she wondered if they were real – that twinkled in the mirror like mischievious sprites.

Kit smiled and pulled her hair to one side, so that it exposed her neck a little and fell in a thick strand across her breast. She raised her eyebrow and giggled as she noted the blue-black mark on her neck – one of Fox's specialities. Sapphire blushed more.

"You look wonderful, Saf. I wish I could look so beautiful."

Sapphire laughed. "You are beautiful, Kit, very beautiful. Why don't you try something on?"

Kit gasped in horror and flung her hands up to her face. "Oh … no, my lady, I couldn't possibly. It isn't right for us to dress this way."

Sapphire ran her fingers over the fine material and found herself taking pleasure in the way it slipped across her skin.

"Don't be silly. Try one on and we will take it. We'll put it on Fox's tab."

Kit blinked again. She didn't understand the term. Sapphire smiled at her. "Find me some of that fancy underwear you mentioned, and a dress for you. Come on."

Kit giggled and left the dressing room quickly.

An hour later they left the shop with several bags full of beautiful things. Sapphire wondered how the hell they would get it all home. It wasn't as though they could put it in the boot of the car and drive back. Kit whistled across the street. A young lad with long dark hair quickly ran to her call, and beamed widely as he noticed Sapphire behind her.

"Yes, my lady, how can I help you today?"

"Raven, I am here shopping with the lady Sapphire. We will be purchasing many things, and I need you to collect them and deliver them all to Master Fox's home once we are done."

He nodded, and bowed at Sapphire ... She was really starting to feel uncomfortable with the whole bowing thing. Kit spun around after depositing the bags with the said Raven. Perhaps he would fly them home.

Next was the jewellery store. Sapphire was in heaven. She was not really a keen jewellery collector but, after living with Charlie and watching her design fabulous pieces, she had an appreciation and awe for the trade. The shop was an Aladdin's cave filled with gems, gold, and silver in intricate designs. She had no idea where to start looking.

They had received the same warm welcome from the shop owner as they had from Violet at the dressmaker's shop. He was a young man – again very handsome – with strange purple eyes and a long goatee beard that was plaited intricately down to his chest. He eyed the obsidian necklace that was hanging between her breasts with a glint in his eye.

"This is a very beautiful piece, my lady. The magic surrounding it is strong. Where did you find it?"

Sapphire lifted the obsidian and held it in her hand, feeling the soft warm pulse of its energy. It had transported across with her when she had left Earth – the only thing, apart from her summer dress – that had.

"A very dear friend gave it to me. It is for protection."

He nodded. "Yes, I can see that. It's wonderful, like nothing I have ever seen before."

Kit, meantime, was having a great time wandering down the glass cases and looking at all the beautiful items.

"Here, Saf, come look at this bracelet. It is amazing. Perfect for you."

Sapphire smiled at the jeweller before heading over to Kit. They stood looking down into the case, and Kit pointed to a filigree silver bangle that was very delicate in design, with ivy and vine leaves wrapping around each other in a series of knots. Deep blue sapphires were placed on the bangle and set at intervals within the silver, which gave it the appearance of something quite precious indeed.

Sapphire was so lost in the moment that she did not feel the presence behind her until a warm hand circled itself around her waist and pulled her into an even warmer, firm body. She gasped.

Kit let out a little yelp and spun around.

Sapphire felt her body start to pulse madly, tingles running up her spine.

"You are very naughty, Sapphire, leaving my home when I gave strict instructions to young Kitten here to keep you safely inside." Fox leant in and kissed her neck, and then without any warning of his intention to do so he began running his warm tongue lightly and quickly up to her earlobe, making her legs go a little weak. The action made her feel like he was scenting her, claiming her as his, and only his. He spun her around and faced her, his amber eyes flashing with amusement. He pressed against her and pushed her back on to the glass case. She caught her breath. He was just so goddam gorgeous - unnervingly so.

Kit had stepped back slightly and was breathing a little too quickly. Sapphire sensed her fear.

"I am sorry, my lord," said Kit. "Saf wanted to go out shopping for a while, and I thought it would not take long to show her around and return before nightfall."

His gaze remained on Sapphire, who was now falling into his wild eyes with a renewed lust. She had only seen him last night, but now his touch was making her want him again. He licked his lips and smiled, obviously reading her mind. He kept her pressed up against the glass counter.

"Kitten, you are also very naughty ... but I know how persuasive my lady can be, so you are forgiven just this once."

Sapphire heard her sigh with relief.

"Yes, my lord. I am sorry, my lord ... I will arrange to take Saf back home right now."

He blinked, and broke the energy connection between them. Sapphire shivered and pulled herself out of the spell he had cast over her.

"No ... it's fine, Kitten. You may continue to show Sapphire around. I have other business I must attend to, but make sure you do leave before nightfall or you will be in trouble."

Sapphire saw Kit curtsey from the corner of her eye.

Fox moved in for a proper kiss. He held her head either side with warm hands and kissed her deeply, obviously not giving a damn that they had an audience ... or was he just claiming her in front of them to make a point? Either way, at that moment Sapphire didn't care. Boy, could this man kiss. Slowly, he released her. She smiled at him as he brushed her cheek with the back of his hand.

"Hello, Fox."

He chuckled and released her, allowing her back to move away from the glass counter. She could sense the shopkeeper hovering to one side. He had no idea whether he should approach them or not.

"Show me what you were looking at, gorgeous," Fox said.

Sapphire stepped to one side. Her breathing was starting to return to normal now after the kiss.

"This bracelet. Kit found it ... It is rather pretty."

Fox smiled at her. His face lit up with amusement. "Would you like it?"

Sapphire bit her bottom lip. She already felt as if she had taken too much in his name. This would be too much. Fox answered for her. He moved his head around and looked at the shopkeeper, who jumped up a little on full alert in the presence of his prince.

"Please wrap the bracelet for me, Stag. Send me the bill."

The shopkeeper rushed to the glass counter and fumbled with his keys to unlock it. Sapphire felt like the mistress who was being spoilt with trinkets.

"Fox, honestly, I don't need it ... I'm sure it is very expensive. Please ... I already have several new dresses."

He took her arm and pulled her into his chest firmly. "And you shall have many more, my love. You shall have whatever you wish for. I want you to be happy, and if this makes you happy then so be it."

She looked up at him. "It would make me happy if you were to come home with me. When will you be back?"

He kissed her lightly on the tip of her nose and stroked her back as if she were a cat.

"Soon my love. I have a few things I need to attend to for my father, but I will be home tonight, I promise." He released her gently. She let go of him reluctantly, suddenly wanting to stay in his arms longer. He smiled and brushed away a hair from her forehead.

"Enjoy shopping. I will see you soon. Be good." He stepped back. The air around him shimmered, and then he disappeared. Just like that. Again.

Kit touched her arm and made her jump.

"I am sorry, Saf. I didn't mean to get you into trouble. I can take you back if you would like."

Sapphire shook herself. The bubble of Fox magic she had just been inside had left, and she was now in the shop with Kit and Stag staring at her. The said shopkeeper was holding up a pretty white bag with blue ribbon tied around it for her. The bracelet, she presumed.

He handed it to her and bowed. "Is there anything else I can help you with, my lady?"

Sapphire took the bag and stared at it. It looked so pretty just in the box. "No, thank you. I think that's enough jewellery for today."

He smiled and dipped his head. "It has been a pleasure and an honour to meet you today, dream traveller."

Sapphire smiled at him. She was getting used to people calling her that now. After all, that was what she was – or had been for a while. The dreaming had stopped for now.

Kit appeared at her side.

"Would you like to go to the market now, Saf? We can eat there as well, if you are hungry."

Sapphire nodded. She was starting to feel a little hungry now. Being with Fox, even for the briefest moment, had worked up her appetite again.

They left the shop. Kit had taken the bracelet and handed it to the waiting Raven – their butler for the day – who had appeared again outside the shop. Kit held her arm again and sighed as they walked up the street.

"It is wonderful to see Master Fox so in love with you, Saf. He is a different man now. He is ... complete. He has been alone for a very long time."

Sapphire looked across at her sweet face. She was smiling, as if imagining a fairy tale story in her head.

"He makes me very happy, Kit. I have never known a man like him."

Kit giggled and blushed. "He is the most handsome of our men, I do envy you."

33

Sapphire nudged her playfully as they walked.

"I'm sure you will find a handsome man for yourself one day, Kit. You are a pretty young thing. You must have all the guys falling over themselves for you."

Kit blushed a little. "Oh, not really. There are many beautiful people here on Shaka, but maybe one day I will find love like you. That would be nice."

Sapphire watched her. After seeing the wash of different emotions cross her expression, she wished it for her too. If every woman could feel the way she did with Fox the universe would be a very happy place indeed.

They arrived at an open marketplace with stalls crammed next to each other that were selling everything, from fresh vegetables and herbs and flowers to animals. All the produce was brightly coloured and inviting. It was the most abundantly supplied of places. People milled around, haggling and laughing and buying their wares, with happy smiling faces. Sapphire soaked up the atmosphere. She could see every person surrounded by the most amazing colours. Their auras were strong, vibrant, and pulsing. Her second sight was in full force here on Shaka, and for a while it made her head spin with its intensity.

Kit noticed her wavering a little and pulled her to a stall with chairs and tables at the front, a place to eat and drink. The smell of hot foot wafted invitingly from behind the trestle tables laden with tempting treats.

"Sit, Saf … you looked tired suddenly. I will order us something to eat. Is there anything you fancy?"

Sapphire sat down heavily at one of the tables. She did feel a little weary. Perhaps she was picking up too much energy from the people around her.

"I really don't mind, Kit. You choose. I could kill a burger and fries, but I'm sure they don't sell those here."

Kit laughed and wandered up to the food seller.

Sapphire people-watched for a while. She tried to ground herself by slipping off her shoes and placing her bare feet on the ground to connect to the energy beneath her. She closed her eyes for a moment and breathed deeply, remembering the meditation Pearl had taught her as she pulled the energy up from under her feet. She felt an intense rush of white heat rise up her legs and fly up through her body and out of the top of her head. She instantly felt clearer and opened her eyes with a start. "Well, that certainly did the trick."

Kit was standing looking at her with wide blue eyes. "Oh, my lady, are you OK? You are glowing with the brightest light I have ever seen."

Sapphire smiled at her. "I'm fine, Kit: much better now. You were right about the magic in this land. I think it just zapped me."

Kit sat and watched Sapphire. Her lips were parted, and she was looking around and shaking her head slowly.

"I have never seen anyone consume energy like that before. You are truly amazing, my lady."

Sapphire laughed and stretched her arms up over her head. She was feeling a little giddy now. "Well, I shall have to do this more often. I feel amazing now, and starving."

The food arrived quickly and Sapphire was pleased to see that Kit had ordered them both a large bowl of what tasted like chicken and vegetable stew, large hunks of fresh bread, and some sweet waffles that were set to one side and smothered in honey. She had also ordered them a glass of cool, crisp lemonade.

They both tucked in. Sapphire was as happy as a pig in shit. It had turned out to be a good day after all, and Sapphire was glad she had made a new friend. Kit wasn't Charlie, but she was sweet and fun, and that was a start. She wondered how old she was exactly.

"Kit, tell me, how old are you?"

Kit was finishing off her stew and mopping up the gravy with a hunk of bread – a girl after her own heart.

"I'm not sure, exactly. Age is not recorded here on Shaka, and we all age differently. We tend to mark our lives with rites of passage."

Sapphire took a sip of the delicious lemonade and reached for the waffles that were giving her the 'Eat me quick' look.

"Really? How does that work?"

Kit smiled at her. "Well, we have landmark stages in our lives. For the women it is in three stages: Maiden, Mother, and then Crone."

Sapphire laughed. "I feel like an old crone sometimes," she said.

Kit laughed. "Oh no, my lady. I believe you are very much in the maiden stage of your life, as am I."

Sapphire regarded her thoughtfully. "So what about the men?"

Kit pushed her empty bowl to one side and dipped her finger in the honey on the side of her waffle. She licked it slowly and looked up, as if for inspiration.

"Well, that is fairly straightforward, but some of the men never reach the final stage of passage. They are adolescent and then they are men. That's it."

Sapphire laughed. "Sounds about right. I am assuming that Fox is in the 'man' stage."

Kit laughed with her. "Of that I have absolutely no doubt, my lady: there was a large ceremony with the Oracle for Fox when he became a man. The journey can be hard for them: they must prove themselves in battle ... and of course there is an initiation ceremony, which some men do not pass."

"Really? What happens to them?"

Kit fidgeted in her seat a little. "They are often killed, and leave this world for the afterlife ... but, luckily, most of the men here are very strong."

Sapphire raised an eyebrow. The waffle was delicious. She had eaten most of it already. "So it kind of sorts out the wheat from the chaff?"

Her words sounded harsh, but Kit nodded. "Yes, it does, my lady. That is the way of our world. The strongest survive, the weak do not."

They finished their pudding in silence. Sapphire thought about what Kit had told her: how this world was a balance of nature, just like in the animal kingdom. She thought about Earth and how much humans had changed that balance, had changed the way people lived. The old were living longer due to modern medicine, and new life was being born with the help of artificial insemination. She wondered if that was why it was becoming so overpopulated: whether humans had actually tipped the balance of their world and changed the magic by consuming too much of its natural energy source ... these were heavy thoughts.

She shook her head and pushed the thoughts to one side. The food was gone, and Sapphire felt nicely full. Her energy buzz had died down a little now, and she felt back to her old self.

She slipped on her shoes and smiled at Kit. "Shall we grab those bits you needed and head back?"

Kit pushed herself up and smiled. "Yes, it won't take long." Kit paid for the food. Sapphire noticed that the coins she left on the table were a solid rough gold with the mark of a pentacle on them. Magic coins, perhaps?

They wandered back slowly, and Kit collected various wares along the way: vegetables, and a pheasant that was hanging by its limp feet looking very much dead. Raven appeared again and Kit handed over her bags. She slipped him some of the gold coins before he disappeared again with all the bags. Sapphire wondered how the hell he would get them back home.

They walked back to the castle gates. The day had passed quickly, and the sky was starting to turn a pink and hazy orange as dusk approached. Their horses were waiting for them at the gate, and the young lad attending them handed Sapphire the reins to Amber as he smiled a little shyly. He helped her up and untangled her dress for her so that she could slip her feet into the stirrups. Kit mounted Midnight with a jump that was catlike. She made it look easy. They took off as the sun slipped down over the horizon.

As she thundered along the road Sapphire felt the same exhilaration she had earlier when riding. The beautiful landscape rushing past her was starting to turn a grey-blue as the daylight disappeared. They arrived at Fox's grand house just as night fell and the house was before them, lit up like a welcoming beacon. Sapphire hoped Fox would be home soon. She missed him already. Kit took the horses into the stable, and indicated to Sapphire that she should go in and freshen up while she took care of them before they turned in for the night.

Sapphire wandered back to the house and noticed another building to the side of the house that she had not realised was there before. She would ask Kit what was inside it later.

Chapter Three

As Sapphire entered the hallway she noticed that candles had been lit and a fire was burning in the room to her right. Fox had shown her around his home after her arrival on Shaka. The house had a large kitchen, a living area, a study, three bedrooms, and a bathroom. It was simple but luxurious, and right now was humming with a warm, homely feeling. The magic here was strong. She wondered if he too had fairies in the cupboards who came out at night and lit the candles and the fire in the fireplace. She laughed at the thought and headed up the stairs to freshen up.

As she reached the bedroom she was surprised to see the clothes she had brought earlier were sitting on the bed. The bag with her new bracelet had been placed next to them. Raven, their appointed butler for the day, had obviously been busy.

She had bathed that morning, but wanted to wash and change. She slipped out of her clothes and went into the bathroom naked, and filled the sink with warm water. Using a soft sponge, she began to wash herself. She missed her hot shower, but found the ritual of bathing this way soothing. She dried herself quickly and found the mouthwash Fox had given her. When she had first arrived she had asked him for a toothbrush and toothpaste. Apparently there was no such thing here, but the mixture of herbs and something else she couldn't place – in a light green liquid – did the job. In fact her mouth was totally refreshed after swilling it around. This would make a killing back on Earth: it was much easier than standing and brushing for three minutes.

Feeling much better after her ride, and now clean again, she headed back into the bedroom and looked for the new underwear Kit had found her. At least they had decent undies on Shaka. They were pretty and lacy, in a blush pink. Sapphire slipped on the underwear. There was no such thing, it seemed, as a Wonderbra, but corsets were the thing here. She found the matching pink corset to her knickers and twisted it around to tie up the lacing at the back. Kit appeared out of nowhere beside her.

"Here ... let me help you, Saf."

Sapphire jumped a little. One of her breasts was poking out. In her fumbling, she covered herself with her hands, strangely shy in front of this young woman. Kit smiled at her sweetly and stood behind her, and twisted the corset back around and shuffled it up so that Sapphire was now fully covered. She started to pull and tie the lacing. Sapphire felt like a stuffed chicken as Kit pulled her in tightly.

"You have wonderful breasts, Saf. Mine haven't even started to grow properly yet. No wonder I cannot attract a man."

Sapphire laughed. "I'm sure they will arrive at some point, Kit. To be honest, mine have been rather a hindrance most of my life. Men couldn't look me in the eye back on Earth. They just stared at my tits a lot, which can be very frustrating."

Kit was laughing now. She had finished with the corset, and stepped back to face Sapphire.

"Which dress would you like to wear tonight, Saf? I think the pale pink would look nice for supper. Master Fox should be home soon... I can style your hair for you."

Sapphire felt a swell of emotion in her chest. It was just like standing with Charlie getting dressed to go out. Her friend always did her hair for her.

Kit frowned. "Are you OK, my lady? Did I say something wrong?"

Sapphire shook her head and looked down at her feet. "No, of course not, Kit. It's just that my best friend at home used to do my hair for me, and I really miss her."

Kit nodded and smiled again softly. "I understand. It must be hard for you ... I miss my family and friends, as I do not see them often now that I serve Master Fox."

Sapphire looked up into her deep blue eyes. This girl was so young, and away from her family too. They seemed to have more in common than Sapphire originally thought.

"Then we shall have to keep each other company and be each other's friend, now, shan't we?"

Kit nodded enthusiastically. "I would like that, Saf, very much."

Kit helped her to dress. They laughed as Sapphire wiggled into the dress. It was made of silk and fell to her ankles in beautiful, flowing folds. The dress was cinched at the waist to give her the appearance of an hourglass. It had an Empire line shape that set off her wonderful cleavage to its best advantage, and long sleeves that fell into points just past her wrists.

Kit made her sit at the dresser and started to brush out her hair. Sapphire closed her eyes and enjoyed the sensation. She could feel static crackle across her scalp as she did.

"Would you like me to paint your face, Saf? You are beautiful without paint, but it would look pretty against the pink of your dress."

Sapphire opened her eyes, and was shocked to see that her hair had been suddenly decorated with tiny white flowers and braids that were twisted and knotted in places up on top of her head.

"Paint my face?"

Kit smiled and nodded. She left the room and came back. Her hands were full of pots with various coloured creams inside.

"Oh, you mean make-up."

Kit looked confused but nodded.

Sapphire clapped her hands. "Yes, please. God, I've missed my mascara. Do you have any mascara?"

Kit laughed. She placed the pots down and began to mix one of the darker brown creams with a tiny brush. "I am not sure what that is, Saf, but let me show you."

After a very short time Sapphire looked at herself in the mirror. Kit had applied a silky golden-brown shade to her eyelids and then used a black kohl on them, giving her the appearance of an Egyptian queen. Another black liquid had been brushed on to her eyelashes ... mascara. She had touched her cheeks with a pale pink blush, and had applied a hint of the same colour to her lips. Sapphire looked amazing. With her hair and new dress she felt like a princess. Fuck! She most probably was a princess now.

Kit was beaming at her. Her own cheeks were flushed now. "You look so beautiful, Saf. Master Fox will be pleased."

Sapphire smiled at her, and turned around and held Kit by the forearms. "Thank you, Kit. It looks wonderful. I have had the best day today. It has been so much fun spending time with you."

Kit lowered her eyelashes and smiled. The blush on her cheeks grew darker. "It has been a pleasure, my lady, and an honour. I am so glad we can be friends." She looked up again and sighed. "I must start to prepare the food. Would you like some mead while you wait?"

Sapphire sat up straighter and laughed. "Only a small one, I think, Kit ... but yes, that would be nice. I think I'll sit in the lounge for a while next to the fire. Do you have any books here I could read?"

Kit blinked. "Books? Well, yes ... I think Master Fox does have some. I will have a look for you." She left the room with a rustle of skirts.

Sapphire stared at herself for a moment. She looked so different: a new person on a new world. But today had been one of the best days since her arrival.

The first few weeks with Fox had been amazing, of course, but she realised now that they had been wrapped in a bubble of lovemaking and she had not really integrated with her new home at all until her visit to the tavern yesterday – and now seeing the town and its people.

She licked her lips. The lipstick Kit had applied tasted like cherries. Perhaps it was made from cherries ... It was delicious. She took the beautiful silver and sapphire bracelet from its box and slipped it on to her wrist. It twinkled in the candlelight. She stood up and walked barefoot down the stairs to the living room. She found a pile of books on the table next to the fireplace, and a small glass of mead placed beside them. The smell of cooking started to waft from the hallway. Kit was obviously working hard already. She must have some seriously strong magic in her as well - she did everything superquick.

Sapphire settled herself in one of the soft leather-backed chairs. A large church candle was placed on the table next to it and it gave off a decent amount of light for her to read by. She wondered why a place like this did not have electricity – but, then again, Fox could conjure light from nowhere, so who needed it? She browsed through the pile of books and flicked through the pages to see which one she might find interesting. They seemed to be fiction: fantastical stories of people and places she had never heard of. Some were detailed catalogues of flowers and herbs, and she also found a book which described various types of battle tactics and fighting skills.

The last book she looked at had a soft leather binding the front cover was etched with a symbol that looked like a chalice. The cup was overflowing – one side with flowers, the other side with vines. She opened it, and raised her eyebrows. The first page showed a picture of a man and woman having sex in the missionary position. She giggled and turned the other pages. The writing was in another language. It looked like Arabic, but was far more delicate and very pretty. Other pages were filled with more sexual positions, and some were pretty graphic. At one point she turned the book upside down to try and figure out what, exactly, they were doing. It was like the *Kama Sutra*, but better. No wonder Fox was such a skilled lover if he had studied this particular gem. A warm hand touched her neck lightly, making her jump a little.

"Interesting reading, my love?"

Sapphire blushed hotly. She looked up into the sparkling eyes of her man, who was standing next to her. He was dressed in black leather trousers and waistcoat, with a cotton shirt. The waistcoat was undone, and was decorated with leather lacing and beads. He looked hot as hell. Sapphire slammed the book shut, feeling as she would have had she been caught out looking at her parents' porn. Fox chuckled and crouched down beside her. He lifted his hand and traced a fingertip across her cheek, his eyes never leaving hers. Tiny sparks of light travelled across her skin, and she shivered at his touch.

"You look beautiful, Sapphire. Spending the day shopping was obviously good for you."

Sapphire smiled at him. "Thank you – and yes, I have had a good day – but I'm glad you are back. I missed you."

He leant forward and kissed her softly on the lips. As he moved back he licked his bottom lip, obviously tasting the cherry. He raised an eyebrow and smiled at her. "Shall we eat?"

He helped her up and wrapped his fingers between her own. His hand was warm, and sent shivers down her spine. Sapphire carried her glass of mead with her, and Fox led them out of the living room into the kitchen. This also served as a dining area, with a long wooden table that had six chairs placed around it. Kit was nowhere to be seen, but the table was now laden with food: the pheasant was cooked and browned to perfection, surrounded by various vegetables.

Sapphire heard her stomach growl again: she was permanently hungry lately. They sat at the table, Fox at the head and Sapphire to his left. He poured himself some mead, and then began to dish up the food for them. He smiled at her as he did, a gentle smile full of love and lust. Sapphire felt her chest swell with emotion, she felt so wonderful in his presence.

"Where have you been today?" she asked him as she took a bite of potato. It was soft and tasted of garlic and herbs … wonderful.

"With my father."

Sapphire eyed him, a little suspicious of his brief answer. "Mmmh … doing what?"

Fox sipped the mead. He hesitated, it seemed, before answering. "Sometimes he asks for my counsel on matters of the kingdom. I shall be spending a little more time with him in the next week, but you have Kit to keep you company now – and I shall return each evening to be with you, my love."

Sapphire nodded slowly. She sensed he was keeping something from her. "OK, and about that kingdom stuff …" she pouted. "You could have told me that your father is king and that you are a prince. Talk about making me look daft … I had no idea."

Fox regarded her for a moment, the smile still faintly on his lips. "It was not important, but now you know."

She laughed. "Not important? Well that's an understatement, Fox. Being royalty is a big thing on Earth."

He continued to eat, slowly now. "It makes no difference to us. My status here is something I deal with in my own way. My father gives me the freedom to live as I please, and what pleases me the most is to have you at my side and to make you happy."

Sapphire sipped the mead again. It warmed her belly, and was starting to give her the happy buzz she had felt at the tavern.

"Well … that's OK, then. But all day everyone has been treating me like some kind of princess. It was a little unnerving, to be honest."

He looked deep into her eyes – which made her stop breathing for a moment, his look was so intense.

"You are my princess, Sapphire, and one day I hope that you will be my queen. You deserve to be treated with respect and honour.

You are the most incredibly powerful and beautiful woman I have ever known. It is your right to feel worshipped."

Sapphire gulped. Intense, or what? "This is all a little overwhelming for me, Fox. One minute I'm an average human woman living an average human life … next thing I'm thrown into a world of magic and a place in the royal household. Put yourself in my shoes for a second. It's intense."

He leant back into his chair and placed his fingers together into a steeple. "I do understand, Sapphire. This has happened very quickly for you, but it was your destiny. I have been waiting many human lifetimes for you to awaken to your magic, and now that you have and are here with me I am taking advantage of the fact you are now my woman. Forgive me if I have not been forthcoming with some of the details, but my love for you is all-consuming. I wish for nothing more than to live the rest of my life wrapped in your arms."

The atmosphere had become a little serious, and Sapphire was taking in the declaration of his feelings for her with a renewed sense of realisation. She laughed softly and reached across to touch his arm. He relaxed his body at her touch and placed his hands back down on to the table.

"It's OK, Fox, really. The feeling is mutual. It's just a lot to take in … I am still human, you know."

He laughed now, and continued to eat. The atmosphere lifted again. "Mostly human, my love. I can see your energy has lifted again. The magic inside you is growing by the day."

Sapphire finished her plate of food. The pheasant had been delicious. "Pearl did tell me that if I came here things would change for me. In fact she said that the possibilities were endless."

Fox sipped his mead. His eyes were flashing black and gold. "And she was right. Your magic is strong, my love, but I will protect you. Never forget that."

Sapphire frowned. "From what? I am safe here now, aren't I?"

Fox looked down for a second. Just the briefest flash of what seemed like a brush of nerves crossed his face. Sapphire caught it, but could not understand it. He looked up again and smiled.

"Of course you are, my love. You are the safest you can be."

Sapphire suddenly felt a presence beside her, and she realised that Kit was standing just behind her. She stepped forward as Fox nodded his head slightly.

"Would you like dessert now, my lord?" She had begun gathering the plates and was piling them up her arm like an expert.

"Yes, Kit, that would be nice. The pheasant was excellent." She curtseyed and left.

Sapphire watched him with keen eyes. "Kit tells me that the people here are like Elves. The magic in them is all different. Is that why people are treating me like a precious object? Is my magic different?"

Fox took a deep breath. "Yes, that is right. You are very different, my love. You are something no one has seen before. The dream travellers have always been a fairy tale to my people. They have never seen one before. A human traveller has never crossed over to our world. It is unheard of."

She licked her lips slowly. "But Kit has told me there are legends of the travellers and legends of a human traveller. Is that me?"

He smiled. "Kit likes to talk too much – but yes, there are stories."

Sapphire wanted more information. "And stories of battles. She tells me of people who live far away from here who are different from you ... not so good?"

Fox hesitated. "We have had many battles here on our planet, Sapphire. There have been times of war here. Everything has a balance: good and bad, dark and light – the same as Earth, but perhaps somewhat different."

Sapphire looked up for a moment. Her mind was swirling with possibilities now. "Like *The Lord of the Rings*?"

He laughed. "I have no idea what that is, my love."

She sighed loudly and looked back at him. "You know ... Tolkien, the Elves and the Orcs, hobbits, magicians ... Come on, you must know that one."

He laughed. "Ah, yes! Tolkien ... He was one of us many lifetimes ago ... an intelligent man ...a great scribe."

Sapphire blinked. That made a lot of sense.

Dessert arrived. Kit dished them up both a generous serving. It looked like pears with berries and honey. Sapphire would need to find a gym at this rate. Her backside was going to become enormous if she continued eating so much. Sapphire tucked in. The pears were sweet, soft, and grainy. The honey was warm and smooth ... It was utterly fabulous. Fox watched her devour the sweet with an amused smile on his lips.

"Sweet like you, my love. Are you enjoying yourself?"

She blushed and smiled, and licked her lips as she finished off the sweet fruit. "Yes, very much. The food here is delicious. At this rate I will be a fat princess, not a slim one!"

He laughed. "Never, my love. I will help you work it off." His smile became one full of promise. She felt his lust wash over her and make her fidget in her chair.

Fox stood up after finishing his own bowl of sweetness and – ever the gentleman – while standing next to her he reached out for her hand to help her up. She took his hand and he led her back out of the kitchen to the living room. The fire was still burning brightly, and the candles sent flickers of orange light up the walls. It was a scene from a romantic novel, and Sapphire felt like the heroine about to be wooed by her hero. Fox let go of her hand and began to gather cushions, which he threw on to the rug in a little circle.

"Come, my love, rest for a while. Let your food go down. I will read to you."

She laughed and sat down, with the skirt of her dress flouncing around her in a rustle of silk. "What, the *Kama Sutra*? That will be fun!"

Fox smiled and raised an eyebrow. He lifted one of the books from the pile and gestured for her to lie back. She settled into the cushions. Her stomach was full and she did feel the need to digest somewhat before the night turned into something else.

He found what he was looking for, a book she had not seen in the pile before he had arrived home. He sat down beside her and crossed his legs. She watched him as his face lit up with the orange glow from the fire. He was so handsome – his face a beautiful picture of hard and soft lines, and his lips so very kissable. He opened the book, turned to look at her, and winked. She found the gesture oddly funny. He began to read to her.

Women are the most confusing and intricate of the species: they are complex in character, but simple in their needs. When courting a woman, one must always follow certain rules.

He paused and looked at her again. She had raised her arms above her head and had a faint smile on her lips. He had picked a book on female courtship. How sweet.

The rules are simple: never move too quickly, for they can become overwhelmed by the male need to conquer. Tread gently but firmly when making your advances clear. Do not give mixed messages: they can often overthink what you say. Treat them with respect at all times and worship the goddess within them, as all women have an infinite connection with the powerful magical energy of the goddess. Some are unaware of this until they are backed into a corner, but eventually this strength and power will always emerge.

He paused again for effect.

Never underestimate the power of the woman, or this will be your downfall.

Sapphire snorted. "Is that the guide to seduction on your planet, Fox?"

He lifted his hand and traced a finger across her chest, slowly and lightly making her skin jump up with goosebumps.

"They are wise words for we men. This book has helped me out on many occasions. I thought it would make you smile."

She lifted her head, and did indeed smile. "And how many women exactly have you needed to refer to your trusty manual for?"

He continued to stroke her chest. His fingers brushed gently across her clavicle then down again, and pushed just slightly under the silk to touch the top of her breast.

"Is that something you really need to know?"

Sapphire closed her eyes for a moment as his finger slipped further down into her gown, and he grazed her left nipple slightly. She moaned softly. "I'm known to be of a very jealous nature."

He laughed softly, a deep, tantalising chuckle. "You have nothing to be jealous of, Sapphire. You are my only desire."

She opened her eyes again. "But you have had other women, I presume."

He dropped the book into his lap and sighed, the smile still on his lips. "Of course, my love. I am a man, as you know, and we do have certain needs. But, rest assured, they were not important – and I had not been with a woman before you for a long time. Nothing really satisfied me until I found you. Now I am completely satisfied in every single way a man could be."

She swallowed, a little shakily. His hand had slipped completely under her bodice now and was caressing her with an almost casual air.

"The book you found me reading earlier … Has that taught you how to be …" she paused as she tried to find the right words, "Such a wonderful lover?"

He bent down and kissed her lightly on her forehead then moved to her earlobe, where he flicked his tongue softly before moving back away from her.

"It was a gift – but, yes, it has been an interesting guide. The men of Shaka are trained in the art of love."

He had her attention now. She pushed herself up so that she was resting on her elbows. His hand had moved to her neck now – and he was stroking her softly, as she would stroke a cat.

"A gift? From who?"

Fox laughed again and removed his hand. He lay down beside her and turned to face her. She looked down at him. His expression was thoroughly amused, as if he had been teasing her the whole time.

"A woman gave it to me. She was practised in the art of sex – a concubine, if you like. It was a long time ago."

Sapphire wrinkled her nose but laughed. "A prostitute! Goodness, Fox, that's actually quite funny!"

He closed his eyes for a moment. His whole face relaxed, and she thought again how beautiful he was. "As young men we are guided by these women. They help us to understand the female body and what pleasures them. All men of Shaka are taught this way."

Sapphire snorted. "God, I wish the men of Earth had such a thing. Everyone would be a lot happier!"

He chuckled.

Sapphire picked up the book and continued where he had left off.

When courting a young maiden it is required to gain permission from her father to spend time with her alone. Do not take liberties with her until it is well established that she returns your affections: to spoil the flower before it has bloomed is a grave offence.

Sapphire burst out laughing. "You mean to say 'deflowered'! This is a trip, Fox. Surely this isn't for real!"

He laughed, opened his eyes and, after taking the book from her hand, placed it back on the floor. "Actually, it is, but it was written many, many years ago. It is what you would call on Earth a collector's item. I found it in a bookshop and found it most amusing."

Sapphire was laughing, but was pleased he had shared it and some of the other interesting facts about his life with her.

She lay back down and turned on her side so that she could face him. He pulled her into his chest, and his right arm snuggled around her. She felt his chest rise and fall softly as he breathed. She closed her eyes and breathed in his scent.

"Fox, can I ask you something?"

He stroked her back gently. "Anything, my love."

"Do you think we will always be like this ... so happy? Sometimes it feels too good to be true."

He sighed deeply and pulled her closer. "Of course, Sapphire. Don't doubt that you deserve this time. We both deserve it. You have always been special. We were destined to meet. I have always been there in the background waiting for you. Now is our time to be happy."

She smiled and nestled in more. The heat from his body and the fire behind her cocooned her nicely. She desperately wanted to believe him, but somehow there was still a slight niggle in the pit of her stomach. She knew that she was changing and the magic inside her was growing, and there was something else ... something else that she could not understand just yet. But for now she would just trust and believe that her time here – with the man she now loved with a passion – was meant to be, and that all was good in her life.

After a suitable length of time for them both to digest their food Fox kissed the top of her head and moved to sit up.

"Time for bed, Sapphire. Come ... it's late."

She had fallen asleep for a while, curled up on his chest. She stirred and yawned. Her body was heavy. He lifted her up into his arms and carried her up the stairs. She leant into his neck and kissed his warm skin.

The bedroom was lit with candles, and the doors to the balcony were open just a fraction to let in the warm night air. Fox laid her gently on the bed and ran the back of his hand across her cheek. She smiled up at him and stretched.

Very slowly he began to undress in front of her. He took off the waistcoat and shirt, revealing his tanned, firm chest. She watched him, her energy starting to lift. He bent down and kissed her lightly on her lips: her own inner goddess was now suddenly fully switched on. He lifted the long skirt of her dress up slowly to uncover her legs. As he pushed the soft silk up her thighs he placed light featherweight kisses up her calves and thighs. She laughed as he pulled the dress up awkwardly over her head and struggled with the long sleeves. He chuckled, but continued to kiss her skin as it was exposed.

He threw the dress on the floor, and was kneeling over her now. Still in his leather trousers, he began to kiss her with a deeper intensity, with his hands either side of her head and his body just inches from hers. She felt the need to get completely naked and tried to twist around to untie the corset. He pulled back from the kiss, flipped her over in one swift movement, and untied the bodice so that it was now open and exposing her back. She felt her breathing quicken as he trailed down her spine. He was licking her and kissing her, his hair leaving a soft brush of sparks. As he reached her bottom he slid down the lace knickers and stroked her buttocks, making her squirm. She heard him move out of his trousers and they too ended up on the floor. Her knickers followed quickly after.

They were both naked now, the bodice still pinned underneath her. She felt him stroke her hips and thighs slowly, with a teasing promise of what was to come. He pushed his hands under her hips and raised her up backward so that she was sitting on her thighs. He wrapped his arms around her and started to kiss her neck. His chest was pressed against her back, his hands were caressing her breasts … his knees were either side of her now, and she felt his cock hard against her buttocks. She moaned, responding to his touch. He moved her hair to one side and continued to suck her neck – his favourite little trick. One hand remained on her breast and played with her nipple. The other moved down to her pussy, and his fingers were touching her lightly on her clit.

50

She was trembling now as the energy grew between them. She was wet and hot. His finger slid inside, making her shiver with delight. He groaned deeply and pushed his finger in further. She pushed against him and closed her eyes. Sparks of white light flashed before her eyelids, making her head spin. He moved his hand from her breast and lifted her buttocks just far enough to slide himself underneath her. She felt her thighs tremble at the effort of holding herself at just the right angle. She felt him probe gently at her pussy.

Both of them were panting now. He released his finger and used both his hands now to lift her just that little bit higher so that she was upright, but hovering over him. He guided her slowly and eased her down gently. As he slid inside her easily she let out a deep moan as he filled her completely. By using his hands to hold her hips he was able to move her up and down slowly. She had never experienced anything like this before: with her back to him and his body pushed up against her the angle was pushing hard against her clit as his cock slid in and out. It made her want to pass out with pleasure. He leant around and kissed her neck again. She turned to capture his lips. They kissed with a ferociousness that pushed her even further over the edge. He was gasping for air as the pace quickened – and he lifted her up and down, making her body shake with the extreme sensations washing over her.

"Sapphire, you are mine … mine to worship, mine to love … always." He spoke to her in a low, guttural tone. It filled her body with fire, and she knew that at any moment her legs would give way and she would explode.

Fox sensed her need to come, and he pushed her over so that she was now on all fours. Without any warning he growled like an animal, and started to pound her hard. That was all it took. She came with a boiling hot wave of pure pleasure, crying out loudly as he continued to fuck her from behind. He was lost as she was in the moment. Her body quivered as he held her hard against him. She felt his cock grow harder before he too came with one last hard thrust into her. The whole house seemed to shake for a moment, such was the intensity of the energy they created in their joining.

Sapphire collapsed on the mattress … She was panting loudly.

Fox was still inside her. He was holding her from behind, and he had fallen down with her. His face was beside her, and she could feel

51

his breathing coming in fast bursts from his mouth. She started to laugh. He rolled off slowly, and slid out of her in an almost painful release. He too laughed. Everything was just so extreme between them. He stroked her back gently and kissed her softly on the forehead.

"I would like to thank the woman who showed you that trick, Fox... Fuck me, that was amazing."

He chuckled and pulled her into his side.

"No need to thank me, my love. It is you who brings out the beast in me, no one else."

They lay together completely sated and happy after their lovemaking.

Sapphire fell asleep with a smile on her lips, wrapped up completely in his arms. She was the happiest she had been in a very long time.

Chapter Four

Sapphire was dreaming again. She knew she was dreaming, as she was sitting on the edge of a lake that spanned out in front of her. The water was a beautiful light turquoise blue, the sun was shining, and she was dangling her feet into the water. She was sitting on a wooden platform jetty which sat out into the water. The coolness of the water on her feet was refreshing and calming. She was wearing a pair of shorts and a T-shirt, as she would have when she lived on Earth. She looked up at the clear blue sky and sheltered her eyes from the brilliance of the sun with her hands. She felt calm and safe.

As she looked back out over the lake she noticed a small dot on the landscape that was moving slowly towards her. It was a boat. She watched with interest as the boat moved closer. She could see a figure inside the boat, a female. She had long white-blonde hair, which cascaded across her shoulders. Her body was framed in a glow of silver white. She was exquisitely beautiful. Sapphire continued to sit, her feet swishing back and forth in the water. The boat moved closer, smoothly through the water, making no sound at all. Within moments the boat was so close to her that she could see every detail on the woman's face. She seemed very familiar. Her eyes were a brilliant blue that sparkled with flashes of silver. She was smiling at her with a sweet softness in her eyes. The boat came to a stop very close to the jetty. It hovered silently. The woman had her hands placed neatly in her lap.

"Welcome, Sapphire. It is a pleasure to see you on this day."

Sapphire smiled at her. The energy coming from this woman was warm and soothing, like a gentle caress.

"I have a message for you."

Sapphire nodded. This dream was different again from the others she had experienced but she went along with the flow, knowing instinctively that she was safe within this woman's company.

"Yes … what is it?"

The woman sighed. Her hair moved around her head as if a gentle breeze was moving around her.

"That she is coming soon. You are not ready just yet, but you will be. She sends you her love and blessings and tells me that, when the time is right, she will come to you and help you to understand more of what is growing inside you. You must be patient, and keep your guard up in the meantime. For there are many that covet your magic, such is its power."

Sapphire blinked and bit her bottom lip. This woman was talking in riddles. "I don't understand."

The beautiful woman unfolded her hands and revealed a white calla lily, which shone with a luminous glow. She raised her hands up in front of her as if to give the lily to Sapphire as a gift.

"But you will in time. Do not be sad that the child you carry cannot be born as yet, but she will come again. Take this as a gift of her love. Be safe, my child, and remember that I am always with you, watching and waiting."

Sapphire felt a buzz of energy in her stomach, and looked down into her lap. The lily was placed on her thighs. It shimmered in the light. Suddenly, without warning, the boat was gone. The sky had turned cloudy, and a wind began to blow around Sapphire.

She felt the temperature of the water beneath her toes turn warmer, and suddenly become thick and viscous. As she looked down she realised with horror that the water was no longer a beautiful turquoise blue but a dark red, and warm liquid was dripping down her thighs into the lake. Sapphire pushed herself up and dropped the lily. As she stood she realised that she was bleeding. Thick hot red blood was gushing from between her thighs and down the wooden jetty into the lake, which was now a dark, rippling pool.

Sapphire gasped and clutched her stomach. Panic rose in her throat. She felt her legs go weak and her head started to spin. She cried out in pain as a cramping in her belly took hold of her and threw her off balance.

The dream had become a nightmare. She hit the wooden decking hard, and her head bounced off it with a thump. Blood was all around her, and it made her feel sick to her stomach. She lay on the jetty clutching her stomach, which now spasmed with such intense pain that her body curled instinctively into the foetal position. Tears formed in her eyes, and she rocked her body as she tried to understand what was happening to her and why. A reality so absurd and so impossible hit her as she lay there and became soaked in her own blood.

"No, no, this can't be happening," she said to herself. She felt the first promise of unconsciousness waver across her body as her vision swam and her body trembled. The dream felt so real it pushed at her sanity. Her mouth opened in an attempt to scream, and her head thumped loudly like a drumbeat. Without warning she felt herself lift upwards and out of the dream state she had found herself in and hurtle back to reality.

Sapphire opened her eyes. She was thrashing around in the bed she shared with Fox. He was above her, his face a picture of worry. As she whipped her head from side to side he tried to restrain her.

"Sapphire, my darling! It's OK. I am here … Wake up. You are dreaming … Wake up."

Sapphire stared up at him. Her stomach was still cramping, and she felt intense pain travel up to her solar plexus and grip her chest.

"Oh my God, Fox … Oh, Fox, something terrible has happened. I'm bleeding …please help me!"

He was confused, a deep frown etched on his forehead. After pulling down the bed covers he stared in horror as he noticed the bed sheets were now a deep, dark colour between her thighs. Sapphire looked down at herself and realised the dream was a reality: she was indeed bleeding. In fact it looked as if she was haemorrhaging. She cried out in horror, and the tears she had cried in her dream now started to fall down her cheeks.

Fox jumped up from the bed. He was still completely naked, but totally alert now. He charged across the room into the bathroom and returned quickly with some towels. He placed them between her legs and brushed his hand across her forehead, kissing her urgently on the lips as she cried.

"Stay there," he implored her gently. "Don't move. I will get a healer, my love." As he began to dress quickly he called out for Kit loudly. As he pulled the sheets back over Sapphire to cover her he looked into her eyes one last time. There was a deep sadness on his face before he left in a rush through the bedroom door.

Sapphire lay on the bed, looking up at the ceiling. She clutched the towels between her legs and felt them become wet and hot. Her stomach was cramping hard, and the pain was intense. Tears were falling now in hot, wet trails down on to her pillow.

Suddenly Kit was by her side, a worried expression on her face. She stared down at Sapphire and shuddered. "My lady? Oh, my lady, are you OK? What has happened to you?"

Sapphire shook her head and gestured down her body.

Kit lifted the sheets and gasped at the sight before her. Without another word she dashed to the bathroom, and then returned with water and more towels. She helped Sapphire to sit up, and began to remove the blood-soaked towels Fox had placed there. As she helped Sapphire to sit she placed a cool flannel on her forehead, and replaced the sodden towels with fresh ones. Sapphire felt her body start to shake. Kit was stroking her softly with the flannel and looking towards the door, obviously hoping for her master to return with help.

She looked at Sapphire with a sad sympathy in her eyes. "I am so sorry, my lady. I think you have lost your child."

Sapphire blinked back the tears and gulped for air. The pain was starting to subside a little now, but her head was pounding.

"Child? What child?" she wondered to herself. Then suddenly, and with a sharp twist in her chest, Sapphire had the worst realisation of all. She had just miscarried. She had been pregnant and had not even realised. Sapphire groaned loudly and started to cry again, turning to Kit she gasped, "No, no … I can't have been pregnant … could I have been?"

Kit desperately tried to soothe her, stroking her cheek gently with sadness in her eyes. "My lady, please try to be still. It will be OK. Fox will be back soon with a healer. I am so sorry, but it seems that you were."

Suddenly the door to the bedroom was flung open. Fox stormed in, closely followed by an older woman. She was carrying a bag, and her face was alive and alert. Fox rushed to the bedside. Kit stepped back, her head hung low. Fox knelt down beside her and placed his hand on Sapphire's cheek. Her lip trembled as she looked into his beautiful eyes.

"The healer will help you now, my love," he said gently, in the most loving tone of voice that Sapphire had ever heard.

The old woman appeared by his side. She had bright green-coloured eyes and wild grey hair, which was braided and beaded like Fox's. She looked at Sapphire and nodded her head slowly.

"Everyone out, please," the old woman said. "I need to help this woman, and I need the space to do it."

Fox looked up at her and tipped his head in agreement. He stood and left slowly, leaving Sapphire alone with the old woman. Kit had vanished. Sapphire clutched the sheet to her chest. She was crying softly now, and rocking back and forth. The old woman smiled at her kindly.

"Do not be afraid, child. I am Willow. I am here to help you." She placed her hand on Sapphire's stomach and a warming sensation began to flow through Sapphire's body, which instantly soothed her. "There. That's better, my child. Close your eyes now. All will be well if you allow me to help you."

Sapphire did as she said. Willow's hand pulsed with a soft, glowing energy that numbed the pain. After a moment Sapphire could no longer feel anything.

Willow turned to her bag and began to lift various pots and herbs from inside. She found a jug of water that was beside the bed and began to mix them quickly. She offered Sapphire a glass of the mixture.Willow lifted the liquid to Sapphire's lips as she said, "Here… drink this, my child. It will stop the bleeding and make you feel better."

Sapphire opened her eyes and took the cup. She sipped it slowly, between sobs. Gradually she felt her body begin to relax as the liquid slipped down into her belly. The old woman stroked her forehead gently. She sat on the edge of the bed with her and cooed like a mother.

"There, there, that's better. All will be well, Sapphire. Your child was not ready to enter this world just yet."

Sapphire finished the drink. She was feeling fuzzy, but calm now the tears had stopped. "But I don't understand. I had no idea that I was pregnant," Sapphire said, a puzzled look on her face.

Willow smiled gently at her. "Such is the way sometimes. They come when they are ready, but this child was not ready."

Sapphire nodded slowly. She had been such a fool. How could she have been so irresponsible? She had not taken any precautions with Fox, and they had been having sex for weeks now. Time had passed, and she had not had her period. How could she have been so stupid and thoughtless?

Willow sensed her guilt. "Do not be angry with yourself, child. I am sure there were many reasons why this happened, but if you are not ready to bring a child into this world just yet you must take precautions."

Sapphire nodded at her. She was overwhelmed with guilt, and a sense of sadness that she could not have been prepared for. She felt like an irresponsible fool.

"You will need to rest for a few days. However, you are strong and the magic within you will heal any damage done. You will be fine, I promise. I will leave you some herbal tea that you must take once a day, which will help with the recovery – and, of course, I will also leave you something to take for the future if you do not wish to get pregnant again just yet." Sapphire watched her rummage through the herbs. She made up several containers of murky-looking liquid and then a pot of herbs that were dried, which Sapphire presumed that she would need to take as the precaution.

Willow placed her hand on her stomach one last time and closed her eyes and hummed to herself. Sapphire felt a soothing warmth spread throughout her body as she did.

"Yes ... all is well, my dear. Everything is clear now, and your energy is coming back up ... but no lying with your man for a little while, just to make sure." Sapphire nodded solemnly. She wanted to cry again. "These are for you to drink today and tomorrow. Kit will make you the tea each day, to prevent any further accidents. Do not worry, my dear. All is well." With that she smiled down at her and raised her hand, and kissed it lightly.

"It has been a pleasure to serve you, dream traveller. I hope to see you again in the future, under happier circumstances." She left quietly and closed the door behind her.

Sapphire closed her eyes and clutched the sheet to her chest. The towels had been removed, but she felt sticky and dirty. The door opened again slowly. Fox appeared at the doorway. His eyes were glazed and his face was stern. He walked to her slowly, then sat down next to her and held her hand.

"My love, I had no idea. I am so sorry."

58

She gulped back fresh tears. "It was not your fault, Fox. It was all mine. I was not thinking. Of course at first when we were together I thought it was just a dream, and then I became complacent and got carried away with it all. I did not think this would happen. In fact I have not been thinking at all. I've been a fool."

He kissed her lightly on the lips, his eyes sad and hazy as if he too had been crying. "No, my love. It was me who was the fool."

They sat silently for a moment before Sapphire pushed herself up fully. "Fox, would you ask Kit if she could run me a bath? I need to wash."

He jumped up immediately. "Of course, my love ... anything you need."

Within minutes Kit was at her side and helping her up into the bathroom. She realised that Fox had left her alone again. She sensed that his own guilt and grief were overwhelming for him, and that he had left the house.

She could feel their connection still as strongly as ever, but his pain was making her feel even worse. Kit helped her into the bath. She was still numb from the work Willow had done, but stepping into the hot water soothed her a little. Kit had asked her if there was anything else she needed before hovering at the door to leave. Sapphire watched her with a blank expression. All of a sudden she didn't want to be alone.

"Will you stay with me, Kit, just for a while?"

Kit jumped back into the room. "Of course, Saf. I will stay with you as long as you need me. I thought you might want to be alone for a while."

Sapphire shook her head sadly. "No, I would like you to sit with me. I don't want to be alone right now ... I'm feeling rather strange."

Kit pulled a chair beside the bath and sat down, her hands in her lap. "It must be the shock, my lady. It is a hard thing for any woman to bear."

Sapphire began to wash herself slowly. She was over the whole thing about being nude in front of another person now. Kit was her friend and she needed female company.

"Is Fox OK?" she asked as she washed away the last remaining evidence of what had happened.

"He was very angry, Saf – with himself, I feel, not with you – and of course also very shocked. But I am sure he will be fine – as you will in time, my lady. I am sure you can try again when you are ready."

Sapphire looked up at her with a stunned expression. "I'm not ready for a baby just yet, Kit. This was a total surprise … something that should never have happened."

Kit lowered her eyes and fiddled with her hands. "Oh, well … that's also absolutely fine. It is your decision."

Sapphire lowered herself into the water to wash her hair. As she bobbed back up she found Kit behind her with the shampoo. Kit started to wash her hair for her, and massaged her scalp. Sapphire closed her eyes and let the slow rhythm of Kit's fingers take away the tension in her head.

"I had a dream last night, Kit. A lady came to me. She told me this would happen – that a child was coming, but it was not ready yet. Now I understand what she was trying to tell me. It was a horrible dream." Kit continued to wash her hair.

"Who was the lady?" she asked.

Sapphire sighed deeply. "I don't know, but she has come to me before. She spoke to me on Earth several times … maybe she is like a guardian angel, or something."

Kit rinsed her hair out with a jug of warm water. It washed over her face and made her close her eyes tightly. "Why was the dream so bad, Saf?"

Sapphire rubbed her eyes as Kit applied another cream – conditioner of some kind.

"It just ended badly. I was bleeding in the dream … then I woke up and found that it was in fact real."

Kit massaged her head again, slowly and tenderly. "I am sorry, Saf."

Sapphire remained silent. She was feeling as if a heavy stone had become lodged in her chest. Although her body was no longer in pain she felt that something had indeed been ripped from inside her. Kit helped her out of the bath, and she dried herself slowly while Kit brushed out her hair. They did not speak any more about what had happened, and Sapphire was glad to remain silent.

She dressed in a long, simple skirt and a gypsy top in a dark purple. She was eager to find Fox again. She was worried about him. Kit had left to make something to eat for her, although she had no appetite. She had no idea what time it was – although time had little relevance, it seemed, here on Shaka. As she walked to the balcony to look out for Fox he reappeared by her side and made her jump at his sudden presence.

He drew her into his arms and held her close to his chest. He was breathing heavily, and his body was trembling slightly.

"You need to rest, my love. Lie down on the bed."

Sapphire looked up into his eyes, which swirled with a new darkness she had not seen in them before.

"I'm fine, Fox, honestly. I feel OK. Willow helped. She did say I needed to rest, but I don't feel like sleeping right now."

He kissed her lips tenderly and squeezed her tighter. "I will stay with you today. My business can wait."

She pushed away from him gently. "No, you must continue with your day as planned. I'm fine … please."

He shook his head, his eyes growing darker. "I will not leave you to grieve alone."

Sapphire blinked. She was finding the whole thing totally unreal.

"I did not even know I was pregnant, Fox. I have nothing to grieve for. It was a mistake. I'm not ready for a child … it was a blessing that it did not happen."

He looked shocked for a moment, but nodded. She realised that he was taking this harder than she expected. Perhaps he wanted a baby. The thought scared the crap out of her. He took her hands and looked down at her, a frown still on his face.

"Whatever pleases you, my love, but I will return soon. Kit will stay with you. Call for me if anything changes. I will come to you immediately." She believed him. His magic could transport him anywhere he wished very quickly, and the thought that he was never far away soothed her. He kissed her again, hard. It felt as if his need to protect her was even stronger now after this event. He left shortly after.

Sapphire stood very still in the bedroom, alone for a moment. The bed had been stripped and remade while she had been dressing, and everything was as it had been the day before. But she was different now: her energy had changed again, and she realised that the niggling feeling she had felt the day before had gone. Why had she not sensed the creation inside her? She did not know why not, and even more confusing was this question: why had Fox not sensed it? Perhaps the child had not wanted to be discovered just yet. As the lady on the lake had told her … the time was not right, but that the child would return. When that would be she had no idea, and was in no hurry. She had never thought about children when she had lived on Earth, probably because the ideal partner had never entered her life. Her last relationship had been very unstable, and she had never wanted to bring a child into the world without the right father figure.

She recalled the other piece of information that the lady had told her: that she needed to protect herself again, because others were coveting her magic. She shuddered at the thought that someone else besides Ebony might be out there, waiting to make their move. She wanted to live a normal life so badly, but nothing had been normal since her dreaming had started. However, she knew there was no going back and was glad she had crossed over to Shaka to live here with Fox. Her love for him was so consuming that she could never imagine him not being in her life. The choice of him coming to Earth and losing his magic – the essence of who he was – did not even cross her mind. She would never ask that of him. He was perfect to her. His magic was his birthright, and she had no right to take that away.

She walked down the stairs slowly. Her body was feeling lighter than normal. The drink Willow had given her seemed to have healed her completely.

Kit was in the kitchen. She looked up and smiled as Sapphire approached her. She had made pancakes – and the smell of them wafted wonderfully from the plate, which was piled high and smothered in honey. Sapphire had absolutely no appetite, but her stomach growled. Kit pulled out a chair for her and she sat down silently. She wished she could call Charlie and talk to her … tell her about everything and listen to her advice, hear her laughter … anything to make her feel slightly more human again. Kit pushed the plate of pancakes towards her slowly. A mug of steaming herbal tea was placed next to it, along with another dish with cheeses and ham. Sapphire looked up at her and tried to smile. She took one of the pancakes and started to eat slowly. Her appetite grew a little as the soft, sweet taste melted on her tongue. Kit sat beside her and watched her.

"Please, Kit, eat something with me. You must be hungry."

Kit shook her head. "No, my lady. I do not eat with you, but I will later."

Sapphire took another bite of the delicious pancake and pushed the plate back towards her.

"I insist, Kit, that you eat with me. We are friends ... equals."

Kit smiled sweetly and took a pancake. She was obviously hungry. They ate in silence for a while. Sapphire reached for some of the cheese and ham. She was actually starting to feel a little better.

"Would you like to rest in the garden for a while, Saf?" asked Kit. "The day is warm, and there is a beautiful tree at the far boundary that would give you some shelter from the sun. I could read to you, and perhaps show you some of my paintings."

Sapphire sipped the tea. "You paint?"

Kit smiled a little shyly. "Yes, my lady. Sometimes – when I am waiting for Master Fox to return and I have done all my chores – I paint. It is very relaxing."

Sapphire was pleased to hear she had her own free time to do as she pleased.

"I would love to see them. That would be wonderful."

They finished eating. Sapphire actually managed to consume three pancakes, and some of the cheese and ham. Her energy was lifting back up again by the minute.

The morning had felt like a bad dream. She wanted to distract herself, and was glad Kit had suggested going outside. She followed Kit out into the gardens. She had offered to help carry the blanket and books, but Kit had insisted that she take it easy. They walked to the edge of the garden wall where a huge old beech tree towered above her. It reminded her of the tree in the woods near her old home... it was beautiful and majestic, and cast a cool shadow on to the grass. Kit threw the blanket out on to the grass and placed the books to one side. She dashed back to the house to return with cushions and an armful of canvasses, which were obviously her paintings. Sapphire settled herself down on the blanket and leant back on to one of the cushions. Her body was suddenly starting to feel a little tired again.

Kit was animated and excited now at the thought that she was about to show Sapphire some of her work. Sapphire rolled on to one side and propped her head up on one hand. Kit laid out her work in front of her.

Sapphire was amazed at how good it was. Some of the works were fine pencil drawings that were intricate in detail. Others were landscapes in watercolours. Kit explained to her where some of the landscape drawings were from, and on which part of the land she had seen this particular waterfall or that meadow.

The last picture made Sapphire gasp. It was a pencil drawing of Fox. He was standing in profile against a moonlit sky. His eyes were cast down, and there was a sadness within them. It was if Kit had captured him perfectly at an intimate moment, when he had not been aware of her presence. Sapphire looked up at her and found Kit blushing, her eyes downcast.

"This is beautiful, Kit. Has Fox seen it?"

Kit started to gather up her artwork, and said, "Oh, no, my lady. I have not shown him any of my work."

Sapphire was shocked to hear this. She knew the girl had a thing for her master, but could tell that it was purely an innocent crush.

"You should, Kit. You are a fine artist. He would be impressed as I am."

Kit looked up, smiling widely. "Do you think so? Would you like me to draw you?"

Sapphire laughed … the first laugh of the day. "Oh, my goodness, Kit. I don't think I would be a very good subject."

Kit stood up quickly. Her face was glowing now. "Of course you would, my lady. You are very beautiful. I will go and get my pencils and some paper. You can rest while I draw you … You will be like Sleeping Beauty under the tree." She ran off at the speed of light.

Sapphire watched her go, and lay back down. She didn't feel like reading … she didn't really feel like doing anything. She closed her eyes again and waited for Kit to return. Perhaps she could just doze for a while. Her mind was still numb. Although Kit had been able to distract her for a while with the paintings, what had happened this morning was still pushing into her thoughts. She rested her hands on her belly and breathed slowly. Her thoughts drifted to Fox, as always. His pain and hurt for what had happened had been clearly etched on his face. She opened her eyes again as Kit stood over her with her hands full of arty things. She was smiling sweetly.

"Stay just like that, Saf. You don't have to move. I will draw you as I see you."

Sapphire returned the smile the best she could. She felt fatigued now and did want to sleep for a while. She placed one hand above her head, kept the other still on her stomach, closed her eyes, and sighed deeply. She felt the warmth of the air on her skin, and the shadow of the tree kept her cool from the sunshine. It was not long before she drifted off.

Sapphire was dreaming again. She was the observer this time. She could see Fox and Bear galloping hard on horses. Midnight was striding at a fast canter and Fox held his head down as the horse pounded the ground beneath him. Bear was at his side. They seemed to be pursuing someone or something. Sapphire could see the rolling landscape of Shaka around them: a vast gully, with mountains either side. Ahead of them she could see a group of riders moving away … three or four men on horseback. They were dressed in dark clothing, and their faces were obscured by hoods. Suddenly they were cornered into a section of the mountain with nowhere to run. Their horses came to an abrupt stop and they leapt down from them, ready for a fight.

She watched with horror as Fox and Bear jumped through the air to engage them. The fight began and the men became a swirling mass of bodies, so fast was their movement. Sapphire could not make out clearly who was who. She caught glimpses of Fox as he battled. He was carrying a big heavy sword that he swung around his head as he connected with two of the men at once. It was a bloody scene. Sapphire gasped and jumped. Her eyes flew open.

"Saf! Are you OK?" Kit was next to her and holding her hand.

Sapphire was panting, with tears in her eyes. She blinked as she tried to bring herself back to reality. Kit watched her with a worried expression, her paper and pencils discarded to one side.

"I'm OK, Kit. I was dreaming again, about Fox and Bear. They were fighting."

Kit stroked her hand gently. "Oh!" exclaimed Kit.

Sapphire pushed herself up and licked her dry lips. She was shaking a little. The dream had, as always, seemed so real.

"Here, my lady, drink this," said Kit, and passed her a glass of cool liquid. It tasted of orange and lemon. Sapphire gulped it down. Her throat was dry and a little sore.

After regaining her wits she looked across at what Kit had been drawing. She must have been sleeping for some time, as the picture was practically finished. It was beautiful. Kit had captured Sapphire lying under the tree with her head to one side, her lips slightly open, her hair tumbling across her shoulders, and her body in a soft slumber. Sapphire wondered if that was how people saw her: a young woman with voluptuous curves and a tiny frame surrounded by ruffled skirts, and her neck and shoulders exposed from the gypsy top. She did look like a sleeping beauty.

Kit smiled at her again. "Do you like it?" she asked shyly.

Sapphire pushed herself up to sit fully. "It's lovely, Kit. You have made me look very pretty."

Kit laughed softly. "You are, my lady. You are." Kit gathered her things and began to collect the cushions into a pile. Sapphire watched her. She was feeling very heavy and sleepy.

"I think you should rest, Saf," said Kit kindly. "You look pale. I will make you some supper soon. Come, let us go back to the house."

Sapphire realised that some time must have passed, as the day was nearly over. The sky was starting to turn a light pink and the sun was lower in the sky. She pushed herself up and started to walk slowly back through the gardens to the house. The dream troubled her. Was it a premonition? She had not dreamt for weeks, but now she had dreamt twice in one day. Was it beginning again?

Kit helped her up the stairs and fussed around her. She helped her to undress again and placed a simple white slip dress over her head so that she could climb back into bed. She gave Sapphire another drink – a potion, it seemed – to help her rest. Sapphire placed her head on the pillow and curled up into a ball as she hugged her body. She wished Fox was here again, holding her close to his hard, warm chest.

Kit stood in the doorway and smiled at her kindly. "If you need me just call. I will be in the kitchen."

Sapphire nodded, with sad eyes. The numb feeling was starting to spread throughout her body from the potion Kit had given her, and her eyelids were becoming heavy. She did not even see Kit leave before she fell into a deep sleep once more.

Chapter Five

Two days later

Fox entered his bedroom silently. The room was dark except for one candle burning softly beside the bed. Sapphire was asleep, curled up beneath the sheet. Her hair was the only thing poking out in a tumble of dark-blonde tendrils. He paused to undress before climbing in beside her. She stirred slightly, but was in a heavy slumber and did not wake.

He felt a heaviness in his chest he had not felt in a long time. It was sadness: deep, consuming sadness. He pulled her gently towards him and cradled her in his arms. She murmured his name softly and nuzzled into him, her eyes still closed. She looked peaceful and beautiful. It made his heart swell more. His woman had been carrying his child, and he had not even realised. How this could have happened without him sensing the new life inside her was beyond comprehension. He felt torn inside with guilt and with such a deep sense of sadness. She had seemed to be numb to the fact that she had lost the child, and was by no means in a hurry to have a baby.

The thought troubled him a little, but then he too had never contemplated the idea until it had presented itself. He wanted this woman to be his wife. Now the thought played heavily on his mind. If they were indeed to produce another child in the future he wanted it to be when they were joined officially in wedlock. It could not come sooner for him: she was his, and he would propose to her as soon as the time was right. The events of the last few days had fatigued him, and he winced slightly as he moved to a more comfortable position on his back with Sapphire pressed against his chest.

The scouting party that Bear and he had intercepted two days ago had been very close to their kingdom. It was a troubling thought. He knew that things had changed again for them. Scouts on the warpath had never approached so closely before: he had caught the thoughts of one of the men before he had killed him. They were searching for

Sapphire. Their intention was to capture her and return her to their queen on orders that she was not to be harmed.

He did not know why they would want Sapphire, but his instinct told him it was the same reason Ebony had tried to steal her away from Earth. The magic inside her was causing great ripples within his world. News had travelled fast that a powerful dream traveller had entered Shaka. More than ever before, Fox knew his job as guardian was going to be a hard one.

He stroked Sapphire softly across her arm. Her skin was warm and silky ... It was beautiful. Kit had told him on his return that Sapphire had slept heavily for the last two days: the potion Willow had left was working its magic to heal her from the miscarriage. He felt his body grow hot with arousal for her, such was her effect on him, but he knew that it would be some time before he could lie with her again after what she had been through. Right now he just wished to hold her and sleep.

Bear was on guard outside. Fox's friend had been magnificent when they had attacked the scouting party: he too had taken a few hard blows before the enemy had been seen off. Fox knew he would heal: the cut from a knife was still apparent on his right arm, but this would be gone by morning. Kit had been there waiting for his return, her face a picture of worry. She had helped him to bathe and dress the wound. He sighed deeply and squeezed his beautiful woman closer to his body. He found such comfort in her presence. He would never let anyone harm her or take her away from him again. Ever.

Sapphire woke to find Fox wrapped around her. She smiled at the sight of him sleeping peacefully. He was completely naked. She took in every inch of his wonderful face and body while he breathed softly, unaware she was awake. Daylight filtered through into the room. The air was warm and soothing. Every day seemed to be summer here. Her own body felt refreshed and light. The memory of what had happened before he had left her was a slight cloud within her mind, but the rest of the nightmare had gone. She had no idea how long she had been sleeping, but sensed it was longer than just one night.

She traced her finger across the lightly tanned skin of his chest and through the hair that travelled down towards his navel. He moved slightly and licked his lips, those wickedly wonderful lips. By moving her hand very slowly she wove tiny circles across his skin and watched with amusement as he became aroused in his sleep. She followed her fingers with soft, light kisses and breathed in his scent of patchouli and sandalwood. Her body was starting to wake up to the idea of jumping his bones. He started to stretch his muscles, and flexed slightly under her touch.

"Good morning, beautiful," he murmured. His hand moved down to her head, where he pushed his fingers into her hair. She continued to kiss him slowly, taking her time.

As she reached his morning glory he pushed his fingers further into her hair and pulled her back slightly. "Sapphire, no. It is too soon."

She blinked and paused her trail of kisses. He had never, ever stopped her before. She looked up. His eyes were still closed, but a smile was on his lips. She suddenly felt very guilty and ashamed. He seemed to sense her change in energy and his eyes opened. They flashed a deep amber and black.

"You know I would love nothing more than to ride you senseless, my love, but I feel we should wait – at least until you have finished taking the herbs Willow gave you."

Sapphire nodded slowly. She pushed herself back up and leant on his chest. She looked into his face, her expression blank. "You are right. I'm sorry."

He frowned a little and pulled her into him. "Shh … Don't ever say 'Sorry' to me. You have done nothing wrong, my love. I am glad to see you feeling better and more like your old self again."

She chuckled, a little glad that he was not chastising her for being wanton after such an awful event. "I didn't hear you come back last night. It must have been late."

Fox kissed the top of her head, making her feel safe and protected in his arms. "It was late. Kit told me she had given you something to help you sleep. You have been sleeping for two days, but I am here now and I do not need to go out today. Perhaps I will need to go tomorrow, but for now you have me all to yourself."

Sapphire could not believe she had missed two whole days, but was glad she had slept away the heartache. She smiled. "Good. I want you all to myself," she said.

He stretched and lifted his arms up above his head, and Sapphire found herself relishing the sight of his nakedness before her. He bumped her off himself gently, pulled the sheet back fully, and looked down on her handiwork with a grin. He jumped out of bed and she watched his naked backside walk gracefully towards the bathroom. She sighed.

"I will take you to one of my favourite places today, Sapphire. We can spend the day there together."

She sat up and did her own little morning stretch. Her body was feeling really good today - the sleeping potion had worked wonders.

"OK. I'll get dressed."

Shortly after they dressed, they went down to the kitchen. Fox draped his arm around her shoulder as they descended the stairs, and Sapphire could not have felt more cherished.

Kit was busy making breakfast. She smiled, her face lighting up with pleasure at seeing them standing in the kitchen doorway together.

"Good morning, Master Fox. Good morning, Saf. I am so glad to see you up and about again."

Sapphire smiled at Kit. She had already laid the table with tempting treats for them. Sapphire's stomach growled in response.

They sat to eat. Kit had placed a mug of steaming herbal tea at her place and urged her to drink before she ate. Sapphire presumed it was more of Willow's healing medicine. It tasted slightly bitter, but she drank the whole thing like a good girl.

"We will be out all day today, Kit ... If you would be kind enough to put some food together for us to take ..."

She curtseyed, the smile never leaving her face. "Of course, Master Fox."

Sapphire got stuck into the eggs and muffins Kit had prepared. As usual, everything was utterly delicious. Fox watched her eat with a smile. She always had a good appetite. Everything seemed back to normal so quickly, but that was a good thing.

"Will it be far to this place you want to show me?" Sapphire asked between mouthfuls.

"No, my love. I will take us. No riding for you today." He chuckled softly as he too devoured breakfast.

She lowered her eyes and hesitated a little. "You don't have to treat me with kid gloves, Fox. I'm fine."

He took a sip of the tea Kit had made him before answering. "I know, my love, but we travel by magic today."

She nodded and, satisfied, sat back in the chair. They left the kitchen shortly after. Sapphire was dressed today in the green skirt and bodice she had bought at the dressmaker's. She felt very much more like her old self again. Her energy was humming softly within her belly, and she could sense the magic around her once more grounding and refreshing her with healing vibrations. Fox stood before her dressed in his leather trousers and waistcoat. His arms were bare. She frowned as she spotted the slight trace of a pink scar on his arm that she had not noticed before.

A cloth bag that held their little picnic for the day was strapped across his chest. He reached for her hands and interlocked their fingers.

"Ready?" he asked.

She stopped frowning and smiled up at him as she anticipated the journey with a tremble in her gut. The air around them shimmered slightly as he drew his magic around them. A soft breeze lifted her hair for a second as she closed her eyes and felt them lift upwards and away from the house.

Flying away on a magic carpet suddenly took on a whole new meaning … Awesome.

Chapter Six

Sapphire opened her eyes and found herself standing beneath a huge willow tree. Its branches hung low over them, almost touching the ground. Around them was a vast meadow full of pretty flowers in all the colours of the rainbow. Fox smiled and released her so that she could step back from him to take in the view. It was breathtaking.

"It's beautiful here, Fox. How far are we from home?"

He removed the cloth bag and placed it on the floor. "Not too far... within the boundaries of my kingdom ... but few come here. It is a place I often visit to meditate and clear my head."

She reached up to touch one of the willow branches and felt its energy travel down her arms into her feet ... such strong magic.

Fox began to lay out a blanket for them, and indicated for her to sit. She lifted her skirt so that it flounced around her legs as she sat cross-legged before him.

He mirrored her and reached across to touch her hair gently with his fingertips. His touch made her shiver as always.

He smiled at her a slightly wry smile full of desire. "How are you feeling today, my love?"

Sapphire played with her hands in her lap. "I feel good ... much better. I'm glad you are with me today. I missed you."

He moved to stretch his legs out before him and leant back on to his forearms to look up at the tree canopy. The sunlight filtered through, dappling his face with golden light.

"You are always in my thoughts wherever I am, Sapphire."

She nodded. "I had a strange dream the other day while I rested. I saw you and Bear chasing men on horseback. You were fighting ... It was a little scary."

He frowned and looked at her intensely his eyes swirling with dark flashes. "Really?"

"Yes. I'm starting to dream again. After what happened the other night the dreams seem to have come back."

He looked away for a second. She caught a glimpse of something in his expression that worried her a little. "Sometimes my dreams are premonitions. I hope that one doesn't come true."

He shook himself as if a dark shadow had passed over him, then smiled at her again. The softness returned to his face. "I'm sure it won't, my love. Come lie with me for a while." He lifted his arms for her to settle into his chest. She crawled across and nuzzled into his side. They both lay back on the blanket and looked up at the sky for a moment. It was so peaceful. Sapphire could hear birds chattering in the branches above them, and a gentle breeze lifted the hair around her face in a soft caress. In that moment she felt like she did not have a care in the world.

"I have been thinking that I should take you to see the Oracle to see if she can give us some understanding of the magic that is growing within you. I sense it changing each day," Fox said.

Sapphire nodded, and lifted herself up slightly so that she could face him. His face was a picture of beauty, and his strong features were highlighted in the dappled sunlight.

"If you think it would help…"

He brushed a stray hair away from her face. "I believe it would."

She traced her fingers across his arm. The tattoos that covered them were interwoven delicately in swirls and soft colours. She paused at the fading scar on his bicep.

"I've never noticed this scar on you before, Fox. When did you get it?"

He watched her cautiously. She sensed his obvious hesitation before replying. "I caught my arm yesterday while riding. It will heal soon."

Sapphire traced one of the tattoos that swirled around his bicep. "Do these have any meaning?"

He licked his lips slowly as he contemplated the question. "They are part of my magic. Some are symbols of power, and others tell stories of my life."

She was fascinated by the way they curled and blended into each other. "They are beautiful, like you," she said, as she smiled at him.

He pulled her towards him and kissed her softly, his tongue probing her mouth with an urgency that made her whole body start to hum. Very gently he pushed her over so that she was lying on her back. His hand travelled across her stomach as he kissed her. She felt her body become limp and fluid. God, this man could kiss. Time slipped for a moment as Sapphire dissolved beneath him. Just as she thought he would begin to push further he withdrew, making her gasp slightly.

"Sapphire, I have something I need to ask you."

She blinked, still recovering from the kiss. "Yes?"

He kissed her one more time, very slowly – a light kiss that just touched her. She felt his body tremble slightly as if he were cold. As he withdrew again she noticed a new expression on his face. He was nervous. She could see it in the slight turn of his brow and the flicker of his eyes that darted from her face back to the floor again. Her heart started to beat a little faster as she sensed his anticipation grow.

"I know this may seem a little soon for you – and I was going to wait – but I cannot wait any longer."

She watched him toy with what to say. She was feeling a little nervous herself now. What the hell was he waiting to ask her about? Fox slid his fingers under her bodice so that they splayed, warm and firm, against her belly. His other hand was holding her head. She stared at him wide-eyed and held her breath.

"You are the only woman I have ever truly loved. You are my love, my life, my everything ... Will you do me the honour of being my wife?"

Sapphire raised her eyebrows in shock. She really hadn't seen that one coming. The air around them seemed to become thick with tension for a second. Everything went quiet.

She smiled at him softly, her heart still thumping in her chest. "Of course I will, Fox. I love you."

The smile that appeared on his lips was full and radiant. He kissed her again, hard, like a man possessed. They lay together on the blanket under the beautiful willow tree, wrapped around each other, kissing over and over again. Sapphire felt she had been waiting for this perfect moment her whole life, but had thought that it would never be possible. Fox withdrew his kiss gently and reluctantly. It seemed from the way he was smiling at her as if his world had suddenly been lit up by the brightest sun of them all.

"You have made me a very happy man, Sapphire."

After eating and resting some more Fox suggested they head back. Sapphire felt as light as a feather. She was so totally and utterly happy. He transported them home in the blink of an eye.

As they wandered hand in hand across the garden and back to the house Sapphire noticed someone standing at the doorway. Fox tightened his grip on her hand slightly, which made a slither of anxiety snake its way up her arm and into her chest.

The man standing waiting for them was as black as midnight. His head was shaved and his body was big and bulky. He was covered in tattoos that were very similar to Fox's, but these seemed more masculine and the lines harder. His face was darkly handsome and the fullness of his nose and lips gave him an aggressive 'Don't fuck with me' look. He was dressed in some kind of body armour made from leather and looked like a formidable warrior, and he was certainly someone that Sapphire did not want to upset. In one hand he held a rather large sword, which was balanced tip down on the grass.

Fox released her hand and strode forward ahead of her. The man smiled a wide grin that showed perfect white teeth.

"Wolf! It has been too long!" They clasped each other's forearm. They were both smiling now.

Sapphire sighed with relief. Fox knew this man, and he was obviously no threat to them. The anxiety held in her chest melted like a snowflake on her skin. She stood behind Fox now, a little timid in this strange man's presence.

Fox turned to face her, still smiling. "Sapphire, this is Wolf. He is the captain of my father's army."

Sapphire raised an eyebrow. "Nice to meet you."

Wolf bowed slightly, his eyes lowered. "It is an honour to meet you at last, Sapphire."

Fox reached for her hand. "Go inside, my love. I will follow shortly."

She hesitated for a moment. It seemed he wanted to talk to this man alone. She did as she was told although she felt a little sulky, as she wanted to find out why the captain of the guard was visiting on this day. Fox was acting just a little too strangely for her liking and the appearance of this man just added to her sense that something was not quite right.

Kit appeared in the hallway. She was holding a glass of clear liquid out for Sapphire, a smile on her pretty face.

"Here, Saf. You must be thirsty."

She bustled Sapphire inside and shut the door, so that Fox and Wolf were now out of sight and out of earshot. Kit almost pushed her into the kitchen. Sapphire was starting to feel that someone was most definitely not telling her something. Kit was flying around the kitchen now, seemingly preparing more food.

"Did you have a pleasant day, Saf?"

Sapphire looked over her shoulder. She was waiting for Fox to reappear. He did not. She smiled, and tried not to waste her energy worrying about what was happening outside.

"Actually, yes, Kit. I have some news!"

Kit stood still for a second, a bowl in her hand. Her face was lit up with anticipation and excitement. "What news?"

Sapphire smiled. She suddenly felt like a little girl, shy and unsure. "I'm engaged!"

Kit almost dropped the bowl as she rushed towards Sapphire, her eyes wide.

"Fox proposed today," Sapphire said with a laugh.

Kit gasped and put the bowl down. She grabbed Sapphire and squeezed her tightly in the biggest hug humanly possible. They both laughed. Sapphire was thrilled by her obviously happy reaction to the news.

"Oh, my lady, that is the most wonderful news! A wedding! Oh, my, there will be so much to do. We will have to start planning very quickly. I am so pleased for you both. Master Fox is so very in love with you, and now you are to be his wife. It's wonderful, wonderful!"

She continued to babble. Sapphire was caught up in Kit's enthusiasm, which created an involuntary lump in her throat that threatened to create fresh tears of emotion. Sapphire's thoughts had turned to Charlie, Pearl, and her mother, and how she would have loved to tell them that she was now engaged to a prince. The last part would have made Charlie fall about laughing. It was a bittersweet thought, and one that caught her unexpectedly off guard. She fought back the tears that threatened to spill any minute across her cheek.

"Are you OK, Saf?" Kit asked her suddenly. Her chatter came to an abrupt halt as she noticed Sapphire's change in demeanour.

Sapphire realised she must have zoned out for a moment. Her face must have said it all.

"Yes, I'm fine." She shook herself slightly to remove the sad feelings of missing her friends and family. "You can be my maid of honour, Kit."

Kit stopped and stared at her. "I do not understand what this is, Saf."

Sapphire smiled. "You would stand at my side when we are married and help me on the day ... You would basically stop me from ruining my make-up if I cry, or catch me if I trip on my dress... that kind of thing."

Kit beamed in response. "Oh, my lady, that would be such an honour!"

Sapphire smiled widely at her. She would have loved to have Charlie dressed up in some fluffy dress at her side as well, but that just wasn't going to happen. Kit continued to chatter to her as she prepared the food. The thought of what Sapphire had just proposed had removed any sadness from the conversation. Sapphire had one eye on the door, and was waiting for Fox to return. She felt a nagging feeling that he was keeping something from her, and that the impressively larger-than-life Wolf was part of the secret.

Fox had taken Wolf into the armoury so that they could talk in private, away from Sapphire. He knew why the captain of the guard was here at his home, but it was a troubling thought for him that Sapphire knew nothing of the storm that was heading their way.

"How many more have been seen scouting the area?" he asked the captain.

Wolf was seated opposite him on a chair that Fox had found for him when they had entered the building to the side of his home.

"Three more parties have been stopped from entering the kingdom boundaries since yesterday, my lord. I have sent scouts of our own to cross the border and intercept them if possible, to find out what they want."

Fox sighed deeply. "I know what they want, Wolf, but they cannot have it. Under no circumstances must they cross into our lands. Send news to your scouts that I need more information as to what is happening with their own army and if, indeed, they are intending to cause us more trouble."

Wolf nodded slowly. His skin was black as night. It glistened slightly, which made his muscles look even more defined.

"Your father is asking for you to return to the castle: he wishes to speak to you on this matter. Fox, do you sense something more sinister brewing?"

Fox looked Wolf in the eye and frowned. "Something sinister and dark, Wolf. We may need to prepare the rest of the army. I am sensing they may actually be stupid enough to attack."

Wolf raised an eyebrow, his chest rising as he let out a low whistle. "There has not been an attack on Calafia for many years, my lord. Why would the queen do such a thing now?"

Fox shook his head as he paced with agitation. "She has caught wind of the fact that Sapphire is a dream traveller – and a powerful one, at that. I believe she wishes to harness that power for her own means, but it will never happen."

Wolf stood. "Of course, my lord, you will be protected at all times. Be assured of that."

Fox ran his hand through his hair. Worry was etched on his face. "Tell my father I will visit him soon. I must get back to Sapphire: she will start to suspect something is wrong if I do not return to her now."

Wolf bowed deeply at the waist. "My lord, I will send news as it arrives."

Fox followed him out of the armoury and watched him leave on his horse. Dust floated in the air behind him as he cantered into the distance. As he headed back into the house his mind raced with this news of more scouts crossing into their lands who were looking for Sapphire. He needed to visit his father and then take Sapphire to see the Oracle. The proposal he had made just hours earlier was now feeling overshadowed by this dark cloud. He also wanted to tell Conloach of his engagement, and that a wedding was to be planned as soon as possible.

He did not want to wait long. His desire to officially make Sapphire his wife pressed even more heavily on his heart now.

Chapter Seven

Sapphire was waiting for him in the kitchen. She stood as he entered, her face etched with lines of worry. She knew something was amiss.

"Is everything OK?"

Fox went to her, pulled her into his arms, and kissed the top of her head. "Of course, my love. Wolf stops by from time to time to update me on any business from the kingdom."

She raised her head to look at him. "But you have already seen your father. Shouldn't he already be updating you on 'business'?"

Fox squeezed her to his chest. She wasn't going to let this drop. "Yes, of course, but Wolf was passing and thought he would drop in."

She raised her eyebrow. She wasn't buying his brush-off.

"I need to let my father know about our engagement. I will visit him later. There is nothing to worry about, Sapphire."

She nodded and seemed satisfied for the moment. He hated lying to her, but he wanted nothing to cloud the happiness they had felt this morning. They ate with Kit, a feast of meats and salad that she had prepared for them. Sapphire seemed to be back to her old self again, and Fox kept up the pretence that all was well. After they had finished he stood to leave for his father's castle to give him the good news.

"Shall I come with you?" Sapphire asked him as he went up the stairs to freshen up before leaving.

He stood halfway up and turned to face her, smiling. "No, my love. You rest here. I won't be long."

She sighed and watched him with thoughtful eyes. "OK, but don't be too long. I worry when you are gone."

He bounded up the last few steps into his bedroom, leaving her standing at the bottom with a slightly forlorn expression on her face. It was killing him to do this. He had never wanted her to feel unsafe here on Shaka, but now things had changed again for them. He washed and dressed into fresh clothes quickly, wanting to get to the castle and back again before the evening was gone. He found

Sapphire in the living area, sitting in one of his big high-backed chairs. She was reading one of his books. She smiled as he stood in the doorway. She was the most beautiful thing he had ever seen, with her face lit up just by his presence. The fact that she glowed so much when he was around her pulled at his heart even more.

"I will be back soon, my love."

She nodded, and he left without delaying further.

After he had gone Sapphire stood up quickly and walked with haste to the kitchen to find Kit again. She was washing up the plates and pots and singing to herself. Determined to find out what was going on behind her back, she confronted Kit with a directness she did not know she possessed.

"Kit, tell me what is going on. I know something is up. I can tell Fox is not himself. He is hiding something from me."

Kit turned to face her. A slight blush was starting to creep into her cheeks. "Nothing is wrong, Saf."

Sapphire approached her slowly.

"Kit, please … we are friends. I need to know if something is going on that Fox is keeping from me. It's not fair to keep me in the dark."

Kit looked down for a moment and bit her bottom lip before looking Sapphire in the eye.

"There have been scouts spotted in the area who have been dispatched from the neighbouring kingdom. Wolf came by to let Master Fox know that they had been sighted, and apparently they were hostile and clearly on the warpath. I honestly don't know anything else."

Sapphire sat down again at the table and contemplated this news. "Thank you, Kit, for being honest with me."

Kit stopped her chores and wiped her hands dry. She sat down next to Sapphire and, smiling, placed her hand on to her arm. "He only wants you to be happy, Saf. He is not trying to hide anything from you. He's just taking away any worry."

Sapphire sighed deeply. "I don't want him to have to lie to me just so that I don't worry, Kit. That's not how relationships work, you know … and, especially if I am to be his wife, we have to be honest with each other."

Kit nodded. "I hope that Master Fox won't be too angry with me for telling you."

Sapphire laughed. "Of course he won't, Kit, and if he is he will have me to answer to. Honestly, stop being scared of him. He is a pussycat underneath all that brawn."

Kit giggled.

"Would you like me to help you finish the dishes?" Sapphire asked.

Kit stood up quickly.

"No, Saf, it is not your place. Please go and rest for a while until Master Fox returns."

Sapphire was finding this whole lying around being a princess thing a little irritating. She was used to being an independent girl and, quite frankly, being the lady of the house was getting on her nerves a bit. She knew Kit would hear nothing of it, so decided to go out into the garden for a while until the sun went down.

She wandered around the gardens and took in the last of the sunshine. The sun was slipping slowly down over the horizon … beautiful pinks and oranges cast their glorious hues across the haze of blue. She still marvelled at the sight of the two moons that rose in the Shaka sky each night and stared up at the sight of them as they gradually appeared on the horizon.

As she walked towards the back of the house she remembered the building she had seen when they had gone to the stables, and decided to go and investigate. When she pushed it gently she found the door was open. The building was quite large from the outside and, as she entered, she gasped at the sight before her. The area inside was a stone-tiled floor that covered a wide space, with a few chairs around the edges. A long rope was suspended from the ceiling at one end, and two large wooden pillars that each had several knives stuck in them stood tall from the tiled floor like barren tree trunks.

This was not the cause of her gasp. It was the array of weapons that covered the walls – which were held in place in their own spots by hooks and nails – that had made her gawp. This was an armoury, and it was fully stocked. It was like looking at a medieval torture chamber: every sort of weapon – from swords to crossbows, and chains with nasty-looking spiky bits on the end – decorated the entire length of one wall.

The opposite wall was covered in a huge tapestry. It was absolutely stunning in detail and told the story of a battle, with men and horses coming together in a vast gully that was surrounded by mountains on each side. As she stood closer to the tapestry she was surprised to see that some of the figures fighting were in fact female. So ... the women of Shaka could also kick ass, by the looks of it.

Sapphire found the whole thing both totally mesmerising and utterly horrifying at the same time. She crossed to the wall of weapons and inspected them more closely. They all looked extremely sharp and well cared for. A large broadsword caught her eye. The hilt was decorated in swirls and symbols she did not recognise. A huge emerald sat in the centre that glittered as if it were alive.

A smaller sword was beside it, and she reached up to take it down. As she lifted the sword from its hook she felt a shiver of energy run up her arms. Magic. She felt a rush of air across her face, and her whole body trembled for a second. She gripped the hilt of the sword in both hands and smiled wickedly. It felt good to hold – light, even. She started to have some fun, and swung it around over her head. She was surprised at how easily she could hold it up. This was excellent. Suddenly she was in her own world of playing at being a medieval knight and she laughed at herself as she danced around, swinging the sword in an attempt at a parry.

A cough at the door made her stop abruptly. Bear was standing in the door frame, an amused smile on his face. Sapphire lowered the sword and blushed fiercely.

"You looked good, Sapphire. I shall tell Fox to watch his back."

Sapphire took the sword back to the wall and placed it next to the broadsword. "I didn't hear you come in. It's good to see you, Bear, but Fox isn't here at the moment. I'm not sure how long he will be."

Bear stepped into the armoury and started to light the torches that were placed at intervals around the walls.

"Fox asked me to keep an eye on you while he was gone."

She turned to face him. "Really? Babysitting duty ... how nice for you."

He laughed loudly. "Not at all, Sapphire, but Fox gets twitchy when you are alone."

She placed her hands on her hips and cocked her head to one side. "Does that have anything to do with the fact that scouts have been sighted recently, and that he is now fearful for me?"

Bear blinked. She knew she had caught him out. He lowered his eyes for a second and smiled.

"Well, yes … that may have something to do with it."

Sapphire pulled two chairs into the middle of the room and sat down. She indicated for Bear to do the same. He walked towards her, still smiling.

"Bear, tell me … does Fox always overprotect his women?"

Bear sat. His large frame just about squeezed on to the seat. "Only when they are a dream traveller and he is their guardian – oh and, of course, when he has fallen completely and madly in love with them."

She smiled. "Fair enough."

Bear leant forward and rested his head on his hand so that he could look directly at her.

"You must not be angry with him for wanting to protect you, Sapphire. You are the most precious thing he has ever found, and he does not want to lose you."

She nodded slowly. "So tell me exactly what is going on, then. First Wolf turns up today, then Kit tells me that scouts have been spied – and now you are here on guard duty while Fox is not in the house. Truthfully, Bear … it's me, isn't it? Someone is looking for me."

He leant back again and sighed deeply. "Fox will tell you, it is not my place. But, yes, I am here on guard duty – although by the looks of things you are just fine without any of my muscle needed. You have a strong arm."

She laughed, and the atmosphere lifted slightly. "I would love to learn how to fight properly. By the sounds of it I may just have to defend myself again at some point without the aid of magic."

He looked thoughtful now. "Now that's not a bad idea. I could teach you – and Fox, of course. He is a fine swordsman." She found the thought oddly exciting. "Of course Fox may object somewhat to his woman learning how to swing a sword. Women do not learn the art of war on Shaka."

She frowned. "But there are women on the tapestry fighting."

He looked across at the hanging that was now twinkling in the torchlight. "They are not of this kingdom – but, yes, they are warriors. In fact they were feared by some men, such was the strength and skill they possessed in battle."

Sapphire smiled at him again. "You should meet the women of Earth. They can put up a pretty good fight, especially after a few beers."

He chuckled. "I can assure you, Sapphire, no harm will come to you here."

She wished she could believe him but it seemed that the safety of Shaka, which had seemed so certain to her when she had decided to cross over, was now not so sure. She regarded the man sitting in front of her and bit her lip with hesitation before speaking.

"Fox proposed to me today, Bear."

He sat back in the chair and beamed at her. "Well... congratulations are in order, then, Sapphire. We should celebrate."

His smile made her feel happy again. It was a time to celebrate, and the fact that he was here to protect her did indeed make her feel less edgy.

"Let's go inside and find something to drink, then."

Bear nodded enthusiastically. "A girl after my own heart," he said, and grinned.

Fox returned to find Bear and Sapphire in the living room laughing. His time at the castle had been a mixture of good and bad news. His father was delighted for him at Sapphire's acceptance to his proposal, and had agreed to marry them within a week. News of the scouts, however, was not good news. Conloach had agreed that they were clearly looking for trouble, and Sapphire was the prize. He would prepare his warriors for any attempt to take Sapphire from them: she was as precious to the kingdom now as she was to Fox. He stood in the doorway for a second watching Sapphire. Her face was lit up by the fire that burned brightly in the fireplace. She had obviously been drinking mead again, and he could tell she was slightly drunk. Bear noticed him before she did.

"Fox! Congratulations. Sapphire tells me you are to be wed. Come drink and celebrate with us."

Fox could not help but smile at his friend – who was supposed to be guarding his fiancée, not plying her with drink.

Sapphire jumped up and rushed to him, and flung herself into his arms. "I missed you."

He kissed her hard on the lips and brushed a hair away from her eye. She was swaying a little. "I can see."

She hiccuped, and giggled.

"Bear, you are a bad influence. I leave for one minute and you get my lady drunk."

Sapphire kissed him again, and pulled him closer to her. She was buzzing with that special mix of magic and sexual energy she uniquely possessed. It made his body twitch in response.

"Don't be a bore, Fox. Come on … Have a drink with us. Bear has been keeping me company while you were away – and on your orders, if you remember."

His eyes flashed with amusement. He crossed the room while holding Sapphire by the waist. She was quite clearly having trouble standing on her own, which was obviously the result of too much mead. He helped her into the chair and took the tankard Bear held out for him.

"I think you may have had enough already, Sapphire."

She pouted and grabbed her glass, which spilled some of the contents on to the floor. "I'm fine. Stop nagging."

Bear roared with laughter, and clinked his tankard with Fox's. "Congratulations to you both. I can tell she will keep you on your toes, Fox!"

Fox sat next to his wife-to-be and she snuggled into his side and put her feet up on the arm of the chair. He untangled the glass from her hand and placed it on the floor, thus removing the threat of more spilled mead.

"Thank you for taking care of her while I was gone, Bear, but I think I may need to talk to my woman alone now."

Sapphire giggled. "Oh, no. I'm his 'woman' again now. I'm definitely in trouble again, Bear. Naughty Saf!"

Bear laughed and stood up. "Of course, Fox. Enjoy the rest of your evening." He bowed with a grin on his face and left the room.

Sapphire grabbed the glass again, gave Fox a look of defiance, and took another sip of the delicious mead. She had been having a whale of a time with Bear. He was one funny man – and he, for one, did not chastise her for drinking too much.

Fox watched her drink. He kept his irritation at her rebelliousness in check before taking the glass from her once more and moving it further away on the table beside them. He kissed her softly on the top of her head and pulled her close, which distracted her from the amber nectar.

"I am glad you are happy, Sapphire. My father is very pleased we are to be wed. He has agreed to marry us within a week."

She jumped and stared up at him, wide-eyed. "A week? Shit, that's quick!"

Fox smiled and placed his tankard on the table next to her glass. He was not in the mood to drink. "I want you to be my wife as soon as possible."

She licked her lips slowly and lifted her hand to trace a line across his cheek with her fingertip. The gesture instantly softened his mood just that little bit more. Her expression changed again before she spoke, her eyes narrowing slightly.

"I know what's going on, Fox. I know about the scouts. I know that things have changed for us again, but you don't have to worry. Bear is going to teach me how to fight – and if anyone tries to take me away from you they will be sorry." She was slurring her words slightly. Each word was spoken softly, like a determined child. He blinked and took her hand, and kissed her fingertips lightly.

"Is he, now?" She nodded at him, her eyes misty and smiling once more. The deep blueness of her irises pulled him in momentarily and made him lose track of where he was. He shook his head and released himself from her hypnotic stare. He searched her expression for a second, looking for clues as to how much she really knew. "Nothing escapes you, does it?"

She grinned. "Nothing," she said, and giggled again.

He twisted her around gently, took her face in his hands, and stared into the depth of those amazing blue eyes.

"No one will ever separate us again, Sapphire. I promise you that." He kissed her with soft tender kisses that made her squirm against him.

He desperately wanted to lie her down on the floor and make love to her right now, but knew he must abstain. She pushed her fingers

86

into his hair and pressed her chest against him. Her slightly drunken state had switched her buttons on, and she was kissing him now with a heated passion. He could feel her body starting to tremble slightly, and her skin was becoming hot to touch. He pulled back reluctantly. He was breathing heavily, because she was so utterly intoxicating to him. Even in her slightly drunken state she could turn on all his buttons.

She opened her eyes and he was lost in the violet-blue depths. In one quick swoop he lifted her from the chair and carried her up the stairs to the bedroom. She smiled up at him, obviously thinking he was going to have his wicked way with her. The house was dark now, lit only by candlelight. He opened the bedroom door with his foot and strode across to the bed, and placed her down so that she bounced slightly. Sapphire was panting softly now, her body completely aroused. He could see flashes of her energy sparking off her skin in gold and red pulses. She stared up at him, waiting for his next move. With a naughty smile on her lips, and lifting her arms up above her head, she stretched. He watched her breasts inch up slightly over her bodice. She was teasing him.

He started to undress quickly, removing his waistcoat and shirt so that his chest was bare. She continued to smile at him lazily, and waited patiently with excitement fizzing in her belly to see what he would do next. He knew exactly what he was going to do next. Slowly, taking his time, he started to undress her while he placed soft kisses on her skin at the same time as he revealed her bare flesh.

She closed her eyes and sighed. When she was completely naked, and when her clothes had been thrown carelessly on the floor, he moved up her body on all fours and kissed her on the mouth. She moved her hands down and started to fumble with the buttons on his trousers. He stopped her. She moaned a little in protest. He released her from the kiss and began to stroke her body with his right hand, gliding his fingers across her breast – then across her stomach, down to her groin. She squirmed beneath him, wanting more.

"Greedy girl," he thought. He smiled at her, a dark predatory smile. He slipped a finger inside and felt her quiver deliciously around him, her muscles clenching tightly at his intrusion. God, this woman turned him on. He moved his head to her neck and nuzzled her so that she moved her face to one side. She was whimpering softly as he played with her gently, teasing with a rhythmic glide in and out of her soft, warm body.

He started to kiss the soft skin on her neck. She always smelt so good. His tongue was sliding over her skin and savouring the taste of her. She trembled beneath him. He could sense her need to come but kept her dancing on the edge, and pulling his finger out slowly before sliding back in again – this time switching his energy on and drawing his magic from inside to travel up his arm into his hand. As he sucked on her neck he felt her gasp as his magic began to flow from his fingers into her body. She pushed her hips up higher as he moved his magic steadily down his arm into his fingers. He was completely turned on just by touching her and pleasuring her in this way. She was moaning loudly now, and her her head was turning to kiss him. He withdrew from her neck and looked down at her as he pushed another finger inside her. Now she opened her eyes and looked up at him with surprise on her face. He smiled at her. His eyes were flashing a deep gold and black, his magic flowing freely around him.

"I am going to make you come now, Sapphire, but I will not touch you."

Sapphire frowned a little. She was panting hard now, wanting more, wanting him. He released his fingers from inside her, and slid them out with painful slowness. She groaned and tried to grip him closer again. He took her hands and placed them up above her head and shook his own head slowly, the dark smile never leaving his lips.

"Watch," he said.

She was hot and sweaty, and her body was shaking from the pressure he had built up inside her. Her eyes drifted to follow him as he moved down her body. He was just inches from her skin, and his mouth was hovering above her groin. She was practically burning with heat now, in anticipation. He looked up at her one last time, and licked his lips slowly, suggestively. Sapphire watched him. Her whole body was alive with the need to feel his touch.

Very slowly, he lowered his head. His lips were just above her groin, which was at fever pitch with excitement. Just the warmth of his breath was pushing her towards the edge of oblivion. He pulled his magic from inside him and pushed it out – with a sigh – from his mouth and over her. She watched him, fascinated, as swirls of gold

88

and deep red escaped his lips and brushed across her skin. It touched her in the most wonderfully deep and intimate way. She watched the area of his attentions start to glow as if he had set her on fire – and then felt pressure start to build up slowly as if he were actually inside her, filling her body with his wonderful cock.

She closed her eyes and flung her head back on to the pillow as the pressure pushed deeply within her. The heat continued to throb outside and inside her, growing hotter and more insistent and making her head spin. Suddenly her body began to spasm, and she came so hard and with such intensity she thought she might shatter like glass into millions of tiny pieces. The bed shook, and she gripped the headboard and arched her back up as her climax spiralled up from her groin to consume her whole body in a rush of heat.

She heard Fox speaking to her in his own language, a string of words that seemed to be a spell of some kind. His voice caressed her body, causing her to climax again. His magic spread through her veins like molten lava. She did not think she could actually take much more, the intensity was so great. Her head began to spin and her hips bounced back down on to the bed again. She thought she would black out at any second. Suddenly – without warning – Fox was kissing her softly again and again, murmuring her name, and talking to her in his beautiful wild tongue.

Slowly, with a gentle softness, she felt her body become her own once more. He was grounding her, bringing her back from the magical orgasm he had just created without even touching her. He released her and gently slipped her back on to the bed. She opened her eyes and blinked as she gasped for air. She was now completely and utterly sober. The effect of the mead had gone, replaced by the most amazing sensation of being totally fucked senseless by the magic from this wonderful, amazing man. Fox was sitting next to her on the bed but not touching her, she could hear him chuckling softly.

She turned to face him. He was smiling – but, she sensed, with some discomfort after his little show. The evidence of his own arousal was hard against his trousers. His aura glowed brightly, a deep burnt orange and red that radiated heat.

"Oh, my God, Fox! How did you do that?"

He stroked her cheek softly. "Magic, my love. Magic."

Despite his obvious need for some kind of release Fox asked for nothing in return from her that night. After kissing her softly he had left her in bed and wandered into the bathroom to wash – in some very cold water, she assumed. He had returned to her naked and silently climbed into the bed. He lay with her under the sheets and spooned her perfectly, his strong arms holding her closely. She felt as if the world had been turned upside down again, but right now – at this moment, completely satisfied and sated – she did not care. All that mattered was that he was hers, and that she felt safe within his arms.

Chapter Eight

Fox had insisted that they eat and dress quickly the next morning so that he could take her to seek audience with the Oracle. Sapphire was nervous, but keen to see whether she could give them insight as to what danger may be heading their way. She was dressed in a beautiful blue gown made from the lightest of silks. Kit had braided her hair, which was pinned back either side, with the remaining locks flowing across her shoulders. Fox held her hands as they stood outside his house. The sky was darker today, with a promise of rain – the first she had seen since her arrival here. It made her feel slightly anxious, as if the sight of rain promised something more sinister on its way.

"Ready, my love?"

She smiled up at him and nodded. "Ready as I'll ever be."

She felt his magic tremble inside her belly and she closed her eyes, ready to be transported to the Oracle's residence. Within seconds they were standing outside a beautiful crystal glass building. Two soldiers stood like formidable statues outside on guard. Fox smiled reassuringly at her as they walked towards the entrance.

"We are here to speak with the Oracle," he said to the soldiers. They bowed, and moved aside without saying a word. Sapphire felt the immense pressure of magic all around her. It caressed her skin and made her shiver slightly in anticipation. As they entered the building Sapphire felt her eyes grow wide with wonder. The hall was beautiful, and it glittered with a soft sheen of crystal. Fox gripped her hand tightly, and she sensed his own anxiety as they walked across a large marble floor into a room that housed many young women who were sitting facing a plinth.

Sapphire blinked in surprise. Seated on a throne-like chair before her was the same woman as the one she had seen in her dream the night before her miscarriage … the same woman she sensed had spoken words of wisdom to her on Earth. Her guardian angel was in fact the Oracle. The Oracle smiled at them both, her face lit up with the most amazing brightness. Sapphire had never seen anything quite so beautiful.

"Welcome, Fox ... Welcome, Sapphire. It is such a pleasure to see you both on this day."

Sapphire was positively gawping now. Fox bowed deeply from the waist. Sapphire had lost all her senses and stood staring, wide-eyed.

"Oracle, blessings to you on this day. We have come to seek your wisdom, and to share the good news of our engagement."

Sapphire wanted to laugh out loud, because the Oracle clapped her hands together with glee like a child who had just opened the perfect Christmas present.

"How wonderful!"

Sapphire sensed Fox fidget slightly beside her. His hand was pulsing heat. He was indeed nervous. The Oracle addressed Sapphire directly with sharp, curious blue eyes.

"Sapphire – dream traveller – how are you finding your new home here on Shaka?"

Sapphire gulped. She was suddenly feeling very overwhelmed in the presence of this woman. "Good, thank you. Everyone is making me feel very welcome."

The Oracle smiled, and her hands returned to her lap. Her eyes flashed with silver sparks and her hair lifted and fell around her in an eerie, non-human way.

"I assume you are well recovered from your loss now, Sapphire?"

Fox, clearly unsettled by the direct line of questioning, tightened his grip on her hand.

"Yes, thank you. I'm fine," Sapphire answered her in a whisper.

The Oracle tipped her head to one side to gauge Sapphire's response and, seemingly satisfied, continued with her inquisition by saying, "And what is it that you wish to ask me?"

Fox loosened his grip slightly. "The queen from our neighbouring kingdom has been sending scouts to search for Sapphire. Are they planning to attack?"

The Oracle smiled serenely. "The balance on our world was tipped on Sapphire's arrival. Darkness and light are now being challenged once more. I am afraid I see a future filled with struggle and battle for you both."

Sapphire swallowed hard, trying to dislodge the lump that had suddenly appeared in her throat.

"But I also see hope and happiness for you. The outcome, however, is, as yet, unclear to me. I know this is a heavy burden to carry, Sapphire, but you are the key to restoring balance once more... not only the balance between good and evil, but also the awakening of consciousness. Your choices in the future will not only affect Shaka but, indeed, your home planet Earth. It is your destiny."

Sapphire remained completely still. Here she was again, being faced with the fate of everyone around her in her hands.

Fox sighed deeply. "How soon, Oracle?"

The Oracle continued to smile at them both, as if the news she had just given them was not disturbing at all. "Soon. You must prepare for war, guardian, to protect your wife-to-be and her magic. The magic she holds will come to fruition during the next full moon. This is all I can tell you for now." She stood up slowly. The bright light shining around her grew just that little bit brighter, which temporarily blinded Sapphire.

"I look forward to attending your wedding ... such a joyous occasion. Do not worry, Sapphire. There will be no fight before this wonderful joining."

Sapphire blinked. Her sight was coming back slowly. "Well, that's something," she mumbled to herself, while trying not to sound disgruntled.

The Oracle laughed softly. It sounded like a wind chime catching in the wind. "Yes, it is. Oh ... and there is just one more thing you should know. Ebony is hiding behind the queen. Her power is growing, and she is waiting for the right moment to strike again."

Sapphire felt Fox start to shake slightly as his anger grew in waves around him.

The Oracle seemed unperturbed by Fox's obviously unhappy response. "But do not fear, my children. You will know what to do with her when the occasion arrives."

Sapphire could feel her legs start to become quite unsteady beneath her. The news that the Oracle had so calmly delivered to them suddenly was causing a mini panic attack to swirl around her chest, which made it difficult to breathe.

Fox sensed her sudden distress, let go of her hand, and wrapped his arm around her waist to steady her.

"Thank you, Oracle. Your wisdom and guidance are gratefully received, as always."

The Oracle tipped her head forward, her lips still in a sweet smile on her beautiful face. "It is a pleasure, Fox, as always, to guide you. I shall see you both very soon."

Fox held Sapphire close to his body and bowed his head. She felt him guide her backward, away from the Oracle and the news they had just been given.

Sapphire stumbled slightly as she moved away. Her mind was racing. There was so much to take in, so much to deal with. This was worse than being on Earth trying to face Hecta, worse than struggling with her travelling, and worse than the fact that magic now coursed through her veins and ruled her world.

Suddenly they were outside, and she felt her whole body start to tremble as if she were falling into the tight grip of shock. Fox held her against his chest and, without another word, he transported them home before Sapphire could collapse in a heap at his feet.

Chapter Nine

On their return home the heavens opened. Rain poured persistently from the sky, the temperature had dropped, and Sapphire could sense the change in energy deep within her body. Fox had taken her upstairs and urged her to rest for a while. She did not resist him, as she suddenly felt very weary from the news they had been given. Her mind was racing with the possibilities that lay ahead of them now.

Kit appeared and helped her to undress so that she could sleep for a while. "Are you OK, Saf?" she asked tentatively as she helped her into the bed.

Sapphire looked up at her and smiled weakly. "Not really, Kit, but thank you for asking."

Kit frowned and sat on the edge of the bed next to her. "What did the Oracle tell you?"

Sapphire lay her head back on the pillows and sighed deeply. "Pretty much that everyone around me will be affected by my actions and choices, as usual. It seems to be part of the package now. Same shit, different day. Not the news I wanted, by any means, Kit."

Kit reached for her hand and held it, clasping her palm reassuringly. "I am sure that must be a heavy burden, my lady. But I know you are strong and kind in spirit, and I am sure that whatever you do it will be the right thing. Try not to trouble yourself too much. All our paths are undefined in the future. We have many choices, you know."

Sapphire blinked at her words of wisdom. Kit was so young. How she could possibly know such things was beyond her.

"Focus on the positive, Saf: your wedding, all the wonderful things that can come from this joining, your happiness with Master Fox ..." She was smiling reassuringly, and trying hard to raise Sapphire's spirits.

"You are very sweet, Kit, but right now I just feel like utter crap... but I'll be fine once I've had a rest."

Kit nodded, and released her hand gently.

"Where is Fox?" Sapphire asked. After they had returned to his home he had kissed her gently before leaving her with Kit.

"He has left for the castle, Saf – I believe to speak with his father and Wolf."

Sapphire closed her eyes. She just wanted to sleep and wake up with none of this impending doom over her head.

"Yes … well, that would be wise, considering that I seem to have started a fight with the neighbours without even realising."

Kit paused for a second before leaving the room. "Everything will be OK, Saf. I promise you it will all work out in the end."

Sapphire nodded, her eyes still closed. "I hope so, Kit. I really do."

Sapphire fell asleep quickly once Kit had left the room, her body utterly spent from the visit to the Oracle. She felt her breathing change and her body slip into the heaviness she was becoming accustomed to when she travelled. There was no doubt that she was dream travelling again, as she realised that she was now in Charlie's home – her old home on Earth.

She was walking through the hallway. Everything was freshly painted, and there were bright new pictures on the walls. It was dark, but she could see quite clearly as she walked up the stairs with light, quiet footsteps. As she reached the landing she could see inside her old room, which was now furnished with a new bed and wardrobe. The bed was made, with a pretty blue throw across the bottom. Her heart lurched as she noted it was empty of all her belongings, but of course they had been destroyed in the fire and she no longer owned anything from her previous life.

She crossed to Charlie's old room and pushed open the door silently and tentatively. Charlie was asleep in the bed with Nathan. The sight of her friend brought tears to her eyes. She was sleeping soundly, and her face was a picture of peacefulness and calm. Her curls, slightly longer than she had worn when Sapphire lived with her, tumbled across the pillow. Nathan was cuddled up against her. He too was sleeping soundly. The room was almost the same as she remembered but with new pieces of furniture, including a beautiful mirror that stood in the corner and which was tall enough for the person standing in front of it to see their entire reflection.

"Good for admiring a new outfit," Sapphire thought, and smiled. She desperately wanted to reach out and touch Charlie to speak to her, but knew this would not be wise. She crouched down beside her and just watched her for a moment, the tears still in her eyes. Charlie stirred in her sleep. A soft moan escaped her lips. She was frowning slightly now. Sapphire watched in wonder as she lifted her hand in her sleep as if to reach out for her.

"Saf?" Charlie said her name clearly.

Sapphire jumped back in surprise. Her energy trembled within her belly and suddenly, without warning, she was standing in the garden of Foxglove. The garden was bathed in moonlight. It looked as beautiful as it always had when she had visited Pearl. With excitement Sapphire walked to the front door of the cottage and pushed it open.

As she entered the hallway she was greeted by a collection of tiny sparkling lights. As she blinked to focus she saw that the sparkles were in fact tiny sprite-like fairies. They buzzed around her head and chattered excitedly at her sudden appearance. Sapphire laughed out loud now she could actually see Pearl's little helpers. They followed her up the stairs. She stood outside Pearl's bedroom door with an excited anticipation in her belly. She pushed the door open slowly and found herself looking at the woman who had helped her so much on Earth. Pearl was sleeping peacefully in her bed, a slight smile on her lips. She looked much younger than her years, and her skin was a soft silver in the moonlight. As Sapphire stepped closer she stirred and suddenly opened her eyes. Sapphire stopped breathing for a second and watched Pearl blink in the darkness.

"Sapphire? Is that you?"

Sapphire found it hard to believe that Pearl could actually be aware of her presence. She rushed to her side and crouched down beside her.

"Yes! It's me, Pearl. I'm here!"

Pearl pushed herself up. Her eyes were now firmly locked on to Sapphire. She beamed at her, a smile so wide she was positively radiant.

"Oh, Sapphire! It is wonderful to see you again. How are you?"

Sapphire reached out to touch her face, and a sparkle of gold light flickered across her skin as she did so. Pearl gasped a little, but continued to smile broadly.

"I'm fine, Pearl. It's so good to see you as well. I have missed you terribly."

"And I have missed you, Sapphire, but I knew you would return at some point. I hope that life for you is good."

Sapphire reached for Pearl's hand and took it, relishing the warmth of her soft skin.

"It is different, Pearl – very different – and things are changing again for me. The magic inside me is growing strong. There are people on my new world who intend to take me away from Fox again. I so wish you were there with me to help me, but I know that's not possible."

Pearl sat up and held her hand in a firm grip, as if she too did not want this moment to end. "I can see the new magic around you, Sapphire. It is so beautiful ... and can I see something else? Have you lost something recently?"

Sapphire sighed and sat on the edge of the bed with her. "Yes, I lost a child. It was quite a shock. but I'm OK now. Fox and I are to be married very soon."

Pearl raised her eyebrows. "Well, that is news. I am sorry to hear of your loss, but so glad to hear that you and Fox are to be married. I wish I could come. It would be wonderful to see you in your bridal gown."

Sapphire felt tears begin to prick her eyes. She so wanted Pearl to be there too. This sudden trip back to her old world was unexpected and, now, very overwhelming.

Pearl touched her cheek softly. "I am so glad you came, Sapphire. It has been a while since you left. I was wondering how you were."

Sapphire blinked back the tears and asked, "How long?"

Pearl sighed softly. "Six months," she said. "Your lovely young friend Charlie has missed you terribly – as have I – but she is very happy, and the cottage has been fixed and tidied. She is enjoying her life with her young man. She went on a long holiday with him not long after you left. I think she was rather surprised by the amount of money you left her."

Sapphire laughed. "Yes, I'm sure she was, but I'm glad everything is good in her life. I just saw her with Nathan. I think she sensed me. It was strange being there again. I had no idea so much time had passed here."

Pearl released her hand, gently, and patted it, kindly. "Time is different from place to place. You will learn that in time."

Sapphire wanted to stay with Pearl so badly, but could feel her energy starting to shift again. The room around her was starting to blur at the edges.

Pearl looked up suddenly, as if she too were aware of the shift. "It is time for you to go back, Sapphire. But remember, I am always here for you if you need me, and I hope to see your wedding in my dreams. Take care, my dear. Give my love to young Fox." As Pearl caught her gaze again Sapphire felt a sharp tug at her chest, as if the light that connected her to her body when she travelled was pulling her back again.

"I will see you again, Pearl."

Pearl nodded and smiled as she leant back into her pillows. As Sapphire felt herself shift away back on to her new world she noticed that a single tear was sliding quietly down Pearl's cheek. She closed her eyes and allowed her body to move away again. Her chest felt heavy, but her heart felt full.

With a pop in her ear, she felt time shift and move – and she was once again back in Fox's bedroom, on his bed. She lay very still on her back and looked up at the canopy above her. It was still raining outside. She could smell the fresh, cool tones of grass and flowers that had been awakened in the rain. Slowly she stretched and lifted herself up. The day was grey outside and she had no idea what time it was, but sensed that Fox was still absent.

She dressed in a long skirt and blouse and went back downstairs to find Kit. She was in the kitchen reading.

As Sapphire approached she looked up and smiled. "Did you rest well, Saf?"

Sapphire took a chair next to her at the table and sat down. "I was dreaming again. I went back to Earth and visited my friend Charlie and spoke with Pearl. It was wonderful to see them both again."

Kit stared at her wide-eyed. "That must have been incredible. It is such a gift to be able to travel when you sleep."

Sapphire smiled weakly. "A gift and a curse, Kit. It can be very emotional."

Kit nodded and put her book down. "I cannot even imagine how it must feel for you, Saf, but I hope that the time you spent with them both was a comfort."

Sapphire nodded. "Yes … actually it was, Kit. I'm glad they are both OK. It was wonderful to actually speak with Pearl. She has strong magic of her own, and was able to see me."

Kit pushed back her chair and stood up. "Can I get you anything, Saf? Are you hungry?"

Sapphire shook her head. She felt empty inside. "No, I'm not hungry at the moment, Kit. I think I will go outside for a while until Fox returns."

"But it is raining quite heavily, my lady. When the rains come they can last for a few days. It may be wise to stay inside."

Sapphire watched her expression of concern and felt a swell of emotion in her chest at her kindness. "No, I'll be fine. I need to clear my head."

Kit found her a long cloak and watched Sapphire leave the house. She looked a little worried as she headed out into the garden with the hood pulled up over her head. Sapphire wondered if Kit was more nervous of her going outside than the possibility of her getting wet. Suddenly nothing felt safe any more, but she knew that Fox had undoubtedly posted guards around the borders of his home and that no harm would come to her here. She wandered to the bottom of the garden to the beech tree.

The rain was pouring heavily from a darkened sky but it felt cleansing, and hearing the cool droplets falling from the tree made her feel oddly soothed. She stood next to the huge trunk and rested against it as she looked up into the canopy above her and breathed the fresh clean air in deeply. She closed her eyes and drew the energy from below her up into her legs and body. It tingled up her spine, making her head spin for a moment. The weariness from earlier began to disappear, and she felt a new surge of hope wash through her body. She would ask Fox to start teaching her how to defend herself and focus on the positive things that were about to happen in her new life. She would also get Kit to speak to Violet about making her a wedding dress. With her eyes still closed and her back against the tree trunk she started to visualise how her dress would look, and how wonderful it would be to become Fox's wife.

Suddenly, without warning, she felt a jolt within her solar plexus. A hot, burning sensation began to grip her in her chest, and she realised that the obsidian was pulsing out of control against her skin. Her eyes opened wide. Standing not far in front of her was a dark shadow. With sudden horror flooding through her brain she realised that it was Hecta who stood before her. He was surrounded by darkness, and dripping wet.

She gasped, and her hand flew to her chest in fright. He stepped towards her smoothly, with no sound. Sapphire felt her adrenalin kick in. Her breathing was coming now in quick, frightened bursts. Hecta stepped forward and removed the hood of his cloak. He smiled at her – a dark, lazy smile. His eyes were flashing red and black.

"Greetings, Sapphire. Such a lovely afternoon for a stroll."

Sapphire gripped the tree trunk and looked around her for help. There was not a soul to be seen in the mist of rain.

"Leave me alone, Hecta."

He grinned, revealing perfectly straight white teeth. "I mean you no harm, Sapphire, but I am here to warn you that it will not be long before events unfold to take you away from this place. It will be stupid to fight, and to make others suffer because of you. I am here to advise you that it would be best to let go of your guardian before he is destroyed."

Sapphire felt her anger begin to rise in response to his words. As usual, this horrible man was making her want to strike out. "No one is going to take me away, Hecta, or harm Fox – or anyone else, for that matter. You can try to frighten me, but it won't work. Now leave me alone before Fox sees you."

He chuckled, but made no further attempt to move towards her. "We shall see about that. You can so easily put an end to this, Sapphire. All you have to do is give yourself to the queen, and it will all go away. No one else will have to be harmed."

Sapphire blinked as she tried to control the energy that was now pulsing around her. "What do you mean by, 'No one else'?"

He turned his head, lifted his arm, and pointed across the gardens in a slow sweep.

101

"The guard came to a rather unfortunate end when he tried to stop me coming over the boundary to speak to you. Such a shame ... He was only young."

Sapphire felt her eyes grow wide as she noticed a dark shape slumped on the ground next to the wall. The sheets of rain made it difficult for her to work out exactly what it was. With renewed horror she realised that he was in fact speaking the truth. The guard was lying lifeless on the ground, with pools of blood surrounding him.

Sapphire cried out as she gasped for air. "No!"

Hecta moved a little closer. Now she could see his eyes clearly, and the hatred within them. "More will come to this end if you do not give yourself up to the queen, Sapphire. Maybe even the little Kitten you have hidden in your house. Now that would be a terrible shame."

Sapphire pushed her back from the tree and lunged across at him. He looked confused for a moment, and stepped back just a fraction.

"You dare to threaten me again, Hecta ... I will personally kill you if you try to touch anyone else, you horrible man."

He laughed again and turned his back on her. Sapphire, not knowing what to do, stood shaking from head to toe. As he walked away she could hear his laughter fade into the rain – dark, ominous laughter that shook her body with fear and rage. He was gone. He had disappeared in the grey mist, leaving Sapphire shivering in the rain.

She could not move for a moment. The shock of seeing him again had rendered her paralysed. She shook her head and forced her body to move forward. She ran across to the body lying by the wall and crouched down to see who it was. A young man with long, dark hair lay lifeless before her. His face was perfectly still, and the rain was washing the blood away from the knife wound in his chest. Sapphire started to cry. She tried to lift him, but he was too heavy. She stood up again and ran as fast as she could back to the house, calling out for Kit as she did.

As she reached the entrance to the house Fox appeared from nowhere. He strode towards her with wide, purposeful steps. Sapphire reached out for him and almost collapsed as he grabbed her and pulled her into his arms.

"By the gods, Sapphire! What is it? I felt your fear and came straight home. What has happened?"

They stood in the rain while Sapphire cried into his chest with deep, shaking sobs.

"It was Hecta ... he was here. He has killed a young man who was standing guard. He is over there by the beech tree. I could not lift him. Oh, God, Fox ... I'm so sorry. This is all my fault."

She felt his energy swell around him. His breathing was rapid. He took her forcefully towards the house and yelled for Kit as he kicked the door open. Kit appeared, looking wide-eyed and scared.

"Kit, please help Sapphire. She has had a shock. I will be back in a moment." He disappeared again out into the rain.

Sapphire felt herself being pulled inside by Kit to the lounge, where she slumped down into one of the chairs. Water was still dripping off the end of her nose.

"Oh, my goodness, Saf! Are you OK? What has happened?"

Sapphire looked up at her with misery filling her body. "Hecta has killed a man ... he was outside. It was awful. Oh, God, Kit ... This is my fault, all my fault."

Kit stood perfectly still for a moment, shock on her face. She began to help Sapphire out of her cloak, which was now soaking wet.

"Oh, no, my lady ... This is not your fault. You could not have stopped Hecta. He is powerful and evil. It was out of your control."

Sapphire sniffed loudly. Kit had managed to untangle her from the cloak and was holding her hand tightly. Her eyes were flashing with worry.

"I will get you something to drink, Saf, to warm you up. Wait here."

Sapphire didn't think she would have been able to move again if she had tried. This was like another bad dream. People had been hurt before because of her, now someone had actually been killed. The tears continued to fall steadily down her cheeks. She was awash with guilt, anger, and confusion.

Kit reappeared with a tankard and gestured for Sapphire to take it. She grabbed the drink and gulped it down. It was mead, sweet and soothing to her troubled mind. She heard the door slam and jumped in her seat. Kit also jumped at the bang.

"Kit! Help me a moment!" She ran out into the hallway.

Sapphire took another gulp of mead. It was starting to create a warm sensation in the pit of her stomach, and she realised Kit must have put something into the tankard to help her calm down.

Fox appeared again at the doorway. His body was trembling with rage. He crossed the room to her and crouched down as he placed his hands either side of Sapphire's face. He kissed her with a passion she knew was due to his relief that she had not been harmed.

"Are you OK, my love? I have called for Wolf and Bear, and will double the guard around the house. I cannot believe he actually came to my house and threatened you."

Sapphire sighed deeply. The mead and whatever potion Kit had given her had now restored her calm, and her head was clearing.

"That man is dead now because of me, Fox. How can I ever make up for this mess? I'm sorry I came here, sorry I have caused all this heartache again."

He took her shoulders and gripped her tightly. There was a frown on his face, and his eyes were swirling with dark flashes of gold and black. "Never say that, Sapphire. This is not your fault. None of this is your fault. You have done nothing wrong. I have been careless."

Sapphire shook her head slowly. "No. You have done nothing but try to protect me constantly since I arrived. You even tried to shelter me from the fact that the queen had sent scouts out to try and find me. This has to stop, Fox. No one else should be killed or harmed just because of who I am."

He continued to hold her shoulders, his face troubled and dark. "As your guardian I should have foreseen this. It is I who should be sorry, but it will not happen again. The king's guard are now on full alert, and I will not leave you again."

She smiled at him, a soft reassuring smile. She knew that he would constantly blame himself rather than think that she was at fault. "I think we both underestimated Hecta. We have been wrapped up in our own little world and believed that we were safe here on Shaka, as we have been in the past. But that has changed now, and the reason it has is due to the fact that my magic has changed. It has grown to such a point where I must be shining like a star to all around me. I cannot hide, Fox. I have to confront the queen, and Ebony. Hecta told me this would all stop if I just went to her."

Fox stood now and started to pace back and forth before her, his hands on his hips. "No! I will never allow that to happen. Sapphire, you have no idea who Ebony is or the levels to which she will go. She intends to take your magic for herself. It would destroy you."

Sapphire remained calm, although she had the intense urge to punch something. Hard.

"And she has no idea who I am, Fox. I'm trusting my abilities now. I'm trusting that I can handle this. The Oracle herself said that we would be faced with battle and torment, but she also foresaw happiness and hope. I am choosing the last bit. I refuse to be kept hidden and safe just because I'm precious to you. If it comes to a fight then I will be there to fight it."

He spun around and stared at her. She had never seen such ferocity in his eyes before, never seen such fierceness aimed at her. "I cannot lose you, Sapphire, not now. It would break me."

She stood up slowly and crossed the room to him. He hesitated as she held out her arms and folded herself around him.

"And you won't – I promise you that – but you can't protect me from what seems to be my path, Fox, no matter how strongly you feel about me and no matter how much I love you. This gift of dream travel – and the magic I have growing inside me – is bigger than both of us. I sense it is bigger than anything we could ever have imagined."

He held her to his chest. She could feel his breathing start to slow to a calmer pace, and his chin came to rest on her head. The smell of patchouli and sandalwood washed over her as he surrounded her with his energy.

"Fox! I came as quickly as I could. What can I do for you both?"

They both jumped as Bear entered the room, closely followed by the huge, dark shadow of Wolf. Fox released Sapphire gently and placed his arm around her shoulder.

"Thank you for coming, my friends. Hecta has been here. He killed the guard posted in the garden. I will need you to double the guards and be extra vigilant. It seems we underestimated the threat growing outside our kingdom."

Bear approached them, concern on his face he dipped his head in agreement. "Of course, Fox ... we will do anything we can do to help. You need not fear now, Sapphire. We will make sure no one enters your home again."

She smiled weakly at them both. Just seeing the two great warriors standing before her made her feel slightly better, but her heart had broken just that little bit more at the death that had occurred earlier.

"Thank you, Bear. Thank you, Wolf. I feel safer already."

Wolf stepped forward. He looked as if he had ridden hard to get to them. He was soaking wet from the rain that still seemed to be pouring relentlessly from the sky.

"I will personally make sure that the best warriors are placed on guard outside the perimeter," he said reassuringly.

Sapphire snuggled into Fox and tried to find some comfort against his warm body. "What happened to the young man Hecta killed?"

Wolf looked down for a moment before raising his eyes to hers. They were filled with sadness. "He will be taken back to the castle and given a warrior's burial." She nodded slowly.

"Please let his family know that I did not intend this to happen, Wolf. I would never have willingly put him in harm's way."

Wolf blinked. He looked confused. "It is our duty to serve you, my lady, and sometimes that duty results in death. It is the way of the warrior."

Sapphire felt weary again and slumped a little against Fox, who gripped her tightly.

"Thank you again, my friends. I think Sapphire needs to rest now. I will speak with you both again soon." They both bowed and left the room.

Fox gathered Sapphire into his arms – he lifted her up with ease – so that he could carry her upstairs. It was dark now. The bedroom was lit with candles, and the balcony doors were closed tight against the rain. Sapphire closed her eyes. She knew that if she opened them fresh tears would start to fall. It seemed that lately, all she did was end up back in bed after another unexpected episode of stress. But right now it was the only thing she wanted to do. Fox placed her on the bed and began to undress her slowly. He spoke to her softly in his native tongue: gentle, soothing words that he whispered sweetly, like a lullaby. She pushed herself under the covers and allowed him to tuck her in. He kissed her softly on the cheek, lips, and head, while weaving a spell of rest within his magical words. She felt him sit beside her for a moment and stroke her forehead.

"I love you, Sapphire, more than words can say. I will never let anyone harm you, ever."

He kissed her one last time and then left the room.

Chapter Ten

Sapphire woke the next morning with a naked Fox wrapped around her. He was spooning her body perfectly from behind. His leg was thrown over her, his arm pulling her closely to his chest. She could feel every part of him pressed against her, the rhythm of his magic pulsed steadily against her skin, like the beat of a drum. When she opened her eyes she noticed that it was still raining outside, and the room was a dark dismal grey. Fox shifted against her. He could sense her waking up, and his body reacted automatically instantly becoming alert.

"Sapphire, my love, did you rest?"

She stretched a little, and he released his grip so that she could turn to face him. He looked at her with sad slightly sleepy eyes. She kissed him gently and pushed her fingers into his hair to pull him closer again. He responded eagerly, and the kiss deepened. His passion ignited instantly at her touch. Reluctantly she withdrew slowly from the kiss and traced a finger across his cheek.

"Yes, I rested. No dreams."

A smile appeared slowly on his beautiful lips. "Good. You were restless. I was afraid you may have been travelling without me."

She sighed and kissed him again, a light, soft kiss. "No, I slept heavily. I feel better now. Are you OK?"

He nodded and licked his top lip slowly. "Of course, my love. With you safely by my side I am happy."

Sapphire pushed herself up, her hair falling across her shoulder in one long lock. "Good. Today I want to see the dressmaker and get this wedding sorted."

He laughed, his face lighting up again. "My beautiful Sapphire … always the positive creature. You shall have whatever you wish. I will send for Violet."

Sapphire frowned for a moment. "I would like to go to Calafia and see her at her shop, Fox. I am not going to be a prisoner in my own home."

He took the lock of hair that had tumbled across her breast and placed it to his lips, then kissed it and breathed in her scent.

"You have no fear, have you?"

She smiled at him. "Not any more, Fox."

He pushed her back down on to the bed and held her hands above her head. She gasped a little, but smiled up at him.

"As you wish, my love." He kissed her then softly at first, then harder and deeper. She sensed his need to claim her. The events unfolding before them were making his need to be close to her even stronger than usual. It had been a few days since her miscarriage, and they had not actually had the chance to be together properly. Suddenly her heart started to race as his hands slipped down her body, skimming across her breasts, and touching her stomach. He continued to kiss her, his tongue probing further into her mouth, causing her body to squirm beneath him. His hand glided across her thigh, his fingers finding the soft curve at the top of her groin. She felt him push against her leg, his own arousal hard and hot against her skin. He released her mouth and she moaned with pleasure. She desperately wanted to feel him inside her, to feel his body connect with her own.

With a rapid intensity the desire between them quickly grew to a smouldering fire. Fox turned to her neck and started to suck the soft skin in slow, deep pulls while his fingers explored her opening, which was now slick and wet with desire. He rolled on top of her and lifted his head, looking down into her eyes for a moment. His own eyes flashed deep amber and gold reflecting his need to connect with her. A smile was now etched firmly on his lips. She lifted her hips up to meet him and in one quick, deep push he was inside her completely. Sapphire groaned and wrapped her legs around him. She pulled him deeper inside, and crushed his buttocks with her thighs. It felt utterly delicious to have him inside her again. It had been too long.

As he watched her the whole time, his face a picture of wonder, he began to slide in and out of her body ... long, slow strokes which stoked the fire that began to burn deep within her. Sapphire pulled him back down to her so that she could kiss him again as he made love to her. She did not care if it was too soon, she did not care one bit. She wanted this so much: to feel him connect with her again, to

109

feel every muscle ripple against her body. His magnificent cock filled her body completely and made her body tremble all over. It made her feel complete once more and take away the tension and unease that had been unwittingly dragging her down emotionally and physically.

He rode her for some time, and pleasured her with such passion it made her head spin. She felt her climax start to build slowly, painfully, wonderfully. The magic inside her pulsed and shook like a wild animal, it too seemed very happy to be reunited with her soulmate. Fox gradually picked up the pace and started to pound her body, like he had no control any more and could not stop himself. He lifted his head and moaned loudly as their energy linked in one big flash of white light. It surrounded them both with a shower of silver sparks as they both came at the same time and washed over them, making them both gasp with the sensation of complete release. Sapphire released her legs and finally lay still beneath him, his body pinning her heavily to the bed. They were both gasping for air now. Fox rolled off slowly to her side, his arm resting on her belly.

She turned to face him and smiled. "I love you, Fox."

He lifted his arm and turned to face her, smiling with a sweet satisfaction on his lips. "And I you, my love … my only love."

After bathing and dressing slowly they went back down the stairs to find something to eat. Sapphire felt like something had been healed inside her that morning during the sweet release of climax with Fox and that she was now whole again. She could sense that Fox had also found some sense of balance return between them now that they had reconnected their magic and their bodies during their lovemaking. It hung in the air between them like a blanket of insence, thick and sweet. Kit was in the kitchen with Bear, who was tucking into a huge plate that was overflowing with food. They both looked up and beamed at them as they stood in the doorway.

"Good morning, Master Fox. Good morning, Saf. I hope you both slept well."

Sapphire still felt slightly flushed from her morning wake-up session with Fox, and blushed a little more. She knew that the magic surrounding them would give no doubt to whoever was looking at them that they had been up to some serious mischief.

"Yes … we did, thank you, Kit. Is there any food left for us? We are both starving."

Bear eyed them, with a wry smile on his lips. "I can see that you would be. It is good to see some colour in your cheeks, Sapphire."

Fox chuckled and grabbed one of the chairs, pulling it out for Sapphire to sit down. She lowered her eyes and smiled. Nothing seemed to escape his friend.

"Any problems last night, Bear?" Fox asked his friend. Bear continued to eat his breakfast with gusto. Sapphire reached for some pancakes that Kit had placed before her. Her stomach growled loudly.

"No, nothing to report, Fox. All seems quiet on the border now. Wolf has had men patrolling continuously, and new scouts have been sent out."

Sapphire ate quietly. It troubled her that more men were putting their lives on the line for her whilst she had been sleeping and making out with her man. Kit was quickly at her side, pouring her some fresh tea.

"Good. We are going to Calafia today. I will need you to escort us, Bear. Sapphire would like to buy her wedding dress today." Kit jumped a little and sloshed the tea.

"Oh, Master Fox, can I please come with you?" She began to mop up the spilt tea, blushing furiously.

Sapphire smiled at her. "Of course you can, Kit. I need you to try on some dresses, as you are maid of honour."

Fox smiled and raised an eyebrow. "Well, that is wonderful news, Kit. Yes, of course you can come. I am sure Sapphire will need your help." He began to tuck into the food Kit had laid out for them.

Sapphire felt a wave of unexpected happiness wash over her as she watched Bear and Kit at the table with them, eating and drinking as if they were family … Her new family. Despite the events of yesterday – and the awful tragedy of the guard's death – today felt like a new beginning, something to look forward to. She was damned if she was going to let Hecta and this queen she did not even know spoil her wedding plans. No one had the right to do that to her and Fox. No one.

They finished their breakfast and headed out to the stables. Sapphire noticed that the garden was suddenly very full, with strange men scattered around who looked very formidable in leather armour. Each one was carrying either a large sword or a crossbow. She shivered a little, but felt comforted by their presence. The rain had turned into a soft mist, and they were dressed in cloaks to keep themselves warm and dry. Fox helped her up on to Amber. There seemed to be several new horses in the courtyard today. Kit and Bear mounted their own horses quickly and with ease.

Fox jumped up lightly on to the magnificent Midnight who stamped his feet and champed at the bit, eager to take off. He held the reins lightly and patted his neck. "Be still, my beauty. We have company today. I will take you out soon for a proper run."

Sapphire smiled at him. He looked sexy as hell mounted on his black horse. Fox took the lead and Sapphire followed, with Kit and Bear bringing up the rear. As they headed out of the grounds Sapphire was aware that several other riders followed them at a distance. Fox was taking no risks today: they had a full escort all the way to the city.

Fox had kept Midnight at a respectable trot until Sapphire had pulled up beside him and grinned before kicking Amber into a canter. He laughed at her recklessness and caught her up quickly. The journey to Calafia took no time at all after that. On reaching the city they left the horses at the gate and entered through the wooden gateway, which had several more guards in place today. The castle grounds were bustling with activity despite the change in weather.

As they walked through the myriad of streets people bowed and smiled at them. Fox held her hand tightly and smiled at her reassuringly. They entered Violet's shop and left Bear standing outside on guard. Violet smiled as the door clanged to announce their appearance.

"My lord! It is a pleasure to see you and Lady Sapphire today. How may I help you?"

Sapphire began to remove her cloak, which was now a little damp from the journey.

"Sapphire will need a wedding dress, Violet, and Kit is to be her maid of honour. We are to be married very soon."

Violet's eyes flashed brightly with joy. "That is wonderful news, my lord. Of course … whatever you need."

Fox turned to Sapphire and kissed her lightly on the lips. "I will leave you with Kit for a while, my love. I will not be far away. I have to speak with my father – but Bear will be outside, and I will be back very soon. Enjoy shopping."

She smiled up at him, grateful for his acceptance of her wish to come to the city today despite the possible danger. Kit had started to rummage through the rails with Violet. They were both chattering about which colour would suit her best, and pulling out fine silks and velvets for Sapphire. She watched him leave, and her stomach churned a little at the thought of him not being by her side for a moment. He paused at the doorway and looked back at her with those beautiful amber eyes.

"I will not be long, and if you need me I will be here quicker than you can blink."

She smiled at him and nodded. Relief washing over her.

"Saf! Look at this! This would be wonderful as a veil … would you like a veil?"

Sapphire laughed and turned to Kit, who was holding up the most exquisite piece of ivory lace. She felt a quiver of excitement flicker in her chest, and realised that she wanted nothing more than to lose herself in the task of finding herself the perfect wedding dress.

Sapphire stood in front of a large mirror and stared at her reflection. It had not taken long for Violet and Kit to find her the perfect materials for her dress. Violet was pinning her with deft fingers at a speed Sapphire had never seen in a human before. Her dress was made from ivory-coloured silk, which clung to her body perfectly. A bodice, scattered with diamonds in swirls and patterns of tiny flowers, twinkled in the candlelight. The dress fell to the floor. More diamonds decorated the hem, as if stars had been sprinkled at her feet. A long coat of almost transparent material fitted over the top to cover her bare arms. It was plain except for a design resembling vine leaves and ivy stitched in silver thread around the sleeves, which trailed down into the long, pointed cuffs. Kit had pinned her hair up, which allowed soft tendrils to fall to her shoulders. The lace veil clipped into place with a tiara, which also glittered and shone with tiny diamonds and sapphires. Sapphire truly felt like a fairy princess. It was as she would have dreamt her most perfect dress would be. She smiled at them both as they cooed and bustled around her. Kit was dressed in deep red. It suited her dark hair and fair complexion perfectly. She looked beautiful.

"It is perfect. Thank you, Violet. Kit, you look amazing."

Kit blushed a little. "I feel wonderful, my lady. Thank you for this gift."

"You are most welcome, Kit. I'm glad you will be at my side when I marry Fox."

The door clanged, indicating another customer. Bear strode in, a grin on his face. "You look beautiful Sapphire – and you, Kit. Fox will be mesmerised."

Sapphire blushed a little, and began to remove the veil. "Violet, would you please help me undress and finish the alterations as soon as it is possible? I believe Fox has arranged for us to be married within days."

Violet nodded in reply. She was unable to speak due to the many pins she still had sticking out of her lips.

"Fox is on his way back, Sapphire. He wishes for you to return home shortly, where he can keep an eye on you."

Sapphire smiled. She was still flying high on being bride for the day. "We won't be long, Bear. You can keep Fox outside until we have finished undressing. I don't want him seeing my dress before our wedding day."

Bear chuckled loudly and left the shop. The door clanged loudly as his head ducked under the door frame. Kit and Violet helped Sapphire remove the beautiful wedding outfit, and in no time at all they were ready to leave. Kit held her hand for a moment, and stared at the fingers on her left hand.

"I wonder what your wedding band will be like, Saf?"

Sapphire shook her head. She had not even thought about a ring. Fox had not given her an engagement ring, as was the custom on Earth.

"I don't know, Kit. Fox has not even mentioned a ring." Kit looked amused, and dropped her hand gently.

"Your ring will be made from the magic that connects you when you are officially married, Saf. It will be a permanent mark on your finger. It cannot be given before the ceremony."

Sapphire raised her eyebrow. "What do you mean when you say, 'A permanent mark'?"

Kit smiled shyly. "You will see."

Sapphire sighed. She didn't understand at all. They thanked Violet, who was already busy creating her own magic with the new dresses, and left the shop.

Fox was standing outside when they entered the street. He was leaning up against the wall and talking to Bear. His face lit up when he saw Sapphire approach.

"Did you find what you wanted, my love?"

She stood before him and looked up into his handsome face, feeling the love radiating from him in gentle pulses.

"Yes, thank you. We did."

He took her into his arms and held her close, kissing the top of her head gently. "Good. We are to be married in two days ... My father will come to the house. The ceremony will be conducted at night, when the moon is full."

Sapphire smiled. "I can't wait," she said.

They left the city shortly after. The sky was beginning to clear, the rains had stopped, and a strong breeze rippled across the fields as they cantered home. Sapphire was beginning to feel a renewed sense that all would be well. She was excited at the thought of the wedding, and knew that it could not come soon enough for either of them.

On arriving back at Fox's grand house Sapphire found another collection of strange people bustling in the gardens. She was surprised to see them working hard at creating a platform near the fountain. Chairs were also being placed on the grass, and women carrying flowers and ribbons were creating an aisle to the platform in pretty floral pathways. Fox helped her down from Amber and watched her with bright eyes. His excitement was spilling over and making him shine with a soft, golden glow.

"There will be many people attending our wedding, Sapphire, with a banquet after. My father insisted. I hope you don't mind."

She laughed. "I doubt we had a choice – but no, I don't mind. I'll try not to trip up and make a fool of myself when I walk down the aisle."

Kit was at their side, after helping Bear to settle the horses.

"Come, Saf, I need to talk to you about the wedding feast. There is a lot to organise!" She practically dragged Sapphire back to the house, giggling like a school girl. Sapphire could not help but get caught up in her joy. This was probably the most exciting time of her life.

The rest of the day passed quickly with Kit in the kitchen, discussing what food they would prepare for the wedding banquet. She told Sapphire that the cooks from the castle would be coming tomorrow to start preparing for the following day. They would bring their own makeshift kitchen. Sapphire was starting to feel a little overwhelmed by the time it was supper.

Fox had been drifting in and out of the kitchen throughout the afternoon to check on them. She had no idea what he was doing in between, but presumed he must be spending time with Bear and Wolf talking wedding security and man stuff. She wondered what he would be wearing for the ceremony and, indeed, what the wedding would actually consist of - she had no idea how a wedding would be performed on Shaka.

Her thoughts drifted to Pearl and Charlie, and how much she would have loved them to attend. It saddened her that her own mother would know nothing of her new status – and that she may be back on Earth, wondering if her daughter would actually come home at some point. The letter Sapphire had left her had consisted of a very vague story – that she would be travelling with a new man she had met for a few years, but she would try to contact her when she could. At the time she had had no idea if this was even possible, but after her dream travelling to Pearl she knew that there may come a time when she could in fact see her mother again.

Kit was dishing up a stew that she had whipped up as Fox and Bear entered the kitchen again.

"I hope you have made double helpings, Kit. I am starving," Bear announced as they sat at the table.

Fox sat beside Sapphire and reached for her hand. He kissed her fingertips lightly, his eyes shining brightly. He looked as excited as she felt at the impending wedding.

"Of course I have, Bear. I know how big your appetite is." They began to eat. The same happy atmosphere that had filled the room at breakfast comforted Sapphire once more.

"What will actually happen at the ceremony, Fox? Do we need to write any vows?"

Fox looked up as he chewed a mouthful of food and smiled softly. "My father will conduct the ceremony, my love. You will not need to worry. He will tell you what to do. If you would like to say anything, please feel free. There are a few rituals that we must perform, but nothing you need worry about. I will show you what to do."

She raised her eyebrow and contemplated the thought of having to jump over a broomstick, or dance around naked in front of a bunch of strangers.

"I trust that we don't have to conduct anything too embarrassing in front of our guests."

He laughed as he reached for the wine Kit had poured him. Bear was already on his second helping.

"No, my love, nothing embarrassing. Weddings here on Shaka are a very happy event. The ceremony won't take long."

She nodded, and let her mind wander across the endless possibilities of what might actually happen.

"We will be well protected. Wolf has the best soldiers on guard, and they will all be patrolling the perimeter of the gardens throughout the celebrations. You have nothing to fear, Sapphire."

Bear slugged back a glass of wine and chuckled. "The entire guard will be on-site, Sapphire, plus me to protect you. Nothing could get through, even if it tried."

She felt reassured by his words, but hoped he was right. Her thoughts had been troubled by the death of the guard the day before, and it niggled in the pit of her stomach that Hecta may turn up again to ruin everything. Sapphire's brow furrowed suddenly as she remembered something very important.

"Who will give me away?" They all looked at her, a little confused for a moment. Sapphire took a sip of her wine and placed the glass down slowly. "When a couple are married on Earth the bride is usually 'given away' by her father – but of course my father died, and I don't even know anyone who would do that here for me. I would feel a little weird, walking down the aisle on my own."

Fox ran his finger across her cheek and smiled. "Bear would be honoured to walk you to the altar, my love – wouldn't you, Bear?"

Bear beamed enthusiastically. "Of course, Sapphire. It would indeed be an honour – although this is a strange custom, I must say. Usually the bride arrives with her ladies, and no man is in attendance until she is wed to her man."

This was news to Sapphire. She looked across at Kit, who smiled and lowered her eyes, looking a little shy.

"You can walk with me as well, Kit. You both might need to hold me up if my legs give out with all the people staring at me." They all laughed. Kit nodded, her cheeks flushed.

After supper Bear left to speak with Wolf, who was apparently outside waiting to talk to him. Kit bustled around the kitchen, tidying up. Fox took Sapphire's hand and led her into the lounge, where they could sit and digest the food before bed. Sapphire sighed deeply as he drew her into his lap and threw her legs across him as he wrapped his arms around her waist.

"Are you nervous, Sapphire?"

She smiled up at him and watched his eyes sparkle with humour. "A little. I really have no idea what is going to happen, or if it will be anything like our weddings at home."

He kissed her softly on the lips, a tender kiss that sent shivers down her spine. "The ceremony is straightforward but may be a little strange for you, as magic is a big part of the joining. I want you to be prepared for that – but I know nothing will really surprise you any more, my love. All weddings are conducted under a full moon, to cleanse and bless the couple and to amplify the magic of the joining. I believe the Oracle herself will attend, which will bless our marriage in ways that the average person on Shaka would never have. We are truly honoured."

Sapphire nodded and nestled into his chest. The warmth of his body comforted her anxiety a little.

"The Oracle said my magic would manifest during the next full moon, at the same time as our wedding. I hope nothing weird happens."

He chuckled softly. "Whatever happens, my love, I know it will be a blessing. Stop worrying."

They went to bed that evening happy and full of excitement. Fox made love to her with a tenderness and passion that made tears fill her eyes with love and pride. She was to be his wife in two days. It was the most wonderful feeling ever. As she lay in his arms in the dark she wished for nothing more than for their wedding to be a joyous occasion, with no drama or problems. She hoped and prayed it would be so.

Chapter Eleven

The next day was filled with more strange people wandering in and out of the house and gardens, preparing the ceremony area, cooking, and cleaning. Kit had not been wrong about the castle kitchen turning up with their own banqueting team: there were so many chefs and cooks in attendance that Sapphire was beginning to think the whole city would be turning up tomorrow night to watch them get married. Flowers were being placed everywhere: there were beautiful white roses, lilies, and vines woven around the chairs and placed in ornamental pots that covered the garden, which made it look like something out of a film set. Fox was by her side thoughout the day, and he introduced her to some of the people instrumental in making this all happen for them. Her head was buzzing by the time the day was over.

They were walking through the gardens as the sun started to slip down over the horizon. He was leading her to the beech tree, away from the groups of people still setting up the sumptuous preparations for the wedding. He squeezed her hand gently as they reached the wall that indicated the end of his land. She noticed that several guards were in attendance close by.

"Are you happy, my love?"

She smiled at him. She had noticed that his energy had expanded even more in the last few days. His love for her was obviously growing by the moment at the thought of their wedding tomorrow.

"The happiest I have ever been, Fox. This is too much ... all of this for us. So many people working so hard ... I can't believe how much has been achieved in such a short time. This would take months on Earth."

He chuckled and drew her into his arms as he breathed in deeply. "We work quickly here on Shaka, and you are worth it."

They watched the last of the sun's rays slip beneath the horizon. The sky was clear and Sapphire hoped that tomorrow would be a good day, with no rain. Beautiful pinks and oranges splashed the sky with the promise that it would be. They stood for a while wrapped in each other's arms, taking time to enjoy the quiet after such a crazy day. They wandered back to the house as the sky turned black. All was quiet now. Everyone had disappeared, but Sapphire knew that Bear was somewhere out there, walking the perimeter with other guards. They had constant company now. Kit was nowhere to be seen. She still had no idea where Kit slept and where she disappeared when she and Fox were alone. They went up stairs to the bedroom to turn in for the night.

Sapphire giggled as she undressed. "You are not supposed to spend the night with your man before your wedding day on Earth. I hope we don't get into trouble."

Fox stood behind her and helped her lift her dress up as he kissed her gently on the neck. "That's a stupid tradition, and I think we should get into as much trouble as we wish," he murmured between kisses.

Sapphire leant back into him and felt his hands stroke her naked skin in a slow, gentle caress. "I agree, but I still feel a little naughty."

He spun her around and stared at her, his eyes dark with passion.

"Naughty but nice, my beautiful Sapphire." He picked her up and kissed her hungrily before throwing her on to the bed. She laughed as he stripped quickly and jumped on to the bed to join her.

"Tomorrow you will be my wife, Sapphire, and tonight I will remind you exactly why you have chosen to take me as your husband." The intensity in his eyes made her quiver in anticipation. As he claimed her lips once again she had no doubt whatsoever that he would do just that.

Sapphire dreamt of a battle that night: a great battle, with hundreds of warriors on horseback. She was observing the scene before her and watching in horror as they clashed in wave after wave of swords and battle cries. She saw Fox fighting like a demon warrior, his eyes flashing in anger at the enemy who poured towards him and slashing down man and beast as they surrounded him. Bear was to his right, Wolf to his left. They were all working hard to stop the dark force around them.

She woke up with a start and sat upright in the dark. She realised that she was panting from shock. Fox stirred beside her and reached out for her. He touched her skin and made her jump a little more.

"Sapphire? Are you OK, my love?"

She blinked as she tried to refocus.

"Yes, I'm OK. I was dreaming." She felt him sit up beside her and pull her into his arms. Her heart was still racing, but the warmth from his naked body started to calm her immediately.

"A bad dream?"

She nestled into his chest, and felt him kiss her softly on her hair and rock her gently.

"Yes."

He did not press her further, and she did not wish to tell him what she had seen. He was murmuring to her in his strange language and lulling her back to sleep. She closed her eyes again and shivered a little. She did not want anything to ruin her big day, so she tried to visualise a happy day and remove the memory of the dream. Before long she drifted back to sleep, only aware now of the man she loved pressed to her body and radiating a love so strong it made her feel safe again in his arms.

Sapphire awoke the next day to sunshine streaming in from the balcony windows. Fox was standing next to the bed fully dressed, and smiling at her lazily. She smiled back at him and stretched like a cat, revealing her naked body to him.

"Good morning, my beautiful bride. I hope you managed to get some rest last night."

She sighed and nodded. The dream had gone, but it lingered at the back of her mind like a bad penny. "You're up early."

He nodded, and finished buttoning his waistcoat. "Yes. I want to speak to Bear about the last few arrangements before tonight, just to be double sure everything will go smoothly."

Sapphire pushed herself up and yawned. "OK … I won't be long. Tell Kit I will be down in a minute. I'm starving."

He kissed her softly and brushed her cheek gently, the smile still on his lips as he took in her nakedness.

She blushed a little as she remembered just how much he had proved to her last night that he was definitely the right man for her. Her body was still a little sore and tender from his relentless lovemaking. She watched him leave the bedroom and stretched one more time, feeling like a naughty mistress. As she wandered towards the bathroom she noticed that several boxes had appeared by the door that had not been there the night before.

121

After washing and dressing she opened the largest box that had been placed next to the dresser, and was pleased to see that it was her wedding dress, folded neatly between sheets of paper. It seemed to glow with a life of its own in the box. Magic surrounded the material in a soft glow of golden light. She ran her fingers across it, and the glow shimmered and twinkled like fairy dust ... amazing. Violet had done the most incredible job in creating a dress in such a short time, plus whatever magic she had applied to it to make it just that little bit more wonderful.

Kit suddenly appeared at the bedroom door. She was flushed, and beaming like a crazy lady.

"Good morning, Saf ... such a beautiful day. The sun is shining, and everything is coming along nicely. Would you like something to eat? Master Fox said you were hungry."

Sapphire looked up at her momentarily overwhelmed by Kit's enthusiasm and energy. She really was the sweetest thing.

"Yes, I am, Kit: starving, in fact. My dress is here. When did that arrive?"

Kit skipped across and looked down into the box with wide eyes. "It came early this morning, Saf. It does look wonderful. Violet has spun some special magic into the thread for you. She really is the most talented dressmaker in all of Calafia."

Sapphire stood up and smiled. "I can see that," she said.

Kit reached down to touch the fabric tentatively. It sparkled at her fingertips. "I shall hang it so that any creases will fall out before tonight, my lady. You will look so beautiful ... I am so excited."

Sapphire watched her with happy eyes. She could see Charlie mirrored in her enthusiasm. She missed her friend terribly.

"Thank you, Kit. That would be wonderful. I'll go find some breakfast."

Kit began to unfold the dress, humming softly with a smile on her lips.

"There are pancakes and eggs all laid out on the table, my lady. I will be down shortly."

As Sapphire descended the stairs she was suddenly aware of more people inside the house. Her eyes grew wide as she realised that the entire hallway was dressed with flowers and rose petals which covered the marble floor, creating a pool of white at her feet.

A young girl smiled at her and curtseyed as she reached the bottom of the stairs. Sapphire paused, and wondered if she could actually walk across them.

"Good morning, my lady. Such a fine day for your wedding."

Sapphire smiled at her, a little shyly. "Thank you. Yes, it is." She tiptoed across the hall to the kitchen, trying not to mess up the petal arrangement too much as she did, and was grateful that no one else seemed to be inside the house. Her stomach rumbled as she eyed the plates of food Kit had laid out. She sat down to eat and was quickly joined by Kit again, whose eyes were shining brightly.

"We can take a ride later if you like, Saf. Master Fox said that you may wish to take some air while the final preparations for tonight are finished."

Sapphire nodded. "Yes, I would like that. It's a little overwhelming having all these strangers around."

Kit bustled around the table, pouring her some fresh tea and loading her plate with more food. "I know it is strange, but very exciting. We have not had so much company in a very long time. Master Fox will join us for the ride, of course, and Bear. I am afraid he will not let us ride alone."

Sapphire licked her lips. Honey from the pancakes was dripping down her chin a little. "OK. I suppose it would be too much to ask for some time alone at the moment, considering everything that has happened lately."

Kit nodded. A little frown appeared on her forehead. "Yes. We still have to be careful, my lady."

After breakfast Sapphire headed out to find Fox. The rose petals had magically stayed put, despite the fact that she felt as if she had trampled over them for a second time. Kit was beside her as they walked out to the stables. Sapphire gasped at the view before her. The garden was now teaming with people finishing the wedding site. The whole area had been transformed, and trellises covered in white roses now created a shield around the platform and chairs. It was totally beautiful and breathtaking. This would be one mother of a wedding.

Fox strode towards her, beaming. She watched him with hungry eyes. He looked magnificent today, the most handsome she had seen him: his eyes were bright and flashing with gold.

"Let's ride for a while, my love … take some time out from all of this."

She rushed to his side and, smiling, wrapped her arms around him. "Yes, I think that would be a very good idea."

They saddled the horses and headed out, leaving the garden full of people behind them. The sun was warm and the air a soothing, cool caress as Sapphire cantered behind Fox, who took the lead. Bear and Kit followed closely behind them.

They did not go far today. Fox took them to the pool and waterfall she remembered on their first trip out after her arrival on Shaka. She laughed as they came to a sudden halt, with the horses snorting and kicking up the earth under their hooves as they arrived in the woods. Fox jumped down from Midnight and patted his rump heartily. He walked across to Sapphire and reached up to help her down.

"Would you like to swim today?"

She was panting a little heavily after the ride, but laughed as she slipped down his body to the ground.

"I would actually love a swim, but not without a bathing suit. I'm not ready to show my naked butt to Bear and Kit just yet."

Bear laughed as he came up beside them after taking the horses to a nearby tree to tether them to graze. "That would be a fine sight to see, Sapphire, I am sure."

Fox punched him on the arm, but smiled at his teasing. "Bear, would you and Kit please give us some time together alone for a while? Sapphire and I would like to swim in privacy."

Bear nodded, still grinning. Kit was standing beside her horse and smiling, with a blush in her cheeks.

"Of course. I will take Kit to the edge of the woods, where I can keep watch. Call if you need me."

Fox took Sapphire's hand and led her across to the pool. His eyes flashed with desire and promise, and she could not help but giggle. "I hope they give us enough time to get dressed again before they come back."

Fox smiled at her, his lips curling into a seductive promise. "We will have plenty of time to enjoy the pool and have some privacy, my love, I promise you."

She watched him undress in front of her. He never took his eyes away from her own. He kicked off his boots and removed his shirt. As he slipped out of his leather trousers he stood up, naked and glorious, and put his hands on his hips. Sapphire smiled widely and began to unbutton her blouse: she was up for this little game. As she stepped out of her skirt Fox winked at her, turned quickly, and took three long strides before diving into the pool with a whoop.

Sapphire laughed happily and followed him, feeling like a naughty little girl. Her breasts were bouncing as she took a running jump into the pool. She folded her legs up into her arms and jumped into the water, making a loud splash. Bubbles rose around her as she held her breath. She kept her eyes open so that she could see Fox under the water. The pool was crystal clear, and she could see him in front of her – a quick flash of strong, naked legs and firm buttocks – as he swam away from her towards the waterfall. She bobbed to the surface and sucked air back into her lungs as she laughed at the sudden plunge back into clarity that the cool water had slapped into her head.

She swam quickly across the pool to Fox, who was under the waterfall with his head thrown back. His eyes were closed, and sparkles of water were flooding across his face and hair. He looked amazing. She kicked her legs and grabbed him, which made him bob under the water again. They tangled around each other like octopuses, grasping legs and arms in a tight embrace. After coming up for air again they were now behind the sheet of water and in a cool cavern. They were both laughing. Fox was holding her up now and treading water. His eyes sparkled mischievously, and she could tell his mind was on other things.

He smoothed her hair back from her face and gazed at her for a moment, his eyes wandering across her features. There was a curl on his lips that indicated his appetite was rising. She watched him, mesmerised, as he pulled her closer and kissed her, gently at first … soft, wet kisses. His tongue just grazed the tip of her own. Her body started to switch on all buttons, ready for lift-off. Despite the fact that they were in deep water Fox seemed to have no trouble holding her up and caressing her at the same time. Her thighs were wrapped firmly around his waist, her arms around his neck. She felt him grow hard against her belly and she squirmed against him. Was this an appropriate thing to be doing on the day of her wedding, while people waited for them nearby?

As he moved her further back she found that her spine was now pushed against something solid: the wall of the cavern. It was covered in moss, and was cool and wet against her upper body. Fox was moaning softly into her mouth, but the kiss had turned into something much more. She could feel his magic awaken and start to pulse around them. She was so turned on right now that she didn't care that Kit and Bear were out there somewhere, probably close by. Fox lifted her up, and with slow precision pulled her back down on to his very ready cock. She threw her head back and groaned out loud. The sensation of being so full made her body quiver and tremble in delight.

"My beautiful Sapphire, you make me so happy," she heard him whisper into her ear as he began to pump her in long, firm strokes. The internal fire was being stoked again nicely. She could see sparks again in front of her eyes.

The waterfall created a shield to the outside world. He made love to her in the water, slow and sweet at first, whispering to her in his musical tones. Her eyes closed, and her body vibrated in a finely tuned throb. Gradually, and with an exquisite sense of urgency, he picked up the pace. He moved in and out of her, making her head begin to swim in the world of 'I am starting to rise out of my body and will explode any minute' magic. Sapphire felt her body start to ignite in tiny sparkles of serotonin. She groaned loudly, knowing she was now close to climax.

As he sucked on the soft skin of her neck she felt him start to throb uncontrollably inside her. He was also ready to come, and dancing on the edge of oblivion. The thought pushed her over the edge, and she felt herself give in to the exquisite sensation of pure white-hot orgasm. They came at the same time, the cavern lit up for a moment in silver light as their magic ignited. He cried out her name and they slipped under the water again, enveloped in bubbles and cool, clear water. Sapphire lost all her senses for a second, and was then gulping in air above the water on the other side of the waterfall. She gasped and blinked wildly as she tried to regain some form of sanity. Fox held her tightly, with her back now against him and her legs floating limply like a jellyfish after her climax. She could feel his chest rising and falling quickly at the exertion of holding her up. She shook her head to clear her mind so that she could tread water and help him. He nuzzled her neck and kissed her softly.

"I needed that," he said.

She giggled and wrapped her arms around his neck, behind her head. "Me too, more than I realised," she agreed.

He kissed her one more time, then pushed with strong legs across the pool and dragged her with him to the water's edge. They clambered out. Both of them were now slightly unstable after their tussle in the water. Fox was laughing softly, just as amused as she was by the irony of what they had just done.

"Well, that was a swim I won't forget in a hurry," Sapphire said, grinning.

Fox pulled her up. He seemed to have regained his strength quickly – and he held her tightly, having noticed that her legs were still in jelly mode. She was shaking now, not from being cold but from the after-effects of just losing all her inhibitions in the water – and from being fucked silly against a cavern wall ... another first for Sapphire.

"Sit, my love. You need to ground."

She almost fell in a heap at his feet – a hazy, very satisfied smile firmly painted on her lips. She felt him cover her with a soft towel that had suddenly materialised from nowhere. He crouched down beside her and rubbed her back soothingly, as though she were a small child.

"Better now?"

Her body started to slowly return to its normal state of equilibrium. She could still feel the wonderful warmth within her groin and belly that he had created just moments ago. The sensation was, as always, totally delicious. Water dripped from the end of her nose in tiny splashes on to the towel.

"Would you like to rest for a while, Sapphire?" Fox asked her gently.

She looked up into those naughty amber eyes, which were now twinkly with an amused glint, and sighed. "I don't think I could go anywhere if I tried right now, I hope we're not needed for a moment."

Fox laughed. He began to gather his clothes to get dressed again. He slowly slipped his leather trousers back up over skin that was glistening wet. Just watching him do this was pressing all her buttons again. Holy shit, this man was hot. And in a few hours from now he would be hers. All hers.

"We have time, my love. The ceremony does not start until nightfall. My father will start the entertainment for the elders before we return."

Sapphire wrung out her hair and tipped her head to one side. The towel had dried her nicely, and the warmth from the sun was finishing the drying process on her arms and face.

"What entertainment?"

He sat back down next to her with his shirt on but undone, and revealing his perfectly wonderful tanned chest. She could feel heat beginning to rise in her body again just from looking at it. She often found it difficult to focus on anything else when Fox was semi-naked.

"Before the ceremony we welcome our guests and eat. It is all a preliminary ... nothing to worry about."

Sapphire reached for her clothes, suddenly wanting to get dressed quickly. This was news to her. "OK ... so we really should be getting back soon, then, if people are arriving."

He ran his finger across her cheek and licked his lips slowly, which made her quiver again.

"Relax, my love. My father will take care of the guests ... It will not be a problem if we are a little late."

Sapphire raised her eyebrow, suddenly feeling a little panicked at the thought of even more people turning up before she had even managed to change into something a little more presentable. She would most definitely need to bathe and wash her hair before the ceremony after their little dip in the pool.

He leant forward and ran his finger across her forehead, kissing her softly at the same time. "Stop frowning and relax."

He pushed her back on to the grass, gathered her into his arms, and held her against his chest. She had only just managed to put her top back on, and was still naked from the waist down. He trailed his fingers across her thigh and made goosebumps jump up like tiny soldiers standing to attention. He pulled her leg up across his thigh and kissed her again while he held her in place, so that he could indulge for as long as he liked. Sapphire gave in. He was just too good at this, and right now she just wanted to hold him, kiss him, saturate herself in Fox essence, and calm the wedding jitters that were suddenly skipping around in her belly.

"I want you all to myself for just a little longer, my beautiful Sapphire," he whispered into her ear between kisses.

Sapphire sighed as he moved to her neck, her chest. Melting slowly, like marshmallows in hot chocolate, she allowed herself to let go for a moment and enjoy this time alone with her wonderful, magical, sexually fucktastic man.

It was indeed a wonderful moment.

Chapter Twelve

They returned to the house some time later. Sapphire had actually drifted into a comfortable snooze while she was lying on Fox by the pool in the sunshine for a while. He had woken her gently with kisses that made her body tingle with excitement. It was late afternoon by the time they returned home. The sun was still shining, but had dropped considerably on the horizon.

Sapphire was feeling slightly embarrassed that she was not dressed appropriately for receiving guests, and felt she still had 'I've just been fucked' hair. Her cheeks were flushed and her eyes wide when she noticed that many more people had arrived while they had been enjoying some time alone. Horses were being taken to the stables, and so many strangers wandered around looking as if they all had a purpose. Kit and Bear had been waiting for them at the edge of the woods when they had returned from the pool. Bear was grinning a knowing smile, and Kit was blushing furiously. Sapphire did not know who was more embarrassed. Fox looked as if he did not have a care in the world. In fact he looked positively smug. They dismounted close to the house and the horses were taken from them as soon as they arrived by the same young lad Sapphire remembered from the castle gates. He smiled at her shyly, and she felt as if she had a sign over her head saying, 'I'm a naughty girl'.

Oblivious to her thoughts, Fox draped his arm across her shoulder and kissed the top of her head. "Go and freshen up, my love. I will speak to my father. We will eat soon. I am sure you are as hungry as I am now." He smiled at her with a wicked glint in his eye.

Sapphire looked down to hide her blush. "When do I need to get ready for the ceremony?"

He kissed her once more, softly, on the lips this time. The contact sent happy signals to all the right places. She felt as if she was on horny pills today. How was she going to keep still during the ceremony, if he kept touching her this way?

"Later, my love. Do not fret ... There is plenty of time."

Kit suddenly appeared next to her and took her hand. "Come, Saf, I will help you change for the entertainment."

Sapphire quickly found herself standing in their bedroom with Kit rushing around, running a bath, throwing clothes on to the bed, and generally trying to organise her. She positively whizzed like a spinning top on amphetamines. Sapphire wondered whether they actually had such a thing here on Shaka. Kit practically shoved her into the bathroom.

"Would you like to wear the green dress or the pink, Saf?"

Sapphire lay in the blissfully hot water as she washed her hair out. "I really don't mind, Kit. Whatever you think would be appropriate."

Kit appeared again at the doorway. She looked like a child waiting for Santa to arrive. Her face was flushed and her hair slightly ruffled.

"I think the pink, my lady. It will set off your eyes beautifully. But of course tonight will be the time you will shine, when you wear your wedding dress."

Sapphire was really beginning to love this girl. She was so sweet and generous, like a little sister who looked up to her with all the innocent enthusiasm of a child.

"And you will look fabulous in your dress, Kit. I hope we have time to get ready later."

Kit nodded, her eyes sparkling. "Of course we will, Saf. Don't worry, I have some help for later. Let me help you with your hair."

Sapphire felt as if a whirlwind had suddenly whipped her up and transformed her into something new, as she found herself standing in front of the mirror gazing at her reflection again. Had she just lost time? One minute she was in the bath, the next minute she was dry and fully dressed, with her hair being carefully pinned and curled by Kit. Yes, definitely time travel.

Kit smiled at her. She had also managed to change very quickly and was wearing a deep blue dress that fell in soft waves around her feet. Pink and blue ... they looked like two fondant fancies standing next to each other. Sapphire smiled at Kit. She was a little nervous now at the thought of having to finally face the many guests. The irony was that she knew none of them except her new small family, which consisted of Bear, Kit, and Conloach.

Kit wrapped her fingers around her own and squeezed gently. "Don't be nervous, Saf. I will help you."

Sapphire could have cried at that moment. She had not realised just how emotional this could be. The whole thing had been created so quickly. Fox, on the other hand, seemed to be taking it all in his stride.

She wished Charlie were here with her big bag of weed, so that she could take a quick hit to calm her nerves. Kit seemed to read her mind and led her out of the bedroom, down the stairs, and into the kitchen. She sat Sapphire at the kitchen table and began mixing something together.

She handed it to Sapphire with a smile. "Drink. It will make you feel better."

Sapphire laughed, a little shakily. "Is it that easy to see I'm actually now crapping myself?"

Kit cocked her head to one side and frowned slightly. She had no idea what that actually meant.

Sapphire wondered where Fox was, and who exactly would be waiting for them outside. Voices and soft music were now coming from the garden. Her belly did another little flip as she sipped the tonic. It slipped down her throat and hit her stomach with a warm sensation and instantly gave her whole body a calm, soothing hug.

She smiled at Kit, who nodded with approval. Her energy lifted and she thankfully felt that at last she could face the crowd.

Kit stood next to her and held out her hand. "Ready, Saf?"

They walked out of the house across the sea of petals, which were still in place – definitely magic rose petals – in the hallway, and were faced with a crowd big enough to fill a theatre. Sapphire felt her throat constrict tightly. Her mouth was suddenly very dry. Kit gripped her hand tightly and urged her forward. Everyone was staring at them. Everyone. She noticed Fox standing with his father near the many tables, which were now weighed down with food of all descriptions.

Fox's smile was as big as the sun. He had changed into a linen shirt and trousers that hung just right on his tall, lean frame. He looked as edible as the food. Sapphire smiled as he approached her, and the crowd parted to allow him through. Kit released her hand. It seemed as if everyone had stopped talking for a moment. You could have heard a pin drop. Even the music had stopped for a second.

He stood in front of her and stared into her eyes as he took her in, every inch of her, which made her cheeks blush just that little bit more.

"You look beautiful, my love, Come, let's eat." He kissed her softly on the lips before taking her hand and leading her to the top table. It had two large, throne-like chairs behind a long table, which was covered in food of every colour of the rainbow. Sapphire heard her stomach growl. He grinned at her and pulled back her chair so that she could sit. As she sat down the crowd began to chatter and the music started again. Sapphire sighed in relief. She noticed that everyone was dressed in the finest clothes. Beautiful people surrounded her in a sea of colours.

Fox's father approached and smiled, a slightly amused look on his face.

"Sapphire, you look beautiful. I am honoured to wed you on this glorious night."

Sapphire smiled at him. He always looked so imposing. She was still a little afraid of him, even though she knew he would never harm her. He took his place to her left, and Fox took his own place to her right. Their guests began to sit, and suddenly they were being served with wine and food. The atmosphere was buzzing. Sapphire realised that she had little appetite despite the fact that her stomach was growling in protest. Fox turned to her with a piece of cheese on his fork and held it up to her lips.

"Eat, my love," he insisted. His eyes were hungry, but not for food. Even his tone of voice was uncurling her from the inside out. She fidgeted in her seat, because she knew that although their guests were busy enjoying the feast they were watching the interaction between them. She took the morsel slowly and chewed as she focused on the eyes of her husband-to-be, which flashed at her with amusement, want, and lust. Slowly she began to relax, and Fox handed her some wine.

"Not too much, my love," he said. "I know how mischievous you can be when you are intoxicated."

Sapphire smiled, and looked out of her peripheral vision at Conloach – who was by her side, eating heartily. Bear was seated beside Fox, and Kit was beside him. It was like a scene from a medieval banquet, and she really did for that moment feel like queen for the day.

Time slipped by, and they ate and drank while their guests chatted. The music was being played by a small group of musicians by the wedding platform. It was a soft, sweet melody that carried on the breeze. It calmed Sapphire, and reminded her of something very old indeed.

When they had finished eating, a group of young men and women appeared, dressed in white silk that barely covered their bodies. They were, of course, all very beautiful. Fox took her hand and kissed her knuckles softly as he watched her with dark eyes filled with passion. She squirmed again. The music began to change into something new – a steady drumbeat – which caused the guests to quieten and turn to watch the group as they began to dance.

Fox leant across and whispered softly into her ear, "Our people dance to evoke the spirit of love and lust before a marriage. It helps to bind the magic before the ceremony. You will enjoy this, my beautiful Sapphire." His breath was warm against her ear, his voice deep and soulful. She felt her body tingle in anticipation.

The dance began, a slow, sensual display of bodies that twisted and turned in time to the drumbeat. They wrapped around each other like sea horses underwater, fluid and supple. Sapphire watched them, her mouth slightly open at the display of sexual energy that began to rise from the dancers. It was erotic and fascinating to watch. She could see flashes of red and orange energy starting to spark from them as they wove their magic.

The drumbeat picked up and Sapphire could feel the intense energy of the dance in her belly and groin. Fox was stroking the palm of her hand, which was in her lap, with slow, feather-light teases.

He leant into her neck and softly nipped her earlobe. "The magic binds us together in body and in soul. Beautiful, isn't it?"

Sapphire gasped slightly, feeling very flushed. She wondered what the hell the ceremony would actually consist of now, and was starting to feel a little anxious that it actually would be a case of stripping naked and dancing around a bonfire. She shook her head, and heard Fox chuckle at her side. She had not expected anything like this. Her body was responding to the magic in ways that she would normally only expect in privacy. She gripped Fox's fingers, which were weaving their own magic up her arm, and took a deep breath as she tried to still her inner goddess – who was smiling lazily at her with a very happy smile indeed.

Suddenly the drumming stopped, and the dancers fell to the floor in a dramatic flurry of silk. The guests clapped and cheered, which broke the erotic spell they had woven. Sapphire blinked. She grabbed her wine and took a gulp, hoping it would help to calm her spangled, horny nerve endings.

Conloach stood suddenly, making her jump. Fox gripped her hand to steady her.

"Honoured guests," said Conloach, "I welcome you tonight on this special occasion of the joining of my son Fox to his beloved Sapphire. The ceremony will commence shortly. I ask you to relax and enjoy the evening while we prepare."

Sapphire felt her palms suddenly become very hot and clammy. Fox released her hand and stood. He looked down at her and smiled softly, his eyes flashing black and gold.

"Time to get ready, my love. I will see you again shortly. Kit will help you."

She stood slowly on shaky legs. She definitely needed some more of the tonic Kit had given her earlier.

The sun had slipped down over the horizon just as the dance had finished, and she noticed that tiny lights were now sparkling in the trees and around the chairs and platform like fireflies. Everything looked surreal and very, very beautiful. Fox led her back to the house, closely followed by Kit and Bear. He kissed her one more time before he left her in Kit's care. The kiss was a slow, sweet promise of more to come. Her legs felt as if they would give way any minute.

Kit was grinning at her now. She took her back upstairs to the bedroom, and the magic began. Several young girls were now in attendance to both her and to Kit. They smiled and giggled at Sapphire with knowing eyes as they helped her to undress and change into her wedding dress. Kit gave her another drink to calm her nerves.

Sapphire felt herself lift up and leave her body. She felt momentarily that she was observing the whole thing from afar, and that she was looking down at herself being pampered and primped for the ceremony like a precious object. One of the girls was rubbing a soft glistening ointment across her arms and chest. It glistened in the candlelight and smelt of jasmine and oranges … it was utterly intoxicating. Sapphire felt her libido lift again. Was everything about sex during this wedding ceremony?

She felt her dress being lifted up and over her head. As it fell about her body it seemed to wrap itself around her with a life of its own and bind itself to her skin in a swish of sparkles. Sapphire gasped and felt a burst of heat within her chest. It expanded outwards and seemed to scatter itself around the room. Kit and the girls stood back hastily, apparently shocked by this new wave of magic, and stared at her open-mouthed. Sapphire felt the dress almost shiver with excitement as its magic connected with her own. She felt a shift within her groin, belly, and head all at the same time. Something had changed within her as she had put on the dress. She could see it in their faces, feel it within her bones.

Kit stepped forward and reached out to touch her, a look of pure amazement in her eyes. "Oh, my lady, you look absolutely radiant. The magic within you has changed. You must look!"

Sapphire felt as if she had taken something illegal again, something that had switched on another level of vibration that she never knew existed. Hesitantly, she crossed the room with Kit and stood to look at herself in the mirror. Staring back at her was a stranger – a stranger who looked like her but different. A beautiful woman with hair that was almost white-blonde gazed at her. Her eyes were the colour of the deepest blue sapphires, with silver flecks surrounded by a dark black ring. She was haloed by a purple, glowing light that pulsed and flickered from her head to her toes.

Sapphire laughed almost hysterically. That couldn't be her. No way. Kit was still staring at her, open-mouthed. Sapphire shook her head and watched her newly coloured hair wave and shine in the light. Her eyes were glowing with a new wisdom and desire. She looked hot … hot as hell, and not human at all. Sapphire smiled, and her lips curled up at the edges. She felt utterly fabulous, and horny as hell. Holy shit!

Suddenly the room was a buzz of action again. The girls began to dress her hair, apply make-up to her face, and pin her veil … and they covered her arms with the long, beautiful coat, which slipped on to her arms with a twinkle of fairy dust.

"I must be dreaming again," Sapphire thought, as she watched from afar. "This is not real … This cannot be happening."

Kit was dressed in her red dress. She looked utterly beautiful in an innocent and sweet way. She sparkled in a soft pink haze, such was the magic being created around them. Kit stood next to her as she stared into the mirror again at the end result. Sapphire did not recognise herself. It was if a new woman was standing gazing back at her. Her hair was falling in soft curls laced with tiny diamond crystals that glittered in the light. The tiara seemed to glow softly on the crown of her head and the veil shimmered eerily in the mirror. Everything about her seemed to be made from magic, a new kind of magic. She was transformed, ready to connect to her magical man as a new woman who had manifested before her very eyes. Kit smiled at her, radiant and beautiful, her dark hair glistening like silk. They looked like yin and yang, dark and light. Sapphire felt as though she would wake up at any moment.

Kit reached for her hand. "It is time, my lady."

Sapphire seemed to glide on an invisible wave of magic as she descended the stairs. The house was strangely quiet. It was dark outside now, but she could see the twinkling of lights in the garden and hear the sweetest music lifting across the lawn in an almost sad lament.

Bear was standing at the doorway. He was dressed in black, his hair braided with gold beads, his beard combed and tidy. He looked very handsome. His eyes grew wide as he saw her approach.

"Sapphire!" He almost gawped at her.

She smiled, a new sense of calm spreading up from her belly to her head. This was real. Even he could see the change that had taken place. Her magic was expanding around her. Kit suddenly handed her something. She looked down and saw two white calla lilies tied with white silk ribbon. It made her stomach lurch at the memory of her dream, when the Oracle had appeared and offered her the very same flower as a gift from her unborn daughter. Kit smiled at her shyly. Bear offered her the crook of his arm. He was beaming now, his grin huge and infectious. They left the house and stepped out into the garden.

All around them became still – everything was holding its breath – as they moved across the lawn towards the platform, where Sapphire could now see Fox with his father. He had his back to her, and was kneeling down as if in prayer. As Bear guided her slowly down towards the makeshift altar with Kit to her other side she could hear gasps from the guests as they too noticed her change in appearance. The music continued to weave its spell of soft gentle tones, with a woman singing in the strange language which she had heard Fox speak to her on many occasions.

She felt as if she were flying now. Her legs were not her own, and everything was moving in slow motion. Conloach looked up and into her eyes. His lips twitched into something that looked like shock for a moment, then into a smile that made him look younger in years. Sapphire smiled back at him. Bear hugged her arm tightly. As they moved closer to the platform Kit took the lilies from her and smiled at Sapphire sweetly. The air was thick with magic, and the scent of incense clung to the gentle breeze that lifted her veil softly behind her.

Fox stood slowly and turned around. He was dressed in black. The material seemed to shimmer slightly in the moonlight, which was now casting a silver sheen across the garden. A simple waistcoat covered his chest. His arms were bare, and his tattoos were glowing and pulsing with his magic. His hair was wild and dark, and decorated with silver beads and feathers. Around his neck was a necklace which hung low on his chest – a large clear crystal that glittered in the light. His eyes widened, and he shuddered for a second as if thrown off balance. It was the first time that Sapphire had ever seen him dumbstruck. He looked utterly beautiful, magical, sexy as hell, and good enough to eat.

Sapphire smiled at him as Bear released her. She stepped up on to the platform. Fox continued to stare at her, and she felt his heart beat within her body. It pulsed loudly, thudding faster than she could ever remember feeling before. His eyes were dark and huge. The amber-like liquid was gold, and swirling and dancing with a fire that seemed to consume her from the inside out. He shook his head slightly, and a slow, sensual smile began to spread across his face. He licked his bottom lip slowly and sighed. As he lifted his hand he reached for her face and touched her cheek softly in wonder.

"My beautiful, wonderful Sapphire, I see you."

Sapphire unexpectedly felt an immense urge to cry. Her bottom lip trembled slightly, as he leant forward and kissed her softly, a gentle kiss that sent sparks of light scattering around them. Behind them the guests gasped. Conloach stepped forward. Fox released her lips and grasped her hand, the smile radiant on his lips. They turned to face the crowd.

"People of Calafia, behold the magic created here tonight. This special joining of my beloved son and Sapphire, dream traveller, will now begin," Conloach announced.

Sapphire caught a glimpse of something to her side. She swivelled her head for a moment and could have sworn that she could see Pearl standing at the edge of the garden, her face lit up with happiness. She blinked and looked back at Fox, who was glowing now like a golden beacon. His body shimmered in and out of focus, and the smile on his lips was almost voracious.

"Tonight I give blessings and love to this couple, who commit themselves to joining not only in marriage but in magic and blood."

Sapphire twitched suddenly. Had he said 'Blood'?

Fox gripped her hand and sent a warm pulse of soothing magic up her arm. It landed in her belly and then fizzled down into her groin, making her shiver involuntarily. She suddenly felt like a bubble had been placed around them and they were no longer surrounded by strangers but were alone, standing in the garden under the moonlight. The heat between them intensified and built up, with tiny red-hot flames that flickered and teased at her ankles

Conloach began to speak in his native tongue. Sapphire could hear his voice, deep and musical, in the background. Fox stared at her, his eyes boring into her soul. He spoke to her, but not out loud: she could hear him in her head.

"Sapphire, my love – my only love – do not be afraid. This will be the most wonderful and magical experience you and I have had so far. You are by far the most intoxicating and beautiful woman I have ever seen ... my glorious, magnificent bride."

She felt as though she were floating on a sea of silk, soft and sensuous. Her whole body was buzzing like a hummingbird. Fox squeezed her hand, and she shook herself and brought her body back into reality.

Conloach was standing in front of them now, a rather large knife in his hand. Sapphire suddenly felt as if she were the sacrificial lamb waiting to be slaughtered. Fox steadied her and gave her a reassuring grin. Conloach lifted her left hand and she felt her body go limp for a second. Fox placed his hand around her waist to steady her. After lifting his right hand he placed his wrist underneath her own. Sapphire watched with almost horrified wonder as Conloach lifted the knife up into the air. It glinted ominously in the moonlight. Sapphire felt that her heart might, at any moment, jump out of her chest.

"Let the blood of Fox and Sapphire be a token of their commitment to each other, and join them in their love forever."

Sapphire felt Fox turn her wrist over. Both of them were now holding their wrists up towards Conloach, who suddenly seemed to have grown taller. Sapphire thought she would faint any second. Fox pushed his magic into her body in a strong surge of love. It calmed her for a moment, and she became quite comfortably numb. Conloach brought the knife down and, with a quick slash across both their wrists, he nicked the skin lightly just enough to bring a crimson line of blood to the surface. Fox turned his wrist to hers and placed the cut to her own. She felt her whole body shudder when their blood connected and mingled as they touched. She could see her skin begin to light up as Fox's blood and magic entered her veins and trailed lazily like a snake up her arm into her body. She watched in amazement as the same trail travelled up Fox's arm as her blood flowed into him.

He closed his eyes and groaned. Sapphire felt her mouth pop open. Her groin clenched in the most sensuous and surprisingly delicious response to his magical blood. The breeze around them seemed to whip up for a moment and created a mini whirlwind, which made her veil lift as though she were underwater. It was the most utterly shocking and totally erotic moment of her life. The very ground beneath them seemed to shiver and shake for a second. The magic pulsed between them and then settled like a soft cloud around their bodies and gradually subsided in its intensity.

The crowd before them seemed to have gone into some kind of trance. Nothing felt real any more. Fox opened his eyes and smiled at her. His eyes were even darker now. Sapphire felt his energy within every cell of her body, and it felt mighty fine indeed. Everything was clearer, stronger, like it might have done if she had just changed into a vampire. Perhaps she had. She cocked her head to one side and smiled, totally intoxicated by this new magic.

Fox chuckled softly and lifted his wrist from her own. She watched, enthralled, as the cut disappeared and healed instantly ... Magic.

Conloach was speaking again in his own tongue. Fox released her waist and took her hand, his eyes never leaving her own.

He whispered into her head ... a soft, sweet caress. "We are joined now, my love: forever bound. Our blood has sealed our magic together, and our love. Nothing can ever break this bond, even in death."

Sapphire gasped out loud. This was seriously heavy shit. But she was alive with excitement, alive with magic. This feeling was beyond anything she could ever have imagined.

"I ask Fox and Sapphire to now make their vows known to all who stand before them, and before the goddess and the Oracle."

Sapphire was shaken back into reality. Was the Oracle here? She looked out across the crowd and noticed that she was indeed at the ceremony. She was attended by her priestesses and guards and was standing ethereally at the edge of the garden, glowing like an angel. Her face was lit up with the most beautiful smile, serene and calm. She nodded slightly as Sapphire caught her gaze.

"Fox, do you take this woman to be your wife in this lifetime and the next? Do you promise to protect and cherish her at all times, to love her and only her, and to accept the punishment if you fail in this promise?"

Fox did not even blink as he replied. "I will take this woman Sapphire, dream traveller, to be my wife and my only love in this lifetime and the next, and accept punishment if I fail in this promise."

Sapphire briefly wondered what the punishment would be if he did fail, but quickly dismissed the thought. Conloach looked at her expectantly. She suddenly felt her mouth become completely dry. Fox waited with bated breath. She sighed deeply and tried not to burst out into tears.

"I will take this man, Fox, to be my husband, and I promise to love him as I do now with all my heart forever."

He smiled at her, despite the fact that she did not say she would take any punishment if she did not comply. That was just a little too weird for her right now. Conloach nodded.

"I ask for the blessings of the goddess and the Oracle to create the rings that bind them to their promise, and which forever show others of this commitment."

Sapphire was quickly aware that the Oracle was now standing on the platform with them. The light emitting from her was almost blinding for a second, until she seemed to turn down the switch and Sapphire regained her sight.

"Blessings, Fox. Blessings, Sapphire. I am so happy for you both and give you, with love, my gift of the rings that bind you."

Sapphire watched her raise her arm and point her finger down towards them. Fox interlocked his fingers with Sapphire and raised their hands upwards so that the Oracle could touch them. Sapphire felt the now-familiar tingle of new magic at her lightest of touches. Her eyes grew wide with wonder as she watched a pattern begin to form in flickers of silver light across her ring finger. Fox seemed to be receiving the same on his ring finger, like a magical tattoo that wrapped and wove itself around her skin. It travelled up to her wrist and wrapped around her like a snake as it caressed her skin in soft licks that made her body squirm with pleasure. Her eyes closed under the pressure of such strong magic. The pattern continued to spiral and twirl across her skin, and almost made her moan out loud. She heard Fox sigh loudly, as if he too were being seduced by this new magic. Sapphire felt as if her eyes would roll back into her head. It was just too intense.

Just as she thought she might self-combust in front of the whole crowd the flow of magic stopped and the energy changed again. She let out the breath of air she had not realised she was holding in and opened her eyes and found Fox staring at her, a huge grin on his face. He gripped her hand tightly, as if afraid to let her go for fear she may faint. As she looked down at their hands she gasped out loud as she saw, plain as day, a tattoo that shimmered in the moonlight. It was in the shape of vine leaves, flowers, and hearts, which wrapped around her ring finger and trailed across her hand, under her wrist, and up her arm as they wound around and around. Fox had a matching tattoo that mirrored her own. This was just a total headfuck, but in a good way. Sapphire grinned back at him … her first tattoo, and it didn't even hurt. In fact it was one of the most pleasurable experiences she had ever had.

The Oracle positively beamed at them, which made her appear childlike for a brief moment. She turned around gracefully, and the unseen breeze around her made her hair rise and fall around her shoulders.

"Behold the final bond between Fox and Sapphire. They are now man and wife in blood and magic. The most sacred of vows have been taken and marked for all to see. May their joining be a happy and joyous one for the rest of their life together."

A great cheer rose from the guests, and Sapphire felt her heart clench in her chest at such a response. Fox gripped her hand tightly. She could feel waves of happiness flowing from him into her body. She felt elated and high from the electric atmosphere that seemed to have risen around them. Her legs were beneath her, but felt strangely disconnected from her body.

"I pronounce you now man and wife under the laws of Calafia, and bless you both on this night." The Oracle turned as she spoke and bowed deeply to them both before vanishing in a flash of white light before their eyes.

Conloach stepped forward again, smiling broadly. "Congratulations to you both. Fox, would you like to speak now?"

Fox nodded and turned to Sapphire, his eyes full of such happiness it made her heart swell. "My love, is there anything you would like to say to our guests?"

Sapphire suddenly felt as though she were five years old again, standing on stage at the Christmas panto. "No, you go ahead."

He kissed her hand, his eyes still firmly watching her every move. He turned to face the sea of guests, who all stood silently in anticipation.

"Good people of Calafia, I am honoured by your presence to witness my marriage to my beloved Sapphire. Please enjoy the night before us … dance, drink, and be merry. As your prince, I give thanks to you all for your valued service, and hope that you all welcome her into your hearts and love her as I do. Blessings to you all."

143

The guests clapped and cheered. Sapphire beamed with delight. This was just too wonderful. The music began once more, and the ceremony was over. Sapphire felt as if someone had switched a different light on to the garden. Suddenly everyone was laughing and beginning to relax. Fox took her hand again and pulled her into his body in one swift movement, so that she was pressed flat against his chest. Her breathing quickened at his closeness and he smiled down at her with those dark, haunting eyes that flashed gold and black, like a simmering volcano.

"Would you do the honour of dancing with me, Sapphire, my beautiful wife?"

Sapphire laughed. She had never felt so happy.

Conloach stopped them as they moved to step down from the platform. Fox hesitated, and looked confused for a moment at his interaction.

"Sapphire, I would like to thank you for coming to our world and making my son so happy. It is a pleasure to have you as my daughter. May you always be as happy as you are now." He bent to kiss her on the cheek.

She felt quite overwhelmed by the gesture, and choked back fresh tears. Fox nodded to his father and pulled her down into the crowd, who were now getting into the party mood. The musicians, accompanied by the dancers they had watched earlier, had begun to play a tribal beat. The energy jumped up a notch to something she recognised from her first meeting with Fox when she had dreamt of him at the fire, surrounded by men and women losing themselves to the beat. The party was most definitely starting.

Bear and Kit were waiting for them as they stepped down. They were both smiling widely, their faces animated and excited.

"Congratulations to you both. Sapphire, you look beautiful. Fox, you had better be a good husband or you will have me to answer to." Bear grabbed his friend and hugged him roughly.

Fox laughed and thumped him on the back. "You have no doubt of that, my friend."

Kit stood beside Sapphire and looked at her with tears in her eyes. "Oh, Saf, you look radiant. I am so happy for you both. I wish you both the happiest of lives together as man and wife."

Sapphire took her hand and smiled at her kindly. She desperately felt that she wanted to cry, but took a deep breath and held back the tears of joy. "Thank you, Kit. I understand now what you meant about the ring."

Kit beamed and laughed. She raised Sapphire's hand so that she could admire the magical tattoo that now covered her ring finger and wove its way delicately up her arm. It glistened beneath the silk of the cloak she was still wearing.

"Each ring is unique to the couple who are married. Yours is so beautiful, Saf … I have never seen such strong magic before."

Fox was pulling her further into the crowd, eager to have his way with her to the music. She kissed Kit on the cheek before he pulled her off her feet. She was still laughing happily as he took her away.

Fox swept her across the lawn through the myriad of guests, who all approached them with smiles and a chorus of "Congratulations," and "Blessings to you both." The very air around them seemed to vibrate with the happiness she felt deep within her soul. She was truly married to him, to Fox – the magical, beautiful man who she had fallen in love with in her dreams. This was real, in a strange, weird, and wonderful world that she had fallen into not so long ago.

As their guests began to drift and sway with the music around them Fox led her to the edge of the garden. She noticed that fires were now lit around the boundary of his land. They were beacons in the night that gave notice to all who could see for miles around them that a great celebration was taking place.

She was almost panting as he drew her into his chest and held her closely to him with heat radiating from his body in the most sensuous, soft caress. He wrapped his arms around her and placed his chin on to her head as he hugged her almost too tightly. She could hear his heart beating erratically in his chest in time with the drumbeat.

"Can you remember, my love, the first time we met in your dream? The time we danced at the summer solstice and you touched me for the first time."

She smiled as she closed her eyes, remembering the moment like it were yesterday.

"I was in love with you then, from that first touch, from the first moment you saw me. I visualised this time now, that we would be joined as man and wife. It was my greatest fantasy, and now it is real. I thank you for showing me true love and giving yourself to me in the most honoured way a man could ever ask."

She sighed as she thought how much had happened between them in such a short time, how much she had changed since that night, and how much she loved him.

She pulled back slightly and looked up into his eyes. They glistened in the moonlight, and she was lost for a moment, in the depths of his love and lust for her.

"I thought you were just a dream then, Fox. Even this tonight seems like a dream, but it is real and I am lost for words to express how I feel. It consumes me."

He blinked, his eyes bright with wonder. "I love you, Fox. Always have, and always will."

He kissed her then with a passion that took her breath away. They were wrapped around each other in a desperate need to consummate the vows they had just made. Sapphire felt his hands move to her shoulders as he pushed the cloak away from her shoulders and slipped it down her arms. He was kissing her hard, bruising her lips with his urgency. She felt the cloak slip to the floor. With a low moan in his throat he released her for a second and stared at her. There was a slither of a smile on his lips that spoke of a passion so strong it made her groin clench deliciously in anticipation. He pulled away from her just slightly and held up her arm as he admired the tattoo that sparkled up her hand and arm. His newly acquired mark mirrored her own in a striking line across his beautiful skin.

"Your magic has grown strong, my love. You are one of us now, forever bound by magic."

She smiled shyly, still overwhelmed by this new wave of spellwork that had been woven between them.

He raised an eyebrow and tilted his head to one side, and his smile became something more dark and sensual. "You owe me that dance now, my wife."

Sapphire giggled and threw her head back. She felt suddenly wanton and playful. "I think I do, my lord. Let's dance."

They joined their guests and danced the night away, just as they had when Fox had visited her on Earth at the festival and they had been surrounded by strangers as they moved to the beat while the tension between them built up into an almost unbearable frenzy. Sapphire could feel the magic between them swell and rise in a haze of heat as Fox moved against her in a slow, sexual display of foreplay. He created their own private bubble within the crowd, and Sapphire knew that before long it would become too much and they would need to move to somewhere private.

Her dress swirled around her as he spun her around and dipped and twirled her in time with the music. The other guests seemed lost in their own world of pleasure. It was intoxicating and fascinating to her to be surrounded by so many people again who were lost in a world of music, dance, and sexual energy. She wished Charlie and Nathan were here with her to enjoy this wonderful and amazing party – the best party she had ever been to. Her party. She became liquid within his arms … felt him caress her bare skin with the lightest of touches as he danced behind her, his hips pushed into her buttocks. His lips on her neck kissed her softly as he whispered to her and spoke in his soft, haunting language. He was saying her name over and over, like a mantra.

Sapphire had no idea how much time passed as they danced and kissed. She did not care. She did not care at all. Nothing mattered except the man pressed against her, who would be worshipping her long into the night.

She had no idea that this time of sweet happiness would be changing again very soon, that her world was about to tip upside down again.

No idea at all.

Chapter Thirteen

The sky was beginning to turn a deep grey-blue as dawn approached. The party had gone on long into the night, a frenzied coming together of people she did not know and did not really understand. Their guests had slowly begun to leave, and Sapphire was starting to feel utterly spent despite the download of magic she had received earlier. The adrenalin from the evening was still coursing through her veins, coupled with the intense magic she had inherited from her joining with Fox and stepping into her new power. The music was now a sweet, haunting lament which was lulling the last guests into a sleep-like state. Fox was still holding her and swaying slowly against her back. They had been dancing for hours between the odd break for mead and more food. They had partied hard.

It seemed ironic to Sapphire that this part of the wedding had seemed so similar to one back on Earth. She was dog-tired, and wanted nothing more than to wrap herself around her man and fall into bed. Fox sensed her fading energy and pulled her close.

He nuzzled her neck with his nose and breathed in her scent. "Time for bed, my love."

She nodded, and her eyes closed. She was feeling sleepy, but jittery with wanting him. He swept her up into his arms and carried her across the garden, which was now virtually empty of guests. She had not even noticed people begin to leave. Kit and Bear were nowhere to be seen, she felt a little guilty that she had not even had the chance to say goodbye to them. She allowed him to carry her effortlessly back into the house. It was silent now. The faint glow of dawn filled the hallway, which was awash with the crisp smell of fresh rose petals that were crushed beneath his feet as he ascended the stairs. Her body felt limp and exhausted but a small fire burned within her groin, waiting to be ignited. It simmered quietly, patiently, deep within her.

Fox kicked the bedroom door open and strode to the bed, and placed her down on to the mattress gently. He closed the door behind them and turned around slowly. She watched him with heavy eyes, her body pulsing softly in the dim light of dawn. He moved across the room with stealth-like grace. He was all animal and predatory eyes flashing seductively, and there was a dark smile on his lips that made her heart flutter softly in her chest. She stretched out on the bed and, sighing deeply, kicked off her shoes. She felt as if she had been in a dream for the last few hours, what with the ceremony, the dancing, and the heat of the energy that had been building between them for so long.

He began to undress slowly before her, unbuttoning his waistcoat and throwing it on the floor ... he was now standing, bare-chested and magnificent, next to the bed. Her heart began to race and her breathing became rapid, leaving her lips quickly in a soft hiss. She was so tired, but her body responded to him immediately as he drew closer. Slowly he bent down and ran his finger across her lip. It travelled down to her neck and grazed her chest softly. It sent shivers down to her groin in a slow, almost painful trail. Fox smiled again and stood up. He was unbuttoning his trousers now and pushing them down slowly, tantalising her with his beautiful body.

His eyes sparkled brightly. His hair was wild and dark, the beads and feathers intricately woven into the braids glowed with a soft pulse of magic. Sapphire moaned softly. Just watching him undress for her in such a manner was making her smoulder like a furnace. He bent over her with his hands either side of her head, his body completely naked and glorious, and his wonderful cock standing to full attention. She did not even know if she had the energy within her to pleasure him but her body was switched on completely, and she realised that she was actually panting out loud. He kissed her very softly, his lips just grazing her own and his tongue flicking across her top lip briefly, before he withdrew and began to undress her.

She closed her eyes and lay still, feeling the heat of his fingers brush against her skin as he turned her over so very gently to unbutton the trail of buttons at the back and release her from the confines of her dress. She felt her energy shudder and shiver as he slipped it over her head, and the magic within the thread almost sang in a sweet sigh of contentment as he released her from the silk.

Her face was against the mattress, her hair tumbling across her shoulder. The veil and the tiara were long gone: he had removed those when they had danced earlier. She was wearing only lace underwear now, and her back was bare to him. He began to place soft, light kisses across her shoulder blades and to stroke her back with his long, lean fingers as he moved down her body. His hair caught her skin in a silky caress and she moaned softly as he coaxed the fire within her and blew cool air on to her skin between each kiss. She squirmed with pleasure: she had no control now over her body as it moved to the rhythm of his dance across her skin. His hands moved to her underwear. He was kneeling over her, his legs either side of her as he peeled them down slowly, softly. It was almost torture.

"Sapphire, you are so very beautiful. Your skin, your smell … your very presence consumes me, my love … my only love."

His words whispered against her mind in a gentle caress as he stroked the back of her body with his hands, his tongue, his hair – which slid across her buttocks as he moved down her legs and circled his tongue behind her knees, the action making her grip the sheet beneath her. With a sudden rush of cool air that swept the entire length of her body he pushed his fingers gently inside her. His head was suddenly at her neck again, his body pressed against her as she lay on her front, her chest flat against the mattress. She moved her buttocks in a soft sway, without hesitation or embarrasment against him. She was so hot and wet now, as he slid his fingers in and out in a soft, soothing rhythm and coaxed the fire within her upwards and out, that she felt like her skin was burning, igniting like a torch. He sucked on her neck and licked her in long, slow strokes, his breath hot against her skin.

"Oh, God, Fox … please!" she whimpered.

He chuckled softly and pressed himself against her as he pushed his hips against her buttocks to demonstrate just how much he wanted her. She was like molten lava beneath him, unable to move, close to climax – just from the magic of his fingers, which danced inside her.

"Patience, my beautiful wife, patience," he crooned into her ear.

She felt him slide down and push her legs apart as he lifted her up slightly so that he could gain access to the most sacred of places within her body, which was moving of its own accord beneath him. He slid his fingers out and pulled her up further. Her eyes fluttered open as he pushed himself inside her in one long, firm stroke. She groaned loudly, still gripping the sheet as though her life depended on it. This was the most exquisite and amazing feeling, being filled completely by her beautiful husband, as he pushed deeper and deeper until she felt his pelvis flat against her backside. Fox held himself still within her body as he reached the very deepest point of her, settling into position.

"I am going to make love to you now, Sapphire. I want you to stay still and wait. Do not come yet, my love."

She felt herself swimming in an ocean of pure, undiluted pleasure as he began to move again, sliding in and out of her. He held her hips firmly, the weight of his body pushing her further into the deep mattress.

He made love to her, speaking to her in soft, deep tones in his strange, intoxicating language, whispering her name, plunging deep within her ... then holding still, so that she gasped in shock at how intense it could feel to have him inside her. She began to whimper as he withdrew again and hovered just outside her opening. Her body quivered and shook with need. He gripped her tightly, and her thighs shook with the effort of keeping her buttocks up. Without warning he growled deeply and flipped her over so that she was now on her back facing him, her breath coming in short, rapid bursts as he stared at her. The magic surrounding him now was flashing with bolts of gold and silver light. It was almost frightening in its magnificence.

He was breathing hard, his lust for her consuming him to the point of turning into some wild, crazed beast. Sapphire felt her eyes grow wide - her own magic was now fully awakened. Her body started to shimmer and shine with purple and silver sparks. Fox rose up slightly, and closed his eyes for the briefest of moments before opening them again and groaning loudly as he pushed himself completely and fully inside her. She cried out as he fucked her hard now, pounding her with thrust after thrust. She thrashed against him, her energy suddenly lifted to the point of ecstatic agony. Her body pulsed and sang with absolute white-hot pleasure. She felt every nerve and cell within her body start to crumble and disintegrate as her climax grew in thick, hot pulses up from her groin to ignite throughout her entire body. Fox continued to pound her relentlessly as she came undone beneath him and shattered into a million tiny pieces.

He cried out her name as he finally found his release within her and filled her completely with his magic, which spilled over them both in wave after wave of carnal heat. They were lost for a moment within the magic of their joining, and Sapphire was totally overwhelmed within the heat of her climax. She felt Fox collapse on top of her, his body slick with sweat, his heart beating hard against her chest. She wrapped her arms and legs around him and kissed his hair. Tears pricked her eyes as she felt him kiss her cheek softly. She loved this man with a passion that consumed her so much it hurt.

He rolled to her side and gathered her within his arms.

"My beautiful wife," he whispered to her as she fell into a deep and totally satisfied state of sleep.

Chapter Fourteen

Fox stirred and opened his eyes slowly. He was wrapped around his new wife like ivy: his face nuzzled into her neck his legs and arms draped across her body pinning her to the mattress. She was sleeping soundly, her body warm and soft. He kissed her hair and sighed deeply. This beautiful woman was now his, forever. He could feel the pulse of her magic within his veins. The blood exchange at the ceremony had connected them permanently now. He smiled and stretched and unwrapped himself from her body with some reluctance, she felt so damn good.

He kissed her softly on the shoulder, moved away from her, and slid off the bed to freshen up. The new day was bright and warm. Air blew gently through the balcony windows, indicating a fine day outside. He walked across to the adjoining bathroom naked, with catlike grace. He would leave Sapphire to rest for a while. It had been a long day and night. She was, most likely, exhausted. Fox, on the other hand, felt himself buzzing. He was relishing this new-found energy that she had gifted him.

He began to fill the bathtub with water, a smile still firmly on his lips. He knew that he would need to speak with Bear and Wolf at some point today and check that all was well regarding the dark presence looming at the borders of their kingdom. His thoughts drifted over the past few days. He frowned a little as he wondered if this new state of bliss would be shattered at any moment by an attack from the queen. He shook his head, and pushed the thought aside. For now he wanted to enjoy being with his wife and to forget such things. He stepped into the hot water and began to bathe, his lips parting with a groan at the memory of making love to Sapphire early that morning. She was so totally intoxicating, and now she was his wife. His body hummed at the memory of her sweet, soft skin against him as he consumed her completely. With a wry smile he watched his body begin to respond to the thought. He would let her sleep a little longer, then wake her in the best possible way.

Sapphire was acutely aware of Fox leaving her side as he slipped out of the bed. She had woken the moment he had untangled his long, lean body from hers. Her eyelids were heavy. She felt as if every single muscle in her body had been worked out by some mean gym instructor. She could hear water running in the bathroom. Fox was taking a bath. She stretched out and, yawning, rolled on to her back. She wanted to sleep but her energy was switched on now, and her body was tingling in a very aroused manner.

A slow smile crept on to her lips as she ran her hands across her naked body and remembered Fox making love to her earlier that morning. Her body responded again as the muscles in her groin clenched slightly, and made a soft moan escape her lips. What was it with this man, this husband of hers? Her connection to him was growing stronger and stronger. She was constantly in a state of arousal now, it was almost painful and sometimes completely overwhelming. After blinking her eyes open she stretched one more time before pushing herself up in bed. She could hear the soft flow of water in the bathroom as Fox bathed. She wanted to be with him, and felt her heart start to quicken in pace at the thought of sitting astride him in the bathtub and riding him like a stallion. The almost reckless way her body responded to him and the way her sex life had turned around from being non-existent to ridiculously frequent made her laugh out loud. Who was she now? Not the Sapphire she remembered before entering the world of dream travel and magic that was for sure.

Feeling extremely wanton, she sauntered across the room naked and stood in the doorway to the bathroom. She found her man lying in the tub, his arms across the sides, his head thrown back, his eyes closed with a sexy smile on his lips. Perhaps he was thinking the same thing she was. She noticed his erection standing to attention in all its glory just out of the water. It was perfectly obvious that he most definitely was. On sensing her presence his eyes flew open, and the smile became dark and greedy. She smiled back at him and tipped her head to one side coyly.

"Good morning, husband."

He sat up a little. The water sloshed around him and his eyes moved across her body as he hungrily took in the view.

"Good morning, my beautiful wife … care to join me?"

She did not hesitate and walked towards him slowly, swinging her hips softly from side to side for full effect. He watched her with amusement in his eyes.

"I thought I would let you sleep for a little longer before waking you," he said.

She stepped into the water, her eyes locked to his and her body pulsing now with desire.

"I'm wide awake now."

Her eyes sparkled mischievously as she moved gracefully through the water on her front and rested her arms on his thighs, with her breasts touching his legs in the most delicious caress.

Fox sighed deeply and shifted his body slightly so that he could accommodate her better. His erection pushed against her stomach as she slid up him slowly, the sly smile still playful on her lips.

"Good. I am glad, my beautiful wife. I was looking forward to waking you up in the best possible way, but now that you are here in the bath with me I can wash that amazing body of yours and enjoy you even more."

Her lips parted slightly and her body trembled a little against him. It aroused him even more. She looked amazing today. Her newly changed hair – a breathtaking white-blonde – seemed to sparkle in the light. It made her eyes look even darker. They too had changed drastically since the new surge of magic had taken hold. They were still the darkest blue he had ever seen, but flashed with silver sparks, and the dark ring around her irises indicated she had become slightly less human from the magic flowing through her veins.

Sapphire continued to smile at him lazily. He had never seen her look so radiant, so full of desire. She pushed herself up out of the water so that he had a perfect view of her wonderful breasts. She reached across and took the sponge and body wash as she sat on the side of the bath and began to lather her hands. He watched her intently as he felt his body start to throb in anticipation. She sat astride his legs and reached down and began to wash his chest and stomach … and, slowly, with a smooth sliding action, took his cock into her hands and massaged him with a firm grip … up and down, up and down.

He growled softly, his eyes burning now with need. "I was going to wash you first, my love."

She laughed and threw her head back. Her eyes were flashing at him. Who was this new woman? What had happened to his bashful Sapphire? Fox closed his eyes as she pulled his hips up out of the water and started to run her tongue across his abdomen. He could not help but groan out loud with pleasure as she trailed leisurely down towards his waiting erection. His breathing quickened and his heart rate sped up rapidly as she flicked her tongue across his cock. His hands moved to her head, and he grasped her hair tightly at the roots and pulled softly as her mouth closed around him. His breath sucked into his lungs as she continued to pleasure him, which made his body tense and flex against her. She was good at this. Very good. Sapphire quickened the pace. Her tongue and mouth were dancing around his arousal in an unrelenting rhythm. He knew that if she continued this onslaught he would come any minute. He was gasping for breath, and he pulled her head back suddenly as he felt his body start to quicken to stop her from tipping him over the edge.

"Too much?" She was laughing with her eyes, her smile a cheeky tilt on her lips.

Fox let out a deep sigh as he tried to catch his breath. "Never, my gorgeous woman, but I want to pleasure you this beautiful morning... and if you carry on sucking my cock like that I will not be in any fit state to do so."

Sapphire rose gracefully out of the water while still holding him in a light grip, and cocked her head to one side. "And how do you intend to do that, my lord?"

Fox felt his blood fizz hotly in his veins. God, this woman was making his head spin today. He grabbed her by the waist, which made her release her grip and squeal in delight. After claiming her lips he kissed her ferociously, and pulled her up and on to him. He pushed his hips upwards and into her soft, sweet pussy in a quick, hard thrust. She gasped and pulled back and stared at him with wide beautiful eyes, an expression of shock and lust on her face.

"Like this, my lady."

Sapphire stared at her reflection in the bathroom mirror, a very satisfied smile on her lips. After Fox had thoroughly fucked her to the point of oblivion in the bathtub he had helped wash her hair and finish washing with slow, carnal strokes. He was dressing next to her now, his body flexing and contracting with grace as he pulled up his leather trousers. She brushed out her hair and marvelled at her new appearance. She looked hot. Totally hot, and deliciously different. Her body was supercharged today. She could sense the new magic inside her pulsing and soothing her muscles in the most wonderful way.

Fox stood behind her and took the brush from her hand as he smiled at her in the mirror, his face still slightly flushed from their coupling.

"What would you like to do today, my love?"

She closed her eyes for a moment and relished the feeling of him brushing her hair out. "Anything that involves being with you."

He chuckled. "So easily pleased, my beautiful Sapphire." He twisted her hair gently and began to plait the long blonde locks into a braid that fell heavily down her back. She smiled as he tugged it playfully.

"Actually … there is something I want you to teach me, Fox."

He raised an eyebrow, mildly amused, before kissing her neck softly. "And what may that be, my love?"

She turned around slowly to face him as she looked up into his beautiful amber eyes. "I want to learn how to use a sword."

He laughed as he held her arms lightly. "Why would you want to learn how to wield a sword, my love?"

She bit her lip and looked down shyly. "Just in case."

He leant down and touched her forehead with his own. He was breathing softly. "Not necessary, my love. Nothing is going to happen. No one will ever harm you, I promise."

She hesitated before moving away slightly to look up at him again. "How can you be so sure, Fox? I may need to defend myself one day. I know that it's highly unlikely, but I want to learn. I want you to show me."

He shrugged his shoulders, his eyes flashing gold and black. "If you insist, my love. It would be a pleasure."

They quickly finished the breakfast Kit had left out for them and went out to the armoury. Sapphire noticed that the garden had returned to its previous state, and all signs of the wedding ceremony the night before had vanished. No doubt a serious amount of magic had been involved in making that happen. She followed Fox with a sense of excitement into the armoury, pleased to be allowed to enter

157

the world of medieval knights with her man. As Fox stood in the centre of the room with an amused smile on his lips she scanned the wall, which was covered in weapons. Her mouth fell open slightly in anticipation.

Fox walked towards her and rested his head on her shoulder, his arms wrapping around her waist from behind.

"Anything take your fancy, my love?" He was laughing at her, but she did not care. She felt the overwhelming urge to learn how to defend herself and the new magic inside her was buzzing with agreement. Despite the carefree days she had spent with him so far she felt a coldness spreading in the pit of her stomach that told her something was brewing, and it wasn't good.

"They all look a little scary to me, but I want to know how to use them."

He squeezed her gently and kissed her hair. "All of them?"

She chuckled. "Just the ones that you think I can master quickly."

After releasing her slowly he walked to the wall and paused, and looked up at the various choices of weaponry. He reached up, took a long, pointed spear-shaped weapon from the wall, and turned around, a glint in his eye.

"This is a bisentō spear. You can use this on horseback, or in battle against your opponent."

Sapphire eyed the long spear with caution. The blade on the tip of the wooden spear looked extremely sharp and dangerous.

"The Japanese on your Earth used these many hundreds of years ago."

Sapphire raised an eyebrow and blew out a long breath. "Like a ninja!"

He chuckled and started to move, slowly raising the spear above his head and swinging it around him in slow circles. It swished in the air with deadly precision. "Yes, like the ninja."

Sapphire watched him move. He was all muscle and sinew, he danced with the spear in a way that seemed almost non-human. She was fascinated and shocked at the same time. He picked up the deadly dance and twirled and turned, slashing the air around him. He looked magnificent and formidable. It was strangely a massive turn-on.

He gradually slowed the pace and his smile flashed sexily at her, as if he could sense her arousal.

"Weapons do that to me too, my love. Here, try ..."

She stepped forward and took the spear from him, then looked down at her dress and frowned.

"It's going to be virtually impossible to do anything in this dress, Fox. I wish I had some jeans and a T-shirt."

He laughed and turned back to the wall to find another weapon to play with. "Sapphire, you are more than capable of manifesting whatever you wish to wear now. Your magic is strong. Just visualise what you want and make it so."

She held the spear in both hands. It felt surprisingly light, but the thought of actually using it against someone troubled her somewhat. She thought about Fox's statement: that she could indeed imagine herself something more suitable to wear. She tilted her head to one side and thought about it. Why not? Everything seemed to be different about her today. Perhaps she could just magic herself a new wardrobe.

She closed her eyes and took a deep breath. She held the sword upright and stood imagining herself warrior-like, clad in trousers and suitable armour. She felt a shiver of air surround her body and a trembling within her belly. When she opened her eyes she found Fox was standing in front of her now with a large broadsword in his hands, his eyes flashing darkly a sensual smile on his lips. He whistled softly in approval at what he saw.

"Good choice, my love. You look hot as hell."

She glanced down and was shocked to see herself wearing black leather trousers. Her body was trussed up in a black leather corset that was slightly padded, and her arms were covered in long black gloves that were fingerless. She felt like Xena, the warrior princess.

She laughed, stepped forward, and moved the spear towards Fox. He stepped back, his eyes wide and excited.

Suddenly, out of nowhere, she felt her body begin to tremble with a new kind of magic. Her body moved of its own accord and began to spin and turn. The spear became one with her as she jabbed and thrust the blade. This was excellent fun. Fox watched her, his mouth slightly open. Sapphire felt a deep sense of knowing within her, as if she had done this before. Maybe she had. It felt easy, familiar, and thrilling.

Fox began to move with her in a strange, deadly dance. They stalked each other playfully, with Sapphire thrusting the spear before spinning around to face him again. He was laughing now, the huge sword swinging around him. In the back of her mind she sensed the danger involved in playing this game … but it felt right – comfortable, even. The spear caught the sword and clanged loudly as she jabbed again. He raised his eyebrows, a grin flashing onto his face.

"Good, Sapphire. You have a natural warrior's instinct … again… like this." He showed her how to move quickly and gracefully, and how to block and attack. It was a massive adrenalin rush. Sapphire was in her element. They danced around each other, playful but determined. Fox called instructions to her every now and then.

"Excellent, Sapphire! Keep your balance. Do not overextend, and remember to stay focused on your opponent. Feel what they intend to do within your body. Anticipate their next move in your bones. Trust your instincts."

Sapphire was working up a sweat. Her energy was excited now and buzzing around her veins in a flurry as she worked the spear. They practised like two experienced warriors, spinning and moving with a speed that was not human. Everything flashed before Sapphire in a slow-motion blur. She knew that this new ability was formed from the magic that was growing strongly inside her, and it excited her even more. She laughed out loud as she struck close to Fox and nipped his shoulder, just slightly causing his shirt to tear at the sleeve.

"Impressive, Sapphire. Very impressive!"

She spun around, breathing heavily, to face Bear – who was now standing at the armoury doorway, his arms crossed at his chest and a huge grin on his face.

"Fox, you should be worried. Your new wife has the speed and strength of a trained warrior. Who would have thought it?"

Fox laughed, and placed the broadsword back on to the wall. His own breathing was heavy and laboured from the workout with Sapphire.

"Be my guest and test her new-found skill, my friend."

Sapphire smiled broadly, her eyes flashing with amusement. Bear stepped forward and sauntered across to the wall, which he casually scanned for an appropriate weapon. He stopped at the mace, looked over his shoulder, and winked at her. Sapphire watched him remove the ball and chain and, chuckling, weigh it in his overly muscular arms. After

160

reaching up to place the spear back into its holder she too scanned the wall for a new weapon.

Fox pulled out a chair and sat down to watch them both. He was waiting to see what would happen next. This was indeed an unexpected turn of events. His wife was a born fighter.

Sapphire turned back to face Bear, a set of knives in her hands. They glinted wickedly in the light. Each knife had three points and a hilt, which made them appear forked and particularly deadly. Bear was swinging the mace slowly around his head now. It made a soft whooshing noise that promised something much more powerful than the slight swish in the air. They circled each other slowly. Sapphire could feel her magic begin to swell and tremble again within her belly.

"Take it easy on him, Sapphire. He may be out of practice."

Bear laughed loudly before taking a step forward and swinging the deadly lump of iron at Sapphire's head. She dodged it easily and spun around as she twisted the knives into a graceful parry that connected to the chain, which caught Bear off balance. He swore under his breath as Fox laughed at him from across the room.

"Beginner's luck," he growled.

Sapphire chuckled and danced lightly. She teased him with a display of flashing steel as her arms spun, ready to attack. Bear moved back, a surprised expression on his face. This woman really knew how to wield a set of knives. They parried and spun around the room. Bear was really trying hard now to keep up with her. Fox watched, fascinated, as Sapphire outwitted him with each turn. She was fast and precise ... and formidable, sexy, and deadly. After some time Bear dropped the mace with a loud thump on the floor and held his hands up in surrender, just as Sapphire twisted around and raised her right hand to hold the three-pronged knife to his throat.

She smiled at him panting heavily. "Gotcha!"

Fox stood up, clapping slowly, a wide smile on his lips. "Bravo, Sapphire. Bravo!"

Bear smiled back at her, shaking his head. She lowered the knives slowly, and dipped her head to indicate that the fight was over.

"Never have I seen such skill from a woman, Sapphire. You are truly a wonder." Fox stepped up behind her and wrapped his arms around her waist, breathing in her wonderful scent mixed now with adrenalin and sweat. "My wonderful, deadly wife."

Sapphire laughed. She was totally buzzing from the adrenalin pumping around her veins. This new-found skill was amazing fun. Once she was an ordinary woman working in a coffee shop on Earth; now she was a ninja from *The Matrix*. Awesome.

Bear was still shaking his head in disbelief. "Kit told me you were both in here. I thought you would be spending the day in bed and not battling each other with arms for the day, considering you were only married yesterday."

Fox smiled. "My wife requested a lesson, but – quite honestly – it seems she needed very little tuition."

Sapphire kissed him softly, the knives still in her hands. "I just felt the need to see if I could defend myself, Fox. It was fun."

Bear regarded the pair of them. "Well ... there is no doubt you can do that, Sapphire. But you need not worry. No harm will come to you here."

Sapphire stepped away slowly from Fox to place the knives back on to the wall. "I wish I had your confidence in that, Bear, but I feel somewhat differently."

The three of them stood silently for a moment. Unspoken words hung in the air.

Fox smiled. "I think that is enough for today, Sapphire. Let's eat and then go back to bed."

Bear laughed, which broke the sudden shift in mood. "I agree with the eating part, my friend."

They headed back into the house together. Sapphire noticed that although the day was warm and bright in the distance a strange cluster of clouds, dark crimson in colour, was gathering on the horizon. It seemed odd and out of place, and made her feel uneasy. She also felt the obsidian necklace nestled between her breasts start to pulse and heat up softly against her skin. Fox and Bear were laughing and joking and had not noticed her hesitate as they headed back inside.

As she held the obsidian in her hand and felt the soft pulse of warning against her palm she knew something dark and sinister was heading their way. And it was coming soon. Very soon.

Chapter Fifteen

The afternoon had passed quickly. Bear had stayed to eat with them and Kit. It was a happy affair, with much laughter at how Sapphire had kicked both their arses. After Bear had left Kit had disappeared with a shy smile on her lips, leaving the house empty. They had retired to the bedroom and made love for the second time that day, slowly and leisurely.

Sapphire was stretched across Fox, her head on his chest, her leg thrown over his own long limbs. He was drifting into a gentle and peaceful sleep. She was wide awake. His breathing was slow and rhythmic ... his skin so warm and smooth against her, and pulsing with his amazing magic.

She could smell his signature scent of patchouli and sandalwood. It filled her with a sense of belonging. He had been stroking her back gently with his long, nimble fingers, a feather-light touch that was soothing and sensual. The stroking had stopped as he had fallen asleep, and Sapphire could sense him fall into his own dream state. Usually it was Fox who observed her in her own dreams and travelled with her. This time Sapphire could sense him travel without her. His eyelids began to flutter as his dream began. She watched him, mesmerised, as his face twitched slightly. She wondered what he was dreaming about as her gaze followed the sharp, handsome lines of his beautiful face.

Although she felt alert and more than wide awake she closed her eyes and placed her palm on to the side of his face as she probed with her mind to see if she could in fact see what he was dreaming. With a sharp jolt of light behind her eyes Sapphire suddenly found herself observing Fox from afar. She was inside his head, watching his dream. It was slightly unnerving, and a little exciting. This was something new to her – to be conscious, but within his dream state.

Fox was driving a beautiful red Mustang. It was open-topped, and the road before him stretched out as far as she could see. It was a long, winding road that spread out like a thin line within a desert landscape. He was dressed in jeans and a T-shirt with his hair tied back and a bandanna wrapped around his forehead, which made him look like a sexy biker back home on Earth. She noticed with excitement that she was sitting in the passenger seat next to him to his right. She was dressed in shorts and a vest top, her long white-blonde hair flying in the wind around her face.

The landscape whizzed past them. There were huge rock formations in the desert around them, dotted with cactus and the odd flowering plant. It looked like somewhere in America. A map appeared in her lap. She probed deeper and saw that they were indeed in the Nevada desert. Sapphire was puzzled by the dream. Why would Fox be seeing a place on Earth that he had never been to with her before? They were travelling hard and fast. It seemed as if they had a purpose.

Fox turned to look at her, a smile on his lips. "Not far now, my love."

The Sapphire in his dream looked back at him, her eyes flashing dark blue and purple. "Yes ... I sense we are near, Fox." She suddenly looked up – directly, it seemed – at Sapphire, who was observing from afar. She smiled and winked. "It will be safe there," she said.

Sapphire gasped as she watched herself shimmer and shine in the bright light of the sunshine. The magic surrounding her body was alive and vibrant, even in the dream. Sapphire felt her head tighten suddenly, and a loud pop in her ears made her open her eyes wide again. She was back in the bedroom, watching Fox sleeping. A slight smile was etched on his perfect lips. He stretched slowly, and she felt his mind start to awaken again. She watched him become fully conscious once more as his eyes opened slowly.

He sighed deeply and licked his bottom lip slowly. "Hello, beautiful. Did you sleep?"

She bent down to kiss him lightly on the lips as she savoured the sweet taste of his magic. "No, but you most definitely did."

Fox stretched again, and blinked. He removed his arm from around her waist and pushed himself up in the bed. "Yes, I did. I had the strangest dream."

Sapphire nodded. "I saw."

He frowned, and raised his arms above his head for one last catlike stretch. "Did you, now?"

Sapphire traced a finger across his chest, revelling in the muscles that rippled as he moved slightly.

"Strangely, yes. I could sense you were dreaming, and took a peek."

Fox regarded her, confusion on his face. "Interesting. What did you see?"

"We were in an open-topped Mustang and driving through the desert in America. It seemed we knew where we were going."

His mouth popped open in surprise as she described his dream exactly as it had happened. "Remarkable. It was the strangest dream I have had yet. You were with me, but I had no idea where we were. I knew you were not actually travelling. It seemed more of a premonition. Perhaps it was."

Sapphire started to rise from the bed. She suddenly wanted to get up and get moving again. "I think it was something in the future, but back on Earth. I think we are going back home soon."

He reached to catch her before she jumped out of bed again. "But this is our home now, my love." His hand was on her wrist, and made Sapphire pause.

"Earth will always be my real home, Fox. The reason I came here was to stop Ebony from taking my magic, from hurting my friends. But I have known all along that this change within me was intended to be used on Earth, not here."

He continued to hold her wrist lightly, his face now troubled. "When were you going to tell me this?"

"When the time was right and when I was ready, Fox. Don't fret. Everything will be OK." She slid away from him, smiling softly. She did not want to trouble him. But now, having seen his dream and seeing a future that had yet to happen, it was perfectly clear to her that she would be going home again.

It was beginning to make sense to her now. The pieces of the puzzle were fitting together and the bigger picture was taking form. She had begun to understand back on Earth when she had spent time with Pearl at the safe haven of her home that the magic growing inside her was intended for much bigger things. It had been maturing and growing inside her since her arrival on Shaka, and with the change that had taken place on her wedding night she knew it was almost ready.

There was one thing that needed to be done before she could return to Earth and finish what she had begun. She had to remove the threat that was looming in the darkness, destroy this enemy who was waiting to attack her: Ebony. She was the only thing that could prevent the magic from completing its task. Sapphire knew they must tackle this one issue, and tackle it sooner rather than later.

Fox watched her in a daze as she began to dress quickly. His mind was spinning with this new piece of information. It troubled him deeply. She seemed intent now on something he knew could only mean more danger for both of them.

"Sapphire … You are scaring me a little, my love."

She paused as she pulled up her new leather trousers. "Don't be scared, Fox. I have never been clearer on what I have to do. Get out of bed. We have to go and see your father."

Night had fallen by the time they reached Calafia and Conloach's castle. Sapphire was animated and excited: Fox was feeling slightly more hesitant about the whole thing. He had followed her without question to the castle but had no idea why Sapphire was keen to seek his father's audience. As they approached his father's private chambers, Fox pulled Sapphire aside for a moment. She blinked up at him, her eyes wide and vibrant, her magic pulsing steadily around her in waves of purple and white flashes.

"Why are we here, my love? I need to know what's going on before we face my father."

She held his forearms and smiled up at him softly. "We are here to make plans, to gain his permission to move forward with our attack."

Fox shook his head slowly in confusion, he was starting to feel more and more out of his depth. This new Sapphire before him seemed almost alien to him. She was confident and strong in her actions. It was thrilling to see her transformation, but disturbing at the same time.

He frowned. "What attack?"

Sapphire reached up on tiptoes and kissed him firmly on the lips. "Stop worrying. Come, let's go inside. It will all make sense soon."

The door to his father's chamber opened up beside them before they had a chance to knock, making them both jump in surprise.

Conloach stood in the doorway, formidable as ever, his eyes flashing with amusement. "Enter, Fox. Enter, Sapphire. I sense we have things to discuss."

Fox led the way, dipping his head respectfully at his father as he entered. Conloach's chamber was lit with many candles and a fire burned brightly in the hearth, reflecting orange and red light across the marble floor. Conloach gestured for them to both sit at his huge wooden table – which was, as always, littered with scrolls and various objects of magical interest.

"And to what do I owe the pleasure of this visit, my son – and Sapphire – so soon after your marriage? I did not expect to see you both for at least several weeks." His eyebrow was raised, and a thin smile was on his lips.

Sapphire did not even blush. She twisted a piece of her hair around her fingers with excitement. "Conloach, we need your help. The army must be gathered, and an attack planned quickly against the queen and Ebony. We cannot wait any longer. I know she is waiting to make her move, and time is of the essence here. I have to face her. I need to make sure she is out of the picture so that I can go back to Earth."

Fox watched her. His whole body was tingling with energy. He could sense her excitement and her urge to move quickly. It coursed through his veins and mirrored her mood intensely.

Conloach chuckled softly. "So eager to start a fight, Sapphire. It is not the way we do things here. I need a reason to start a war. Explain your reasons, and I may consider. We have been a peaceful city for many years. I do not intend to change that on a whim."

Fox stood and started pacing by the fireplace. The heat from the flames made him feel even more on edge, the air in the room was almost stifling. He never understood why his father kept a fire burning all year long in his room. But then fire was often used in creating and cleansing magical spells so he assumed this would be the reason behind such a strange habit.

"Yes … Please explain, my love. The last thing I wish to see is you put into danger again, and my people engaged in battle."

Sapphire sighed heavily. She knew this was going to be hard, but necessary. "OK, I will explain from the beginning. Since the very start of my dream travelling I have been receiving different snippets of information. I have been travelling in my dreams to different places and experiencing new surges of magic. None of it made much sense to me the whole time I was on Earth. In fact it scared the crap out of me. The only thing that made it easier was my relationship with Fox, and of course my love for him." She smiled at Fox tentatively, knowing he was more than worried at where this was heading.

"Pearl taught me a lot of things, and she knew – has always known, I think – how important this journey has been. You were the one, actually, Conloach, who made me really understand what this is actually all about."

Conloach stared at her, his face still etched with amusement. "I did? And what exactly have I said to make this all about starting a war on my homeland?"

Sapphire stood up. "You were the one who told me that the magic on Earth was lost, forgotten, and that was the start of it. Pearl then explained to me that our mother still holds that magic deep inside her. She is sleeping, waiting for the magic to reawaken. I hold the key to that reawakening. The magic inside me is what she is waiting for. I need to go back to Earth to help this, to help her wake up again. I feel it growing inside me every day. She needs my help."

She paused, looking up for a second as if for inspiration. "The people on Earth need to be woken up. I can do that. But I need to do this without the constant threat of Ebony and her minions ... and to remove that threat we must make our move here on Shaka, where the magic is strongest. It will reconnect our worlds and open a consciousness that has been waiting for aeons to happen. It will change us all for the better. Can you imagine how amazing it will be to open everyone's eyes for the first time to the beauty of her magic? This is my destiny, our destiny. I understand that now, but I need your help ..."

She faced Fox and Conloach, her face alive and animated with an expression of hope and happiness. "I need both of your help."

Fox was standing with his back to the fire, his outline lit up in a deep red and orange. He was as still as a statue. "My love ... this is a huge thing you ask of us, to put you in such danger. As your husband, I am loath to do this. We are safer here, regardless of your new-found gifts and insight."

Conloach moved around the table slowly, his fingers stroking his long goatee in deep thought.

"If what you speak of is the truth, Sapphire, then this is bigger than all of us. I have always had no doubt that you have come here for a reason. The fact that a human dream traveller even exists at this time on our planet is amazing. Ebony coming back here again after such a long time in exile indicates that there is some truth in what you speak of. She will want this magic for herself. It would increase her own power tenfold and, indeed, could cause havoc across time and space." He paused before addressing his son.

"Fox, I believe your wife has unlocked the answer to her coming here and joining with you. We have no alternative but to do as she says and face Ebony head-on. We will capture her and remove the threat to the magic that can reawaken Earth. Our own world was created from such powerful magic and it is our beginning, and our end. We cannot sit back and do nothing on the edge of such change."

Fox stepped away from the fire towards Sapphire, a deep frown now etched on his brow. "I refuse to put you in such danger, Sapphire. You have no idea what Ebony is capable of. We escaped before by chance. I cannot lose you, my love. I will not do this willingly."

She stood before him now and reached up to touch his face, a smile on her lips. "I love the way you continue to protect me every step of the way, my love ... my guardian. But you know I can defend myself, and this has to happen. It is the right thing to do and, no matter how long I try to run away from it, eventually it will happen. Please, Fox, don't resist me. Join with me ... fight alongside me. I know we can do this. The dream you had earlier today has foreseen us back on Earth – together, happy, and travelling to a place where the magic can start healing Earth."

Fox leant down, rested his forehead on her own, and sighed deeply. Her words were like a knife in his chest, and he could not bear to think of walking into such danger willingly with her by his side. But deep in his heart, he understood that the magic she had been given was for a higher purpose, and it would be selfish of him to think they could hide it from the rest of the universe. As a guardian he knew the code of magic and its trials and tribulations, the balance of things in his world could not be ignored or played with lightly. Everything came with a price. It seemed his wife had to pay a rather large fee in exchange for the magical gifts she had been given.

"Then we have to plan this properly and use every resource we have, not just dive straight into a massacre," he replied.

She pulled his face down towards her and kissed him deeply. Her body had relaxed slightly, now that he had given in to her mad, crazy request. The part of her that was still human was standing up straight with a pained expression on its face, pulling its hair out by the roots. The new magical Sapphire was grinning confidently, champing at the bit for a fight.

So much had happened to her in such a short space of time, but now it all made sense: complete sense. She was about to change the course of not just one world but two. They spent the next hour talking through possible tactics, and how to approach the bordering kingdom without causing too many fatalities to their army. Conloach knew the queen to be a hard woman who, if instructed by Ebony, would not back down easily. At some point during the heated discussion Wolf appeared from nowhere, along with Bear. Both of them were briefed quickly by Conloach, as to what was happening. Sapphire watched the alarm and disbelief forming across their faces as Fox and his father brought them up to date with what was ahead of them. They were quickly brought up to speed, though, and their shock and incredulity eventually metamorphosed into calculated battle plans. Such was the strength and adaptability of the warrior, it seemed, in this strange magical land.

Sapphire stepped back at one point to allow the men more room to look at plans of the kingdom on the huge wooden table. Her husband's face was now fully focused and his eyes were scanning the map, looking for ways they could launch a surprise attack. She watched him intently, looking for signs that he would back out if the task seemed too dangerous. He was the most handsome, ferocious, and sexy as hell warrior she had ever seen. She had no doubt whatsoever that between them they would find a way to capture Ebony.

Sapphire also wanted some peace in her life again. She hated having to constantly watch her back against either the disgusting Hecta or the mad, crazy woman who wanted to steal her new-found magic. Plus the burning excitement in her stomach at the thought of returning to Earth was tugging at her insides.

She realised guiltily that this was what she wanted more than anything. It was as if a homing beacon within her had suddenly been switched on and it was pulsing softly – on and off, on and off – wanting to return to its point of origin. Earth.

Chapter Sixteen

After what seemed like an eternity, Fox said it was time to call it a night. They would resume talking battle tactics tomorrow. He wanted to go home with his wife the troublemaker, and sleep. Sapphire could not be more in agreement. Now that she had started this whole thing she wanted to just lie down and rest for a while.

Fox pulled her into his arms, kissed the top of her head, and squeezed her tightly after he had said goodbye to the other men, who continued to argue over which plan would work best.

"Time to go home, my love."

She felt his magic pulse around them and send a shiver of pure pleasure rushing throughout her body as he transported them home.

They arrived back at the house. The sky was still an inky dark blue, but she sensed dawn approaching fast. Kit had lit several candles, and the house was warm and inviting. Sapphire also sensed the presence of several guards still patrolling Fox's border, and hoped that soon this would be a thing of the past. Good. She wanted her life back, her life with Fox to be free and safe again. Now that they had Conloach and his army to back them she knew that this would at last be possible. They headed to the bedroom. Sapphire felt weary, but her mind was still racing.

Fox picked her up at the foot of the stairs in his usual 'I am here to rescue you' way and kissed her softly, taking two steps at a time. He never seemed to lack energy.

He sat her down on the bed and smiled at her, his dark, predatory smile. She knew he wanted to wipe away the evening's dark cloud, and she felt no reason to stop him. He licked his lips slowly and began to undress in front of her. He seemed to enjoy teasing her in this way before they made love. Sapphire felt her body start to awaken and her magic twitch restlessly as she watched him remove his clothing. He was a fine specimen of a man. Or magical man, whatever the case may be. She never tired of looking at him. As he exposed his chest to her he cocked his head to one side and stopped the striptease for a second.

"Are you tired, my love?"

She leant back on to her forearms and smiled. "Not any more, Fox."

He chuckled and continued to undress as he slid out of his leather trousers. He now stood naked before her in all his glory.

"Now your turn."

She laughed. "Are you not going to help me?"

"Not this time, my beautiful warrior woman. I want to watch you."

Sapphire sensed the talk of battle had excited the beast within him, and it was prowling hungrily beneath his skin. It pressed her horny button big time. As she sat up again she began slowly, one eyelet at a time, to unbutton the corset she was wearing so that her breasts began to spill out before him. She watched his eyes turn a darker shade of gold, and the dark ring around each iris flashed with sparks of light. He placed his hands on his hips with his feet spread apart, dominant and expectant.

Sapphire stood up slowly and slid her hand into the front of her leather trousers. She lowered her head slightly and looked up at him from beneath her eyelashes, a smile on her lips. Fox gasped softly as she pushed open the buttons on her trousers and spread her fingers open seductively. With her other hand she shimmied out of the leather trousers, keeping herself covered modestly while she gracefully stepped out of them. He remained still in front of her. The magic connecting them was pulsing steadily now, heightening the intensity of what was manifesting between them: lust.

Pure and hot, it began to fill the room with its heady heat and scent. Sapphire marvelled at how, each time they came together, it created a stronger bond between them ... how it seemed to make the magic grow fiercer and more powerful. It seemed to have a will of its own now and since their wedding and the blood bond, pushed them constantly to connect as often as they could.

She slipped her hand down further and pushed one of her own fingers inside herself, and at the same time she raised her other hand to her breast and squeezed softly. Fox watched her, his mouth slightly open now, his breath coming harder from his lips. She slid her finger back and forth, teasing him. He remained still as he watched her pleasure herself. Slowly, she removed her finger and placed it into her mouth, sucking it with a deliberately loud smacking of her lips.

That did it. Fox tipped over the edge and lunged at her. He grabbed her by the waist and pulled her against him, a deep growl in his throat. She laughed as he pushed her forcefully back on to the bed and claimed her neck as he nipped her roughly with his teeth. Suddenly the temperature shot up and Sapphire felt the tempo quicken. She had never felt Fox become so wild so quickly with her before. He became animal-like: he was grabbing her wrists and forcing them above her head, pushing his hips against her own and grinding his very hard cock against her groin. Her head fell back with the pressure he was exerting on her. It was almost painful, the way he was gripping her wrists and pushing himself on to her. She felt totally at his mercy, slightly scared, and completely turned on.

Without warning he pushed her further up on to the bed and released her neck so that he was towering over her – his face dark and sensual, his eyes blazing at her. He paused for a second. He was whispering words in his own language in a deep guttural tone, which made her shiver with anticipation. His voice sounded different, as if he were not himself. After pushing her legs apart with his own he plunged himself inside her so hard that she felt a sharp pain in her belly. He continued to hold her down and fucked her fast for what seemed like an eternity. He was clearly out of control.

Sapphire realised that all this time he had been holding back the true beast within him. She had never seen him so dark before. The dangerous edge to her man was unleashed fully tonight. Her magic swelled and spun around her, intertwining with his own, making the pain just a little easier to cope with. He almost snarled at her, his teeth slightly bared. Sapphire felt her body tremble beneath him. She was almost overwhelmed by the harshness of his lovemaking. It excited her, scared her, and made her feel completely at his mercy.

Suddenly she realised her body was responding to this strange sense of fear she was feeling in a rhythm of its own. From deep within the recess of her mind she felt her own beast begin to awaken. Black and sleek – like a dangerous panther – it sprang from within her, and she fought back against him. She bucked her hips, pulled against his hands – which clamped her wrists like a vice – and snarled back at him. The pain became pleasure, and he continued to pound her hard. Their magic grew into a thick, dark cloud almost sinister in appearance around them. Fox was lost to his beast. He continued his assault on her body, and carried on pounding her hard. She pushed back against him. She managed to release her hands from his grip, grabbing his buttocks and scratching her nails across his skin.

He threw his head back and cried out at the pain she had inflicted on him as she drew blood. It seemed to excite him even more, and he claimed her mouth and kissed her hard. They fucked like animals, devouring each other with their mouths and bodies, pushing themselves closer together to the point of oblivion. Sapphire could feel her whole body begin to shake and tremble as her climax grew within her. Every single cell was switched on, ready to ignite.

Fox released her mouth and grabbed her head as he pushed his fingers into her hair at the roots. She looked up at him, deep into his eyes, which had turned almost black. He stopped pounding her for a second, his cock still deep within her. She blinked, confused at the sudden change in rhythm. Her body was just on the edge of the precipice and shaking with wanting to jump over the cliff and dive into pure white-hot climax. The stillness after such relentless torment was exquisite.

The magic surrounding them pulsed strongly, lighting up the room with flashes of red and purple. Then it came, for both of them at the same time: the ultimate climax. Sapphire cried out, unable to contain herself any longer. She could hear Fox howling his own words of pleasure as they both came at the same time. It threw them both into a force of pure pleasure that crashed against them and split them apart at the seams. Sapphire felt her eyes roll into the back of her head, and the last thing she remembered before actually blacking out was Fox shouting out, "Fuck!" at the top of his lungs. Death by orgasm. Awesome …

Sapphire was not actually dead, although the climax she had experienced had caused her to momentarily lose consciousness. Gradually she started to feel her body again, and felt her eyes began to refocus. Fox was above her as she finally opened her eyes. He was panting and covered in sweat, a concerned frown on his brow.

"My love, I am sorry. Did I hurt you?" His expression was one of concern and confusion.

Sapphire sighed deeply. She felt totally and utterly wonderful. She smiled up at him and lifted her very limp hand, and touched his face lightly. "I'm fine … more than fine. That was amazing, utterly amazing."

His expression softened, and he smiled again and leant down to kiss her gently on the lips. "Thank God. I thought I had hurt you."

Sapphire laughed and stretched her body, which felt wonderfully loose and like liquid silk. "Well, maybe a little, but it was good. Honestly, I'm fine."

Fox slumped back on to the bed and let out a deep sigh. "I have never experienced anything like that before, Sapphire. Sex magic is a dark and dangerous thing to delve into. I would never have done that if I thought for a moment that it would damage you. It seemed to take control of me and I had no warning of it until it was too late and I was lost within its depths."

She rolled over on to her side and watched him, the smile still on her lips. He seemed to be at odds with what had just happened between them."Sex magic?"

He closed his eyes for a second, seemingly trying to control his breathing. "Yes, sex magic. It is powerful, and very old. It can evoke the beast within, and take you to places that are often too intense for some to experience."

Sapphire trailed her finger across his chest. She felt wonderful, not damaged at all."Well, I think we should talk of battles more often if that's the result."

He opened his eyes and laughed. "Nothing surprises you any more, does it, my love?" He pulled her into his arms and squeezed her tightly as he wrapped his legs around her. He kissed her again, gently this time, with a soft, sweet probing of his tongue.

Sapphire felt herself melt into this man – who had, once more, taken her to a place she never knew could even exist. They kissed for some time, slowly and leisurely, without the edge of danger they had just experienced.

A new day had dawned around them, and Sapphire knew she would need to get some rest before they actually started making plans again. Wrapped in Fox's arms, she gradually felt her body succumb to sleep. She was totally and utterly spent … in the most wonderful way any woman could be.

Chapter Seventeen

Sapphire was once again dreaming. It had been some time since she had experienced a dream like the dreams she had come to know so well, back on Earth. She knew that this dream was going to be a particularly strange one, as she was standing in a land that could not be real. Everything around her glittered and shone in bright colours and waves of light. Her body felt as light as a feather and she was aware that, although she may be travelling, her real body was still firmly placed at home in bed with Fox.

Her eyes scanned the area as she looked for signs of life. All around her seemed deathly silent except for a gentle whooshing noise, which sounded oddly like someone breathing rather heavily (or like someone with a bad case of asthma). The scene around her was one of a beautiful forest, with wild and strange-looking plants and huge pink and blue spotted mushrooms, dotted around like something on a crazy golf course. It confused her for a second, until she spotted where the whooshing noise was coming from.

Sitting on top of one of the mushrooms was a large blue caterpillar, who was smoking a hookah. He smiled at her lazily, took another lungful of smoke, and blew it out towards her with slow precision. Sapphire smiled back at him – a slightly crazed smile as her subconscious pulled out the image of the blue caterpillar from *Alice's Adventures in Wonderland* from the memory of her human brain. He was here in her dream, smoking his pipe and smiling at her... for what reason she was yet to discover, but it amused her and she started to laugh – a real belly laugh.

The caterpillar paused in his smoking and raised an eyebrow. "Something funny, young lady?"

Sapphire bent over, clasping her stomach, which now hurt from laughing so much. "Sorry ... It just seems a bit strange seeing you here, that's all."

He watched her for a moment before taking another lungful of smoke, and exhaling again with what seemed like boredom. "And why would it be strange to see me here, dream traveller? You willed it, did you not?"

Sapphire stepped closer to him. The smoke lingering in the air had the sweet scent of apples. "Did I?"

He let out a loud 'humph', and sighed deeply. "Of course you did. Don't act stupid, for you are far from stupid."

Sapphire crossed her arms in front of her chest. "OK, so I created this wonderful little scene. Can you give me some clue as to why?"

He nodded slowly. "If you ask me the right questions, of course."

Sapphire frowned. "OK, let me guess. A set of riddles again, as always. Everyone talks in riddles at the beginning of my dreams. Great."

He laughed then, a deep rumbling laugh, which seemed out of place in such a strange character. "But you like riddles, Sapphire, and you always work them out eventually."

She smiled again. "Yes, eventually I do."

He took another suck on the pipe. The smoke was growing thicker around her now. If the scent was not quite so sweet it would be annoying.

"OK. For some reason I have created part of an old story, which I loved to read as a child. Are you here to tell me what I am supposed to do to help with the battle on Shaka?"

He cocked his head to one side and closed his eyes for a moment. After reopening them he shrugged and said, "No."

Sapphire sighed loudly. "Are you here to help me with my new magic?"

He tilted his head back straight and smiled. "Yes," he said.

Sapphire uncrossed her arms. "Good. That's a start. What do I need to do with this magic to awaken our mother on Earth?"

He looked slightly more interested now, and leant forward a little. "Now, that's a good question." He paused. Sapphire waited for him to continue. Another moment passed. He closed his eyes again and seemed to fall asleep momentarily.

"Erm ... excuse me ... I'm waiting for an answer here."

He opened his eyes again and shook his head, as if to restart his train of thought. Maybe he was just really stoned. It was a very definite possibility with all the smoke around him.

"Well, you need to plant them in the right places, of course."

177

Sapphire could feel herself become agitated. This was ridiculous. "Plant my magic?"

He laughed again, before taking another hit on the hookah. "The seeds, my dear. The seeds."

Sapphire watched him stretch forward with his free hand and open his little blue palm before her. On stepping forward for a closer inspection Sapphire found herself staring at a group of what looked like tumble stones in his hand. They glittered and shone an ice blue colour.

"Seeds?"

He pushed his hand forward again and gestured for her to take them. She opened her own palm and watched with interest as they slipped into her hand like diamonds would. As she looked back up at him she noticed that his form began to shimmer slightly, as if he was about to disappear. Sapphire knew her dream was about to end.

"How do I use these with my magic? Where do I plant them? Please tell me what to do."

He smiled at her. The edges of his outline were beginning to fade quickly now. "You will know what to do when the time is right, dream traveller. Keep them safe ... the seeds, they are very important. Travel safe ... travel well, Sapphire, dream traveller." And then he was gone, hookah and all.

Sapphire was left standing in front of the pink and blue mushroom, her head spinning with this strange piece of information. She looked down at her hand and found the seeds staring back at her innocently. The sweet scent of apple filled her nostrils, the smoke from the hookah was growing thicker around her head. It seemed to become denser and denser and surrounded her completely, until she could no longer see anything except white tendrils of smoke. It filled her lungs and made her cough: the sweetness was suffocating. Sapphire closed her eyes and tried to breathe, but the smoke was making this nearly impossible. It felt like she was suddenly trapped within a massive bong and was about to have her first 'whitey'. Her head began to swim, and she felt nausea begin to rise hastily from the pit of her stomach. She bent over and started to retch.

"Oh, shit. I'm going to puke," she said out loud, before she felt the familiar loud ping in her head and blacked out.

"Sapphire! Sapphire ... Wake up, my love ... You were dreaming. Here, drink this."

Sapphire woke up, coughing loudly. She could still feel the sweet, sickly smoke in her lungs. She had never liked smoking much and was now even less enthusiastic about ever trying it again.

Fox was beside her on the bed, holding a glass of water in his hand. She reached out and took the glass, eager to soothe her throat. As she did the tumble stones she had seen in her dream fell from her hand on to the sheets. Fox paused and looked down with wonder at the shining gems. Sapphire gulped the water down as she tried desperately to remove the remnants of the caterpillar's smoke.

"What are these, my love?" Fox was tentatively touching the tiny blue stones, his eyes wide with curiosity.

Sapphire finished the water and sucked in fresh air. It felt like bliss. She gasped a little as she regained her breath.

"Seeds, Fox. They are seeds."

He began to scoop them up into a pile, almost as if he were afraid they would explode at any minute and needed to be removed from the room quickly before they did. Sapphire watched with amazement that, yet again, something real had manifested itself from her dream state. Where the hell had she just been?

Fox looked across at her as she started to laugh. His face was still etched with surprise.

"We need to keep them safe, Fox. They are the key to awakening Mother Earth, believe it or not. Some crazy caterpillar just gave them to me while I was dreaming."

He shook his head in disbelief. "Sapphire, I seriously fear for your sanity sometimes."

Sapphire reached across to the bedside cabinet, put the glass down, and picked up one of the trinket boxes that were placed beside the candle. "Here, put them in this for now." She paused looking at him with a smile on her lips. "As for my sanity, I think that left me a long time ago Fox."

Fox grinned back at her, obviously amused, and nodded. Transporting the tumble stones into the box, he made sure that he shut the lid carefully. Just in case.

Sapphire realised that the day was at its fullest, and time was of the essence. She reached across for her beautiful man and kissed him hard before pulling back slightly and smiling.

"Let's get dressed," she said. "We have a lot to do today."

Fox shook his head in bewilderment but did as she said, pushing himself out of bed so that he could bathe and dress. He had the distinct feeling that everything was about to change again for them both. And that it had everything to do with the appearance of some extremely strange stones that were now sitting, safely hidden, on their bedside cabinet.

Sapphire found Kit in her usual place, working hard in the kitchen. Her face was slightly drawn today, with a look of anxiety. She buzzed around like a bee, cleaning and tidying after what looked like another mass cooking session.

"Are you hungry, Saf? Bear and Wolf arrived early this morning, and I have already fed them both. They are in the armoury."

Suddenly ravenous, Sapphire sat down at the kitchen table and stared at the breakfast things she had laid out for them. "Yes, I am, Kit. Fox will be down shortly … I didn't hear anyone arrive."

Kit smiled at her, a little weakly. "We let you sleep in, my lady. I gather you had a long night."

Sapphire blushed slightly as she remembered her tussle with Fox in the early hours. Kit must think the pair of them had a sex problem if she had been around to hear that particular encounter. She hoped that was not the case.

"It was a long night. Has Bear brought you up to date with our plans?"

Kit had her back to her and stopped for a second, dropping her head slightly. Sapphire could feel the tension rolling off her in anxious waves that clearly indicated her unease with what had transpired.

"Bear told me you are preparing to attack the queen." Kit said, her voice wavering as she spoke.

Sapphire started to fill her plate with food. She was suddenly very hungry. The combination of sex and dream travelling often had that effect on her.

"I fear for you, Saf. It worries me sick that you are forcing your hand in this matter." Kit turned to face Sapphire slowly. "Why must you pursue Ebony? Can't you just wait? At least take some time to spend with Master Fox and be happy."

Sapphire sipped the hot tea Kit had prepared, and shook her head. "No, Kit, we cannot wait. I'm sick of having this constant threat hanging over my head. Besides, there is more at stake than just my happiness and our safety. I have to go back home again soon. Very soon."

Kit looked at her with obvious anguish in her eyes. She said nothing and turned back to her chores. Sapphire hated the fact that she was hurting her new young friend, and she wanted nothing more than to just get on with her life. But that was not meant to be. Tension hung in the air like a heavy cloud between them. It sucked.

Fox appeared at her side looking slightly ruffled, but as gorgeous as ever. She noted that he had slightly dark rings under his eyes today. This new turn of events was obviously taking its toll on him as well as Kit.

"My love ... any food left for me?"

She smiled as he kissed her on the cheek and sat down beside her. "Of course. Bear and Wolf are here already. Kit said they are waiting for us in the armoury."

He nodded and started to load his plate up. His appetite had been spiked as much as hers from all the energy they had used over the last few hours. They ate in silence while Kit went about her business. She disappeared before they had finished without saying another word.

"She is angry with me, Fox. I hate to see it, but we have to do this," Sapphire said sadly.

Fox sat back in the chair. He reached for her hand, took her palm, and traced a circle softly on to her skin as if to distract her. "She cares for us both, Sapphire. Of course she wishes for us to stay away from any danger. You cannot begrudge her that."

Sapphire sighed. "I know. I just wish it could be easier for her to understand."

"She will eventually." He smiled at her and lifted her hand to his lips as he kissed it softly. "Kit will come around, don't worry. Let's go talk battle tactics." He winked at her playfully.

Sapphire grinned in response as they remembered how such talk had ended the last time.

Chapter Eighteen

"Creating a diversion is the only way we can have a chance at capturing Ebony." Fox said. The men were still throwing ideas back and forth between them. Bear wanted a full-on attack at night after scouts had been sent ahead, to give them a heads-up on whether the queen was aware of their plans. Wolf was not so keen, saying that although his men were more than capable in a fight they should send out a first wave of attack and reserve his counter-attack to take the queen's forces by surprise at the furthest reaches of her kingdom. Fox agreed with them both, but had other ideas up his sleeve. Sapphire watched them with fascination. A table had been pulled into the centre of the armoury and was littered with maps of the area again.

"What kind of diversion?" Sapphire asked.

Fox countered, "We need some bait, something to pull her out into the open. I can be that bait ... She wanted me last time. We can whet her appetite and then attack while she is otherwise occupied."

Sapphire swung around to face him, her eyes wide in horror. "Over my dead body. She is never going to be near you again. Ever."

He watched his usually passive woman turn suddenly into possessive wife mode. It was oddly arousing.

"If anyone is going to be bait it will be me. It's me that she really wants. No offence, Fox, but I'm ready to draw her out if necessary."

Fox walked towards her slowly, placed his hands on her waist, and gazed down at her with intense eyes. "I will go in first, my love. Then you can come and rescue me, if needed."

She smiled at him. He was teasing her.

"I am not sure either of you are thinking straight, Fox. It sounds like a bad idea to me." Bear was getting agitated, and Sapphire did not blame him. It sounded like suicide, even to her, but both of them were now keen to draw Ebony out and finish this deadly game of cat and mouse.

"Sapphire and I are the only ones – apart from my father – who have the magic strong enough to transport us to the queen without

182

being detected. It makes complete sense to me. You and Wolf can create the diversion outside while I go in first to find out where Ebony is hiding. I'll draw her out, and then Sapphire and my father can capture her. My father has the power to create a binding spell that will trap her until we decide what to do with her from there."

Sapphire pulled him into her body and rested her head on his chest. "I don't want to put you at risk again, Fox, not after last time. What about Hecta?"

He smoothed her hair away from her face and kissed her forehead softly. "I am a lot more prepared this time, my love. We are on Shaka now, my magic is strong here. Hecta will not be a problem. Besides, we are joined in strength since the blood exchange. I am stronger than I have ever been, thanks to you."

She sighed deeply. She knew deep down that this would most likely be their only chance at capturing Ebony, but the plan troubled her to the core.

"I will ask my father to see if he can foresee when would be the most opportune time for our attack." He paused. "In the meantime, I want to spend some quality time with my new wife. We have not had a honeymoon yet ..." Sapphire looked up at him and blinked with surprise. She had not even thought about such a thing since their wedding night two days ago.

Bear then added his view."I still think it's a bad idea, Fox, but if you feel it is the best course of action, I will go with Wolf to prepare the men. We have scouts in the queen's kingdom as we speak, and should hear back from them tonight as to whether she is also gathering her forces."

Fox was staring at Sapphire intently, a slight smile on his lips. "Good. We shall see you both again soon."

Both warriors left shortly after and Sapphire found her mind was still spinning with a thousand thoughts as to what was about to happen for them all. Fox had taken her out into the garden. They were sitting beside the fountain, wrapped around each other. It had always been a special place in his garden that they could find some peace and balance together.

"Stop thinking too hard, my love. All will be well. We need some time away from all of this. I want to take you away for at least a day, so that we can enjoy our new status and celebrate."

Sapphire squeezed him tightly, revelling in his warmth and the firmness of his chest. She felt guilty at the thought of taking off while others were preparing to fight on her behalf. "Where will we go?"

Fox was trailing a finger across her right breast, kissing her neck softly in between gentle nips with his teeth. It was his favourite thing to do. Almost as if it soothed him. Thankfully now that she was filled with magic she no longer bruised as easily, and he did not mark her skin the way he did when they first met.

"I have a place at the coast. We can spend a night there together. It is perfectly safe - we can go today. I have sent word to my father that we will be back before nightfall tomorrow."

She tilted her head back and sighed softly, his caress making her body shiver with excitement. "Sounds wonderful."

He nipped her skin again playfully. "It will be."

They left shortly after to go to Fox's hideaway. Using magic, they transported themselves to a place in which even Sapphire was amazed to find herself. It was like something out of paradise. A white sandy beach stretched out for miles in both directions, complete with palm trees and an endless panorama that took her breath away. A small but functional hut stood hidden on the hillside, looking out over the coast. It consisted of a simple living area, a kitchen, a bathroom, and a bedroom. Sapphire wandered through the wooden hut – her eyes wide in wonder at the beautiful furnishings and decorations, which were in keeping with the nautical surroundings. Seashells hung on the small veranda as wind chimes, which tinkled in the sea breeze. Fox had changed into loose linen trousers that looked a lot like the fishermen's trousers she had seen on Earth. With his chest bare and his hair tied back with a piece of leather he looked relaxed and at ease and, as always, totally delicious.

"Go and change, my love. There are suitable clothes in the chest by the bed. I will go and find us something to eat." He kissed her softly and stroked her back tenderly, making her skin tingle. The sound of the waves crashing against the shoreline was soothing and, with the combination of sunshine and the scent of the fresh sea air, she also began to relax.

"Don't be long, Fox."

He chuckled, and tucked a piece of her hair behind her ear. "I won't. Do not worry, my love. You are perfectly safe here. We are a long way from civilisation and this place is hidden from anyone who may be looking for us. I found it a long time ago, and have used it many times to find peace and quiet when I have needed solitude."

She nodded, reluctant to let him go even just for a short time. He kissed her one more time softly, on the tip of her nose, then turned on his heel and disappeared in a flash out through the door.

Left alone inside the hut, Sapphire suddenly felt very strange. This was the most beautiful hideaway for a honeymoon and she knew that she needed to make the most of their limited time here. But everything felt totally surreal. She headed into the bedroom, found the trunk at the foot of the bed and looked inside. There were blankets and items of clothing, most of them obviously belonging to Fox. On rummaging through she found several pieces of colourful cotton at the bottom which, she quickly realised, were like sarongs. Although she knew that she could now imagine herself a cheeky pink bikini if she wanted to, she pulled out the material and stared at it for a moment. The fabric seemed to shimmer slightly, and the patterns swirled and shifted slightly as she ran her fingers across the design. Magic. Everything seemed to be made from magic here, including the beachwear. She laughed, and started to strip off her clothes. By the time she had fastened the sarong around her neck and finished plaiting her hair again Fox had returned.

He stood on the veranda with a smug smile on his face, holding up two very large fish. "Your dinner, my love!"

Sapphire laughed, wondering how he had managed to catch them so quickly. "Looks good, Fox. What can I do?"

He hung the fish on the wooden slats that sheltered the veranda from the hot sun, and began to make a fire in the iron firepit that was set to one side of the decking.

"Nothing, my beautiful wife … make yourself comfortable. I will cook for us tonight."

185

Sapphire had gathered cushions from the living area and was stretched out, her arms above her head, her eyes closed as she waited for supper. The smell of fresh fish wafted across from the firepit. Fox had also managed to produce a bottle of wine and salad for them to enjoy (she suspected more magic was involved in this part of the preparation: there were clearly no corner shops in this part of Shaka). The day was passing quickly and, although the sun was still shining, it had dropped slightly on the horizon and the heat of the day was gradually fading.

"This place is wonderful, Fox. I actually feel relaxed for the first time in ages."

He chuckled softly. "I am happy you feel that way, my love. That was my intention." They ate in comfortable silence. The fish was, of course, wonderful, and the wine cold and crisp.

Sapphire watched Fox as he ate. "Please don't be angry with me, Fox."

He looked up at her with an expression of surprise. "I am not angry with you, my love. Why would you think such a thing?"

She paused and took a sip of the wine before speaking again. "Because I did not tell you that I would need to go home again. I know you want me to stay here with you, but it was only really ever a temporary thing."

He smiled at her, a soft smile full of understanding. "It was perhaps just a dream for me that we would be able to live in peace here on Shaka, but I am beginning to understand now, my love, that the magic growing between us is meant for greater things. I was angry at first, yes. But now I accept what must be done. Besides, I know that although you want to be with me wherever I am you miss your friends and family just as much. I cannot deny you your happiness."

She sighed deeply. "I am hoping that once the job is done we can both just get on with our lives together, wherever that may be."

He reached across and softly traced a finger across her cheek. "This is also my wish, my love. More than anything I want us to be safe and happy. It was wishful thinking on my part that Ebony and Hecta would just leave us alone." He smiled cheekily. "I cannot leave you alone, so it is no surprise that they cannot either."

Sapphire laughed. "For somewhat different reasons, I think, Fox."

He leant back while holding his wine glass gently at the stem, a look of contemplation now on his face.

"From the moment I first met you, Sapphire, I knew that my journey as guardian would be a different experience from anything I had ever had before. You are unique ... special. Life with you is never dull, my love. I sense that it will always be an adventure."

Sapphire shrugged. "I just never expected this kind of adventure in my life, Fox. Not in a million years."

He placed the wine glass down and moved towards her slowly and gracefully, his eyes flashing with amusement.

"Enough talking now, my love. We are on honeymoon, and I intend to spend the remaining time we have together alone doing what I love to do the most."

She smiled at him and tilted her head to one side. Her heart started to beat just that little bit more quickly.

"And what is that, my gorgeous husband?"

He was inches from her now, his body pulsing softly in the growing darkness.

"What do you think?"

Chapter Nineteen

Fox showed her not only once but twice what his favourite activity was that night. She felt as if her honeymoon was everything it could have been, and more. He was as always the most attentive lover and, by the time a new day had dawned, she was well and truly satisfied. Fox was sleeping beside her as the new day approached: she had dozed for a while after their intense lovemaking, but was now wide awake and watching the light beginning to filter through the wooden slats of the roof. It seemed that since her shift in magic she needed less and less sleep. At present this did not bother her at all as it meant fewer dreams, which in turn meant less hassle. Her mind, however, was spinning again. She wondered if this feeling of anxiety would ever leave her for good.

She turned to her side and watched Fox sleep. His face was calm and serene, his lips slightly parted, his dark lashes fluttering as if he were dreaming. He was, at that moment, picture-perfect. She wanted to take a photograph of him just as he was right now – to keep – and so that she could remember him looking so peaceful. With a gentle touch she brushed her fingers across his brow and ran them through his hair. He licked his bottom lip slowly, and a smile began to creep around the edges of his mouth as he stretched lazily.

"Good morning, wife."

She smiled in response as he opened his eyes slowly. "I'm still getting used to you calling me that."

He chuckled and stretched out fully, giving her a lovely view of tight abdominal muscles that rippled as he moved. "I shall constantly remind you, my love, of your new status as much as I can, so that you never forget you are forever bound to me."

Sapphire laughed. She sat herself up against the headboard and looked down at his naked body with pleasure. "That sounds almost kinky, Fox."

He raised an eyebrow. He was looking up at her now with an amused smile on his lips. "I am not familiar with this term, my love. Explain."

Sapphire started to blush, the first blush in a while, and the first since her change in confidence. "You know … to be bound … to be tied to someone. The possibilities are endless." She had his attention now, as he turned over on to his side and began to slowly trail his fingers across her thigh.

"Now that sounds very interesting. I could definitely succumb to some binding at some point, my beautiful Sapphire."

His fingers had reached her inner thigh and he was stroking her just so, in exactly the right spot, to start her internal fire again. He moved down the bed slowly. His mouth was now following the trail of his fingers to her thigh. Sapphire closed her eyes as the familiar tingle began across her skin as he kissed her lightly.

"Would you like me to bind you now, my love, or would you prefer to do the tying?"

She gasped as his tongue began to gently probe between her legs. The thought of him tying anything up made her squirm against him.

"I'm not sure I'm ready for that just yet, Fox."

He blew cool air against her, softly, in between light flicks of his tongue. "When you are ready, my love. When you are ready."

She grasped his head as he plunged his tongue further into her and let out a low moan of pleasure. His teasing made her tremble just that little bit more at the thought of him tying her up and having his wicked way with her. Fox continued his tongue dance, sliding his finger inside her and pulling her down on to the bed fully so that he could hold her in place. She felt her head begin to spin at the intensity, and gripped his hair at the roots tightly.

"I would do anything for you, Sapphire. Anything," he mumbled between kisses. His words tipped her over the edge and she climaxed quickly, unable to hold back. He held her tightly as her hips pushed up to meet him, her muscles clenching as she let herself go.

"Oh, my God," Sapphire whimpered. She was trying to pull him away, as her clit throbbed almost painfully. He held her in place and pushed his finger in deeper while lifting his head to look up at her as she continued to spasm around him. His eyes were dark and carnal, his lips curled into a wicked smile as he enjoyed the view of his wife coming undone before him. Sapphire held on to him and allowed her orgasm to roll luxuriously over her body.

"What a way to wake up," she thought wickedly.

He released her swiftly and rolled on top of her – then pushed his more than ready cock inside her slowly, with a smooth, controlled thrust. Sapphire felt her eyes roll back and her body become limp as he started to ride her with the most wonderful rhythm, his pace almost casual in its smoothness. He kissed her again, with a deepness that made her grip on to his buttocks with her thighs, and she felt her body start to respond once more. Fox was insatiable, his need for her overwhelming. She could feel him grow hotter and harder within her, and it made her grip him even tighter in response. It was if she were the oasis in a desert, and his need to drink from her was his only desire. He made love to her in this slow, almost unbearable manner until she could take it no longer and climaxed again.

Fox released her mouth and seized her neck, biting her hard just below her ear as he too found his release. She cried out from the mixture of pleasure and pain it caused throughout her body. Her cry excited him more, and he claimed her mouth again as he pushed deeper inside her. He was still pulsing from his orgasm, which seemed to go and on. Their magic swirled around them in a mixture of gold and silver sparks that lit up the room. Slowly the intensity began to ease, and Sapphire regained her senses. Fox was whispering to her in his beautiful, intoxicating language as he held her against him. He was still inside her, and their hearts were beating fast and loud in the afterglow.

"I really wish I knew what you were saying to me, Fox," she whispered.

He slowly, painfully released her and rolled over on to his back again, a soft moan escaping his lips.

"I cannot translate the words to you, my love. They are all-consuming, and would most probably make you blush fiercely if you could understand them."

She laughed softly as she tried to regain her breath. "In that case I shall just continue to enjoy the mystery."

Fox pulled her into his arms and kissed her tenderly. "There is no mystery, my love, only my all-consuming need to have you wrapped around me at every moment I can." He certainly proved that to her on a daily basis.

After a light breakfast they took a swim in the sea. Sapphire was getting used to swimming naked now, and to the feeling of the water against her bare skin. Her body felt overwhelmingly wonderful, such was the strength of the new magic inside her. They splashed each other playfully, and Sapphire laughed loudly as Fox grabbed her and threw her into the air as if they were two teenagers again. She revelled in this time they had together ... alone, happy, and contented. Because she knew that they must return very soon she made the most of every second of their last day in paradise. Fox seemed to be completely relaxed, despite the impending battle and possible danger they would face when they returned to the reality waiting for them at home.

After their swim they lay on the sand drying in the sunshine. The waves crashed against the shoreline in a rhythmic tumble of aquamarine blue that foamed and turned white and silver as it pulled against the sand. Sapphire turned to face Fox, who was lying with his hands behind his head, his eyes closed, and his lips turned up at the corners in a soft smile. She watched him breathe slowly, his chest rising and falling as if he did not have a care in the world. His skin had turned a darker shade of brown in the last two days as they had rested in this hideaway: his body glistened in the sunshine, tiny droplets of water were still visible on his chest and hair. Every time she looked at him she wondered how she had ever ended up with such an impressive man. On sensing her stare he turned and looked at her, his eyes squinting in the bright sunlight. The dark ring around his irises flashed at her with a touch of laughter in their gaze.

"I sense your thoughts are spinning, my love. Care to share them with me?"

She laughed softly. "I was wondering how I ever ended up with someone so completely gorgeous as you, Fox."

He rolled over. His naked body caused her to become momentarily distracted and slightly breathless. "It was always meant to be, my love. Besides, you are the most gorgeous woman I have ever seen. We are perfectly matched."

She lifted herself up slightly and gazed down at him, taking in every inch of his face, his body, and the pulsing energy that wavered around him.

"You are the only man who has ever made me feel even the slightest bit attractive, Fox. I still find it hard to believe that you want me as you do."

He frowned and lifted his hand to her hair, and stroked his fingers across a tendril that fell across her shoulder. "They were fools, Sapphire. But I am glad you feel worshipped now. I want you more than the air I breathe. Do not doubt this."

She felt her cheeks begin to blush once more, and she turned her head to kiss the fingers that brushed through her hair. "I don't doubt you, Fox. But it still feels strange to me. All of this – my new life, the magical world I have entered – everything has happened so fast. Sometimes I think I will wake up and it has all been a dream, after all."

He pushed himself up now and pulled her into his arms. He smelt of the sea, and the faintest trace of his signature sandalwood. The combination was heady and intoxicating. He kissed her softly and she allowed him to roll on top of her, their naked bodies still slightly wet and rough from sand. Their magic pulsed around them, nuzzling and stroking in an eagerness to connect. The kiss was slow, and filled with unspoken words of need. Fox continued to kiss her for some time, his body hot and hard against her. They had little time left before they must leave, but he seemed to want to fill every moment attached to her by the lips. With some reluctance she pushed him back gently and smiled at him. The dark threads of lust were etched across his face, and he sighed deeply as he acknowledged that she was stopping this embrace from going any further.

"Know this, my love: all the dreams you may have from now on, I will share with you, whether they be real or not. We are real, our love is real – and, whatever we face when we return, we face together."

Sapphire smiled at him. Her heart was beating fast and loud within her chest. She hoped that this love they shared would be enough to shelter them from whatever lay ahead.

Chapter Twenty

They returned to Fox's grand house just as night began to fall. The last few hours at the beach had been spent making love again, and then sitting on the veranda watching the sunset. Sapphire held the memory in a special place in her mind: she never wanted to forget those last moments of peace. As they walked back towards the house she noticed a bustle of activity at the stables, and many more guards around the borders of the garden. Fox held her hand tightly as they approached. She sensed his mood switch immediately, from relaxed to a warrior once more on guard.

Bear was standing in the doorway, his huge frame casting a shadow across the lawn that looked almost frightening in its size.

"Fox, we have news from the scouts. I am glad you have returned quickly. Things have changed somewhat since your departure."

Sapphire felt her chest clench in anticipation as alarm spread in waves across her body.

Bear smiled at her as they entered the house. "You look well, Sapphire. I hope you enjoyed your time away."

She returned the smile, and looked up at Fox with a softness in her eyes. "Yes, I did, Bear. It was wonderful."

Fox seemed distant suddenly, his face now set in a stern expression.

"Sapphire, my love, go freshen up while I speak with Bear. I am sure Kit will be eager to see you again."

She knew he was dismissing her so that she would avoid further worry at the news he was about to hear. It annoyed her slightly that he still felt she was too fragile to deal with whatever bad news Bear may have for them. The carefree man she had only hours before been tumbling with on the beach was gone, and the warrior had returned. Fierce and focused, he needed no distraction. He kissed her quickly on the lips before releasing her hand and heading into the living area with Bear.

She stood in the hallway for a moment, feeling a little lost. The sudden disconnection from his energy making her waver unsteadily.

193

"Sapphire, how are you? I have missed you terribly." Kit rushed from the kitchen and stood before her with flushed cheeks. Her hands were white from the flour that she had obviously been working with before they had arrived.

Sapphire leant in to embrace her, glad to see the young woman who had become her friend. It grounded her again instantly.

"And I have missed you, Kit. It was wonderful to have some time away with Fox, but I'm pleased to see you."

Kit hugged her back, avoiding touching her with her flour-covered hands. "Come, I have made some fresh bread. You must be hungry."

Sapphire followed her back into the kitchen. She looked over her shoulder just once to see if Fox was within sight. He had disappeared again. It troubled her that once more she did not know what was going on around them.

Bear was standing against the fireplace, stroking his beard slowly as he watched Fox pace up and down the living area. His friend was clearly anticipating bad news.

"How many are gathering against us?" Fox asked.

Bear let out a deep sigh. "More than we anticipated. It seems they know we are coming. In fact, it seems that the queen has been anticipating our attack for some time. We have lost the element of surprise, I'm afraid."

Fox slammed his fist down on the table before him, making it shake slightly. "By the gods, how?"

Bear shook his head. "I have no idea. It seems to me as if Hecta already knew exactly what we were planning. Your father is no longer confident that we should even enter their kingdom."

Fox looked across at his friend with despair in his eyes. "We have no choice now, Bear. We must attack before they make their move. I only hope that we can capture Ebony, as we previously hoped. She is their strongest defence."

Bear scratched his chin and raised an eyebrow in contemplation. "Our scouts have seen no sign of her or Hecta, but their army is gathering in force and it seems they mean to move very soon."

Fox felt his anger flare within his chest. The thought of an attack at any moment made him wish they had never left his hideaway. At

194

least there he could keep Sapphire hidden and safe. He knew, however, that this would always be a temporary thing, and that Sapphire would never be truly safe. Even here on Shaka, in his own kingdom, the threat of Ebony loomed over them.

"Dammit. This is not how I foresaw things."

Bear nodded slowly. "I understand your concern, Fox, but do not doubt that the men of Calafia will fight to the death to protect your wife. As will I."

Fox looked at his friend, a thin smile on his lips. "And for this I am in your debt, my friend. I fear this will not end well, but what is unfolding before us can no longer be avoided. I will contact my father and let Sapphire know things have changed."

Bear nodded, and paused before leaving the room. "The men are ready for a good battle, Fox. Do not despair. In fact I, for one, am personally looking forward to chopping off some heads. It has been too long."

Fox laughed. "Your boldness and courage never cease to surprise me, old friend. Thank you."

Bear chuckled as he left. He was leaving Fox to an empty room, and a heart that was heavy with confusion. Could they win this battle? How could they find the priestess who was so strong with magic that even his father was beginning to doubt the odds? He could not lose Sapphire. It was beyond thinking about. He ran his hands through his hair and pulled it at the roots, his brow furrowed in thought.

"Fuck," he whispered to himself, as he tried to find the courage to tell Sapphire what had transpired.

With a bored expression on his face Hecta pushed the young girl from his lap.

"Leave me now, woman."

She stumbled as he shoved her away from him, her face drawn with confusion at his rejection. Only moments before he had taken her hard and fast, in the most passionate way any man could. She stood staring at him as she covered her naked body with her hands and shivered slightly at his sudden change of mood.

"But, my lord, I thought it pleased you to have me here."

He looked up at her with a slight snarl on his lips. "The pleasure is over. Get out."

She bit her bottom lip and held back the tears that sought to tumble down her cheeks. She paused and looked at him with dark eyes, which glistened slightly in the candlelight.

"Did you not hear me? Get out."

The harsh words shouted into her face made her flinch, and then she took a run for the door and left his chamber. He pushed himself up out of the chair and headed to his bed to find his clothes. His body moved gracefully, his strong muscles flexing as he bent to retrieve his shirt and trousers. Despite the fact that he had just fucked the pretty young serving girl senseless – and relieved himself into her – his agitation still spun around him in angry dark threads.

He was done with waiting, waiting to make a move on the woman who had been constantly causing him problems since she had stepped into her power. Sapphire, dream traveller, pain in his arse. As much as he tried he could not get her out of his head. This was not his only problem. Selling his soul to the priestess, Ebony, had been a big mistake. She owned him now, and it was becoming a drain. They had been hiding within the castle walls of the neighbouring kingdom, watching and waiting for the right moment to take Sapphire. But everything that had seemed so simple had become just the opposite. Sapphire had not left her guardian's side since her arrival on Shaka, and now she had grown in power. He had seen the changes in her before her marriage to Fox. Now she was a formidable foe.

Ebony had become impossible, screaming at everyone around her with a temper that flared at even the mention of Sapphire's name. The queen was a tough woman in her own right but even she was beginning to grow nervous as Ebony had demanded that the army begin to gather in force so that they could attack in the morning.

When they had arrived and taken residence – after convincing the queen that they were about to claim a prize so valuable she would be handsomely rewarded – everything seemed straightforward. Now everything had changed.

Even Ebony seemed anxious about the new magic that flared around the human dream traveller. Hecta remembered the first time he had seen her while she travelled. She was indeed a stunning woman, and the magic that surrounded her was something he had never seen before. He had watched from afar for some time as she stumbled from place to place, his curiosity growing as she blossomed. Before he had had the chance to capture her interest, her guardian had stepped in and claimed her. The memory of their first joining angered him even now. Hecta was the highest-ranking gatekeeper, and it had pissed him off that the rules had been broken when Fox had taken her. Never before had there been such a breach in conduct between traveller and guardian. He had fancied the woman for himself, something to play with for a while. If Fox had not taken her when he had, he could have claimed her as his own.

Ebony had sensed his rage, and whispered of revenge to him. He had no notion of her own intentions at the time, or what she was actually coveting within this strange, intoxicating human. Now he knew and it angered him more.

Ebony would not release him from her service until she had what she wanted, and she wanted Sapphire dead. He was torn inside, racked with guilt and frustration. Part of him wanted her, part of him loathed her. His own magic was strong, and he was able to take whatever he wanted in his own realm. Spending time with Sapphire, even in the briefest of moments, had made him turn into a beast. Her rejection of him – even before he had a chance to make himself known to her – had created a resentment that grew thick and heavy in his chest. His desire to destroy Fox was even greater, but he knew in his heart – which had begun to turn darker each day – that he had never wanted to destroy Sapphire. Ebony had taken his anger and changed it into something despicable. He even despised himself right now. Hence, his mood.

They were ready to attack in the morning, and he knew from the scouts who had been entering the kingdom that the men of Calafia would be ready. There had not been a battle between them for aeons. Ebony had changed that: she was darkness and loathing. The magic she held was powerful and manipulative. There was nothing she could not have, except one thing: Sapphire.

Her face appeared in his mind again and filled his head with conflict. She angered him and excited him at the same time. He had no intention of letting Ebony take her and destroy her, but he would not let Fox keep her either. She would be his, and that was the end of it. Somehow he would find a way.

He gathered his weapons and drew his magic within. He took a deep breath before leaving his chamber to find the priestess who was, no doubt, throwing – in her rage – large, sharp objects at some poor person right at this moment. He was ready for a good fight, but he was also ready for some deception of his own. Ebony had underestimated him, and she had no idea he had grown weary of her oppressive disregard of him.

It was going to be a long night.

Chapter Twenty-One

Sapphire watched her husband undress before her, as she had many times since her arrival on Shaka. They had retired for the remaining part of the night after he had told her the news that the battle they had been anticipating was coming for them sooner than they had expected. Fox had left her for a while after Bear had gone. He had visited his father once more, to convince him that they could still have the upper hand if they were bold enough to storm the castle at dawn. He had returned to her looking sad and weary. She hated to see him so distraught, but knew that she could do nothing to change this. Everything was due to her presence here: her magic, her new secret.

The seeds were still safely hidden in the box beside the bed - she had peeked at them before sliding under the sheets. They had glittered at her innocently in the box, which was a beautiful shade of blue that sparkled with a brilliance that made her eyes grow wide in awe. They were the key to the awakening, the planting of a new awareness that only she could nurture. The thought made her tremble, but she was a changed woman now in more ways than one. She knew her magic had transformed her from an ordinary thirty-something woman to a magical creature who could no longer deny her role in the future of her own world.

Fox stood before her, his eyes dark in the candlelight and his body gloriously naked and strong. She reached for him as he pulled the covers back so that he could slip in beside her. The tattoo on her finger and arm shimmered slightly as he touched her, making her skin jump with electricity. Such was the connection between them now: they were forever bound.

Fox pulled her into his arms, pushed his fingers into her hair, and breathed in her scent with a sigh. "Do not be afraid, my beautiful Sapphire. No harm will come to you, my love. I promise you this."

She shivered at his touch as he stroked her softly across the nape of her neck, his fingers coiling around her hair and skimming her skin. "I'm not afraid, Fox."

He kissed her softly and looked into her eyes with a slight frown on his forehead. "Then I underestimate you, my love. And, as always, I am in awe of your strength and courage."

She watched the tenderness unfold within his eyes and felt a wash of pure love rush over her. "I know in my heart that we will be OK, Fox. I believe it: I feel it in my bones. This cannot change our course. I have seen our future. We will be fine."

Fox held her gaze and nodded slowly. He wished with all his heart that this would be true, and that he would have the strength and conviction to keep her safe. He held her close and kissed her again, with a desperateness that made her whimper against him. Fox knew that this battle would be harsh, and that Sapphire – despite her bravado – had no idea what the sight of death would actually feel like. He, on the other hand, knew only too well the darkness that would overwhelm them tomorrow when the battle began. Death was never an easy thing to face, and a life taken was never easy to stomach.

The new day dawned with a heavy blanket of cloud that hung dark and low on the horizon. It blazed dark red and ominous, like blood coagulating against the landscape. Sapphire stood in the garden facing the oppressive skyline, her head held high and her back straight. She was dressed in black leather, and her hair was tied in one long braid that trailed down her back like a rope. Fox was in the stables with Bear, saddling the horses. Conloach would be joining them soon, and the army was gathering nearby. She could sense them approaching, feel the connecting of their energy as it marched towards them. The sun was just beginning to rise, and she could see a flicker of gold within the deep red clouds which whispered of a hope she clung to desperately that all would be well.

On sensing someone approach she turned around slowly to find Kit behind her. Kit had been crying, and her face was ruddy and wet from tears. Sapphire felt her heart lurch at the sight of her sweet face looking so forlorn.

"Please, Kit, don't cry. We will be fine. I'll be home again before you know it."

Kit stood before her, wringing her hands, her face turned down. "I want to believe you, Saf – truly, I do – but my heart is so heavy I think it will break."

Sapphire stepped towards her and took her in her arms, and hugged her tightly. "I promise you, Kit, that we will return. I have a task for you while we are gone: it is something very special, and I need you to be strong."

Kit looked down at her and sniffed. "Anything, my lady."

Sapphire stepped back slightly and took her hands into her own. "In our room in the box by our bed are some stones that must be guarded well. Under no circumstances must they be taken away from this place. Keep them safe. Hide them if you have to, Kit, but make sure no one finds them if we are delayed."

Kit blinked at her, the tears still fresh on her lashes. She nodded slowly. "Of course, Saf."

Sapphire smiled at her. She knew that Kit would do as she asked and guard them fiercely, if needed. Her body trembled slightly as she felt Fox's presence again behind her. He placed his hand on her shoulder softly.

"It is time, my love," he said. "We must leave now. My father is waiting for us."

Sapphire nodded. She kissed Kit lightly on the cheek before turning away. Her heart was heavy, but she felt stronger now than she ever had. Her magic thrummed within her, and the obsidian necklace pulsed hotly against her skin. She could see Pearl in her mind, and drew strength from the knowledge that she was on the right path. It was time to kick some arse and find some peace at last.

Sapphire had no idea how big their army was until they came face to face with the long, dark shadow advancing towards them. Conloach was beside them, mounted on the largest white stallion she had ever seen. He was dressed in black armour, which glistened like oil in the morning light. The energy around him spun and shivered with shades of purple and gold. She had never seen anything quite so formidable in her life. The ground trembled as his army gathered before them. The steady march of a thousand feet and men on horseback made the earth groan beneath it as it sensed the impending battle, and cried out in its fear.

Fox was beside her, dressed as his father was in black armour: his hair, tied back in leather braiding, made him look like a Viking warrior. Two large swords were strapped to his back. Bear was to her left, mounted on what seemed to be a huge shire horse that stamped impatiently as the army grew closer. He too looked as scary as hell. Sapphire gulped. She felt as if she were suddenly in a movie. The scene that was unfolding before her seemed totally unreal and completely crazy.

She shook her head, almost believing that once more she would wake up in bed at home on Earth with Charlie shaking her, saying, "Come on, Saf. You need to get to work." The thought made her want to laugh out loud with hysteria. How had she come to this point in her life? What in the hell had created this madness? She shook her head. She knew that the reality was standing directly before her, and she was not going to wake up from it. This was the real deal.

"Get on with it," she said to herself quite harshly.

Fox turned to face her and smiled a soft smile that, for a moment, removed the face of the warrior from him.

"The army will move forward first, my love. We will follow behind, then slip into the castle with my father. Do not leave my side at any cost. Do you understand?"

She nodded, feeling her body become cold and the familiar grip of fear starting to spread through her limbs.

Conloach turned and regarded her solemnly. "I will transport us inside once the battle has begun. We will have to be as quick as we can to trace Ebony and trap her before she escapes. I sense that she is well aware of our approach, but is lingering within the castle walls. Stay with Fox until I say otherwise, Sapphire. Whatever happens inside keep your wits about you, and if you feel at any point that you are threatened remove yourself in whatever way is easiest for you back to Fox's home. There will be guards here to protect you."

Sapphire stared at him, a slight frown now on her brow. "Whatever happens I will not leave Fox."

Conloach let out a deep sigh and shrugged, as if admitting defeat. "Do as you will, Sapphire. But – remember – you are holding something that is far more precious than any of us right now, and if Ebony captures you all our futures will turn to dust."

202

Fox fidgeted in the saddle. "It will not come to that, Father. Do not pressure her."

Bear chuckled loudly. "None of us will let that happen, Fox. You do not have to doubt that."

Sapphire bit her lip. She felt the fear begin to leave, and a new wave of emotion slip into her body: anger. She held it to her chest and pulled its dark, twisting energy within her, and asked for it to strengthen her. No one was going to harm her, Fox, or anyone else she cared for, during this ordeal. These people may be strange, magical, and powerful – but she was still part human, and an angry human woman was a force to be reckoned with.

They urged the horses forward and joined the huge line of men that were now gathered en masse. Wolf appeared on his own stallion, his eyes flashing black and silver, a flicker of excitement within them.

"We are ready, my lord."

Conloach dipped his head in acknowledgement. "Then let the battle commence."

Sapphire felt her heart lurch forward to the front of her chest as the men kicked their horses, and the army began to advance at a speed she knew was not humanly possible. The sudden change in energy around her was thick and palpable, intense with the gathering of so many men intent on two things: destruction and mayhem. As they sped towards the neighbouring kingdom Sapphire reached out in her mind to try and discover what lay ahead. She felt a tremble within her own power, which indicated the presence of a great force before them that was ready and waiting for their attack.

Fox was to her side on Midnight, galloping like a horse from Hell. His hair was flying behind him, his body rippling with power. She felt breathless at the sight of him. The noise of horses' hooves rumbling against the ground was so loud that it deafened her for a moment. It seemed that the men on foot – who were not far behind them – must have had superhuman strength and speed, because they were able to keep up with how fast the mounted warriors were advancing.

As they moved across the landscape like a plague of locusts Sapphire could not help but feel that she was heading towards a darkness that even she could not comprehend. Everything became dreamlike around her: the rushing of the wind against her face as they cantered forward and the energy that grew around them, shaking the ground beneath her.

Heat built like a furnace within her chest, and she felt her lungs would explode at any moment. She could hear Bear crying out beside her, a war cry that sent shivers down her spine but excited the blood within her veins. Adrenalin pumped fiercely throughout her body, making her muscles groan at the pressure building up within them.

Suddenly the reality of what they faced became clear before her. An army so great it darkened the landscape in a blanket of terrifying blackness lay ahead of them.

Conloach shouted above the din, "No mercy!"

Fox moved ahead of her, and she had no choice but to move aside as he pushed her away from the line of men so that they would not be crushed in the first line of attack. Conloach was to her right, Bear to her left. They protected her at both sides, pulling away slightly so that the army could advance into the wall of men who were waiting to engage.

Sapphire watched in horror as the battle began. The noise was like thunder in her ears: the clash of steel and bone as the first wave hit full strength was like a tsunami crushing the shore with no mercy. The queen's army was just as powerful as Conloach's, and the men equally as fierce. The scene was brutal, bloody, and horrific.

Sapphire could feel her magic swell and expand around her: the obsidian burned against her skin, pulsing with a new intensity that she had not felt before. Her eyes blurred with tears that stung like acid. She was aware of her horse doing all the work for her, following Fox and Conloach without her assistance. Her energy was flashing around her – a brilliant white, so pure and bright it was almost blinding. She had no control over it, and the thought made her dizzy with fear that she would somehow harm those close to her. She could hardly hear anything over the melee before her, but was acutely aware of Fox screaming at her over the chaos to slow down.

Suddenly, without warning, a warrior came thundering towards her. He had broken through – and she watched in terror as the man drew his sword, ready to attack her. Before he could even come close Fox steered Midnight to intercept, and drew both swords from his back. In one quick swoop he raised his arms above his head and sliced the warrior's head clean off with a scissor action that sent the skull flying through the air, blood spurting in thick bursts from the neck. Sapphire felt herself gag, and her head spun at the horror of the scene before her. Death surrounded her as the men fought like demons in hell. Bear caught another warrior, who had tried to advance with his axe, and he removed the arm that had seconds ago held a spear that was aimed directly at him.

Fox was beside her again, eyes wide, his face now splattered with blood. "Sapphire, stay with me," he shouted at her above the thunderous noise.

She followed him away from the line of battle with Conloach and Bear still beside her, the wind whipping her face viciously. As they retreated to a safer distance Sapphire caught her breath, her energy still pooling around her in silver and white flashes.

The battle raged on before them. The army had advanced, so that they were now behind the worst of the fighting. Sapphire could feel her heart beating so fast within her chest that she thought it would shatter and break. She felt sick to the stomach but held fast to her horse, which stamped with what seemed excitement beneath her.

Fox pulled Midnight to her side and reached across to steady her mount. "My love, are you harmed?"

She shook her head, her eyes wide and filled with fear and her body saturated in adrenalin.

Conloach was beside her now. He dismounted quickly from his stallion and reached up for her. "Come now, Sapphire. We must go while the confusion hides us from Ebony ... she will think we are still within the battle."

Sapphire slipped down into his arms, reassured that she could sense Fox following closely behind. Conloach enveloped her within his hold. His body throbbed with power, which rolled over her own magic in intense waves. Fox was behind her, his body now pressed to her back. She could feel his breath against her neck, panting hard and fast in hot bursts against her skin. The air around them trembled for a moment. She felt herself fall into a dark abyss as they travelled across the short space before them into the queen's castle.

Her eyes were shut, and blackness surrounded her. She could still feel the pressure of the two men against her as they transported inside the castle. She was afraid to open her eyes. Her body was trembling now at the intense reality unfolding around her. With a hard jolt she felt herself stumble slightly as her feet hit solid ground.

Fox was holding her close to his chest. All around them was silent. Sapphire blinked and tried to find her bearings again.

"Are you OK, my love?" Fox whispered softly into her ear, his arms still holding her in a protective embrace.

She was aware of Conloach standing beside her, his energy still pulsing strongly in the darkness. She was afraid to speak, so nodded her head quickly in response to Fox's urgent question. He pulled her closer and moved her forward. They moved through the dark corridor silently, Sapphire worried that her breathing was so loud it would alert anyone close by to their presence.

Conloach moved swiftly, without sound, before them. Fox held her hand and pulled her behind him with an insistence she had never felt in him before. As they turned a corner she became aware of a new energy swelling in the darkness. Conloach stopped dead. His head turned and his eyes narrowed to slits. Fox held her back. Sapphire felt she might faint at any moment, trepidation filled her body like a heavy weight. Only the persistence of her pounding magic held her up.

Without warning Conloach disappeared before her very eyes. He had vanished without a trace.

Fox pulled her with a thrust so hard down the corridor that she felt her arm would be removed from the socket. She could not believe that Conloach had just left them without any warning. Why would he do that? Her heart began to beat even faster at the thought of his loss. She could hear a rushing behind them that was moving closer and closer and gaining distance as Fox ran with her through the darkened corridors. He pulled her into a room to one side and held her back against the wall. His sword was drawn, his body rigid against her. He faced the door and waited for the inevitable to happen. She panted heavily with fear as she waited for whoever – or whatever – was pursuing them to burst through the door. Silence rang in her ears for a moment. Then she slowly realised she could hear a low, thumping noise in the corridor … a sound that made her blood turn cold.

Thump! Thump! Thump! Without warning the door flew open, and a sight so terrifying and gruesome stood before her that she felt her mind switch off and her body become limp. The last thing she heard before she shut down mentally was Fox's war cry bouncing off the walls and the clash of steel ringing in her ears.

Chapter Twenty-Two

Conloach stood silently in the darkness, scanning the area for movement. He had removed himself quickly when the beast had approached: he knew that Fox could take care of the diversion that had been thrown at them. He would regroup with them once he had found Ebony. He could sense her close by, her magic throbbing steadily in the darkness. Without Sapphire the binding spell would not hold for long. He needed her magic to close the spell and trap the priestess indefinitely, but for now he would face her alone. He moved with stealth through the darkened room and pushed his senses outwards as he searched for her within the castle rooms. She knew they were stalking her and had taken precautions. The situation was turning from bad to worse, but there was no turning back now: the events unfolding before them could not be undone.

As he entered another chamber he stepped into a swell of magic so strong it almost knocked him off his feet. She was close. As he quickly wrapped a cloak of protection around himself he gathered his wits and proceeded further into the room. Before him, torches mounted against the wall cast an eerie orange glow across the stone floor, which gave the room the appearance of a glowing furnace. His body shuddered with the instinctual reaction to retreat.

Ebony stepped into the light, a slight smile on her cherry-red lips. "Conloach ... how nice to see you again. It has been such a long time since we last met."

He felt her swell of magic envelop him greedily. It was clutching at his protective cloak, and trying to find a weakness and bring him to his knees. The king, however, was strong, and his magic amplified in response as it grew all the more powerful.

He dipped his head in acknowledgement and moved towards her slowly. "Indeed it has been a long time, Priestess. I see you have been busy gathering more power and weaving your mischievous magic around you."

She laughed and threw her head back with glee, the darkness of her hair shone in the torchlight like black silk. "It is a shame that you will not survive this day, magician. You were foolish to think you could trap me."

From the dark shadows beside her another form moved forward. Hecta revealed himself armed with sword and shield, his face animated with excitement. He was surrounded by tendrils of darkness interlaced with flashes of red and gold that flickered and wavered around him.

Conloach watched them carefully. He noted the thread that tied the gatekeeper to the priestess, almost as if he were held by a leash. Hecta had given Ebony his soul – tied himself to her – which made her magic all the more powerful.

Conloach raised an eyebrow and took a deep breath as he steadied himself for what was about to unfold. "You have always been a little too sure of yourself, Ebony … hence your banishment. There is still time for you to stop this madness."

She tapped her foot impatiently. Her magic was pushing even more against his barrier, making him feel slightly nauseated.

"Madness? I think it would be madness to allow the dream traveller to live and give her magic to such a useless cause, don't you?"

Conloach could sense that she had become even more unstable during her many years of banishment. Clearly insane now, she was power-crazy and even more dangerous than he had anticipated. He began to draw his magic within and start the binding spell that would at least hold her in place until Fox and Sapphire came to his aid. Hecta would be another problem, but one he would have to deal with once Ebony was taken care of.

He whispered the words needed to incant the spell and pulled his magic from within to start the binding process. The air around him wavered and bent slightly, which caused the figures before him to shift as if facing a mirror that had been warped by intense heat. The feeling of nausea grew in the pit of his stomach, and the hairs began to rise on his body.

Ebony stopped smiling, and a dangerous snarl began to spread across her face.

"You are a fool, Conloach." She growled at him, her body twisting and shimmering as the magic augmented and took hold.

Hecta stepped forward. His feet were moving slowly and heavily, as if a great force pushed against him. Conloach continued his mantra. His head was throbbing with the intensity of the magic that poured from within. Sparks of light crackled from his body and thrust outwards, and caused the air around him to sizzle and crack.

Ebony shook her head. She raised her hands up to clutch her skull as she tried to shake off the effects of his magic. He knew that he could not hold her for long, and that he would have very little time left to complete the spell once Sapphire and Fox found him. Hecta continued to advance. The sheer weight of the spell upon him was making his face contort with rage. The priestess pushed back, her own magic growing stronger again as her fury bubbled and spilt out from her body. Thick and black, it spread across the floor towards Conloach like spattered blood. She fought back against him as she pushed against the spell, making it bend and wave as he continued the mantra. His voice was growing louder and louder to deafen the buzzing that now filled his head painfully.

Hecta was making progress. His sword was raised and his body was shuddering, but Conloach held fast. He pulled every last remaining piece of strength from within himself to hold them both, while he willed his son and the dream traveller to arrive and support him. In his mind he called upon the Oracle for strength, and he prayed to the goddess that he might complete this task. His body began to tremble and his muscles gave way slightly as Ebony raised her arms above her head and screamed out in frustration.

Conloach knew that at any moment she would break through and the spell would shatter. Determined to hold on to the last, he felt his eyes close from the pressure building up from beyond the lids. His knees began to buckle as the pain of such furious magic pulsed viciously through his veins. He cried out in desperation for his son, while at the same time reciting the mantra.

Blackness surrounded him as he continued to push against Hecta and Ebony. As his knees finally went from beneath him he felt a wave of new magic join the room. A sharp, twisting pain filled his body as the room was lit up with bright, white light that shook the walls and broke his concentration, and made him crumple to the floor.

Chapter Twenty-Three

Sapphire had lost her senses completely for a moment - the sight of such a grotesque beast before her had made her become the helpless human again. She had never seen anything quite like it. Half man, half bull, the creature towered above them like a dark wall of flesh and fur.

Fox had not hesitated, and had attacked the beast with a ferociousness that scared her witless. She had watched for a second, horrified at the way they clashed against each other. Their movements were so fast that they blurred in and out of sight, and she found it hard to distinguish who had the upper hand.

Her body began to shake, and her magic grew stronger as the anger she had felt earlier fed from the bloody scene before her. Nothing would take her man from her now. Sapphire shook her head and took a deep breath, as she visualised the bisentō spear that she had been training with in Fox's armoury. It appeared in her hand as a loud pop sounded in her ears. Her eyes narrowed and heat began to rise in her chest. Everything suddenly became quite clear around her. Fox and the beast slowed down, as if time was standing still. She could distinguish where each of them stood now: its eyes burning bright red, the beast was ready to thrust its sword into Fox.

Sapphire moved with the speed and agility of a creature so nimble and slight that she could not be of her old world. She flew upwards with the spear and came down so hard upon the beast's head that the tip of the spear pierced its skull with a crunch that reminded her of a butcher's knife opening a chicken carcass. Blood splattered across her face hot and thick as she twisted the spear further into the beast's head. As she landed back on her feet with a soft thud, the room suddenly returned to real time.

The beast slumped heavily to the floor with a low, rumbling groan that made the floor shake for a second. Fox jumped back with his sword above his head, ready for the impact. His eyes were wide, his face ashen. He was breathing heavily and he stared at Sapphire, bewildered for a moment at what she had just done.

Sapphire shrugged her shoulders and kicked the black body to make sure it was well and truly dead.

Fox continued to stare before laughing loudly and lowering the sword as he gasped for air. "Sapphire, my love, you never cease to amaze me."

She smiled at him weakly. Her magic pulsed hotly against her skin as the adrenalin coursed through her veins. "I amaze myself sometimes, Fox."

As his laughter grew softer his head tipped to one side, as if he could now hear a new danger approaching. His eyes grew dark, and the flashes of gold within them cast flickers of light eerily against the wall. "My father needs us," he said, and moved closer to Sapphire.

He grabbed her arm and pulled her out of the room and along the corridor. Sapphire stepped into a cloak of magic that was so thick and powerful it made her gag for a moment. It spread along the corridor like a blanket, choking and consuming in power. On entering another room she was faced with a scene equally as terrifying as the one that she had left behind her. Conloach was on the floor in a heap, his magic still pulsing steadily around him. Ebony was above him, suspended in the air like a banshee – and Hecta, with his sword raised, was ready to strike the great magician at his feet.

But most shockingly of all … the Oracle was standing before them, her arms above her head, white light spilling from all around her and lighting up the room like a bolt of lightning that illuminated the room in pure brilliance.

Fox skidded to a halt and caused her to bump straight into him. Sapphire blinked, her eyes blinded for a moment. As Fox raised his sword, ready to attack Hecta, she felt her body lift upwards and out so that she was no longer grounded within the room.

Time stood still again. Hecta was in the perfect pose to strike Conloach. The priestess was ready to break free from the binding spell. Fox was a motionless warrior, his sword drawn to block the gatekeeper from killing his father. Sapphire felt time itself shift and spin around her. She was floating weightless above them all, and looking down with wonder.

The Oracle turned her head and smiled at her, a smile so sweet and pure it made Sapphire feel like sobbing like a baby. Her eyes

211

glittered blue and silver and her hair was silver-white, floating around her head like glitter.

"Sapphire, my child," said the Oracle, "It is time to embrace the power within you and put an end to this scene before you. I give you my blessing and love, dream traveller. Blessed be." And then she vanished.

Sapphire was back inside her body. The room spun before her. The magic was cloying and pawing at her body as Ebony screamed loudly for release. Fox caught the blow Hecta threw down, and sparks cascaded from their swords with a deafening clash.

She sucked air into her lungs, closed her eyes, and pulled down, deep down within her body to find the source of her magic.

Hecta had pulled back from Conloach and moved to the back of the room. Fox stood over his father, guarding him like a lion protecting its cubs. As she gathered her magic and pulled it out – with a painful burst of energy from her chest – the room shook and groaned under the pressure. She focused on the priestess, stepped towards the magician, and placed her hand against his back so that she could suck up the last of his powerful magic and the binding spell, which threatened to break at any moment.

She watched Hecta drop his sword and close his eyes, his own magic swelling around him and expanding and puffing out like a bloated fish. She could see a long tendril of darkness flicker and waver between him and Ebony. It began to break and shatter as Hecta struggled against it. He was breaking free from her grip. Ebony wailed in fury as Hecta broke free from his bonds and her magic diminished slightly as he stepped back, panting.

He looked across at Sapphire directly into her eyes, a strange look of regret in his expression as he mouthed to her across the room, "I am sorry." Then he too vanished into thin air.

Ebony thrashed and spun within the bindings of the spell. She knew her fight had been in vain. Without the gatekeeper to help her she was not strong enough to break free from the magic that Conloach had trapped her in. Sapphire kept one hand on Conloach, holding him steady but drinking from his energy. The other hand lifted high and was aimed at the woman struggling above her. With a deep, gasping breath she freed the magic within her and directed it at Ebony with a cry of triumph. The bolt of pure white-hot magic shot from her to the priestess and she was illuminated for a moment, so beautifully that it took Sapphire's breath away. Ebony stared at her in disbelief, her face a picture of awe and confusion, before she shattered into a million tiny pieces and disintegrated into dust at their feet.

Sapphire fell to her knees, her body weak from the use of such powerful magic. The pulsing of magic around them stopped and caused the walls to groan in relief. Fox dropped his sword and crouched down beside her. His father lay still and seemingly lifeless on the cold floor.

"Sapphire, my love, are you OK?"

She gasped for breath. She was shaking from head to toe. Slowly her strength began to return. Her body tingled all over, and goosebumps were travelling across her skin. The room smelt rotten, like sulphur. All around them was quiet and still.

"I'm fine, Fox. Is your father still alive?"

Fox placed his hand on his father's neck to check for a pulse. His face filled with concern. "He is breathing, but it is shallow. We have to get out of here."

She turned to face the pile of dust before them. It glittered in the dark, like a pile of black diamonds.

"I killed her. I didn't mean to kill her, Fox. I don't know what happened."

As he lifted Conloach into his arms Fox shook his head.

"She is not dead, Sapphire. The essence of Ebony remains within the dust. It must be gathered and taken with us so that we can keep it safe, or she may be able to manifest again."

Sapphire gawped at the pile of dust. How could such a thing happen? It made no sense to her. She nodded slowly and stepped cautiously towards the dust. She then held her hands out and visualised a suitable vessel in which to place the seemingly innocent remains. A small box appeared within her palm, and she quickly bent down to scoop up the pile of glittering powder. It felt hot to touch, and her body shivered as she touched it. Fox had lifted his father on to his shoulder so that he lay slumped across him, still unconscious. This was no mean feat, as Conloach was a big man.

Sapphire handed the box to Fox and stepped back and stared wide-eyed for a moment.

"How do we get out of here without your father to help us?"

Fox placed the box inside his armour and gestured for her to come closer. "I will transport us, my love, but you will need to help me. Visualise us back home, Sapphire. You can make my magic stronger by thought alone."

She nodded and stepped within the circle of his free arm. As she closed her eyes she felt Fox open up his magic. It nuzzled against her softly, a welcome balm to this horrible situation. Once more Sapphire called upon her own magic and felt them shift and fly out of the room. She pictured their home within her mind ... and saw Kit sitting at the kitchen table, her head in her hands, filled with despair.

Her chest tightened, and her head filled with pain for a moment before it released with a sharp jolt ... and she found herself standing on solid ground again inside the house, with Fox clinging to her as if his life depended on it.

They stumbled back from each other, Fox almost dropping Conloach as they landed. Voices began to shout loudly as a new chaos began to unfold around them. Strange men appeared and helped Fox with his father. Fox barked commands at them to fetch the healer. Sapphire was ready to crumple to the floor, her face still covered in blood and her mind spinning like a top. Just as she felt her knees give way the sweet face of Kit appeared before her with eyes bright and wide, and a smile so big on her lips that it made fresh tears begin to fall from her eyes like raindrops once more.

Kit caught her before she hit the ground and held her close, laughing and crying at the same time.

"Oh, Sapphire, you are home ... you are home!"

Sapphire smiled softly and closed her eyes.

It was over. At last the horror of battle was gone and she was home, safe and unharmed.

Chapter Twenty-Four

Pearl looked up from her knitting at the tiny sprite who was buzzing around her head in a frenzy.

"What is troubling you, little one? I am busy right now, my friend." The sprite continued his furious fluttering around her head, tiny sparks of light shooting from his body in a mini cascade of silver glitter. "OK, OK, I will come with you ... but I need to finish this scarf, as the snow has been falling heavily and I want to keep myself warm in the coming weeks."

With some reluctance she placed her knitting to one side and stood up and smoothed down her skirt. She followed the sprite as he whizzed down the hallway. The sprite made the candlelight waver and flicker at the draft it caused as he flew past the glass holders lining the darkened corridor. It was well past midnight. The cool night air crept under the doorway with icy fingers, making Pearl shiver a little as she reached for her shawl.

The sprite circled her head again. He was chattering to her with agitation and a sense of urgency that began to trouble Pearl.

"I'm coming ... I'm coming. Stop your chatter."

She reached for the doorknob and hesitated for a moment. She had suddenly sensed something outside that made her skin begin to crawl with goosebumps. After steadying herself she opened the door and looked outside into the garden, which was covered in a thick covering of white snow. It glittered in the moonlight like a beautiful blanket made from tiny diamonds. All was still, the air crisp and clear.

After pulling on her boots she gathered the shawl around her shoulders and headed out into the garden, her breath coming out in puffs of white mist before her. Her feet crunched steadily across the snow, which was as yet undisturbed and perfectly flat. The sky above her was completely clear and scattered with stars, which blinked and shone brightly against the darkness. Her garden seemed to throb steadily with its own heartbeat: the plants and vegetation were in hibernation beneath the blanket of snow. The sprite settled on her shoulder and clung to her hair. He was hiding behind the grey locks that fell to her shoulders. She could feel his body tremble slightly, and his breath warm and soft against the skin on her neck.

"Do not fret so, my little friend. All is well." As she walked towards the edge of the garden she felt her chest tighten and all her senses come alive. A dark shadow moved across the gateway in front of her and caused her to stop still. Her heart was beating loudly in her chest.

"Who's there?" The sound of her voice seemed loud against the still of the night, and the sprite snuggled closer into her neck.

The shadow moved forward ... tall, imposing, and dangerous. "Such a pleasant evening for a stroll, old lady. It is a shame I cannot enter your garden and admire its beauty more closely."

Pearl stepped forward. Her magic was starting to draw around her in a protective shield. "Show yourself, stranger. It is not polite to hide within the shadows."

The dark shadow stepped forward into the moonlight to reveal features which were now clear in the silver-blue haze that cast a line of light across a man's face. Hecta stared back at her. He was smiling at her, his eyes flashing red and black with amusement.

"Hecta ... what brings you here tonight?" Her body was shaking slightly now, but she remained steadfast and tried to hide her fear now that the gatekeeper was standing so close to her home.

Hecta moved forward further, and placed his hands on the wooden gate. It seemed ridiculous that such a tiny frame could be keeping him at bay ... but Pearl knew it was the wards she had placed around her boundary that held him fast, and not the gate itself.

"Can I not just pay you a visit from time to time, old woman? It has been some time since I visited this realm."

Pearl lifted her chin and placed her hands on her hips. "You are not welcome here, Gatekeeper. You know that."

He tilted his head to one side and smiled broadly, his teeth glinting with a dangerous snarl. "It seems I am no longer welcome in many places, which angers me somewhat ..."

Pearl sighed deeply. "What do you want?"

He remained, leaning casually against the garden gate, and began to tap his fingers against the wooden frame in a slightly agitated rhythm. "What I want, old woman, is beyond my reach just now ...

but soon this will change, and I sense you will be able to help me with that."

Pearl felt her chest grip even tighter. Sapphire ... she must be in danger. Why else would the gatekeeper be here?

"What have you done to Sapphire? Where is she?"

His finger-tapping continued, slightly faster now, as if he were growing even more angered at the mention of her name. "Nothing. I have done nothing to the dream traveller."

Pearl stepped forward, her own anger rising now within her belly. "I don't believe you, Hecta. If you have harmed her in any way you will feel my own anger ... something that you would not like very much."

He laughed and raised his hands to his head, and clasped his hair in frustration. "Such threats, old woman. You are amusing. No harm has come to Sapphire. She is safe for now."

Pearl watched him for a moment. She could sense something else within his mood, something she could not quite understand. He seemed conflicted in his thoughts. Very strange.

"Then leave this place, Hecta. You are upsetting my friends, and – quite frankly – I do not want you lurking at my gate."

He ran his hands across his face as if in desperation. "You cannot stay inside forever, old woman."

Pearl raised an eyebrow and took a deep breath. "Are you threatening me now, Gatekeeper?"

He stepped back slightly so that his face was now in shadow again and chuckled deeply. "I will see you again, old woman. Sleep well." And then he was gone.

Pearl realised she was shaking now from head to toe. The sprite was still attached to her neck, his tiny hands gripping her skin just a little too tightly and pinching her in his fear. She shook her head, turned around slowly, and headed back to the cottage. She sensed a shift within the energy around her boundary and knew that Hecta had left her realm again. After removing her snow-covered boots at the door she closed it behind her and stood in the hallway for a moment, breathing slowly and calmly to regain her sense of equilibrium.

What did he mean by saying that Sapphire was safe for now? What had changed for her? Was she coming back to Earth again? Her head spun with confusion. It had been such a long time now since Sapphire had left them and since her departure life had moved along quietly, with little fuss or bother. Was that about to change? Pearl headed back into her little living room and the warmth of her open fire, and sat down in the armchair. She lifted her hand to find the sprite, who was still nestled within her hair. After prising him out she looked down at her palm at his tiny face, which was staring up at her wide-eyed and scared.

"Do not worry, little one, I will not let him harm you. He cannot enter our home, I promise you that."

He fluttered up on tiny wings to hover in front of her face before flying off quickly and disappearing up the stairs. Pearl picked up her knitting again and began to finish her task. The tick-tack sound of the needles added a sense of calm again as she tried to push away the worry that seeped like a dark fog across her mind.

In the morning she would visit Charlie just to make sure she was OK, and that the wards she had placed around her home when Sapphire had left were still in place.

Just to be safe … just to be sure.

Yes, that is what she would do tomorrow.

Chapter Twenty-Five

Sapphire felt as if she had been beaten with a very large stick, as she tentatively slipped down further into the hot water of the bathtub. She had finally managed to remove the last remaining traces of blood from her face and hair, and let out a deep sigh of relief that she was at last clean from the dirt of battle and safe again. Once they had stabilised Conloach and established that he was out of danger, Fox had returned to the castle with his father and the healer. The house was quiet now. The day had slipped away and the sky was turning darker as night approached.

Sapphire felt weary to the bone. The adrenalin from the battle earlier that day had now drained from her body – and this made her feel as if she could fall asleep right now, in the bathtub. Her eyes were shut and her body was floating in the water as she heard someone enter the room.

"Sapphire, are you hungry?" Kit was standing beside her. Sapphire could sense the soft pulse of her sweet, gentle magic. It felt soothing against her troubled mind.

Without opening her eyes, she nodded slowly. "Yes, actually ... I am a little hungry, Kit."

"I will bring something up for you, my lady. Would you like me to help you out of the bath?"

Sapphire struggled to open her eyes. She sat up a little, and smiled weakly. "No, I'm fine, Kit. Just some food would be nice."

The young maid smiled at her before turning quickly and leaving her alone once more in the bathroom. Sapphire pushed herself up with some difficulty. Every muscle in her body groaned in protest. Despite the strength of her growing magic she felt utterly human right now, and exhausted to the point of passing out. Her stomach rumbled loudly, and she placed her hand against it to try and soothe the gripping pains within her belly.

As she tried to lift herself out she suddenly felt warm hands slip under her arms and pull her up from the water in a smooth, gentle slide. Fox was back. He kissed her neck softly as he gathered her, dripping wet, into his chest. "My love, you are exhausted."

Sapphire wrapped her arms around his neck and noted with amusement that he was now soaking from her wet body. She snuggled against him. His warmth was soothing, his body firm and strong against her own as he carried her back into the bedroom. Fox wrapped her in a towel. He brushed her wet hair away from her face and stared down at her with a look of relief.

"You are safe now, my beautiful wife."

Sapphire smiled back at him and nodded slowly. He plumped the pillows behind her head and rubbed her arms with the towel as if she were a small child. The gesture made her heart swell with love for this wonderful man, who was so precious to her.

Kit returned with a tray laden with food. After placing it beside the bed she watched Fox as he continued to dry Sapphire.

"Will there be anything else you need tonight, my lord?"

Fox continued to stare at Sapphire, his eyes dark and hooded and filled with their own love and the promise of something more.

"No, Kit, thank you. You may leave us now."

She curtseyed, the smile still fixed on her lips.

Fox leant forward, kissed Sapphire gently on the lips, and walked back into the bathroom. Sapphire looked across at the tray and sighed again, wishing that someone could actually feed her and save her the bother of getting up. Fox returned with her hairbrush and sat down beside her. He pulled her up gently and began to brush through the tangles in her long, white-blonde hair. He was smiling at her softly as he brushed with long, smooth strokes through the tangled strands.

"Eat, my love, before you fall asleep."

Sapphire reached across for some bread, broke off a piece, and took a bite. It was warm and soft, and deliciously sweet on her tongue. The taste instantly soothed her.

"How is your father?" she mumbled, between mouthfuls.

Fox stroked her cheek gently, and placed the brush to one side. "He is recovering well. Willow is the best healer we have, and she seems confident he will be back to his old self tomorrow."

Sapphire continued to eat, her energy lifting a little as the food slipped down into her belly.

"So soon? That is good. He is an amazing man, Fox. Without him holding the spell, Ebony would have escaped, and we would not be here now."

After reaching for his own share of the food Fox nodded solemnly. "My father is the strongest magician ever known ... but it was you, my love, who saved us. Your magic and strength of will gave us the advantage."

They ate in silence for a moment. Sapphire was watching her beautiful man with a sense of wonder that he seemed so unaffected by the events that had unfolded earlier that day. She knew without a doubt that he had seen many battles in his lifetime and had been able to process the death and destruction far easier than she had. The images in her head of what had happened were still flickering in and out like a very bad dream. Something she wished never to witness ever again.

"Actually, Fox, I believe it was the Oracle who tipped the balance."

Fox frowned, a look of confusion on his face. "The Oracle?"

Sapphire gulped down some of the water Kit had brought her and nodded. "Yes. She held the spell until we arrived ... Please tell me you saw her."

Fox shook his head slowly and regarded her for a moment. She watched his face flicker with mixed emotions. "I did not, my love."

Sapphire sighed. "Perhaps I'm going mad again."

Fox laughed softly and reached out to touch her face again. He traced a line of sparks across her skin, which made her shiver in response to his light touch.

"The Oracle does not always reveal herself to us all, my love. She is the most sacred of beings and often works her magic in ways that are unseen to the lesser of her subjects."

Sapphire laughed. "So what does that make me, then?"

Fox stopped chewing and stared at her with a hunger, not just for food, in his eyes.

"A beautiful and pure spirit, who the Oracle herself has blessed and watches over. Truly, you are a most special and sacred being."

Sapphire chuckled. "Oh, please, Fox, don't blow my ego up so much. I'm just me."

He shook his head, obviously thinking she would never fully understand just how important she was. They ate in silence for a while, with Fox passing her morsels of food and encouraging her to take more as she faltered.

He took one last bite of food, slowly slid the towel away from her chest, and slipped his hand across her breast ... lingering for a moment on her nipple, which puckered and hardened under his touch.

"You underestimate yourself, my love. Just look at how wonderful you are ... so beautiful, so intoxicating."

Sapphire shivered slightly. She closed her eyes and felt her body respond eagerly to his touch. The piece of bread she was holding slipped from her fingers on to the floor. She felt Fox press down on to her, his lips touching the skin on her neck with the lightest of touches.

"Never forget how blessed you are, my Sapphire ... how wonderful you are." His voice trailed away in her fuzzy mind as he began to trail kisses across her body, softly caressing her with his warm, wonderful tongue. She was so very tired, so utterly exhausted, that as Fox began to make love to her she felt as if she had slipped into another dream ... A dream so wonderful and soothing that she never wanted to wake up from it again.

Sleep had hit Sapphire hard and fast after their lovemaking, and it took her away into a black abyss of silence. Her body and mind were exhausted, but her dreaming did not seem to care. She realised that she had travelled again, and felt the warmth of hot sun on her skin and recognised the smell of incense in her nostrils. A breeze ran warmly across her skin. She was so hot that her body felt covered in a fine sheen of sweat. The sensation was slightly uncomfortable, and she groaned faintly as she tried to open her heavy eyelids to find out where she was.

Sapphire found herself lying on a padded mattress on what seemed to be a rooftop terrace. She blinked her eyes against the brightness of the sun and pushed herself up. She looked around in wonder. A man was calling out in a strange language from across the rooftops, a deep wailing that sounded soothing and mystical: the call for prayers. She stood up, and slowly realised that she was dressed in

222

a long cotton dress in a deep blue that flowed to the floor. She walked silently to the edge of the roof and rested her hands on the stone wall as she looked out across the landscape.

A wide river, its banks lush and green, stretched out from left to right in front of her as far as she could see. Small white boats with huge sails that billowed in the breeze drifted along the water. She sensed a new presence behind her on the rooftop and looked back over her shoulder. A wide smile slipped on to her lips as she recognised her new companion. She reached out her hand for him and took a step away from the wall. Fox stepped forward and gathered her in his arms as he pulled her close to his chest

"What a beautiful place you have brought us to, Sapphire. Do you know where we are?"

She breathed in his familiar scent, and smiled before turning back to look out over the river.

"I think we are in Egypt, Fox. This is the Nile, and they are calling for prayers."

Fox rested his chin on her head and sighed deeply. "A beautiful sound, my love, a beautiful place ... Why do you think we are here?"

She shook her head slowly and frowned a little, just as confused as Fox that she should be back on Earth again – and in such a place. "I have no idea."

Fox squeezed her gently and kissed the top of her head before releasing her. "Shall we take a look around while we are here?"

Sapphire nodded. She had never been to Egypt before, and even if this was another dream she knew without a doubt that being here would later unfold something else that was of great importance. She could feel this knowledge within her bones, deep inside her belly.

They left the rooftop. Sapphire noted with appreciation that Fox was dressed suitably in cream linen trousers and a shirt that was cut to show off his upper body in all the right places. He would stand out a mile, but she did not care. This was her dream, and with all her new magic and understanding she knew they would be safe. They headed down inside the building, which seemed to be a hotel full of tourists and locals who stared at the pair of them with wide eyes. They went out on to the street outside. The sights, smells, and sounds hit them as they stepped out of the cool lobby hand in hand.

Hot air filled their lungs. Sapphire looked around. The bustle of the street before them made her head spin for a moment.

"This way." She pulled Fox with her, took a turn to the right, and headed out towards the river, which stretched out before them. She could feel a pulsing within her chest, and her heart rate quickened as they walked, which guided her as to which way to turn. Fox followed her silently, his grip light but steady on her hand. Everyone stared at them as they walked. Heads were turning, and people were talking about them in whispers. They must have looked like two exotic creatures striding down the street with purpose. Sapphire stopped abruptly at a shop that sold tourist trinkets, paused at the window, and looked in.

"I need to do something before we leave, Fox. It won't take long." She pushed the door open. The bell tinkled above them, and a handsome-looking local looked up with curiosity as they entered. He smiled at them, his eyes growing wide at the sight of such a wild-looking man with his white-blonde companion.

"Welcome. How may I help you today?"

Sapphire looked around the shop, still holding Fox by the hand.

"Do you sell postcards?"

The man stepped from around the counter, smiling broadly. "Yes, of course. We have many. Do you need a stamp?" he asked with a slight chuckle.

Sapphire returned the smile as she noticed the large stand full of pictures of pyramids, sphinxes, and temples.

"Yes, please, and could I borrow a pen?"

The young man nodded, and gestured for her to choose before heading back to the counter.

Fox stood beside her, a wry smile on his lips. "A message for someone, my love?"

Sapphire picked out a card with a 'Wish You Were Here' and a river scene with white feluccas splashed across the front.

She smiled at him warmly. "Yes."

He nodded and watched her walk across to the counter and take the pen from the young man, who continued to beam at her with slightly love-struck eyes.

She quickly scribbled a message on to the card and handed it back to him.

"How much do I owe you?"

He blinked, mesmerised by the beautiful, strange woman before him. "A gift, beautiful lady."

Fox stepped forward a little. Sapphire sensed his energy change, which caused her body to tingle softly. She laughed at his sudden show of possessiveness.

"Thank you."

"You are most welcome," he whispered in response, before she turned on her heel, took a slightly disgruntled Fox by the hand, and dragged him away.

Back out on the street Sapphire chuckled. "I love the way you are so protective, Fox."

He growled softly, pulling her closer, and draped his arm across her shoulders. "I did not like the way he was looking at you."

They headed across the road to the riverbank, which sloped before them in a gentle, green curve. The sunlight hit the water in a dazzling display of crystal lights, the distinct and hypnotic sound of the call for prayers was still drifting in the wind.

As they reached the bank Sapphire stopped still and closed her eyes. She could feel the thrum of her magic inside her as it trembled and skittered excitedly.

"I think this is one of the places I need to bring the seeds to, Fox. I feel it within my body."

He was standing close to her, but not touching. The noise of the street behind them was quieter now, with just the gentle sound of the water lapping against the riverbank.

"Right here?"

Sapphire listened intently for any inner wisdom that may suddenly decide to guide her. Nothing. Just the constant thrumming in her chest and stomach.

"Not right here, but I sense not far away. We need to come back another time. I think this is just a small step in the right direction, Fox."

She opened her eyes and held out her hand for Fox, who wrapped his fingers around her own. She could sense her energy changing slightly as they walked along the riverbank hand in hand. The pull back to Shaka was strong, and she realised that the travelling would be coming to an end very soon.

225

"Thank you for following me here, Fox. I always feel safe when you are by my side."

He squeezed her fingers gently. "I will always follow you, my gorgeous wife, wherever you may go."

She stopped walking and pulled him against her and nuzzled her face into his chest as she felt the heat of the sun on her back.

"Then follow me home again."

He wrapped his arms around her waist, lowered his face to hers, and kissed her lips softly.

"As you wish, my love."

Chapter Twenty-Six

Charlie poured some milk into her extra sweet coffee, leant back against the kitchen counter, and sighed deeply. She had just finished a piece that she had been working on all morning, and was ready to take a much-needed break with a cigarette and some caffeine. She took her steaming coffee mug to the little kitchen table, sat down, and lifted her tobacco pouch ready to make her cigarette just as she heard a knock at the front door. It was 11.30 a.m. and she wasn't expecting anyone today. Nathan was at work and, since Sapphire had left, she had very few unexpected visitors. She shrugged her shoulders, left the tobacco pouch on the table and padded to the front door in her fluffy slippers. It was cold outside. It had been snowing for two days now, and she pulled her woollen cardigan around her body tightly as she reached for the door handle.

"Who is it?" she called out before opening the door. She was always a little more cautious nowadays. Since the fire six months ago she had never quite felt completely at ease. The persistent niggling in the pit of her belly – despite the report saying the fire had been caused by an electrical fault – told her otherwise, and she had vowed never to let her guard down again. As she hesitated at the door she heard a stamping of feet, as if the person outside was indeed covered in snow.

"It's Pearl, Charlie, just paying a quick visit."

A big smile grew on Charlie's face. Since Sapphire had disappeared, the old woman had begun to visit her from time to time. Her visits were most welcome and Charlie enjoyed her company. Sometimes she would go to Foxglove and spend the evening with her, sampling her weird and wonderful home cooking. It was her last link to her friend, which was something she now cherished.

"Oh, crikey, Pearl. Sorry ... I wasn't expecting anyone. I'll let you in ... hang on a sec."

Charlie unlocked the door and pulled it open. She faced a happy-looking Pearl, who was swaddled in what looked like an oversized rug and *Doctor Who* scarf which almost touched the floor in multicoloured squares. Charlie resisted the urge to burst out laughing. Pearl had the most eclectic of tastes when it came to clothing, but the old woman was such a wonderful person she could forgive her for such awful colour coordination.

"Come in ... come in, Pearl. It's so good to see you."

Pearl slipped off her Wellington boots before stepping inside the cottage. Thoughtful as ever, she placed them on the mat before stepping forward to hug Charlie and engulfing her in the scent of lavender and roses.

"I thought you might be out working at the back, but knew you usually have a break around this time."

Charlie beamed at her and, after shutting the door behind them, helped her take off the huge woollen scarf and rug-sized shawl.

"Well, you were spot on with your timing as usual, Pearl. I have just made myself a coffee. Would you like some tea?"

Pearl followed her into the kitchen which, with her occasional visits, had recently become familiar to her. "Yes, that would be lovely, Charlie. Some peppermint, if you have some."

Charlie took a big sip of her own coffee before heading over to the kettle again to give it one more boil before adding the tea bag.

"Such a nice surprise, Pearl. I was thinking about popping over to see you soon. It's just been so cold, I haven't ventured out for a while. I, for one, hate the cold. Much more of a summer girl, that's me."

Pearl watched her from across the table and looked for any signs of recent trouble that may be etched across Charlie's pretty features, but she noticed nothing unusual in her manner. Charlie continued to babble about the cold weather as she finished making the tea.

"What brings you over on such a horrible day, Pearl? Is everything OK?"

Pearl took the mug Charlie handed her, and smiled at her sweetly. "Just thought I would check up on you, my dear. It has been a little while since I visited you last, and I wondered if you had heard from Sapphire recently."

Charlie stopped still, her eyes growing wide as she contemplated the thought of Sapphire actually making contact again. She shook her head, sat down opposite the old woman, and reached for her coffee slowly. "No, I haven't, Pearl. Not a word in six months. To be honest, I'm a bit cross with her. Not a single call or note. I know she said in her letter that she may not even come back, but I didn't believe that for a second. I can't believe that she has actually vanished without a trace again. I keep dreaming about her. Weird, really. Sometimes they seem so real. I actually dreamt she was standing in my bedroom one night. I swear, honest to God, that she was actually standing over me. It was a little unnerving, I can tell you. Nathan thinks I had too much to smoke that night, but sometimes I just feel as if she is still here." She paused and took a sip of the coffee, her eyes misting over a little as she remembered her friend. "I miss her terribly, Pearl."

Pearl nodded and sighed. "I miss her too, Charlie, but I do feel quite strongly that she will contact us again very soon. She may even be back to visit."

Charlie's face lit up suddenly, animated at the thought that her friend may return to see her again. "Oh, I do hope you're right, Pearl. I know that if anyone can sense something like that it would be you."

Pearl sipped her tea tentatively, eyes raised to the ceiling for a second as if she was tuning into some other channel for a moment. Charlie had seen her do this before. It made the old lady look like the crazy old witch she knew she actually was – and she found it a little odd, but comforting at the same time.

"You must understand, Charlie, that Sapphire had no choice but to leave when she did. There were many things happening in her life at the time that could not really be explained, and she did feel that she may not be able to come back … But that time has passed, and I know that she will return very soon. I want you to be prepared for that, and also that she may not be the old Sapphire who you remember."

Charlie leant forward, eager to hear more. "Uh-huh … and what exactly does that mean?"

Pearl smiled and leant back in her chair as she cradled the hot tea carefully in her hands. "It means that some things in this life are transformed and reborn to become bigger and brighter than they were before … like the chrysalis that turns into the butterfly."

Charlie laughed loudly, her curls bobbing up and down as she did. "You talk in riddles, Pearl. Honestly, between you and Saf, sometimes I have no fucking idea what you are trying to tell me."

229

Pearl continued to smile. "Just trust me on this."

Charlie tapped her feet happily under the table, excitement beginning to fill her belly at the thought that Sapphire may just come home again. "Do you think that she and Fox will stay a while if they do come back?"

Pearl shrugged and raised an eyebrow. "Maybe for a while. I am not sure of that, young lady, but I would like to think they will. We shall see."

They sat in a comfortable silence for a moment, sipping their drinks. Pearl looked around the kitchen with keen eyes, looking for signs that the wards had not been broken recently, and that the house was still safe from any unwanted visitors, that is, Hecta.

"Tell me, Charlie, have you had any other visitors recently?"

Charlie looked confused for a moment. "No, only the usual. Why?"

Pearl looked down at her teacup and tapped her finger against the china absently. "Oh, no reason … just wondering."

Charlie frowned, not buying the casual way Pearl was being inquisitive about 'visitors'.

"Is there something else I should be aware of, Pearl?"

Pearl stared at her, the whites of her eyes bright and clear, making Charlie feel a little wary of her suddenly piercing gaze.

"Just be careful, my dear. Only invite people into your home that you know and trust, that's all."

Charlie put her mug down and crossed her arms in front of her chest, head tilted to one side. "Oh, no! You don't just say something like that without good reason, Pearl. Come on. Spill the beans."

Pearl sighed deeply before answering. "I just have a feeling that not only will Sapphire be returning soon, but perhaps some of the bad luck that had been following her before her departure may be as well. I just want you to be safe and alert, Charlie. Just in case."

Charlie blinked back at her. The hairs on the back of her neck had started to rise at the thought of something nasty happening again. She remembered the man at the festival, the lightning bolt, and the fire at the cottage. Pieces of the very weird and strange puzzle began flitting around in her head and creating a very uneasy feeling in the pit of her stomach. She licked her lips slowly. Suddenly they had become quite dry.

"Tell me, Pearl, did you ever get the feeling that there was something a bit odd about Fox? And the fact that some seriously weird shit was starting to happen around Sapphire when he suddenly stepped into her life? I might come across as a little daft, but I'm far from that ... and I know for sure that he had something to do with all the crazy, fucked-up shit that happened just before they left."

Pearl swallowed another gulp of tea, her eyes downcast for a moment. She had opened this conversation up, and knew Charlie would not let it drop. "Well ... yes, Charlie, he was very different – and I will not deny that it seemed more than just coincidence that some terrible things happened around the time they met ... And I wish you would not cuss quite so much, my dear. It is quite unladylike."

Charlie smiled warmly. "Don't change the subject, Pearl. But sorry, yes, I do swear a lot. Sorry for that. I'm just honest with my emotions."

Pearl fiddled with the button on her cardigan and shook her head a little. "Some things are just a little too much for our brains to translate, Charlie. I don't think you are really ready just yet to hear the truth as to who Fox is, and why Sapphire seemed to be having such a hard time."

Charlie was beginning to feel a little agitated now. Pearl had obviously turned up to check whether she was OK ... and that meant there was a possible threat heading her way, now that Sapphire was coming back on to the witch radar. She just wished Pearl could stop treating her like an idiot, and be honest with her for once.

"Pearl – seriously – if there is something you need to tell me then just do it. I'm a big girl. I can handle crazy: my whole life has been one big crazy. Meeting Saf and getting caught up in her weirdness was actually not that strange for me."

Pearl nodded. "I know, Charlie. You are a clever young lady, just as Sapphire was ... I mean is. It is just that I think we should wait for some word from her before we jump into the truth pool."

Charlie stood up and took her mug to the sink. This conversation was turning from casual to strange to extremely mind-blowing. What did Pearl mean when she said, 'Before we jump into the truth pool'? Was there more to Sapphire's sudden road trip with Fox than she had actually thought? The letter Sapphire had left her had been ambiguous, to say the least. It had been left open with a 'Maybe I will show up on your doorstep soon … or just maybe you will never see me again'. If it had been anyone else but Sapphire she would have cursed them to hell and back. The fact that she had also left her such a huge amount of money was also totally weird. Who had that kind of cash? Who would give it all away just like that? It had been six months since Sapphire left, and no word until now. Well, no word from Sapphire. Pearl, on the other hand, was really making her feel her friend had indeed been in contact with her. She needed a smoke to to give her the headspace to be able to think about the riddles Pearl was casting.

"OK, Pearl, I get it. For now you don't want to blow my mind with whatever weird and wonderful truth there is about Saf and Fox… but come on, I can handle it. Just keep me in on any updates you get on your witchy newsfeed. It would be nice to have a heads-up if someone is about to burn down my cottage again."

Pearl twitched nervously. She had no idea if Hecta would actually try to contact Charlie or cause any havoc again. She seriously doubted that he would be that bold. But his last visit to her did have her worried, and she would hate to think that – while Sapphire was out in the vast, unknown universe, travelling around with her guardian – her human friend would be suffering. She pushed the thought to one side and made a mental note to increase the protection around both their homes tonight, when the moon was full again … just to be safe.

"Nothing bad is going to happen, Charlie. I would never allow it, but I do want you to be vigilant. My 'witchy newsfeed', as you so kindly put it, is telling me that we both need to be a little cautious for a while."

Charlie turned to face her with an expression of apology. "Sorry, Pearl, I didn't mean to sound rude. I get a little twitchy sometimes. I do trust you, and I look forward to seeing Saf again – as and when she does decide to make an appearance. To be quite honest, I'm getting a little sick of covering her arse every time her mother calls me, asking where the hell she is."

Pearl finished her tea and pushed back from the table, ready to leave. She had some preparations to do if she were to strengthen the wards tonight. Time was of the essence when it came to performing magic.

"Yes, that is rather unfortunate. I know that Sapphire did not intend to cause anyone worry."

Charlie sighed. She could see Pearl was getting ready to depart just as the conversation was getting interesting.

"Right ... well, I will be off then, my dear. It was lovely to see you, as always. Come see me when you can. I have saved you some lovely home-made piccalilli that I know you would just love next time you visit."

Charlie could not help but smile. The old woman was just a pickle-making machine: her cupboard was already full of home-made produce that Pearl had been giving her from the summer crop in her garden.

She helped Pearl with the floor-length scarf and yeti-sized rug, and made sure the old woman was bundled up nicely before hugging her at the door.

"Take care, young Charlie. I will see you again soon."

Charlie kissed the cool, soft skin on her cheek and grinned at her mischievously. "You will, Pearl. I look forward to trying the piccalilli."

Pearl headed back down the lane. She sensed that her wards were still in place around the house, despite the heavy blanket of snow that covered everything in sight. Charlie was, no doubt, right now throwing around the many possibilities of their strange conversation. She just hoped that the headstrong young woman would follow her words of caution, and keep any unwanted visitors out of her home.

Chapter Twenty-Seven

On their return to Shaka after her last dream, Sapphire had felt restless and fidgety, despite the fact that life was moving on again since the battle with the queen and Ebony, and a sense of peace had returned to her home with Fox and Kit. It was a bright, warm day, and Fox had left that morning with Bear to attend to some 'man business' that she did not need to know about. It made her laugh that Fox still remained so tight-lipped about his day-to-day wanderings on this world. In the past she had often wondered what could possibly need so much attention – but then again, he was the king's son and she assumed that running a kingdom took some time and effort.

Kit was busy making fresh bread in the kitchen and Sapphire watched her knead the soft dough with an expression of boredom, her mind spinning with thoughts of her travelling last night. She needed to speak with Conloach and make sure he was still recovering well. It was bothering her that he was still out of action.

"Kit, I'm going to take Amber over to the city and check on Conloach. I won't be long. Let Fox know where I am if he returns before me."

Kit looked up from her bread-making and regarded Sapphire with thoughtful eyes. "You are troubled, Sapphire. I can see that. But he will be fine. Have no fear: he will recover soon."

Sapphire stood up with renewed purpose and pushed her chair under the table. "I know, Kit, but I need to see him … speak with him. I'll be fine. Don't worry about me."

Kit watched her leave and bit her bottom lip with a renewed sense of worry. She could see the lines of thought etched across her lady's face, and this troubled her more. Sapphire was thinking about returning to her own planet, and soon. This much was clear even to Kit, who had no idea what it must be like to have the gift of dream travel. She wished that Sapphire could feel settled and happy in her new home, and that she no longer needed to carry such heavy burdens. It seemed that this was far from the case.

Sapphire saddled Amber quickly, and headed off at a fast canter towards Calafia. The young mare was full of energy and sped across the landscape at breakneck speed. The feeling of wind rushing through Sapphire's hair gave her a renewed sense of energy. The pull to the castle was strong inside her belly and she knew that the magician would not be surprised to see her.

In no time at all she was at the castle gates. They were heavily guarded, but the men standing at the great gates stepped aside quickly on her approach. She had left Amber with the young stable hand she had met on several occasions now, and she rushed with hurried steps towards the king's chambers. Her magic thrummed strongly as she grew closer to Conloach's room, as if excited to reconnect with him again. Something had changed since the link she had made with him only the day before, when they had joined together with the binding spell. She could almost feel Conloach's energy inside her now, in the same way she could sense Fox when he grew close.

On opening the huge wooden doorway to his chamber Sapphire sighed in relief as she found Conloach sitting up in one of his throne-like chairs. Apart from the slightly pale colour to his cheeks he looked almost like his old self.

Standing near to the fire with her back to them both was Willow, the healer. She turned and smiled at Sapphire as she entered the room.

Conloach watched her with amusement in his eyes as she entered, a thin smile on his lips. "Sapphire, welcome. It is good to see you today, although – as you can see– I am feeling much better, and your visit was unnecessary."

Sapphire approached him slowly, desperately wanting to reach out to him but feeling this would be inappropriate.

Willow walked towards them both with a cup between her hands. "Drink this, my lord. I will return tomorrow."

Conloach looked up at the healer and grimaced slightly as she handed him the cup. "More poison, Willow? Really, is this necessary now I am feeling much stronger?"

Sapphire watched them, amused by the interaction. "Drink, my lord, and stop complaining. You are still a man, albeit made from magic, and need my help to regain full strength."

235

Sapphire stifled a giggle as Conloach regarded the liquid distastefully before downing it in one big gulp. He returned his gaze to Sapphire, a whisper of a smile on his lips.

"Sit, child. Tell me why you felt compelled to visit me so soon."

Sapphire did as she was told: this man always made her feel slightly intimidated. Willow had left the room without a sound.

The more she looked at the great magician, the more she could see Fox within his features. He was strong and handsome, but with a deep wisdom which she knew came from years of living that she would never understand.

"I was worried about you, that's all."

Conloach turned to face her, his eyes twinkling slightly now, and a slight blush returning to his cheeks. It was as if the potion Willow had given him had indeed lifted his energy again.

"And ...?" He paused, waiting for her to continue.

Sapphire could feel the link to him tingling and teasing in the pit of her stomach. It was strangely pleasant, in a safe and comfortable way. "And ... I wanted to talk to you without Fox around."

He reached for his goatee with his long, lean fingers and began to stroke it slowly, leisurely, and nodded his head in encouragement for her to continue.

"What do you need to talk about without my son knowing, child?"

Sapphire looked away from his gaze. She was starting to feel a little uncomfortable under his scrutiny. It was as if he could already read her thoughts, but was taunting her into speaking them out loud.

"I need to return to Earth. You know this already, Conloach, but I'm worried how it will affect Fox, and if it will drain his magic and make him weak again. I do not wish for him to change because of me."

He remained silent for a moment. Sapphire could almost sense his thoughts whirring through his mind as he digested her words.

"You know the risks involved in returning to your homeland, Sapphire. Fox also understands these risks. Do not forget he has been a guardian for many lifetimes. He is well travelled, and can hold his own."

She fiddled with her bracelet and turned her face away for a second, not wanting to look into those deep amber eyes and show her fear to him.

"I don't know how long I will need to stay there. This task I have to complete could take some time ... It is a lot to ask of him."

Conloach reached across and took her hand – a gesture Sapphire found odd, as he was not a man to touch without good reason. He held her hand gently, and traced his finger across the tattoo that wrapped around her ring finger and travelled up her arm to show her link to Fox.

"This symbol binds you together, Sapphire, forever – and in all ways possible. Your magic is linked, and this will sustain you both when you return to Earth. Although the planet you come from will without doubt drain you both, this bond will keep you safe. I cannot predict what will happen to you both when you return for long periods, but I feel sure that whatever lies ahead you will face it more strongly together."

Sapphire watched his finger linger lightly on her skin, making shivers run along the lines of the pattern and casting a soft pink glow beneath her skin. He withdrew his touch suddenly, quickly, making her jump slightly.

"Plus you are linked to me now, dream traveller. Your essence touches my own. My magic will feed you both when you are not here on Shaka."

Sapphire felt her cheeks blush dark red. The thought was just too weird.

He chuckled, as if reading the sudden change in tempo between them. "There is nothing to be ashamed of, Sapphire. The bonds between magical beings is different to the links you humans make together."

She smiled at him softly and shook her head slowly. "I'm sorry, Conloach. This is all still a little new to me ... the magic, the binding, everything ... I feel like I'm stumbling along in the dark sometimes. Fox is my only guide here. Most of the time I feel like a complete idiot when I'm surrounded by you guys."

He laughed out loud, which broke the uncomfortable tension that had crept around them. "You are far from an idiot, Sapphire. I think you have adjusted remarkably well, considering. I remember the first time I met you … You were full of fire and anger then, rushing back to save your friends. I saw you then and realised that my son had met his match – in fact, perhaps even a little too much of a challenge. But now I know that you are more than capable of this task that has been placed upon your shoulders. You may leave with no guilt for my son's well-being – or for my own, young traveller. Such consideration is truly thoughtful, and so very human. I have not seen such compassion since my wife was alive." He smiled again, a full smile that reminded her so much of Fox it pushed at her heart heavily.

"Go now, child. Be safe in the knowledge that I will be watching over you and my son, and that – whatever journey lies ahead for you both – it will be worth the risks."

She hesitated before standing up. "Then I have your blessing to take your son away from his kingdom, and to take him on some wild, mad – and as yet unknown – adventure, that may or may not take both our magic away from us?"

He sighed heavily, the smile still on his lips. "Yes, Sapphire, you have my blessing."

She nodded and walked towards the door. Just as she pulled the heavy door open to leave she heard Conloach stand behind her.

"And Sapphire … know this … your magic will always be with you both. Of this I am sure."

Chapter Twenty-Eight

Fox stood in the doorway and looked out across his lawn as he waited for Sapphire to return. He could sense her approach, and felt the buzz of energy in his chest and groin at her return. He smiled and leant against the door frame in his usual lazy manner as her horse approached in a cloud of dust. She jumped down and beamed at him, her face alight with renewed energy.

"Fox, have you been home long?" She held Amber by the reins and walked towards him, her hips swaying just so in that crazy, sensual way that made his body tingle in all the right places. He pushed himself away from the door and ambled towards her, his eyes dark and soulful and filled with a need to get close to her again.

She was slightly breathless from the ride and looked up at him hesitantly as he stood before her, teasing her slightly, before he took the reins from her fingers with a brush of his skin that left the signature sparks they created whenever they were aroused. He could feel the heat from the horse pulsing softly beside them. The scent of sweat mingling with his wife's own sweet smell filled his nostrils. He bent down slowly and brushed his lips against her cheek, then the crook of her neck, as he kissed her softly.

"Not long, my love. I have missed you," he whispered smoothly. He felt her body soften at his touch, and her breathing quickened just that little bit more. He loved the way he could affect her with just the slightest of touches. It excited the beast within him, made him want to tease her more. Fox led the horse back slowly to the stables. He took her hand within his own and smiled at her softly.

"I hear you have been to see my father … How is he today?" Sapphire looked down at her feet as they walked.

"Good … He is good today. Willow is nagging him to take his medicine. It was actually quite amusing to watch him bend to her rules."

Fox led Amber into her stall and let go of Sapphire's hand before reaching up to remove the horse's saddle.

"I am glad he is feeling better."

239

They stood in silence for a moment. Fox lifted a handful of straw to begin brushing down the wet coat of the mare. Sapphire watched him sweep in long, graceful strokes across the animal's rump as his muscles moved beneath his shirt in strong, gliding ripples. The action was strangely arousing. She shook her head and stepped back for a moment to fully catch her breath. He had his back to her, and she continued to watch him carry out the simple task of rubbing down the horse in smooth, steady strokes.

As she stepped back against the wall of the stable she felt a gentle throbbing begin in her chest that travelled lazily down to her belly and groin. Fox remained silent, but she could see that he too was feeling the rush of energy between them, as his aura changed colour before her eyes to a dark plum that flashed with streaks of gold and red. It was late afternoon now, and the sun was slipping down across the horizon and filtering a hazy gold into the stable, which lit up her husband in a strangely hypnotic glow. Sapphire could feel her breathing become heavy again. The seductive song of arousal filled the small stable as she watched her husband.

"Where did you go today?" Her voice was a soft whisper, her tone slightly rasping. He remained steadfast in the job at hand, his back still facing her.

"With Bear to the edges of our kingdom, to check that all is still well now that the queen has been taken."

Her palms were placed against the wall now. They had become a little clammy, and she tried to steady herself with the coolness of the stone against her fingertips. "And is all still well?"

Fox stopped brushing and dropped the hay to the floor. He patted Amber on the rump, and pushed a bale of hay towards her head so that she could graze. He turned around slowly, and rubbed his hands together. His feet were hip distance apart and his long, lean legs in a position of dominance as he looked across at her with a wry smile on his lips. His eyes were flashing at her now, dark gold and black, and his lids were hooded and low.

"Yes, all is well."

Sapphire did not know why they were suddenly dancing this strange, seductive dance around each other in the stable, but it ignited the flame within her instantly and she was finding it a little difficult to stand still.

Fox took a step towards her, his head tilting to one side, the smile still firmly planted on his beautiful lips. He licked the fullness of the top edge slowly, and took another step closer. "Are you well, my love?"

Sapphire giggled and pressed herself back further against the wall, so that her whole body was flattened against the cool stone surface. "I'm feeling a little flushed after the ride."

He stalked her gracefully, edging closer and closer. Sapphire could hear Amber munching behind him on the hay. The sound of her powerful jaw biting down on the grass was quite loud in the sudden silence.

"You look a little flushed," Fox said. He was standing inches before her now, not touching her but radiating heat and a strong scent of patchouli. She closed her eyes for a second and breathed in. Her mouth had suddenly become quite dry and she gulped, trying to ease the tension in her throat. Before she could open her eyes she felt Fox lean forward, his face close to her own, his breath touching her skin in warm, soft waves as he stood silently in her space.

"You look like that just before you come," he said. His hands were either side of her now on the wall, capturing her against the cool stone. She could feel his heat on the front of her body, and the coolness of the stable wall against her back. She squirmed, sighing softly and enjoying the game. Fox moved in and nuzzled his face against her neck. With her eyes still closed she opened her other senses and took in all that he had to offer. His tongue began to move across her skin in a slow, casual caress ... soft licks that traced a wet line down to her collarbone. His mouth was the only part of his body to touch her, but it created a surge of arousal so strong within her bones that she almost slid down the wall.

He bit down on her neck gently, and swirled his tongue across the skin inside his mouth. She could stand it no more, and grabbed him before she collapsed in a heap. Her hands gripped his buttocks, and he moved swiftly to lift her away from the wall and up against his chest. His body was trembling slightly now, and she felt him grow hard against her. Without hesitation or permission he began to pull her underwear away with a ripping of material that made her groan out loud.

241

"Would you like to come now, my beautiful wife?" he whispered tantalisingly into her ear, his tongue catching the shell of her earlobe slightly as he spoke. Sapphire was panting now. This game they were playing was making her need to have him inside her swell strongly throughout her veins.

"Yes … yes, please," she whimpered as he pushed her back against the wall and trailed his fingers across her thigh.

"Good, because that's exactly what I am going to make you do."

Her dress was hitched up around her waist now, and Fox claimed her lips with a renewed hunger as he reached to his trousers to release himself against her. She was still clinging to his buttocks, her legs now limp and hot as they wrapped around him. He kissed her long and hard as he moved her into position before lifting her up and pushing himself, slowly and carefully, inside her. She was wet and tight around him, and enveloping his cock with an animalistic need that made them both cling harder to each other. Fox groaned heavily into her mouth as he began to move her up and down as if, wrapped around him, she weighed nothing.

Each thrust caused her to give way to him just a little bit more, so that he fitted perfectly inside her body. They were caught in the moment, lost in the heat they had created in their lovemaking. The air around them was thick with the swell of magic and sex. It pulsed softly against the wall and made Sapphire lose her mind as she felt her body mould against him. She matched his movements with enthusiasm, pushing down as he thrust upwards. He was grunting like a beast … his eyes closed, his head back now, his lips slightly parted. Watching the exquisite expression on his face turned her on even more, and she felt the heat cascade upwards from her groin to her head in one quick shudder as she came so hard that her body convulsed uncontrollably around him.

Fox continued to fuck her hard against the wall, his lips glistening, his eyes now open as he pushed himself into her over and over again … until he too fell over the edge and found his own release deep within her womb. The room lit up with a shower of gold sparks as their magic connected and magnified. Tumbled words in his own strange language slipped from his lips as he dropped his head down into her hair and breathed heavily against her. His arms were still wrapped around her tightly, his cock still hard within her body. Sapphire gasped for air. Her body was still sending ripples of pure pleasure across her skin. Slowly and carefully, he eased himself out and dropped her feet to the floor. He held her close, still leaning against the stable wall for support. She was glad for the help, as her legs had gone completely numb and she knew that she would be on the floor if he were not still holding her up.

"Are you still feeling flushed, my love?"

Sapphire began to laugh as he moved back just slightly to look down at her beet-red cheeks, which were radiating heat.

"You could say that."

They returned to the house after straightening up and kissing for a while longer against the stable door. Amber seemed to have been completely unaware of the show that had just been put on behind her. Her need for hay was obviously a far greater concern at the time.

Kit was in the kitchen, and had laid out a virtual feast for them. She smiled shyly at them both as they entered, and gave a quick curtsey before disappearing without comment. Sapphire was famished. Her ride to the castle and the activity in the stable had renewed her appetite, and she dug into the food like a starved person.

Fox sat opposite her, a knowing smile planted firmly on his lips. He always looked so goddam smug after he had fucked her.

"So ... when are we leaving?" he asked.

Sapphire looked across at him suddenly, surprised by the question. "What?"

Fox continued to eat slowly, smiling at her before taking a sip of wine. "We are leaving, Sapphire. When do you want to go?"

She sighed before chuckling softly. "I can't hide anything from you, can I?"

He placed the wine glass down, reached across the table for her hand, and touched her fingertips gently with his own.

"Why would you want to, my love? We are linked in more ways than one. I sense your unrest, your passion, your anger, your love. I know it is time, Sapphire. You just lead the way."

She nodding slowly and continued to eat the wonderful food Kit had prepared. Her belly was full and her heart was happy.

"Tomorrow, Fox. We leave tomorrow."

Chapter Twenty-Nine

It was wonderfully warm and snug inside the coffee shop and, predictably for a Saturday afternoon, absolutely packed with people. Charlie had managed to snag herself a window seat, and sat nursing her second hot chocolate as she looked out of the window. Her feet fidgeted nervously under the table, and she held the mug firmly in both hands to stop them from shaking. She was, for some obscure reason, extremely nervous – to be quite frank – at the prospect of meeting her client, who had insisted on collecting the pieces she had recently commissioned for him in person.

Christmas had come and gone, and the snow outside was still sticking fast and causing shoppers on the high street outside to huddle against each other and take pigeon steps carefully across the footpath to avoid slipping over on to their backsides. Charlie watched them with amusement. She had been waiting nearly half an hour for her client to arrive, and was starting to feel a little stupid – and somewhat peeved that he was so late. She had never actually spoken to the man, but had corresponded by email and received instructions from him as to what he had wanted made.

The materials had arrived via courier. His detailed description of the necklace and two bracelets had been so precise that they verged on anal. When he had sent her the actual gems and silver to work with (which no other client had ever done before) she had been slightly overwhelmed. The stones, an exquisite set of sapphires, had been absolutely beautiful: clean, cut to precision, and perfect. The silver was also of the highest quality, and he had sent drawings detailing how he wanted the finished pieces to look like. They had been hand-drawn, scanned, and sent to her via email. She guessed they had been sketched by a professional artist, such was the excellence of the work.

He had also been very insistent that he come and pick the finished pieces up from her, and that they were not be delivered to his home address in the city. Nathan had insisted she met him in a public place as this sounded odd, and he would not be around that morning to

244

stand as chaperone. At the time the client had requested the meeting she had thought Nathan was being paranoid and stupid, but as she waited in the coffee shop where Sapphire had previously worked she was grateful he had made the suggestion.

She had received the order two weeks before Christmas, and it was to be made for New Year's Eve – a tall order, considering it was her busiest time of year. The price offered, however – and the fact that she did not have to initially pay for any of the costs of the materials – was the deal-breaker. The only name she had for her client was a Mr Monroe: very impersonal, but it seemed that the man must have money as his address was listed in Chelsea, London, and he had already deposited half the payment into her bank account without first seeing the finished product.

The aforementioned product was sitting by her feet in a bag within a bag. The boxes had been handmade for her at an extra cost by a supplier she used for extra special clients. They had been lined with black velvet and were made from cushioned leather, as requested by this Mr Monroe. As the design details had been taken out of her hands this made the job very easy indeed – a doddle, in fact. She had no idea where he had even tracked her down from: he had made no reference on his initial contact to her as to how he had known she was a jewellery designer, or that she worked at the high end of the market. But that was the beauty of good work: excellent referrals.

However, there was a niggling in the pit of her stomach that this particular client was a little on the kinky side. This was mainly due to the fact that the necklace itself was almost like a collar and chain: beautiful, but still on the verge of BDSM. The bracelets resembled tiny cuffs, with the sapphires dotted at intervals along the links. The necklace was the same, scattered with sapphires along its length – and boy, was it long. The whole piece was unique, very odd and very, very expensive. In fact, as Charlie continued to sip her hot chocolate, she revelled in the fact that she could probably take the next six months off with the payout from this one job. She had absolutely no idea what Mr Monroe looked like, but he had seen her website with her profile picture and in his last email correspondence had said he would find her easily in the coffee shop she had directed him to. The place, date, and time had been set, and now she was waiting like a dumb-ass with a bag full of jewels that were worth a small fortune for a man who – it now seemed – had stood her up. She was about to leave, go home, and email the idiot when the door opened and the tiny bell jingled to indicate another customer.

Charlie looked up from her swirling hot chocolate to see whether this could possibly be her man. The figure who had entered was indeed male. Not only was he male, but he was an extremely good-looking male. He was over six feet tall, was dressed in a long black coat (which looked as if it were made from cashmere) that swept to his feet, and had dark hair that swirled untidily just above the collar in that 'Just got out of bed' look. He was standing in profile and looking at the counter but his face was outlined by the overhead fluorescent lighting, which gave her a great view of his features. And boy, oh boy, was this man handsome.

Charlie stared, and her heart started to beat a little more rapidly as he turned slowly to face her. As he looked directly at her across the heads of the other customers she could see him start to smile – a direct smile that just tipped the edges of his lips upwards in a look of near satisfaction. His eyes were dark, his lips full and sensual. He tipped his head at her and headed over. Charlie tried to smile back, but found that her body had gone into some kind of weird sexual overdrive. No one had made her feel that gobsmacked since she had caught Fox in bed with Sapphire the first time he had slept over. This guy was of equal swoon appeal, but with a darker edge.

He was suddenly standing at the table before her, his hands clasped together in front of his body in a pose of someone refined, elegant, and about to pounce. Charlie stared up at him and took in every single curve and edge of his frame. It was tall, imposing, and a little intimidating. He seemed oddly familiar.

"Miss Daines, I presume?" His voice was like black coffee … dark and inviting, promising visions of keeping you up all night. "I apologise for my delay. The drive from London was rather difficult, considering the weather. I hope I have not kept you waiting too long."

Charlie shook her head slowly, still finding it difficult to speak. "No, it's fine. I've been enjoying a sugar fix."

He pulled out the chair opposite her and sat down in one graceful swoop. "Like a panther," she thought absently.

He looked at the hot chocolate in her hand and smiled again. "Ah, yes ... sugar: one of the human cravings I have never fully understood, but could quite easily enjoy myself if I had the time."

Charlie blinked. What the fuck? This guy was superweird. Charlie pulled herself out of the hypnotic trance she seemed to have fallen into and went into business mode as she lifted her hand away from the mug and reached across the table to greet him.

"Charlie. My name is Charlie. It's nice to finally meet you, Mr Monroe."

He took her hand in his own and shook it as he wrapped his fingers in a firm but almost too familiar handshake. When he released her hand slowly she felt her body shiver involuntarily. His hands were cool but soft like a woman's, with something almost sinister beneath the touch.

"I assume that my order is ready. I would like to see it, if you wouldn't mind."

Charlie watched him from across the table. She was glad for the piece of furniture between them. She had the odd sensation of wanting to run away, but jumping him at the same time. It was scrambling her brain, and she wondered if she had drunk far too much wine last night and was still feeling a little tipsy. She shook her head again and reached under the table for the bag.

"Yes, of course. I have it here." She could feel his eyes following her every move, almost sense the burning of his gaze, as she bent down to retrieve the precious parcel. She placed it on the table and leant back, as she tried to steady her breathing. Plus ... the damn necklace Pearl had given her for Christmas was, for some weird and fucked-up reason, burning a hole in her chest. Well, that is what it felt like. She rubbed it as she tried to shake away the feeling of heat that it seemed to be radiating suddenly from under her jumper.

Mr Monroe regarded her coolly from across the table, one eyebrow arched perfectly, as he observed her fidgeting.

"Are you feeling unwell, Miss Daines?"

Charlie stopped her scratching and tried to ignore the pulsing against her chest.

"No, I'm fine. Sorry, I have an itch." She could feel her cheeks starting to blush a deep red. "I have an itch ..." What the fuck was she doing? This man was making her act like a teenager.

He smiled again and reached inside the bag to find his prize. Charlie held her breath as he pulled out the boxes one by one and placed them on the coffee table. She suddenly felt like this had been a big mistake: this was the stupidest of places to exchange such expensive pieces with a man who was pretty obviously used to doing business in a bank vault, not in the local coffee shop. He opened the first box, the largest of the three, which held the necklace. His eyes glittered and shone with excitement, and for the briefest of moments Charlie thought she saw flickers of red cross the dark pupils of his eyes.

He touched the chain and sighed deeply. "Very nice."

Charlie let out the breath she was holding and smiled. He liked it, thank God. He inspected the two bracelets, and held one up in his hand to take a closer look. There was quite a lot of background noise - customers around them chattered and laughed, seemingly oblivious to this strange transaction going on beside them. Charlie was glad for the distraction; he was making her feel positively weak at the knees.

He looked at her again, and snaked his tongue across his bottom lip in a way that suggested she looked like dinner.

"Would you try this on for me, so that I can get an idea of how it will look?"

Charlie felt as if her groin was about to combust. She squirmed in her seat. The heat from the necklace was thumping now against her breasts, and her body was starting to tingle all over. She wasn't sure if it was from fear or extreme sexual attraction.

"Sure ... why not?"

He leant closer, and wrapped the chain around her wrist. It felt heavy and cold against her skin. A tiny shiver of anticipation ran up her wrist as he touched her while he fastened the clasp. It felt as if he had sent a bolt of electricity up her arm that made her skin rise with goosebumps. The bracelet looked beautiful and deadly at the same time. He held her hand lightly, so that he could examine the bracelet against her wrist. The sapphires twinkled in the bright overhead lighting.

"Exquisite, Charlie. You have done me proud."

Charlie smiled weakly. Her body was responding to his touch in the weirdest and most fascinating way, as if she were a bird trapped within the claws of its predator and fluttering in protest. But the feeling was not unpleasant. In fact it was turning her on just that little bit too much. She pulled her hand away quickly, breaking contact, and began to hurriedly unfasten the clasp. Mr Monroe leant back in his chair and continued to smile at her in that 'I am undressing you with my eyes' kind of way.

Charlie suddenly felt as if she wanted to get the hell out of there, take her money, and run. Mr Monroe was the oddest, most fucked-up, sexually attractive man she had ever met, and her body and mind were in compete turmoil from just being in his presence. She did not know whether she wanted to jump over the table and flee out of the door, or jump on his lap and kiss him to death.

He chuckled suddenly, breaking the silence. "I am very happy with the finished pieces, Charlie ... May I call you Charlie? I will have the remaining balance due to you transferred to your bank account today, and will contact you again soon for my next commission."

Charlie raised her eyebrows in shock. "You have more work for me?"

He leant forward again and opened his mouth just slightly, and licked his top lip again in that 'Oh, yes, I can definitely do that to you' gesture.

"I have many things in mind for you, Charlie. I believe this is just the start of a beautiful working relationship together. I have a feeling you can give me lots of things that I want." He paused for a second. "Many beautiful things that I wish to obtain, which I know you will be able to help me with." Charlie was feeling dizzy. His eyes were flashing at her, dark and carnal in a way that seemed very inappropriate.

God, this man seemed very familiar to her from somewhere in her past. She almost felt as if they had met before – but that could not be possible, could it? He stood up suddenly, so quickly and silently that she did not even register the action. The boxes were gone – in the bag, she presumed – and he was standing right next to her, heat radiating from his body. She noticed the sweet smell of some expensive aftershave that she did not recognise. It was overwhelming, intoxicating, and terrifying all at the same time. He bent down and whispered into her ear.

"I will contact you again soon, my beautiful jewellery maker."

Charlie shivered again as his lip touched her earlobe with just the faintest of touches before he withdrew. She stared up at him, aware that she was gawping now.

"Thank you, Mr Monroe. It was nice to meet you," she stammered.

He sighed deeply again and smiled. As he turned to leave he looked at her one last time.

"It was certainly nice to meet you again, Charlie. Oh, and you may call me Hecta from now on."

Chapter Thirty

Charlie had stumbled home from the coffee shop in a daze. Her head was spinning and thumping persistently with a splitting headache. The crystal necklace Pearl had given her had stopped radiating heat as soon as Mr Monroe had left the building. It was still warm against her skin and making her tingle slightly – but the incessant heat had dissipated, and she was glad it had. The sensation had given her the heebie-jeebies and made her feel as if it was alerting her to something seriously abnormal in the air.

When she reached the front door to her cottage she shook her head and tried desperately to find some clarity again. The whole transaction had been fucked-up crazy. He was one strange guy. She unlocked the door and stamped her feet before stepping inside, and almost stood on a bundle of post that had been delivered while she had been out. She picked it up absently, and placed it on the table in the hallway before taking off her boots. Nathan should be home soon, and she was more than glad he would be back before it was dark again. She suddenly wanted company.

The memory of Mr Monroe standing before her in the coffee shop kept playing around and around in her head on a loop. It niggled her that it bothered her so much. There was just something so familiar about him. Was it his eyes? His mannerisms, perhaps? The tone of his voice? She just couldn't place the reason why.

She headed into the kitchen, and decided to down some headache tablets and then have a rummage through the fridge for inspiration in creating the evening meal. Just as she had finished pulling out the last ingredients to make a lasagne she heard Nathan come in through the door.

"Hey, sweet thing, I'm home …" He popped his head around the door and grinned. His face lit up with excitement. "Did you miss this when you came in?"

Charlie looked up from the packet of mince she was about to attack with a knife. "Hey, hon. What did I miss?"

Nathan was holding the bundle of post in his hand. It was unwrapped from the elastic band now, and he was holding one of the items in his right hand and waving it slowly in front of his body mischievously.

"You are so bad at opening your post, Charlie. Not everything is a bill, you know. I can't believe you would have missed it."

Intrigued, Charlie stepped forward to get a closer look. "What is it?"

He was holding it up over his head now, just out of her reach. "Kiss first."

Charlie sighed, smiling. "Oh for goodness' sake, Nat, just give it to me."

He chuckled, and lifted the item higher. Charlie got a peek at it before he pulled it away. It looked like a postcard. Now she really was curious.

"Kiss first. That's the deal."

She grabbed him by the waist and pulled him against her as she ground her hips into him roughly. "You are such a bloody tease, Nat."

She reached for his neck and pulled his face closer to kiss him – a hard kiss with a loud, smacking noise that made him laugh as she stepped back. "OK, OK … Here you go."

Charlie beamed at him as he placed the card into her hand. The picture on the front was a river scene with a large white boat sailing along dark green waters, lush vegetation, and palm trees along its banks. The words 'Wish You Were Here' were splashed across the top. Egypt … the card was from Egypt. Her hands were shaking a little now and she turned it over quickly, her breath catching in her throat. She read,

Charlie, my best friend in the whole world,

I know it's been a while, and I really do wish you were here … but I will be coming home very soon, and I can't wait to see you. I have so much to tell you, but it will have to wait …

Looking forward to catching up over a coffee (or maybe something stronger).

All my love,

Saf xx (PS Fox will be coming home with me).

Charlie looked up at Nathan – who was beaming at her, his beautiful blue eyes sparkling brightly.

"Now you can stop sulking so much, Charlie," he said.

The sky was turning a dark grey and more snow was starting to fall as Pearl made her way back from the local shop to her little cottage. The bag she was carrying was only filled with a few essential provisions, but it was starting to feel a little heavy. She stopped for a moment and placed it on the floor. Her fingers within her gloves were starting to creak and groan, and she suddenly felt very much like the old woman she was. She stretched her back out for a moment and paused as she breathed in the cold air and filled her lungs with the wonderful crisp coolness of the snow in the air.

She wondered when the weather would change. It had been abnormally cold this winter: they had not had snow in December for a very long time. It felt like something was brewing on the wind. A change was on its way, and she knew instinctively that it had something to do with Sapphire's imminent return. It was as if Mother Earth was anticipating the start of something wonderful, and was cleansing the ground before that something would emerge again – refreshed, renewed, and powerful.

Just as she bent forward to pick up her bag again a hand reached out and took the bag before she could take it. She jumped back, a little startled. She had not seen anyone approach her. Standing before her in the grey light of the dusk was Hecta. He was dressed rather dashingly in a long dark cashmere coat. His hair was trimmed just below the collar, and his face was clean-shaven and tidy. His eyes were dark pools of coffee-coloured brown with flickers of red, which sparkled in the dimming light. Pearl stepped back. Her heart began to beat furiously, and her own magic started to swell and grow around her in an immediate blanket of protection.

"That looks heavy, Pearl. Here, let me help you."

Pearl gathered her wits quickly. She knew this was no chance meeting. "What do you want, Hecta?"

He remained perfectly still before her as he held the bag lightly in his hand, a slight smile etched on his lips. "Ah, Pearl ... You always think that there is something I want. Maybe I just wanted to help an old lady carry her heavy burden."

She felt her magic crackle slightly around her. He was pushing at its edges, testing her strength. Pearl felt her chest start to constrict slightly, and her hands trembled a little within her warm gloves. This was not good. Not good at all.

"Now that would be a most unlikely gesture from someone like you, Hecta."

He shook his head and slowly tutted. "I am hurt, Pearl. Why must you always think so badly of me?"

Pearl tried to take a step backward but was suddenly unable to move. Her body became fixed to the pavement. The snow was beginning to swirl around her more thickly now, slightly obscuring her view to the street around her. She had almost made it home, and her lane was within view a short distance away … so near but yet so far away.

He was smiling at her broadly now, and the smile made her feel sick to the stomach. Her head was pulsing, throbbing now, and the sensation was causing her to feel dizzy.

"Leave me alone, Hecta. No good can come from this." Her voice was strangely distant, as if disconnected from her body. It sounded weak and feeble, even to her own ears.

He stepped forward and raised his other free hand slowly towards her. "Ah, Pearl … I am afraid you are wrong on that account. Many good things can come from this meeting and – as you are outside of your wonderful home, with its rather powerful wards – I think that you and I can create something wonderful together for when the beautiful Sapphire returns … And I sense she will be returning very soon."

Just as he touched her – and the bubble of protection around her shattered – she watched his head tilt to one side like a predator surveying its latest catch with curiosity.

"I see it in your eyes, Pearl, and I hear it in your mind. We just need to create the perfect web to catch the fly in, don't we?"

Pearl closed her eyes and let out a gasp of breath as he caught her around the throat and squeezed tight.

"And you are the bait, old woman."

Chapter Thirty-One

It was New Year's Eve, and Charlie and Nathan were at the party of all parties. Simon's house was packed with people and pumping with the heavy beat of house music. Christmas lights were strung around the walls, and a huge tree was flashing with tiny white lights in the hallway that created a winter wonderland scene that rivalled the Las Vegas strip.

Nathan passed Charlie a glass of champagne, slipped his arm around her shoulders, and hugged her body close.

"How are you feeling, gorgeous?"

Charlie giggled, and sipped the cool liquid that tickled her nose with tiny bubbles that exploded as she raised the glass to her lips. They had dropped about half an hour ago, and it had been a dose suitable for the epic night they were about to jump into. She was buzzing nicely already, and knew Nathan had dumped a sizeable amount of the sparkle dust they both enjoyed into her bomb. It was going to be a very good night indeed, if this was any indication of the journey she was about to take.

"I feel goooood, babe ... really good."

Nathan laughed and kissed her on the tip of her nose. His body was radiating heat, and his eyes were wide. His pupils, black and huge, were starting to dilate. "Me too, sweet thing. Not long now: five minutes to go until we bust into the new year."

Across the room Charlie could see Simon standing behind the decks, his head bobbing to the heavy bass beat and a big grin plastered across his face. Caitlin was beside him, dressed in a skimpy white dress with angel wings strapped to her back. The party was fancy dress and, of course, she looked very much the part of the angel at the top of the Christmas tree. Charlie was dressed in a sexy Santa outfit, and the thigh-length red boots she was wearing were pinching her feet slightly. But she didn't care, not one damn bit. She could feel the drug snaking its way through her veins into her blood, and everything was starting to feel lighter, softer, and so much better than before. Nathan looked hot in his black tuxedo. He was Mr

James Bond himself tonight, and he even had the plastic gun in his pocket to complete the look. She couldn't wait to get her hands on the other loaded gun he had in his pants at the end of the party.

As she smiled up at him she sighed happily. She so wished that Sapphire were here to enjoy the fun. It had been two days since she had received the postcard. She was rather hoping that she would be back for the celebration and could see the new year in with them, but that was obviously just wishful thinking. Nathan grabbed her free hand, and pulled her further into the lounge through the throng of dancing bodies to get closer to the small stage Simon was spinning his decks on. The house was literally jumping, and the energy high. Charlie closed her eyes for a moment and allowed herself to be carried away in the rush of wonderfulness. All was good. They danced, champagne in hand, as the seconds slipped by. The new year was rushing towards them in a crescendo of thumping beats that radiated up their bodies, and teased and pushed them forward into an anticipated frenzy.

Simon grabbed the mic. "Hello, party people!" The room yelled back at him as everyone whooped and called out in response. "Are you ready for the beginning of a brand-new spanking hot year?" They yelled back, "Hell, yeah!" The music was cut, and the TV in the corner of the room was turned up full blast. Big Ben appeared on the screen, larger than life. Charlie clung to Nathan, her glass of champagne jostling against her chest, as people around her began to jump as the clock began to chime.

"Ten, nine, eight, seven, six, five, four, three, two, one ... Happy New Year!" The room erupted in party poppers, laughter, and craziness. Everyone was hugging and kissing and clinking their champagne glasses as the new year began. Simon cranked up the music again, and the lights were dimmed so that the lasers could pierce the darkness and cascade over their heads in a green haze. Charlie wrapped her fingers into Nathan's hair and kissed him deeply, her glass still dangling precariously in her other hand. They were lost for a moment in each other, in the promise of a new start for a new year. The party was officially starting, and she could not have been happier.

Sapphire stood on the doorstep of the large house, and raised her hand to the knocker. She paused for a moment. The music from inside was so loud that she knew that not a single person would hear her. Fox stood behind her, his arms wrapped about her waist, his head resting against her shoulder. He squeezed her gently.

"No point, my love. Let's go around the back."

The heat from his body pulsed softly against her, and she smiled and breathed in his scent of patchouli and sandalwood. "Good idea."

They walked slowly back down the gravel driveway and across the lawn towards the back of the house. Sapphire looked up at the sky, and saw the darkness of the night pierced with a thousand tiny stars. She smiled as they walked hand in hand as she remembered the first time she had been to this place, the first time she had jumped down the rabbit hole and met Fox. It all seemed such a long time ago – but here she was again with him, about to see her friends once more. Her body tingled in excitement and fear. She was different now, so very different in every way possible, and she knew that it would be more than obvious.

Lights flashed inside the house and the movement of bodies cast elongated shapes across the darkened lawn. Sapphire stopped and looked up at Fox. His expression was one of amusement and happiness. He could sense her hesitation to enter, and urged her forward with a gentle push.

"She's just inside, Sapphire. Stop delaying the inevitable," he said encouragingly.

She was biting her lip with nerves, but Sapphire released Fox's hand and stepped up on to the decking at the back of the house. She was heading for the French doors, which were open a little (this allowed the sound of the music to spill out into the garden). He followed her silently, allowing her to take the lead but remaining a little in the shadows as she stepped inside.

Charlie was dancing with her eyes closed and her head thrown back. Nathan was beside her, lost in his own little world of niceness. Sapphire watched them for a moment before heading across the room. She knew Fox was close behind her – but that he was allowing her the space to make this moment special just for her. Her magic began to swell around her, and she could sense its excitement at the gathering of such intense energy. She could see a rainbow of colours drifting across the room, spinning and flashing as it pulsed around the guests. They were all as high as kites, and it was making her own energy lift higher and higher. She had forgotten what this felt like ... how the linking of other people's energy with her own made her lift out of her body and dance like a bird.

As she moved across the room, silent and graceful, she could feel the stares of the other people moving around her. Some of them recognised her, some of them did not – but they were all aware of the change in her appearance, of the new energy radiating from her body. It was powerful, consuming, and magical.

Charlie opened her eyes just as Sapphire stepped within a few inches of her. She looked confused for a second, then her eyes grew wide as she looked at her friend for the first time in what seemed like forever. Sapphire watched a myriad of emotions pass across her face as she processed this picture before her. The look was one of disbelief and wonder.

"Hello, Charlie. Happy New Year."

Charlie blinked, and stopped dancing. She stared open-mouthed before launching her whole body at Sapphire and wrapping her arms around her, squeezing so hard that Sapphire thought she might pop at any moment.

"Oh, my God! Saf! Saf! Is it really you?"

Sapphire held her tightly and felt the warmth of Charlie's body, the firmness of her chest pushed against her ... the solid, real feeling of her best friend here in the room with her. Tears began to spring from her eyes as she held her close.

Charlie pulled back and put her hands either side of her face and held Sapphire tightly, as if she were afraid she would disappear again.

"Oh, Saf, it is you! You are real. I can't believe it. How? When?" She was gasping for breath, her own tears forming in little droplets across her cheeks. She frowned suddenly. Her eyes were wandering across her friend's features, in wonder. "You look strange ... so different. Your eyes are weird. What have you done to your hair?" She started laughing. "You look awesome! Fucking awesome!"

Sapphire laughed with her, and kissed her hard on the mouth.

"And you look beautiful, Charlie. So beautiful. It's so good to see you again."

Despite the volume of the music Sapphire could hear her heightened breathing and the loud beat of her heart.

Charlie shook her head in obvious confusion. She grabbed Sapphire's hand and pulled her towards Nathan.

"Nat! Look who's here!"

Nathan opened his eyes and stumbled for a second when he realised that Sapphire was standing with his girl.

"Holy fuckin' shit! Saf!" He grabbed her and hugged her tightly as he laughed loudly. They were interlocked now: the three of them were standing in the crowd of people dancing around them hugging, kissing, and laughing.

Sapphire felt her heart swell fit to burst within her chest. She was home. Home, at last.

Chapter Thirty-Two

The nurse checked her watch again. It was half past one on the first of January: a new day of a new year. The old woman in the bed before her was breathing deeply, her eyes closed, her face a nasty shade of grey. She was hooked up to an IV drip, and a monitor that indicated a shallow heartbeat beeped slowly beside the bed. Such a shame. The old dear had been brought into A & E earlier that evening by a man who had found her on the street, beaten and unconscious. A mugging on New Year's Eve. Such a terrible thing to have happened.

The man who had brought her in had said that she was barely alive and that he could only find a small shopping bag beside her, which had been left discarded by the muggers. What was left in her purse indicated that she lived in the small village of Heckfield, and that she was eighty-seven years old. There was a small slip of paper in the purse that indicated the name of a Charlie Daines, with a telephone number, possibly her next of kin – her daughter, perhaps? They had tried to contact this person without success, but had left a message saying that Mrs Pearl Fellows had been brought into the hospital … and could he or she call as a matter of urgency? It was the early hours of New Year's Day and the nurse knew that it would, most likely, be some time before this message was received.

The nurse checked her pulse one more time, smoothed the white sheet across her chest, and sighed. Poor old thing. She had slipped into a coma, and was oblivious to the world around her right now. Not a pleasant start to the new year for anyone. She tidied the small number of belongings that had been removed from her when she had been cleaned up and put into bed.

A beautiful bracelet lay to the side of her purse. It glittered in the glow of the bedside lamp. There were diamonds scattered around the silver chain of the bracelet, which were interlaced with sapphires. A small frown appeared on her forehead as she touched it lightly for a moment. It looked oddly like one side of a cuff: something that would restrain you. She pulled away quickly as a sharp jolt travelled up her hand like a tiny electric shock when her finger brushed the clasp. She shook her head.

She stepped back and watched with wide eyes as the bracelet began to pulse in the dim light as if it were suddenly alive. The old woman stirred in the bed and moaned softly, as if in pain. Nurse Bourne rushed off quickly to find a doctor. She suddenly wanted to get out of that room and run far, far away ...

Sapphire pulled back slightly from the tight embrace that consisted of Charlie and Nathan to catch her breath. They were positively beaming at her, and their energy was flowing strongly around her in waves of pink and gold so full of love and happiness that it was overwhelming.

"Fox is here with me, Charlie. Come see him."

Charlie nodded enthusiastically, and her eyes lit up brightly against the lasers. Sapphire took her hand and led her back towards the French doors, where she sensed Fox was waiting in the shadows. Nathan followed them. He was jumping up and down in his own world of buzzing energy. He was smiling widely, and nodding his head in time to the music that continued to throb around them.

As they stumbled out of the French doors and on to the decking Fox stepped forward into the light, and Charlie let out a whoop of delight. She practically launched herself at him and wrapped herself around him, laughing loudly. He caught her before she fell on the decking and, laughing with her, held her against him.

"Fox ... Oh, my God, it's so good to see you. I can't believe you are both here. It's the best New Year's Eve present ever. This is awesome."

Nathan joined her, and thumped Fox on the back heartily. "Good to see you man. Happy New Year."

Fox managed to prise the overly excited Charlie from his chest and, smiling widely, hugged Nathan. "And you, Nathan. It is good to see you both, and you're looking so happy."

His face was etched with amusement as he could obviously see the waves of drug-induced energy coming off them in flashes of light, just as Sapphire could. The four of them stood on the decking for a moment, taking in the moment of uniting again after such a long time. Charlie was staring at them both, shaking her head in

261

disbelief. Sapphire watched her process this turn of events. A million thoughts were flashing through her mind at how crazy this must all seem.

"Saf, you are so bad at communicating. I can't believe you only sent one goddam postcard in six months. Where the fuck have you both been?"

Sapphire smiled. It was such a typical response from her friend. "I know, Charlie, I know. It's been a crazy few months. A lot has happened. I have so much to tell you, but right now is not the time…"

Charlie grabbed her hand again and held it out in front of her as she studied the tattoo that now laced up her arm. Open-mouthed, she gawped at the intricate design that swirled and circled from her ring finger around her wrist and up her forearm.

"You have a fucking tattoo! Oh, my God, Saf … A tattoo… and that crazy new hair. It really suits you, but you look so different. Am I just totally spangled, or am I really seeing this?"

Fox was laughing now, his hands in his trouser pockets, and an expression of pure enjoyment etched on his lips.

"It's all real, Charlie. Don't worry about it for now … I will explain later. Let's just enjoy the party and the start of a new year together."

Sapphire interlocked her fingers with Charlie's and rose up on her tiptoes to kiss her friend on the cheek. Charlie was still shaking her head in bewilderment.

"Well … OK, then … Moët all round, then, I think. Nathan, can you go and get us a bottle? There was plenty in the kitchen. I'll wait out here with Saf."

Nathan nodded, still grinning. Fox stepped forward. "I will help you, Nathan. Let's leave the girls for a minute."

Sapphire watched the two men move back inside the house. Fox looked back over his shoulder as he stepped around the door and winked at her. He knew she would need some time alone with her friend.

Charlie dragged Sapphire across to the wooden chairs that were scattered around the hot tub. Blue lights in the edge of the decking illuminated the area in a soft glow and highlighted the steam from the hot tub in electric-blue wisps of smoke. She plonked herself down on one of the chairs and she stared across at Sapphire, who sat a little more gracefully opposite her. She was still beaming, her feet tapping to the music which bounced around the garden from the party that was in full swing inside the house.

"This feels like a dream, Saf. I'm honestly finding it difficult to take all this in. It just doesn't feel real. Fox looks exactly the same as I remembered him – hot as hell and juicy as fuck – but you … You just look so different – like the old Saf, but with this shiny, sparkly coating … Amazing."

Sapphire leant back in the chair and sighed deeply. She was so totally happy that her body was finally beginning to relax. She had no idea how much she had missed Earth, her real home. The journey for both her and Fox to come back to Earth had been quick, but a little draining.

Jumping through space and time had required a fair amount of their magic to pull them through the void intact, especially with the valuable seeds in her possession. They sat in her coat pocket inside a bag made from material that Violet had made for her before they left: a magical case that would protect and hold the precious seeds to keep them safe here on Earth. At this precise moment Sapphire could feel them warm and snug, vibrating at a high-pitched tone against her leg. Fox had wanted to carry them for her, but she knew that they must never leave her side now. They were her burden to carry, and she must keep them with her wherever she went from now on.

"I needed a change, Charlie. The hair, my eyes … it's all cosmetic, really." She paused, watched Charlie digest the slight lie she was telling her. "The tattoo, though, is something really special… Fox has the same on his hand … We got married, and it symbolises our bond to each other."

Charlie slapped her hands against her thighs and opened her mouth in shock. "No fucking way! You got married, and you didn't even let me know. Sapphire Whittaker, you naughty, naughty girl…"

Sapphire laughed and took a deep breath. "I wish you could have been with me, Charlie, but we were caught up in the moment. It happened really fast, honestly. If I could have had you by my side I would have."

Charlie smiled and leant back in the chair, her face shining a rosy pink. She was hot, and her energy was pulsing crazily as she buzzed high and fast.

"Pearl will be cross you guys got married without telling her, I'm sure of that."

Sapphire trembled a little at the mention of the old witch. She wanted desperately to see her, but knew that the visit to Foxglove would have to be at a respectable hour later in the day.

"And your Mum, Saf. God, she has been harassing me constantly. You have a lot of explaining to do, that's for sure!"

Sapphire nodded. She knew this would most likely be a difficult conversation to have with her mother, but that could wait for now.

"I know, Charlie ... God, I know that ... But it's so good to see you and Nathan again. I've missed you guys so much."

Charlie stood up abruptly. "Speak of the devil. Here is my gorgeous man with the champers."

Fox was holding two glasses and standing beside Nathan, who held out two more and who also had a bottle of Moët in his other hand. "Right, let's get the party really going."

Sapphire grinned in response. She was totally up for some good old-fashioned drinking with her friends. Time to get wasted.

And they did just that. The rest of the evening flew by with drink, dance, and a fair amount of debauchery. The house was full of happy party people. Simon, Caitlin, Dave, and Grace had all found their way to Sapphire at some point during the evening. They were as happy to see her and Fox as Charlie and Nathan had been – enthusiastically so. It was wonderful to feel so loved by so many people again, people she had remembered having such good times with.

Her life on Shaka had been amazing, strange – bloodthirsty, even, recently. In addition, she had been totally overwhelmed by the passion and love that had blossomed between her and Fox during her stay there. But now she was home again, with the other people she loved. She felt complete tonight, united with her friends again back on Earth, and she was finally beginning to understand why she was here. To protect them, to enlighten them, to awaken them from the deep slumber they had been in throughout their short lives.

She knew instinctively that the seeds she held were the key to that awakening – not only for her friends, but for everyone here on this planet. The magic they held would grow and flourish, and everything would change for them. How and when this would begin was still unknown to her – but this step across the void had been the first step and Sapphire was eager to see Pearl again, to ask for her wisdom about what the next steps on this new journey would be.

The party was slowly starting to wind down and dawn was approaching fast, casting the sky with beautiful pinks and reds across the horizon. The air was cold and fresh outside the house, and Sapphire was now draped across Fox on one of the chairs by the hot tub. Charlie and Nathan were huddled together in a blanket that Simon had given them when they had finally decided to call it a night and to start to come back down again. Charlie was smiling lazily, smoking a big fat joint that she passed between herself and Nathan. Fox was stroking his wife's neck softly, running his fingers through her hair, making her skin tingle at his touch.

"So I assume you guys need a place to crash, Saf?"

Fox began kissing her neck now. The champagne, it seemed, had actually made him even more amorous than usual, and she could sense his need to consume her again. It felt decadent – and so very naughty – to know the things he would do to her once they were alone again. She sensed it in his touch, and in the lingering of his lips on her skin.

"If that's OK, Charlie. Yes, we need a place to stay for a while."

Nathan took the joint and narrowed his eyes as he took a lungful of the happy smoke. "It will be great having you back, Saf. Plus a man in the house will keep me from being totally henpecked by Charlie."

Fox chuckled.

"Hey, that's not fair! I don't nag you, Nat," Charlie protested.

Nathan blew the smoke out into a perfect ring and laughed, before kissing her on the cheek.

"You can have your old room back, Saf," Charlie said. "In fact a few of your bits that survived the fire are up in the loft. You can have a look through them tomorrow. I knew you would be back – just knew it – so I kept them for you."

265

Sapphire perked up at the thought of seeing some of her old belongings. She wondered what had managed to withstand the ravages of the fire. Hopefully there would be some of her jewellery and knick-knacks that her mum had given her.

The buzzing energy from earlier that night was fading now, and she sensed that everyone was finally starting to fall back to Earth, after flying so high. She also sensed Charlie and Nathan's rising libido, which always seemed to follow such intense sessions. It was time to leave. Plus, Fox was now pushing his very warm hand inside her coat ... and it travelled down south towards the button on her jeans, where he stroked her slowly and started to ease his magic further down to her groin. A sharp breath caught her throat as he ignited the fire that was starting to glow softly at his insistent probing. Time to go, definitely.

"Are you two ready to leave? I think we've had enough fun for tonight," Sapphire asked, while trying to stop herself squirming too much at the pressure that was now building up inside her. Fox had his face buried into her neck now, and her hair was covering his face as he started to suck the tender skin beneath her ear. Good God, he seemed positively drunk. Charlie was smiling at them both now. Watching the scene unfolding before her was obviously causing the same reaction that Sapphire was having, as her eyes were sparkling with that 'Oh, yes, I know what he wants from you' smile.

"Abso-fucking-lutely, Saf. Let's get home and crash."

They left after saying their goodbyes rather hurriedly. Fox was gripping her hand tightly as they walked down the lane, his thumb brushing the inside of her palm in tiny circles and continuing the rush of desire that he was obviously feeling up her arm. She looked up at him with a smile on her face. She was feeling flushed from the champagne, but lucid enough to control the flames of passion that he was sending across her body. His eyes were flashing dark and gold, and he had a wry smile on his lips that spoke words of lust and wanting.

"Are you OK, Fox?" she whispered as they followed Charlie and Nathan, who were laughing and stumbling slightly as they led the way home.

"Definitely," he whispered back, as he licked his bottom lip with anticipation.

She giggled at him. He was positively glowing, with sparks of light around his aura that indicated his heightened state of arousal. She leant in closer and breathed in his scent of patchouli and sandalwood.

"You seem a little drunk," she said. He gripped her hand a little more tightly.

"Drunk on you, my love. Drunk on your happiness. I am pleased for you, but cannot wait to get you alone again. It has been torture to watch you tonight. You are like a wild flower that has blossomed since you were last here. The energy of this place has done nothing but brighten your beauty."

Sapphire laughed loudly. Rarely had she seen Fox so inebriated. She knew that if they did not get back to the cottage quickly he may just find a bush they could hide behind and take what he needed to satisfy his craving.

They arrived back at the cottage in double quick time. Charlie opened the door and stumbled through, laughing, as Nathan smacked her playfully on the backside.

Sapphire stood for a moment and took it all in, seeing the renovated cottage for the first time and sighing in happiness that her old home had been transformed again.

"Do you guys want anything to eat or drink before you go to bed, Saf?" They were standing in the hallway. Charlie was heading to the kitchen, with Nathan trailing behind her.

"No, thank you, Charlie," Fox answered on her behalf. He was tugging at her arm, pulling her towards the stairs.

Charlie laughed.

"You know where to go, Saf. The bed is made ... See you later."

Fox was already dragging her up the first few steps. Sapphire shook her head and smiled at his eagerness. "Yeah, see you later, Charlie. Love you."

Fox practically manhandled her through her old bedroom door. He was virtually panting now, his face alive and animated. As she shut the door behind her he pounced on her, and began kissing her with a furious need to consume. Sapphire let herself go. She did not care now that they had only just arrived, that her friends were downstairs. She wanted to dive into the pool of Fox and let him drown her in his essence. With a frenzied grappling of hands he began removing her clothing, kissing her the whole time. She could hear his breathing become more and more rapid, and the heat radiating from his body enveloped her and made her moan out loud.

"You are so very beautiful, Sapphire. My wife, my love," he began to whisper to her in his strange and intoxicating language over and over, as he stripped naked. He pushed her back on to the bed and he stared at her for a moment, his hair wild and untamed across his shoulders, his eyes dark and filled with longing. They remained like that for a second, suspended in time, as if nothing had passed between them before … as if, like always, this was the first time they had come together.

Sapphire closed her eyes and sighed deeply just as Fox slid down her body and began to kiss her chest, her stomach, lower and lower, before he claimed her with his mouth and tongue.

The room lit up with the brightness of their magic, and she allowed herself to ride the energy flow. She was happy, she was home, and she was about to be devoured by the man she loved. Nothing could be more perfect than this.

Chapter Thirty-Three

Darkness surrounded Sapphire on all sides. Above and below, and all around her, it was a complete darkness so black and cold that she could feel her body weighted down heavily by its presence. She was dreaming again – and had seemingly travelled to a place that was so far away it stretched her body and mind completely, to the point of oblivion. The urge to scream out was strong within her chest – but she could not move, could not even breathe within its confines. Panic was rising within her like a coiled spring, pushing up further and further and trying to burst free from her body, but it was trapped within. The feeling was so utterly terrible that she thought her mind would implode from the pressure.

As she tried to regain her bearings she pulled inside for her magic to help her, pulled it out from the centre of her chest to light the way ahead. Nothing had prepared her for this after such a peaceful and wonderful ending to the night in Fox's arms. As she fought hard to regain control a glimmer of light began to spread outwards from her core and flicker within her mind. Using nothing but her senses, she pushed her magic further from her body to find out where she was. Nothing.

There was nothing around her, just the darkness that enveloped her from all sides. This was a nightmare of the most extreme – the most horrific – feeling that could be endured by anyone. She willed herself to wake up, to break free from this moment in time. As she struggled within the dream she slowly became aware of a new presence within her space. It was a new energy that was drawing closer and closer. She could feel it moving forward like a dark shadow in her peripheral vision.

Suddenly, without warning, the shadow grew lighter. It became a shade of grey that began to form the outline of a person. Sapphire was still unable to move, locked in this dark cell that was closing in on her ... but the person before her gave her hope that she was about to be rescued from this terrible prison. Just as she felt as if she was about to pass out her eyes opened fully, and she could see clearly the shape before her in the darkness. It was a man, and a man she knew well: Hecta. He was like a vision before her in the darkness, hanging suspended in the seemingly never-ending abyss. He was glowing in a strange, unearthly light. His face was clear now, and smiling at her. Sapphire tried to move away from him, but was stuck fast. She had no idea where she was, or why she was here. Fox was nowhere to be seen. She was lost.

"Sapphire, do not worry. I am here to help you." He was moving closer, his face different from how she remembered it ... his hair was a little longer, his clothes the same as a man on Earth would wear. "I can help you return home, Sapphire. This place is visited by very few, and those that do come here rarely return ... but I know how to escape the darkness ... Would you like me to help you?"

Sapphire was screaming inside her head now, pulling her magic from within. She could feel it start to rise as her anger rose fiercely within her chest.

"Leave me alone, Hecta." Her voice was strong within her head, but she had been unable to move her lips. Her magic was pulsing now, and she could feel the bonds of the darkness beginning to waver and break. She flexed against it and felt it begin to crumble slightly.

Hecta tipped his head to one side, aware of her new movement. He was still smiling, a soft smile that made his features slightly more appealing. Sapphire wanted out of this place, away from him and his almost smug smile.

"I know you want me to help you, Sapphire ... I can help you." He was inches from her now. She could feel the warmth of his body, the touch of his breath on her face. "Take this, beautiful Sapphire. It will release you from this place and keep you safe." She felt him place something onto her wrist. It was cool and heavy against her skin. She tried to pull away from him, but was unable to do so.

He leant in closer, and kissed her gently on her cheek. Her mind was screaming out for him to back off and leave her alone, but she could not speak. He stepped back again and blew her another kiss before disappearing into the darkness. Sapphire tried to move, tried to free herself from this awful place. The weight of the bracelet that he had placed on her wrist grew heavier and heavier, and was pulling her down. The magic within her was confused, and skittered around her body as it tried to readjust.

Just as she thought she could not take any more, the darkness around her began to waver and pulse. It moved like wisps of smoke that were starting to dissipate into a soft breeze. Slowly, slowly the darkness was moving away, releasing her from its hold, and a new light was moving towards her. Sapphire opened her mouth and screamed as loud as she could at the top of her lungs.

"Sapphire, Sapphire ... stop. It's OK ... you are OK. I am here, my love. I am here."

Sapphire opened her eyes. Fox was holding her by the shoulders, his face etched with concern. She was in her old bedroom back on Earth, in Charlie's lovely little cottage, and Fox was there with her. She was awake again, and she was home again.

"Where have you been, my love? I sensed you had travelled far away. I tried to reach you, but something was pushing me back."

Sapphire tried to regain her breath. Her body felt heavy and hot, and uncomfortable.

"A place I never want to go to again, Fox."

He hovered above, her his handsome face a picture of concern. "Tell me where."

Sapphire turned her head away from him, closed her eyes for a moment, and sighed heavily.

"A dark place that was so oppressive I could not move, could not think ... Hecta was there." She felt Fox shift his weight. His energy moved into warrior mode, sharp and alert.

"Hecta? How can that be?"

Sapphire suddenly felt claustrophobic, and struggled against his grip so that she could sit up. Fox reluctantly released her, moving away to give her the room she desired.

"I don't know. He appeared in the darkness, said he was there to help me ... He placed something on my wrist." Sapphire pushed herself up, opened her eyes, and looked down at her arm as she lifted her hand slowly, with a deep sense of fear. Sure enough, placed on her wrist was a silver bracelet, twinkling innocently in the dim light of the dawn. She could see the intricate placing of diamonds and sapphires along the length of the cuff. Filled with magic, it glowed

271

softly. Fox grabbed her wrist and remained silent as he held her arm out before her.

"This object has a binding spell surrounding it. The magic is strong. This is not good … not good at all." Sapphire felt his magic begin to swell and pulse around him. He placed both hands against the cuff and pulled gently, trying to prise it apart. A jolt of pain so sharp and hot flashed across her skin that it made her jump back from him in shock.

"Ouch! Shit … that hurt, Fox! Stop. Leave it alone."

Fox looked at her, his face troubled, his brow turned down with worry. "He has bound you to him, Sapphire. He will be able to track you, wherever you are on this plane. We need to get it off."

Sapphire scrambled away from him across the bed, her other hand now placed protectively over the cuff.

"No! Don't touch it again, Fox." He regarded her silently, his hair tumbling wildly across his shoulders, his eyes dark and distressed. "I need to see Pearl, Fox. She will know what to do."

He nodded slowly and watched her moving away from him defensively. "As you wish, my love."

Sapphire looked for her clothes. She needed to get dressed and get moving – to find Pearl, and to find a way to work out what was happening to her. She hadn't even been back on Earth a day, and already her life was being thrown up into the world of crazy again. She felt a slight headache begin to take residence in the back of her skull. This was totally shit. Another thing to worry about.

Fox began to dress behind her, silent and brooding. She sensed his anger and frustration at this new turn of events. After checking that the seeds were still safe within their pouch she took a quick glance at her man before heading for the door.

"I need the bathroom, Fox. I'll meet you downstairs."

She left the room quickly, her heart thumping loudly in her chest. The dream had been as real as all her previous dreams had been, and Hecta had now bound her to him. What did he want this time? The seeds, her magic … or her? He had been different in the dream, almost pleasant and calm … not the Hecta she had learnt to hate so far. Her head was spinning as she shut the bathroom door behind her and sat down on the toilet to relieve herself. She had known that coming back to Earth would be hard, the task ahead of her a heavy burden. But now this … She hoped that Pearl would indeed have some answers, and that Hecta would not just pop up in the kitchen, standing there looking devilishly handsome, with a smug smile on her lips. Or did she?

Fox was waiting for her in the kitchen leaning back casually against the counter, his arms crossed against his chest. His face was impassive, but his energy was wild. He was angry, that much was obvious. The kettle was boiling and he had already found the coffee, a human gesture she found odd but comforting. Charlie and Nathan were still sound asleep, and Sapphire had no idea what time it was. She headed to the kettle and silently filled the cups with coffee and sugar. Boy, did she need some sugar today. Fox remained still beside her, saying nothing. The silence was unnerving, as if the dream with Hecta had already caused a bridge between them.

"Don't be angry with me, Fox."

He sighed. He pushed himself away from the counter, walked across the little kitchen to the back door, opened it, and stood with his back to her, looking out into the garden. The ground was still covered with a scattering of snow and the air was cool and crisp. It filtered inside, touching Sapphire gently with a soft caress.

"I am not angry with you Sapphire. I am angry with the gatekeeper. How dare he touch you, bind you? I hate that he has done this, and that I was not there to prevent it … again."

Sapphire watched his warm breath collide with the cool outside air and move away from his face in white trails. Even with his back to her he looked gorgeous and irresistible.

She silently filled the mugs with the boiling water and picked up the steaming mug of coffee. She followed him across to the doorway and stood behind him, feeling the warmth of his body connect with her energy and nuzzle her gently.

"You cannot be there to protect me every time I travel, Fox. It's just not possible. There was no way you could have helped me in that dark place. He took the opportunity to cross the line, and tricked me."

Fox remained statue-still, the warmth of his breath still sending wisps of mist into the garden.

"I will find a way to remove the bracelet," Sapphire continued. "It's not up to you to find a solution to every single situation I find myself in."

He turned his head and looked down at her, his face like a cool mask of non-disclosure. "It is my job to protect you when you travel, Sapphire. Before you were my lover, before you were my wife – before I fell completely and utterly in love with you – it was my job, as your guardian, to protect you. I have never forgotten that, and never will. That is why I am angry, Sapphire. I am angry, and disappointed in myself that I have failed you again."

Sapphire shook her head slowly, and sipped the coffee. "Stop saying that. You have not failed me, Fox, not for a minute. It's simply not possible for you to be constantly at my side. I have travelled many times without you in the past. Things have changed for me drastically in the time I have spent as a traveller, you know that. We both have to learn to adapt to this. My magic has grown and changed within me. How were you to know that a new path lay ahead of me, that something more sinister would present itself in the shapes of Hecta and Ebony? No one knew, not even your father. So, please … stop punishing yourself. You are no good to me like that."

He blinked slowly as he digested her words. Sapphire remained behind him, her coffee redundant in her hands for the moment (and warming her palms a little too much).

"You are right, of course … as always, my love. I will no longer allow Hecta to come between us. The Oracle warned me of this. She told me to remain clear and focused on the task at hand."

Suddenly he was facing her – and his hands were in her hair, holding her towards him, his eyes locked with hers. "But my love for you has robbed me of all clarity. It makes me doubt myself. I will not forget who I am again, my love, and I will not allow my focus to slip. We will go to see Pearl and ask for her wisdom on this situation, and then we will move forward as planned …" He paused, kissed her softly on the lips, and added, "Together." As he pulled away slowly he whispered, "Always together."

Sapphire decided not to wake the two sleeping beauties upstairs. They would most likely still be in the spiral of comedown after the party, and in need of several more hours of sleep. After finishing her coffee and grabbing some toast she grabbed her coat and called out to Fox, who had been standing in the garden, brooding and silent.

"Fox … Let's go."

He ambled back into the house, his eyes dark and troubled. She noticed that a dark cloak of energy now surrounded him like a blanket of protection for his heart, which was quite clearly struggling.

"I've left Charlie a note that we will be at Pearl's, so she won't worry."

He nodded and took her hand. His skin was cool to touch from the winter air, but there was heat in his eyes for a second that flashed and thawed her a little. He had stepped into role of guardian again and was in warrior mode – disconnected from her emotionally, but ever-present in his need to protect her.

She was glad of this, as there was a strange feeling uncurling within her chest as they left the cottage and headed towards Foxglove – a feeling of unsettled discord. Something was amiss, and it pushed against her skull uncomfortably and made her walk faster and faster as they approached the edge of the village and the woods that hid Foxglove from the rest of the world. As they approached the gate to the cottage Fox stopped abruptly, causing Sapphire to lurch forward as his grip tightened on her hand.

"Something is wrong, Sapphire. The wards are broken … Pearl is not here."

Sapphire frowned, urging him forward. Her need to find Pearl was now causing her heart rate to jump up and down in her chest loudly. Fox pushed her behind him and strode forward quickly, so that he would be the one to enter the garden first. Sapphire followed him, her palms beginning to tingle as she noticed that the garden was quiet and still and without its usual buzzing energy. No birdsong. No magical sounds at all. Just silence.

Fox pushed the front door open and entered before Sapphire could stop him. He shut the door behind him with a slam before she could follow. Sapphire felt her breath rush from her mouth in short, fast bursts. Something was terribly wrong: she could feel it in her bones, and it made her feel sick to the stomach. She fought the urge to follow Fox straight into the cottage and stood awkwardly on the doorstep, her head turning this way and that, looking for signs of danger. This cottage had always been a sanctuary to her, a place of safety and comfort. Now it felt cold and dead, as if the life force that created such wonderful sensations was long gone. After what felt like a lifetime the door opened again. Fox stood before her, his face stern and angry.

"Hecta has been here," he said. "Pearl is gone – but I sense she is still alive, at least. But the magic within her has withdrawn so much that this place has lost its protection and life force. Even the sprites are gone."

Sapphire was trembling slightly. Not from the cold or from fear, but from the growing anger in her belly. "Do you think he has taken her with him back to Shaka?" she asked.

Fox looked down at the ground, his expression filled with concern as he sifted through the endless possibilities of what may have happened here.

"No, he cannot take her from this realm. She is here somewhere, of that I am sure. No one can cross through the dimensions like you, my love. But I fear he has damaged her magic, and taken what he can from this place to make himself stronger while he is here on Earth. The energy here is as draining to him as it is to me, Sapphire." He looked up again directly into her eyes. "He must know about the seeds and our purpose here, and is trying to find a way to stop you."

Sapphire could not believe this was happening. Once more she was being pursued by the gatekeeper. Not only that, but the bracelet was still stuck fast to her wrist and now – without Pearl's assistance – she had no idea how to remove it.

"I will take you back to Charlie's and go out and find her, Sapphire. It is not safe for you here."

Sapphire shook her head. "No, I'll come with you. We have to find her together. You said that to me earlier, Fox. We will do this together."

He raised his head defiantly. "Sapphire, I know how to handle him. I have spent lifetimes dancing with the gatekeeper across time and space. I will find him. You, however, are far too important to place in the face of danger right now. Please … do as you are told for once."

She understood the sense of his words, but the need to find Pearl was crushing her from the inside out. Silently she nodded, and looked up at the lovely cottage – which now seemed so sad – before her. They left Foxglove behind them, and hurried back towards the village. Sapphire felt all the happiness – all the excitement of coming home – disappear from her body in one long sigh of defeat.

This was not how she had foreseen her homecoming. Not at all.

Chapter Thirty-Four

Charlie scratched her head sleepily, pushed the duvet away from her legs, and yawned as she slipped out from the bed and headed to the toilet. It had been one hell of a New Year's Eve party, and she was feeling the after-effects in every inch of her body. After brushing her teeth and taking a leak she headed downstairs. She wondered if Sapphire and Fox would be up yet: she literally had no idea what time it was. As she walked towards the kitchen she noticed that the light on her answering machine was blinking, but decided to pick up her messages after a strong coffee and some painkillers. Her head was starting to pound somewhat savagely, and reminding her of how much Moët she had consumed. Just as she had finished spooning the coffee into her mug she heard the front door slam shut and a cool breeze rushed inside that made her shiver.

"Charlie? Are you in the kitchen?" Sapphire appeared at the doorway, her face flushed and her hair tumbling wildly across her shoulders.

"Hey, honey, have you been out already? I thought you and Fox would be having a lie-in."

Sapphire stood silently, watching her as she poured the hot water into her mug.

"Do you want one?" Charlie nodded at her mug, suddenly sensing something was amiss. For a start Fox was not at Sapphire's side, and she seemed anxious.

"Charlie, have you seen Pearl lately? Fox and I went to visit earlier this morning, but the house was empty and there is no sign of her."

Charlie sipped the coffee before reaching for another mug and frowned. "No, I haven't seen her for a while … not since Christmas. That's strange. She never goes far. Perhaps she went out for a walk."

Sapphire crossed the kitchen to her friend and shook her head slowly. "I don't think she was out walking, Charlie. Something feels wrong … I'm worried about her. Fox has gone to see if he can find her, but I was hoping you might have heard from her."

Charlie shrugged. "No, I haven't heard from her, but the machine is blinking at me so she may have called. It's not like her to ring, though. She usually just turns up, like an apparition at the front door, whenever I am on my coffee break." She laughed at her own joke.

Sapphire remained silent, unusually so. Charlie was still finding it hard to take in her friend's new appearance. Her eyes – for one thing – were flashing today with sparks of silver, which seemed really weird. Charlie thought, "I must be on a hard comedown. Now I'm seeing things."

She tried to reassure Sapphire by saying, "I'll check the machine, Saf. Stop worrying. Honestly, you have been home five minutes and you're stressing over something that hasn't even happened yet. Sit down, and have some coffee."

Sapphire could feel her own uneasiness creeping like tiny insects across her skin and making her even more jumpy. Charlie had no idea how serious this was – no idea that a gatekeeper called Hecta was involved, or that something terrible had most likely happened to their friend. Without Fox by her side she was suddenly feeling very human again, and wanted to burst into tears like a child. She sat at the kitchen table and took the coffee Charlie handed her. The warmth of the mug soothed her once again.

"Honestly, Saf, you are looking really freaked out. Stop worrying. I'm sure Pearl went out into the woods and Fox will find her there picking mushrooms out of the snow, or some such nonsense. I'll check the machine, just for you to stop stressing." She paused as she headed out to the hallway. "Oh ... and, by the way, did I tell you last night how great it is to have you home?"

Sapphire smiled weakly as her friend disappeared around the door frame to pick up her messages. It was great to be home – or it had been, before she had stepped into another nightmare scenario.

The cottage was silent for a moment before Nathan bounded down the stairs.

"Morning, Saf. Or is it afternoon? Where's Fox? Still in bed, the lazy bastard?"

Sapphire smiled at his happy face. As usual he seemed to have fared well, considering the heavy partying from the night before.

"Is there any hot water left? I could kill a coffee."

Charlie appeared at the kitchen door again, her face deathly white. The coffee mug was still in her hand – although it had slipped slightly to one side now, and the contents were spilling on to the carpet.

"Charlie … What the hell, honey? You are spilling coffee on the floor." Nathan was laughing, until he realised something was wrong.

"Saf, you were right, something is wrong. The hospital left me a message late last night. Pearl was admitted into A & E. She was mugged yesterday, and is in intensive care. It's bad … really bad."

Nathan stopped laughing. Sapphire stood up so fast she knocked the chair to the floor, causing it to bounce loudly on the tiles.

"Holy shit," Nathan whispered.

Sapphire reached out to take the mug from her friend, and gripped her hand tightly.

"Get dressed, Charlie. We need to get over there right now and see her."

Charlie nodded, stunned to silence. This was not how she had envisioned the beginning of a new year. Not at all.

Fox had returned to the woods after seeing Sapphire safely to the cottage. He needed a place to ground and meditate, so that he could reach out into the ether and trace Pearl. He had forgotten how heavy the energy on Earth was, and how much it drained him. He also felt the beginning of a hangover, which was something he rarely suffered from on Shaka. This place was particularly alien to his own energy and, even with Sapphire close by linking to him and adding to his own power source, he felt a little weary. The woods, however, were a soothing balm, and the coolness of the winter air and the slight scattering of snow helped his mind become calmer and his body less tense.

He walked slowly through the trees, closed his eyes, and used his other senses to feel what was around him: without using sight everything became clearer to him on Earth. His magic began to thrum around him, tuning into the environment and blocking out any unnecessary information. Coming back to this planet with Sapphire was a task that he had not relished, but would never have turned down if it had meant leaving her side. Now that Hecta had reappeared, and Pearl was in trouble, he was glad he had pushed for them to leave when they did. He wished for a peaceful life with Sapphire, for time that they could build a secure future and a family. It seemed that this would be the last thing they would achieve while her new magic and power grew.

On sensing a group of deer nearby he stopped and waited silently for them to pass so that he would not scare them. Inside his mind he could see them quite clearly, their outline a deep orange aura that shimmered as they moved through the woodland. A new energy source caught his attention as he watched them move away. It was a tree so huge and bright with energy that it connected with his own magic and pulled him towards it like an old friend. When he opened his eyes again he found himself standing beneath a canopy of bare branches that held a thin dusting of snow from the day before.

The tree glistened in the dim sunlight like a diamond-encrusted giant holding out its many limbs and proudly reaching upwards to the sky. His own magic grew excited and jittered impatiently for him to move to the trunk of the tree, which thrummed with its own powerful magic. Fox placed his hands on the mighty tree trunk and felt a jolt of pure white energy travel up from its roots into his body. The effect was overwhelming and quite unexpected, and caused him to shiver from head to toe.

He closed his eyes and saw the residual images that flickered across his mind and played the scenes of others who had visited the tree. He saw Pearl collecting herbs nearby and meditating at the base of the tree on a summer's day, her face happy and vibrant. He saw animals that had nibbled the grass at its base – and then Sapphire herself standing with her eyes closed and forehead pressed against the bark, connecting with the energy that sparkled and shone around her. He smiled at the image of Charlie and Nathan being thrown to the floor one day, as Sapphire absorbed a bolt of energy that knocked them clean off their feet.

This tree was special. It was a powerful doorway to something quite unique on this planet, which was something he had not anticipated: a portal. Fox opened his chakras and allowed his magic to connect to the tree, and the energy below it filled him with powerful waves of refreshing aura. He immediately felt better, cleansed, and renewed. Everything around him remained silent and respectfully still in the presence of such immense power. Fox knew that this place would serve him well if he needed to recharge – and he also sensed that it would need to be protected from Hecta, should he also find it by chance. After stepping back he bowed at the waist, and nodded his head in thanks.

The wood had grown still again, and he sensed another shift in the energy around him. He spun around quickly, pulled his magic close, and threw a shield around his body, suddenly aware of something sinister in the air. Moving towards him quickly like a dark shadow was a cluster of birds. Black as night, they flew silently on the wind – closer and closer – until they hovered a few feet away. Fox could feel the darkness within them, the threat of danger on their seemingly innocent wings.

The wind picked up and the birds suddenly scattered, squawking loudly and creating an unearthly noise that made his body tremble. Hecta emerged from the black shadow, stepped forward and revealed himself, a smug smile on his lips. Fox breathed in heavily and prepared to take action if necessary, hoping that the gatekeeper was not here to damage the energy source that he had just a moment ago tapped into.

"Fox ... fancy meeting you here," Hecta growled.

Fox tipped his head to one side, his hands clenched as he kept a check on the anger that was beginning to swell in his chest. He must remain in control. To lose control now would not help him, Pearl, or Sapphire.

"Where is Pearl, Hecta? What have you done with her?"

Hecta remained perfectly still, his magic swirling around him now in dark wisps of orange and red, his eyes flashing with amusement. "She is safe, guardian. Have no fear."

Fox closed his eyes for a second and caught a glimpse of Hecta's thoughts – a flash of the pain crossing Pearl's face as he had attacked her in the street, her magic struggling to fight him off as she had been crushed beneath his hand as it pressed against her throat. Fox stepped forward, his eyes now dark and focused on the danger before him.

"You have hurt her, Hecta ... not a wise thing to do. You know Sapphire will be angry when she finds her like that, and you know what happens when Sapphire is angry, Gatekeeper."

Hecta laughed. "I am more than aware of your wife's mood swings, Fox. It's a pity she cannot control her temper. She would be quite spectacular if she could just manage her outbursts of emotion a little better." He paused, his smile turning into a snarl. "But then ... she is mostly human, and humans lack such skills."

Fox sighed deeply, his chest rising and falling and puffing out like a bull about to charge. "Your insults will not help you, Hecta. You need to leave this place, and stop causing pain and suffering to the people Sapphire loves. We have danced this dance before, and I am sad to say that you do not seem to have understood that no good can come of it. You will not stop Sapphire from fulfilling her destiny."

Hecta shook his head slowly. A deep growl rose from his chest and escaped his lips in a tone that hung in the air around him. "You really are quite delusional, Fox. I have no interest in Sapphire's 'destiny'." He almost spat the last word out in disgust. "But I am interested in her. She has such an unique form of magic ... it excites me." He paused before smiling again. "I have not been excited by anything for a very long time."

Fox stepped forward now, all reason beginning to slip as Hecta goaded him with such disrespect towards his wife. "You will never have her, Hecta. Never. She is mine, and will never be tainted by your magic, your words, or your touch, despite your pathetic attempt to bind her to you with the bracelet you tricked her into wearing the last time she travelled."

The energy around them both began to heat up, and Fox could feel the tree behind him start to throb and pulse as it sensed the discord between the two of them lift higher and higher.

Hecta raised an eyebrow and looked up at the tree. "Interesting place, Fox. I thought I might bump into you here, and I am rather glad that you are alone. I would hate Sapphire see you reduced to a messy pulp before her."

Fox twitched, and took the bait. Enough was enough. Hecta was ready for the impact as Fox launched himself at the man before him. His anger and hatred unleashed into a fury, which now consisted of fist and foot connecting with Hecta in a blur of blood as he punched him in the head before spinning around and kicking him to the floor. Hecta laughed again as he took the force of the punch with glee. He fed on Fox's anger and allowed his magic to swell around him. The wind began to pick up and leaves flew up from the woodland floor, swirling around them both like a mini tornado. After picking himself up from the floor Hecta brushed himself down, his eyes glinting with sparks of light and shadow.

"Temper, temper, young Fox. You really should learn to control your anger."

Fox knew the gatekeeper was playing with him, and tried to steady himself. The air around him grew cooler and he sensed Hecta pushing against his shield, picking at its edges like a venomous snake sending out its poison.

"You have pushed me too far this time, Hecta. No more games. Tell me where Pearl is, and leave this place before you get hurt."

The gatekeeper threw his head back and laughed loudly, as if he had not a care in the world.

"Your beautiful Sapphire has found her already, Fox, and will have no doubt by now stumbled quite unknowingly upon the second part of my binding spell."

Fox shook with rage. The thought that he had been tricked by Hecta and left Sapphire without his protection made him think of unspeakable things that he wanted to do to the gatekeeper.

"What do you mean, Hecta? What have you done?"

Hecta picked another leaf that had stuck to his coat from the expensive cashmere and flicked it to the floor.

"You are a fool, Fox, to think that you can own such a powerful dream traveller and keep her all to yourself. You are a fool, and you are too late. The spell is cast and she will be bound to me, not you, for eternity."

He stepped back slowly, a new smile growing on his lips. "It was good to see you again, guardian. Until the next time."

And then he disappeared. Just like that.

Chapter Thirty-Five

Tears slipped slowly down Sapphire's cheek as she looked at the pale form in the bed beside her. It seemed utterly incomprehensible that Pearl was unconscious and unable to communicate with her. Charlie sat in a chair on the opposite side of the bed, her head held in her hands. She had failed to contain her own grief at finding Pearl in such a terrible state, and had bawled her eyes out as soon as they had entered the hospital room.

Sapphire reached for the old woman's hand, closed her eyes, and pulled every ounce of magic she had inside her through her fingers and into Pearl's hand. She focused on sending her pure, healing energy, which would help Pearl regain consciousness and pull her out of the spell she had been placed under. For there was no doubt that something sinister and foul had been used against Pearl, and it was not just a human mugging. Dark magic surrounded the old witch, and it covered her in a heavy blanket that seemed to press her further into the stark hospital bed with a weight that was not humanly possible. Charlie was totally unaware of this particular problem and continued weeping, a little more quietly now, while Sapphire did her best to help their friend. She felt the familiar tingle of magic sweep through her body as she tried in vain to lift the veil that clung to Pearl like a heavy mist on a cold winter's morning.

Despite her good intention, and despite her having pleaded to whatever god, goddess, or other magical creature may be listening, her attempt to break the spell was hopeless. She needed Fox to help her, and help her quickly. She could sense the ominous pressure of such dark magic, and knew that the longer it lingered the worse Pearl would get. She let go of Pearl's hand reluctantly, knowing that she would need to use both her own and Fox's strong magic combined to break Pearl free.

"Charlie, go and see if you can find a doctor. We need to find out just how bad Pearl's condition is, and who brought her in."

Charlie looked up, her face tear-streaked, her cheeks ruddy. She was sniffing loudly, but she nodded slowly and stood up quietly.

"I can't believe this is happening, Saf. It's just so unfair. Poor Pearl ... she didn't deserve this."

Sapphire sighed heavily. She wanted to explain everything to her friend so that life for her would be so much easier without all the lies and deceit. But that would not be possible right now. For now her focus would need to be on how to help Pearl.

"I know, honey, but let's get the facts first. We need to find out what they are doing to help her, and if the person who brought her in knows anything else – other than that she had been mugged."

Charlie glanced down at Pearl's frail form one last time and then, hugging herself tightly, shuffled out of the room. As soon as she had left Sapphire sat down on the bed beside her old friend. She took her hand again, closed her eyes, and reached out with her magic through the dark veil that covered Pearl.

"Pearl ... if you can hear me, please hold on. I'm here now, and I will do everything within my power to help you. Just hold on. Don't let go. I will bring you back – I promise you, Pearl. Don't give up." As she opened her eyes again she noticed something shining on the bedside cabinet. It glistened and shone under the fluorescent hospital lights like a tiny fairy light. A small frown formed on Sapphire's brow as she walked around the bed to get a closer look.

As she moved towards the object she felt her chest begin to constrict and pull uncomfortably, making her breath catch within her throat. It was a bracelet covered in diamonds and sapphires, beautiful and intricate in design. Sapphire pulled back and tried to stop herself from moving forward. Her body jolted hard, and she gasped as her hand lifted up slowly with a mind of its own and reached out to touch the bracelet. Her hand kept moving, the hand that was suddenly not her own.

Her mind began to scream, "Don't touch it. Don't touch it," but her body ignored the warning. Before she could stop herself her fingers touched the silver, and the band unclipped itself. The bracelet jumped up from the cabinet, wrapped itself around her wrist, and clicked shut again with a gentle sigh. Sapphire blinked and blinked again. She looked down at her arms, which were both now circled with a silver bracelet ... both identical, both shimmering from the magic that surrounded them.

Just as her mouth opened in a silent scream Fox crashed through the hospital door and entered the room, his face a picture of fear and panic. Sapphire closed her eyes and held the scream within. She had been tricked again by the gatekeeper, and she could feel his touch on her skin. It made her mind recoil and her body rejoice. Fox grabbed her by the shoulders and spun her around roughly. She could hear his voice at the back of her mind as her body started to slump to the floor.

"No, no, no," he screamed. It was too late. He was too late. Sapphire felt as though a blanket had been thrown over her body and she was being dumped in a cold, dark lake. She was lost, lost in the dark.

Fox held Sapphire in his arms and crushed her to his body with all his strength. He slipped down on to the floor and held her to him. She was unconscious, just as Pearl was in the bed behind them. His whole life had suddenly come crashing down around him. Everything that had been crystal clear was now shattered like a piece of broken glass. Sapphire was breathing shallowly against his chest, her warm body sagging against him like a rag doll. He could feel the spell Hecta had spun wrapping around her and encasing her in a shield that even he could not penetrate in his moment of grief. As he rocked her gently back and forth he felt tears begin to fill his eyes. Never in his whole life had he felt so helpless. He had been too late. Too late to stop her from touching the bracelet and falling into Hecta's trap.

His head spun with anger, panic, and confusion. He could not think straight. All that he could do was hold his wife to him, and fight the overwhelming urge to howl out loud with frustration. How could this have happened so quickly? They had only just arrived back on Earth to complete a task, which Sapphire had held herself responsible for. After all the events that had unfolded back on Shaka – and the removal of Ebony as a threat – they had thought they were safe. He had thought they were safe.

Fox buried his head in Sapphire's hair and clung to her body, breathing in her sweet scent. He tried to grasp some form of clarity. What should he do? What could he do to change this disaster into something else? He moved her into his lap, cradled her like a small child, and continued to rock them both back and forth in a soothing rhythm. He so hoped to bring her back to him and to stop this inexplicable scenario from unfolding even more. He whispered to her softly in his own language, and tried to coax her out from the dark blanket that had been thrown over her when she had touched the bracelet.

"Sapphire, my love, my love ... Don't leave me ... stay with me. I am here ... please ..." He could feel his voice crack under the pressure. Even in his own language the words sounded pitiful. He opened his magic fully, pressed his lips to her forehead, and began to push – with all his strength – his very essence into her. He was trying to break the binding spell and shatter any bond that Hecta now had on his wife.

The room flared brightly with white and gold light. Sparks scattered across the floor like the trail of a firework that had hit the ground while still burning. His head crushed with the weight of such powerful magic, and he felt Sapphire's body shudder within his arms. The spell wavered and bent for a moment as he pushed harder and harder ... her name on his lips, his hands now in her hair and holding her close to him.

Just as he felt the spell begin to give slightly – tear at the edges – the door to the hospital room opened loudly behind him, and he was aware of Charlie screaming at the top of her lungs in fear at what she could see ... a sight that no mortal had ever seen before ... a sight that could not be explained with any logic or reason.

Charlie broke the swell of power that he had created as she unwittingly reached out to touch him. Her mortal touch disconnected his source for a second and allowed the binding spell to bounce back again, like a plastic shield that had momentarily given way and folded in on itself. The force behind his magic snapped and the bright light and sparks of power shot out, shattering the windows in the room and causing all the electrical equipment to spark and explode. Utter chaos erupted, and all that Fox could sense – as he realised that the very worst-case scenario had now unfolded – was that Charlie was now screaming at other people who were standing in the doorway, and there was no going back. He had exposed himself in this human world for what he really was: powerful and non-human. And now, in their eyes, extremely dangerous.

Fox opened his eyes and twisted his head around. He watched Charlie before him, her face tear-streaked and her eyes wide with confusion. The staff behind her were shielding their eyes from the remaining sparks of light from his fading magic, and small fires were now beginning to break out from the electrical equipment Pearl had been linked to. Raised voices began to surround him as the staff rushed around the bed and tried to take control. A cool breeze rushed across his face from the now-broken window and brought him back to his senses. Charlie grabbed his arm and shook it roughly. Anger now flashed in her expression, which swarmed with a million judgements.

"What the fuck, Fox? What the hell just happened? Are you OK? What is wrong with Saf?"

He could sense her disbelief at what she had just witnessed, and could see that her energy was a swirl of confusion. How could he explain this? He pushed himself up to standing. He then lifted Sapphire up and looked back down into her face – which was void of all articulation, as if she were sleeping within his arms - a sleeping beauty under a dark and mysterious spell.

"I need to get Sapphire out of here, Charlie. You have to help me get her out of here."

Charlie gawped at him. "Like hell you do, Fox. What have you done to her? What was that flash of light?" She stepped away from him, suddenly afraid.

He took a deep breath and picked Sapphire up so that she lay across his arms, her head hanging limply like a broken doll.

"Charlie ... I ... need ... you ... to ... move." Each word was spoken slowly and precisely, his tone dark and dangerous. Charlie's eyes widened in surprise and, almost involuntarily, her body moved further away. Fox pushed his magic further from his body and managed to sidestep her and push past security, who had now suddenly appeared in the doorway. As he literally ran down the corridor with his wife hanging lifelessly in his arms he could hear people yelling at him to stop, but his stride was firm and his pace fast.

He fled the human hospital and the people within it. He needed to escape this nightmare that had unfolded and to find a place of safety, so that he could regain his wits and work out what to do next. He knew of only one place that existed in this plane which could give him this safety, and he fled with all his speed and strength towards it.

He had to get back to Foxglove – and get there quick – before he was arrested, or worse.

Chapter Thirty-Six

Sapphire felt as if she were dreaming again. She could feel that her body was weightless, and moving at great speed. She was aware of someone holding her, but was not sure who this person was. Her mind was cocooned in a soft cloud that made her feel suffocated but soothed at the same time. She could hear voices shouting, and sense many different people around her. Slowly the voices began to fade and she could no longer sense the other people, just the warm body holding her close and carrying her through the darkness. Shards of light pierced the darkness, like flashes of lightning in a stormy sky. They made her flinch and groan at the pain they caused behind her eyelids.

The person carrying her squeezed her tightly, and she felt a swell of something familiar that connected with her heart break momentarily through the dark cloud and touch her chest in a fleeting twist. Fox. It was Fox who held her. She smiled, and sighed with relief. He would find her in this dark place. He would bring her out of this abyss in which she was floating – this dark oubliette that seemed to suck her further down into its bleakness.

She felt a shift in the energy around her – and was suddenly floating silently in the dark cloud that felt like a soft and comforting bed of feathers. A light began to appear in the corner of her vision. It grew into a thin line that moved towards her faster and faster. It was terrifying and mesmerising at the same time. The light grew brighter and more ferocious, and shattered the black shadow that hung around her. It pressed against her body and enveloped her as it crashed through her skin into her nerve endings. It was exquisite, and terribly painful.

Sapphire felt the wave of light explode from within her and shatter the blanket that had surrounded her in one giant crash. She opened her eyes and, panting hard, sat bolt upright. Her vision returned and she was back in reality, in a bedroom in a place that she knew. Fox sat beside her, his wild eyes glowing amber and black. It was the first time she had ever looked into his eyes and been afraid.

The power within his eyes was all-consuming and powerful beyond comprehension, and they shone so brightly she almost did not recognise him.

"Fox."

He blinked once, and became the Fox she knew once more. His energy pulsed around him in bright white with flecks of gold and red. Suddenly it withdrew and the room became still again, the light fading just as quickly as it had appeared. He tipped his head to one side and smiled, a slow, soft smile that crept at the edge of his lips and made her heart clench tightly.

"My love ... you are back."

Sapphire looked around her at the room, which was starting to fade with the coming dusk. She was in the guest room at Foxglove, and all around the room she could now see tiny sprites who sparkled and spun like fireflies in the dimming light. Fox pulled her into his arms and buried his head into her neck as he breathed heavily.

"I thought I had lost you," he whispered.

Sapphire wrapped her arms around him and she revelled in the feel of his hard, warm body against her again. She had no memory of anything other than standing beside Pearl in the hospital, and now this. What the hell had just happened? She pushed him back gently and looked up into his face, noticing the dark shadows that now touched the edges of his eyes.

"What are we doing here? What happened?"

He shook his head slowly, as if in despair. He looked away from her for a second, and seemed to be trying to regain his composure ... the warrior she loved suddenly lost and unsure.

"Hecta tricked us both. He had laid a trap at the hospital: the second part of the binding spell. You had no chance to avoid it. You were taken from me, and for a moment I thought I had lost you. But, with the help of the energy of the sprites here at Foxglove, I have managed to remove part of the spell he had cast. But ..." He paused as if afraid to carry on.

Sapphire raised her hand and brushed his cheek tenderly. She could feel his anguish, his fear, and something else. Was it shame?

"I used my magic in the hospital," Fox continued. "I panicked. I blew up the room Pearl was in. It was utter chaos for a while. Charlie saw me. She saw me using my magic and thought I had hurt you. I had to flee with you, my love, bring you here to safety. Many humans witnessed what I did. I had no time to rectify this situation, Sapphire. You were my only concern."

Sapphire sighed heavily. Holy Mother of God. This was definitely a big crock of shit. Fox looked back into her eyes and waited for her response. He wrapped his fingers into her own and pulled her back towards him, pausing for a second before kissing her softly on the lips. She felt a flare of magic pass between them that reignited their bond. He withdrew slowly and remained silent.

"Well ... that is what we would call back here on Earth, Fox, 'One big fuck-up'."

He laughed softly and kissed her again.

"Is Pearl OK? Where is Charlie now?" she asked in a whisper of a voice. He had obviously been through enough already, and she did not want to make more of a mess of this than it already was.

"I assume the staff at the hospital took control, and Pearl is still unconscious. I have no idea where Charlie is."

Sapphire shook her head as she tried to clear the last of the fuzziness that had overcome her. The sprites who had not so long ago departed from this place now buzzed around her head, chattering noisily. They were desperate to find out where Pearl was, and were working themselves up into a frenzy of worried confusion. Fox looked up at them and spoke in his own words – calming them and scolding them at the same time, it seemed, because they took flight and scattered back out of the door and down the stairs.

"I have to speak to Charlie. I need to find her. She will be going insane after what she saw."

Fox nodded slowly. "I will speak to my father, Sapphire. We both need his help now." He lifted one of her arms slowly and her jacket slipped back away from her wrist, revealing one of the bracelets that was still locked in place. Sapphire stared at the object, her mind not understanding. Had he not just broken the spell and brought her back to him?

"The spell is still in place. I broke through the first layer ... but it is strong, and I need his help to remove the cuffs." He was standing now, and paced the room. He was looking around suddenly at the objects placed around him as if he were looking for something. Sapphire watched him, her head spinning. Her own magic was starting to return now, and it snuggled against her as if it were also afraid. It made tiny butterflies skitter inside her chest and send goosebumps across her skin.

Fox grabbed the mirror that was lying on the dressing table. "I can use this to reach across to Shaka for my father. I will be back, my love. Stay here for a moment." He brushed her cheek softly with the back of his hand and left the room quickly, taking the mirror with him. Sapphire assumed that after using all his magic on her he could not just jump back to Shaka and speak to Conloach in person. The thought unnerved her.

She moved slowly off the bed and headed back down the stairs, despite Fox's insistence that she stay put. She needed some air and desperately wanted to clear her head, which was starting to pound again. It troubled her immensely that she could not remember anything apart from standing beside Pearl in the hospital room. She tried in vain to push back into her memory for any further information, although a small piece of her was grateful that she had not witnessed the chaotic scene Fox had described after using his magic.

Sapphire could not begin to imagine how much that must have fucked with everyone's brains. Humans were not able to comprehend that magic was actually real: she herself had found it almost impossible at the beginning, when she had started to dream travel. Pearl had warned her of the dangers it could cause to the train of thought of mortals if they actually knew what was going on around them on their own world – and what was happening in the other worlds that were scattered around our vast, unknown universe. It would be mind-blowing, literally.

As she reached the bottom of the stairs she could hear Fox in the kitchen, and it sounded as if he was swearing – in some unknown language, anyway. She poked her head around the door and found Fox pacing again, a deep frown etched on his forehead.

"No luck?"

He cursed again, this time in English – which, despite the predicament they were in, sounded quite funny coming from him. "I cannot get this mirror to scry for me, no matter how much I try."

Sapphire cocked her head to one side. She suddenly remembered the black crystal Pearl had used – what now seemed like years ago – when she had first discovered that Hecta was stalking her.

"Pearl has something that you might have better luck with. She used to keep it in the dresser over there."

Fox nodded and began rummaging through the drawers. The sprites returned and flittered around him. He batted them away and grumbled at them to stop bothering him. A smile appeared on his face as he found the black obsidian stone that Pearl had scried with so long ago. He set it down on the table, sat down, and placed his hands either side of the dark stone.

Sapphire watched him tune in. His energy began to flicker again, and she watched his eyes start to glow an unearthly green. His magic was changing again, and she could sense he was trying hard to disguise the fact.

Hecta had really gone to town on the both of them. He had tired Fox, and trapped her with his madness. Sapphire was really beginning to feel quite tired of this whole thing. She wished he would just leave her alone for good. What in the hell did Hecta want from her? The bracelets on her wrist started to tingle, and she felt a shock of electricity run down her arms into her groin. She gasped, a little taken aback. If that's what he wanted he had another thing coming.

She shook herself back into the room and waited for Fox to finish his call. He remained silent, and was probably communicating with his father through some telepathic method that she was unfamiliar with. She left him in the kitchen and headed out to the garden. She really needed to clear her head. The sprites followed her and whizzed around her hair, making blonde wisps sweep across her face. They really were being rather persistent.

Just as she had sat down on the bench by the gate to recover her breath and her sanity some car lights swept up the lane, and the sound of doors opening and closing with a thud made her jump up again. Charlie and Nathan were striding with purpose towards the gate. In the soft light of dusk Sapphire could see that Charlie was not only anxious, but as angry as a wasp that had just been swatted. This was not good, not good at all. She swept through the gate, closely followed by Nathan. Sapphire stepped out from beneath the honeysuckle that had shielded her.

"Charlie, I'm here."

Charlie spun around and knocked into Nathan, who staggered for a second. "Saf. Holy shit. What the hell happened? Are you OK? I thought you might be here. I went home and found no trace of you, and thought Fox must have whisked you away from us again." She paused and looked around, with anger flashing in her eyes. "Where is he?" Sapphire stepped towards her friend and clasped her arms tightly.

"Charlie, it's OK. Look at me. I'm fine. Fox did not hurt me."

Nathan was breathing heavily, and standing behind his girl with a look of total perplexity on his face. He had no idea whatsoever what was going on. Poor Nathan. Charlie looked so very confused. She scanned her friend's face as she searched for some reasoning behind what she had seen.

"But ... I saw him holding you. He was glowing with this light that was just so unreal ... I don't understand what happened. He blew up all the equipment in the hospital room. The glass in the windows exploded. It was like something out of a horror movie." She paused, and her bottom lip trembled as if she were about to burst into tears. "I thought he had killed you." Nathan wrapped his arms around her and squeezed her close, the only thing he could do in this crazy situation.

Sapphire smiled gently. "As you can see, Charlie, I'm fine. Fox did not kill me, or try to hurt me. He was helping me."

Charlie blinked, and a single tear fell from her eye across her cheek. "I don't understand, Saf. Please tell me ... What the hell is going on?"

Sapphire nodded, her mind clearing now and her inner wisdom stepping forward to the forefront of her brain.

"You both need to come inside. I need to talk to you, and I think you will need to sit down to hear what I have to say."

Chapter Thirty-Seven

Sapphire led the way back into the cottage and closed the door behind them. Charlie and Nathan stood awkwardly in the hallway, with Nathan looking around in fascination at his surroundings. The cottage was lit with candles now and the temperature had gone up – no doubt due to Fox's magic, which Sapphire could sense was pulsing in the kitchen.

"Go and sit down in the lounge. I won't be a minute."

Nathan nodded, and guided Charlie into the adjoining room. She had seemingly gone into shock, and was looking quite ashen.

Sapphire slipped quietly into the kitchen. She found Fox standing with his back to her, looking out of the window.

He turned around slowly, and smiled at her weakly. "I sense we have visitors."

Sapphire nodded. "We need to tell them, Fox. It's time to cut to the chase." He tipped his head to one side and frowned, not understanding her terminology. "It's time for the truth, Fox. They deserve to know."

Fox stepped towards her, his body moving like a graceful cat. He licked his lips slowly. His eyes, having returned to their normal amber and black, flickered with sparks of light.

"As you wish, my love." He paused for a moment. "I have spoken to my father. He has told me what needs to be done to break the binding spell and to help Pearl, but it won't be easy." He reached out to take a piece of her hair between his fingers and caressed it casually, as if delaying the truth. "In fact, it will be almost impossible without some help from your friends."

Sapphire sighed and nodded. "Let's get this over with, then."

Charlie and Nathan were sitting holding hands on the small sofa opposite the fire. Both looked as nervous as hell, and slightly shell-shocked. As Fox entered the room behind Sapphire, Charlie winced slightly, her fear of him from earlier still evident on her face. Sapphire bent down and took her friend's free hand and smiled into her face with as much kindness as she could muster. Fox remained standing, his energy pulsing around him freely now. There was no longer any reason to hide who he really was.

"Charlie ..." She paused, and her eyes swept between her two friends. "Nathan ..." They remained stock-still, like two frightened rabbits ready to take flight at a moment's notice.

"What I am about to tell you will no doubt be a shock – and seem totally unreal – but I assure you both that it is real ... very real, and I need you to both be open-minded and not freak out."

Charlie opened her mouth as if to speak but shut it quickly, her eyes flickering between Fox and Sapphire like someone on speed.

"When I left you six months ago I did go travelling with Fox, but not to any place that you will ever know. Fox is not from this world, and he is not human."

Nathan leant back in the chair and let out a deep breath. Charlie gripped tightly on to her hand. "I have changed in so many ways since I left you both that it is probably not possible for me to fully explain everything to you. But know this: Fox is not to be feared, and neither am I. We are just different from you, different from everyone on this planet."

Charlie let out a small squeak. "Is he an alien or something? What has he done to you, Saf?"

Fox chuckled from behind her, and Sapphire spun her head around and frowned at him. She looked back slowly at her friend, who looked scared shitless, and smiled once more.

"No, Charlie, he is not an alien. But he is magical – something not of this world – and unfortunately there is someone else like him here now who is trying to hurt Pearl and me. His name is Hecta, and he is also born from magic."

Nathan closed his eyes and started to laugh, a nervous laugh that caught in his throat. "You have got to be kidding me, Saf. Come on: that's just total bullshit."

Fox stepped forward and Sapphire felt his energy expand. "Sapphire, you cannot explain this to your friends. It is beyond their capability to understand such things. This is a bad idea."

Charlie let go of her hand, a flicker of realisation suddenly registering in her mind.

"Hecta? Oh, my God. I know someone called Hecta. He asked me to commission him some jewellery before Christmas. Weird name, I thought ..."

Nathan looked at her and shook his head. "You can't be buying this, Charlie. You saw the magic tricks Fox did last time we saw him, babe. It's just illusion. What Saf is trying to tell us is the stuff of movies and story books, that's all. Someone mugged Pearl – and I really don't know what you saw at the hospital, but it just can't be what Saf is trying to scare us with ... It can't be."

Charlie looked at Fox, back at Sapphire, then at Nathan. Her expression changed from fear to disbelief to understanding.

"I've always known there was something odd about you, Fox, from the first time I saw you. It's in your eyes: they're not normal. The way Saf changed when you were around ... at the festival ... the night of the storm ... when I was attacked by that lunatic ... the lightning bolt ...

"I saw it. I know I did. No one believed me, though. They thought I was just crazy on drugs. Now it all makes sense ..."

She stood up slowly. Sapphire allowed her to move away from her and stepped across towards Fox, who stood quite still before her. Charlie reached up to his face and touched his cheek. Her fingers brushed his skin lightly, and a trail of light flickered across her hand as she did. She was mesmerised, fascinated, as she saw him for the first time ... really saw him. Nathan remained seated as he watched her, his breathing now quickening. Fox's magic began to swell around him and Sapphire's energy responded in the same glowing light, so that they both now lit up the room in a myriad of bright sparks. Charlie stepped back. Just as Nathan stood up to grab her she fell back into his arms and let out a gasp.

"Holy Mother of God," she whispered before she quite dramatically, and in total Charlie style, fainted in his arms.

Sapphire stood in the kitchen making tea. The memory of Pearl doing exactly the same thing for her making her chest constrict. Nathan had taken Charlie upstairs and put her to bed. He was now sitting at the kitchen table with Fox. They were both silent. The sound of the kettle whistling as it boiled made the only sound in the room. Sapphire poured the water into the teapot and fetched cups and milk to the table.

She placed the items on the table before the two men and laughed in her head at the scene before her. Fox, now fully exposed, had dropped his shield and was glowing softly in the candlelight. Nathan was fidgeting beside him, not knowing where the hell to look. She took a seat and pushed a cup towards Nathan, who looked up at her with slightly fearful eyes.

"Have you got anything stronger, Saf? I think I need it."

She laughed out loud. "I'm not sure Pearl would have any whiskey, Nat. But I am sure Fox could mix something up that might help, if you like."

Fox allowed a wry smile to grace his lips. Nathan shook his head slowly. "Seriously, Saf, I've taken some serious drugs in my time, but I have never seen anything like that before. You really are telling us the truth, aren't you?"

Sapphire nodded and poured herself some tea. She added some sugar for good measure.

"Yes, it's true. That's as much as I can tell you for now, anyway: any more information would most likely blow your mind."

Nathan laughed. He reached for a cup and looked across at Fox. "Whatever you can add to the mix would be greatly received, Fox. Show me what you've got."

Fox shrugged and placed his hand over the cup. His fingertips glowed again as he tipped some of his magic into the liquid. Sapphire watched him, smiling. It was strangely comforting to be able to show her man for what he really was to her friend.

Nathan took a sip and shrugged. "Tastes good, man."

Fox leant back in his chair and raised an eyebrow. "I would advise you drink it slowly, my friend. It's a strong brew."

Sapphire felt as if she were at the Mad Hatter's tea party, sharing magical cocktails with the most unlikely guest. Her mind switched back to Pearl and the situation at hand.

"So, what can we do about Pearl? How can we help her? I have no doubt we won't be allowed back in the hospital again after the showdown this afternoon."

Nathan had slipped into some mild semi-stoned state. His body had started to relax, and his energy was shifting before her eyes. She looked across at Fox, who shrugged again.

"I told him it was strong."

Nathan sighed deeply and took another sip. A smile was now sitting lazily on his lips.

"Whatever you plan to do it will definitely not involve you being able to see Pearl in the hospital again, either of you. For one, Fox blew the room up. And two, Charlie told them you had killed Saf. You are both screwed."

Fox looked bewildered for a second, then cast another 'I'm sorry' look at Sapphire.

"What did your father say?"

Fox took his own cup and leisurely poured himself some tea. After taking a sip he looked at them both before speaking. "The only way we can break both the binding spell and the dark shadow Hecta has locked Pearl into is to either kill him or make him undo the spells willingly."

Nathan hiccuped and chuckled. "What, are we hit men now? This is just too crazy, Saf ..." He paused, blinked, and shook his head. "Fuck. I feel totally stoned."

Sapphire sighed deeply. This wasn't helping. "OK ... so now you have totally zapped both Charlie and Nathan we need a serious plan to get us out of this situation, Fox. You had better think of something else because, sure as shit, neither of those things are likely to happen."

Fox narrowed his eyes at her from across the table. "I am totally willing to erase the gatekeeper from existence to keep both you and Pearl safe, Sapphire. Have no doubt of that."

Nathan was slipping down in the chair slightly but pushed himself up, his eyes growing wide.

"Wow ... a gatekeeper. What the fuck is that?" He looked at Sapphire and smiled again. "Oh, and I totally believe him, Saf. I certainly wouldn't want to piss Fox off ... especially now."

Sapphire stood up. Her patience was running thin. "Fox, we can't kill Hecta. Believe me, I've tried several times and failed. He is like a shadow, appearing and disappearing." Her eyes flicked to her husband for a moment. "Just as you do, Fox. And – I'm guessing –

he is just as hard to kill as you are. As for him willingly breaking both spells, I just don't see it happening. He is mad, crazy, and totally fucked-up. We have to think of another way."

Nathan seemed to be flowing well with the magic now, and raised his head to face her. "What does he actually want from you, Saf? Maybe you could bargain with him ... give him something to make it worth his while."

Fox shifted in his chair. "Sapphire will give him nothing, Nathan. What he wants from her cannot be bargained for or traded. We have to kill him."

Nathan shrugged. "Just a thought." He laughed again, and took another sip of the tea. "I hope that I wake up in a minute and this has all been a bad dream."

Sapphire paced the kitchen floor. "I could try to speak to him. The last time I saw him – when I travelled – he seemed different. It might be worth a try. I need to know what he wants from me exactly. Nathan has a point, Fox."

Fox stood up abruptly and made the table shake. "No. He will not touch you, go near you, or speak to you ever again, Sapphire – not while I am still breathing."

Nathan looked at them both, his mouth open slightly in awe. He had no idea what was happening again.

"Oh ... For God's sake, Fox, stop it. Stop making this a testosterone match. I can look after myself, you know that. My magic is as strong as yours now, and different from either of you. I just need to entice him back again. We need to trap him the same way he trapped Pearl, and me."

Fox was angry now, and the energy grew thick and strong around him. "You are insane to think you can reason with him, Sapphire. You do not know him as I do. He wants you for himself. Not just your magic, not the seeds. He wants you, Sapphire. You."

Nathan had shrunk back down into the chair again, feeling a little out of place in the middle of this domestic. Sapphire felt sorry for him. He was stoned on magical tea, his head was spinning from all that had been revealed, and now this heated conversation was spinning around him. She needed some time out. In a huff, she left the room to check on Charlie and left Fox standing behind her in the kitchen.

300

She heard Nathan cough with embarrassment.

"Take a load off, Fox. She will be back in a minute."

Sapphire stormed upstairs, taking two steps at a time. She was crazy angry at both Hecta and Fox now. Did this always have to turn into some sort of macho showdown between the two of them? The bracelets on her wrists began to throb again, and her obsidian necklace was doing backward somersaults against her chest. She was irritated and frustrated, and had lost all sense of clarity again. When she pushed open the guest room door she found Charlie lying on her side, her blonde curls lying across the white sheets like a cascade of water. Sapphire pulled in her temper and sat down on the bed next to her friend. She brushed the hair from her face gently. Charlie stirred, and whimpered softly.

"Hey, Charlie … How are you feeling now?"

Her friend opened her eyes and blinked up at her. She smiled a little. "I'm OK, Saf. I just needed to take a step out for a second. Where are Fox and Nat?"

"Downstairs, trying to work out what to do next." She moved back a little to allow Charlie to sit up. "Oh, and Fox has managed to get Nathan stoned on his magic. Great … just great."

Charlie looked confused, but smiled back at her. "Oh, sweetie … this is all just a bit too crazy, isn't it?"

Sapphire nodded and took Charlie's hand in her own. "Honest to God, Charlie, I just wish sometimes that I could turn back the clock and change everything. I love Fox, I really do, but since he arrived in my life nothing has been simple."

Charlie was wide awake now, and yawned a little. Her energy was also lifting again after all the shock.

"I cannot begin to even imagine what you have been going through, Saf. All this time who would have thought that you had met and married someone who wasn't even human? I'm still trying to get my head around it. I think I might need some serious therapy after this is over."

Sapphire laughed. Only Charlie could make light of the situation in this way.

"I'm going to need both your help, Charlie. I need you to go back to the hospital and check on Pearl … make sure she is OK. I can't go back there now, not after this."

Charlie sighed. "No, you certainly cannot, babe. We don't want Fox blowing anything else up and freaking everyone out. I'm assuming they thought it was some crazy electrical fault. You did persuade me several times that I was seeing things, Saf. But now I know and there is no going back. It does make a lot of sense now. All of it." She pushed the duvet away from her legs. "This guy – Hecta – what does he look like? If it's the same man who asked me to make him the jewellery then he has some seriously weird issues ... he's kinda creepy."

Sapphire stood up as Charlie shifted her legs to the floor.

"He's tall, dark – oddly good-looking, considering he is such a creep – and his eyes will be like Fox's ... only dark, really dark."

Charlie looked up at the ceiling for a second. "Yep, that's him. Sexy bastard, but disturbing at the same time. Coffee-coloured eyes that – now I think about it – kept flashing with red." She shook herself, as if shaking off something that smelt bad.

"Ugh ... just thinking about him makes me feel weird. He was charming, but there was something about him that made me either want to jump his bones or run for the hills."

Sapphire's eyes widened. This was just strange. She had never thought of Hecta in any other way than disgusting, but looking through different eyes she could see how he could have changed his real appearance and enchanted any human woman.

Charlie gasped and grabbed hold of Sapphire by the forearms. "I made two bracelets for him, and a necklace. Well ... it was more like a collar and chain, really. Kinky ... sort of BDSM."

Sapphire closed her eyes as she listened to Charlie babble. She stepped away from her friend and uncovered her arms.

"Are these the bracelets, Charlie?"

Charlie's eyes grew wide as she looked down at the offending pieces. "Yes," she stuttered. "How did you get them? Why are you wearing them?"

Sapphire withdrew her arms and covered her wrists again with her jacket.

"Hecta tricked me into wearing them. They bind me to him with a spell that, at the moment, Fox has only managed to half break."

Charlie regarded her curiously. "Oh, shit," she said.

302

Sapphire smiled weakly. "Yes ... oh, shit. And – believe me – I'm not happy about it, and neither is Fox. In fact he is fuming, and seems to have lost all reason and is totally gunning for Hecta."

Charlie placed her hands on her hips, her famous 'Take no prisoners' stance coming back into play.

"Well, I don't blame him. That guy, whatever he is, has seriously bad vibes – and I, for one, will make sure he comes nowhere near me again." She moved towards the door. "I need to freshen up, Saf, then I'll head back to the hospital and check on Pearl with Nathan. Are you staying here with Fox for a while?"

Sapphire watched her leave the room, her curls bouncing down her back as she headed towards the bathroom.

"I'm not sure what we will be doing, to be honest, Charlie."

As her friend disappeared Sapphire heard the front door slam shut and she felt a shiver of energy travel up her spine. Something was wrong. The energy in the cottage had changed again.

Sapphire hurried down the stairs and found Nathan standing at the door, his energy sparkling around him. He was still being affected by the magical tea. He turned around slowly to face her and smiled apologetically.

"He's gone, Saf. I tried to stop him, but he wouldn't listen to me."

Sapphire felt the blood drain from her face. "What do you mean?"

Nathan stepped towards her and reached out tentatively to touch her arm. "He said he was going to find Hecta, and finish this." He watched her face for a reaction, any reaction. "I think he means to kill him, Saf. He was crazy angry."

Sapphire could not believe that Fox could be so stupid.

"What's happening now, for goodness' sake?" Charlie had reappeared, and looked much better now that she had splashed her face with water.

Sapphire sighed and ran her fingers through her white-blonde hair – which was now glowing brightly along with the rest of her, as her magic thrummed angrily.

"My stupid husband has decided to go on a mission to find Hecta and kill him, Charlie."

Her friend opened her mouth, closed it again, and shrugged.

"I can't think of anything to say to that, sweetie."

Sapphire felt her body grow stiff and cold. Neither could she right now, but the anger within her swirled and gathered within her chest and made her hair lift with static. Both of her friends stepped away from her warily.

Nathan lifted his hands up in an 'I surrender' gesture.

"Saf, stay cool ... Don't lose your temper. Your eyes are glowing. That cannot be normal."

Charlie was breathing a little more heavily now, and fidgeted a little on her feet.

"I'm sure he will be back soon, Saf. He can't seriously be thinking about killing someone. That's just not legal."

Sapphire closed her eyes and counted to ten in her head, reining in her temper so that she didn't zap them both.

"Unfortunately, Charlie, you have absolutely no idea what Fox is capable of ... and the fact is that neither he nor Hecta care one damn bit about our rules here on Earth. Not one damn bit."

Epilogue

Fox stood in the woods and closed his eyes. His body trembled with rage – pure, undiluted rage – and it created a whirlwind around him that crackled with electricity. The trees around him whipped their branches loudly, sending leaves and twigs scattering across the woodland floor. Small animals in the vicinity scampered quickly away in terror as they fled this sudden disruption to their habitat. Fox did not care whether he started a tornado, a fire, or a flood: he was beyond consoling. He wanted Hecta dead and removed from his life.

During the entire time he had played guardian to the dream travellers he had never faced such extreme emotion. He could not bear the thought of losing Sapphire, and it removed all reason from his mind. With the spell attached to her she could not see clearly. She did not know the gatekeeper as he did. He would finish this once and for all, and put an end to this cat and mouse chase.

Fox pulled the energy from the ground below him, moved towards the tree he had found earlier that day, and reached out for its power source. He would need to be fully charged before he faced Hecta, and this time he would not hold back. The Oracle had foreseen this, and she was right. If he was not careful he would lose his head, and lose Sapphire for good. He was not prepared to lose either, even on this strange, dysfunctional planet that sucked his energy like a parasite. He would beat Hecta in this fight, and remove both the binding spell and the dark shadow that was draining Pearl's life force. He had not told Sapphire, but when he had found her in the hospital room he had realised that Hecta had plugged into her source of magic and was killing her slowly – like a vampire feeding on his prey.

Waiting to negotiate and bargain with the gatekeeper was out of the question, but he had not the heart to tell Sapphire the reason why. His father had told him that the spell – once completed – would take Sapphire away from him for good ... and she would be bound to Hecta forever, despite their blood bond and the love they had for each other. He could feel their connection already fading slightly, and it made his blood boil with fury.

He found the huge beech tree, which glowed in response to his magic as he approached. His eyes were glowing dark gold and black, and he reached out and touched the bark with both hands and plugged in. The sky above him crackled, and a low rumble of thunder groaned across the horizon.

It was time. Time to finish this.

Printed in Great Britain
by Amazon

38762694R00176